HIT-GIRL IN HONG KONG

DANIEL WAY WRITER
GORAN PARLOV ARTIST
GIADA MARCHISIO COLORIST
CLEM ROBINS LETTERER

MELINA MIKULIC DESIGN AND PRODUCTION
RACHAEL FULTON EDITOR

FRONT COVER GIGI CAVENAGO
BACK COVER MATTEO SCALERA WITH MORENO DINISIO

HIT-GIRL and KICK-ASS created by MARK MILLAR and JOHN ROMITA JR.

IMAGE COMICS, INC.
Robert Kirkman – Chief Operating Officer
Erik Larsen – Chief Financial Officer
Todd McFarlane – President
Marc Silvestri – Chief Executive Officer
Jim Valentino – Vice President

Eric Stephenson – Publisher / Chief Creative Officer
Jeff Boison – Director of Publishing Planning & Book Trade Sales
Chris Ross – Director of Digital Sales
Jeff Stang – Director of Direct Market Sales
Kat Salazar – Director of PR & Marketing
Drew Gill – Cover Editor
Heather Doornink – Production Director
Nicole Lapalme – Controller

IMAGECOMICS.COM

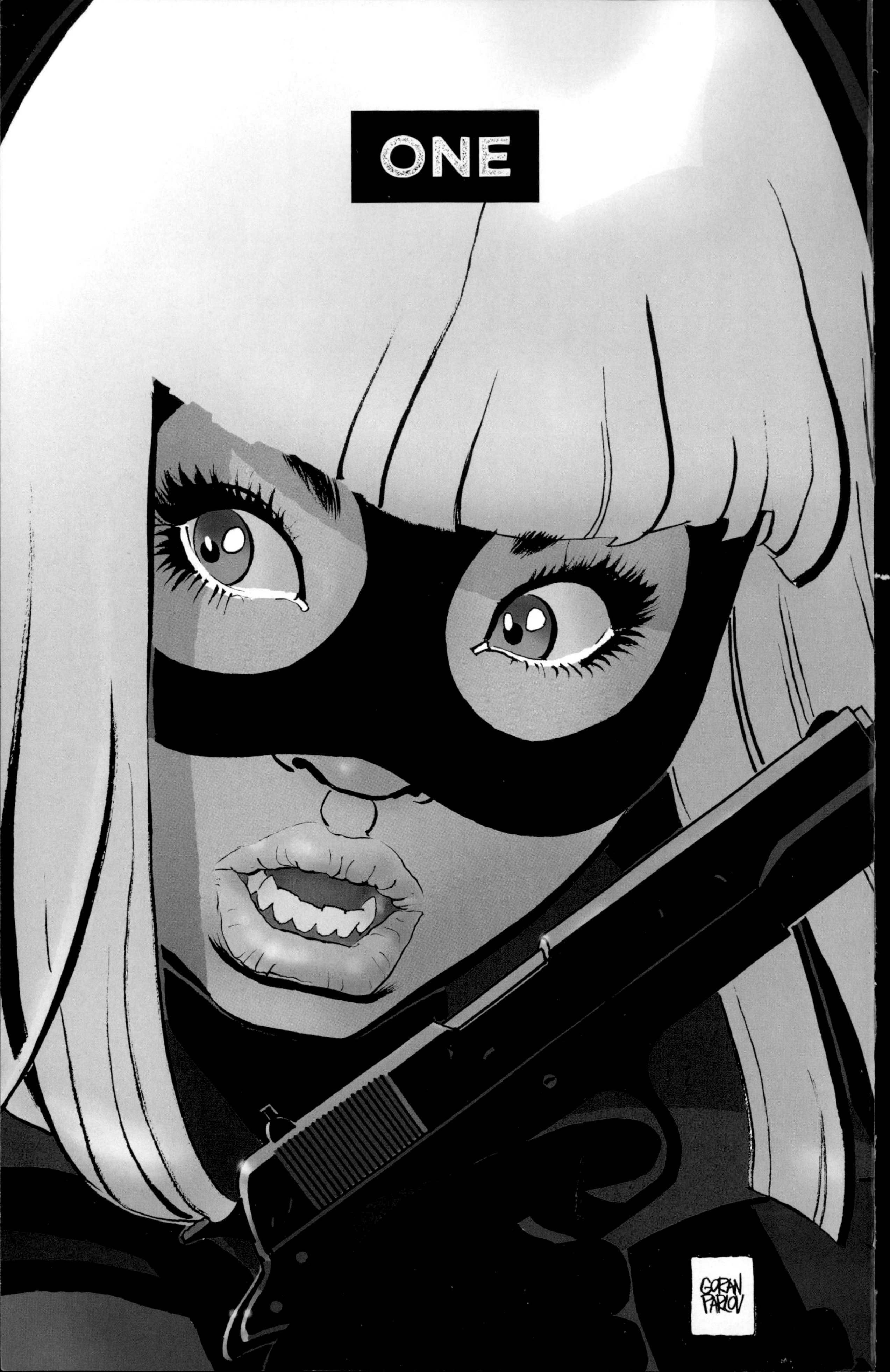
ONE
GORAN PARLOV

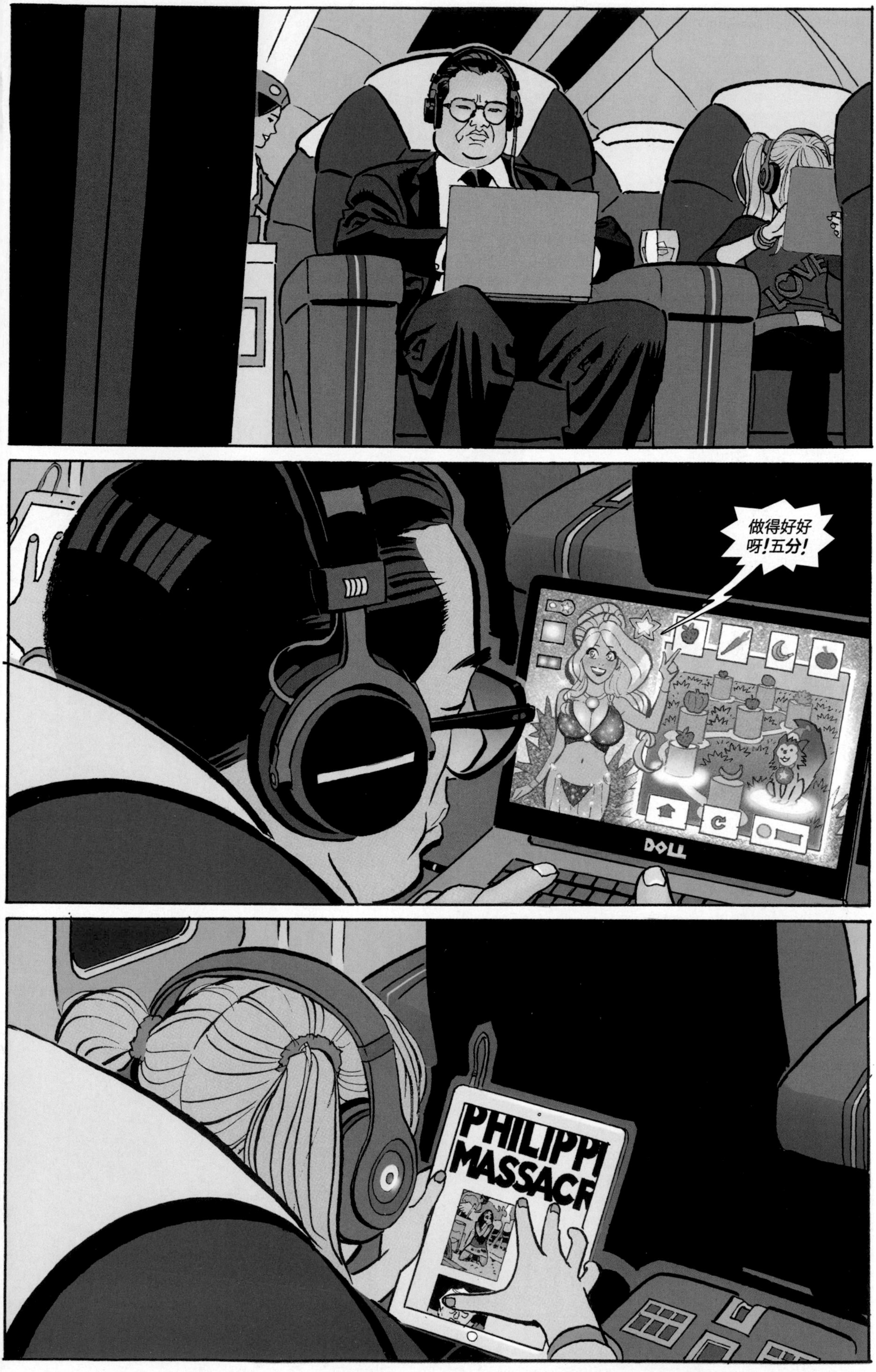
LOVE
做得好好
呀！五分！
DOLL
PHILIPPI
MASSACR

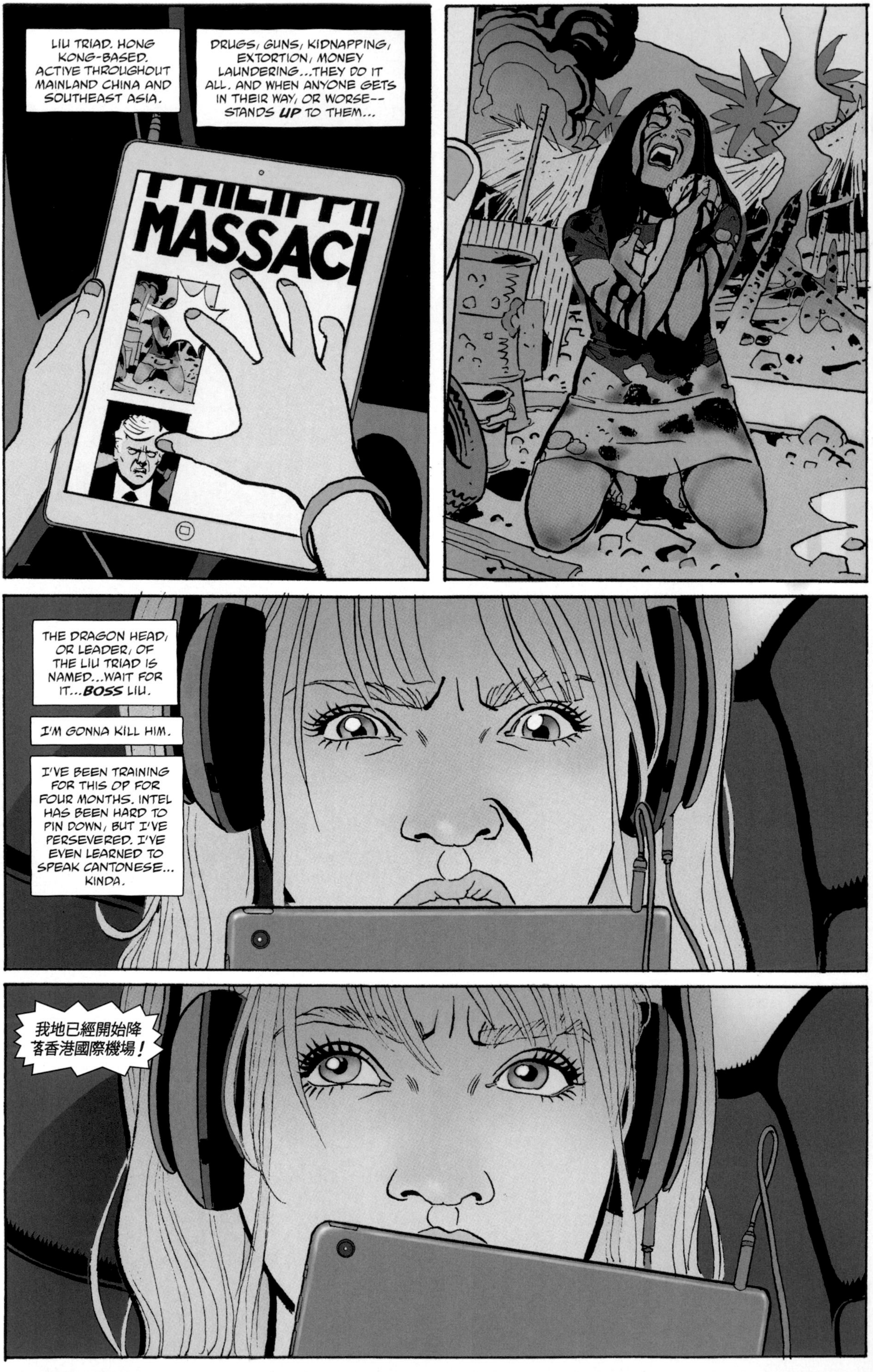
LIU TRIAD. HONG KONG-BASED. ACTIVE THROUGHOUT MAINLAND CHINA AND SOUTHEAST ASIA.
DRUGS, GUNS, KIDNAPPING, EXTORTION, MONEY LAUNDERING...THEY DO IT ALL. AND WHEN ANYONE GETS IN THEIR WAY, OR WORSE--STANDS UP TO THEM...
PHILIPPI
MASSACI
THE DRAGON HEAD, OR LEADER, OF THE LIU TRIAD IS NAMED...WAIT FOR IT...BOSS LIU.
I'M GONNA KILL HIM.
I'VE BEEN TRAINING FOR THIS OP FOR FOUR MONTHS. INTEL HAS BEEN HARD TO PIN DOWN, BUT I'VE PERSEVERED. I'VE EVEN LEARNED TO SPEAK CANTONESE... KINDA.
我地已經開始降落香港國際機場！

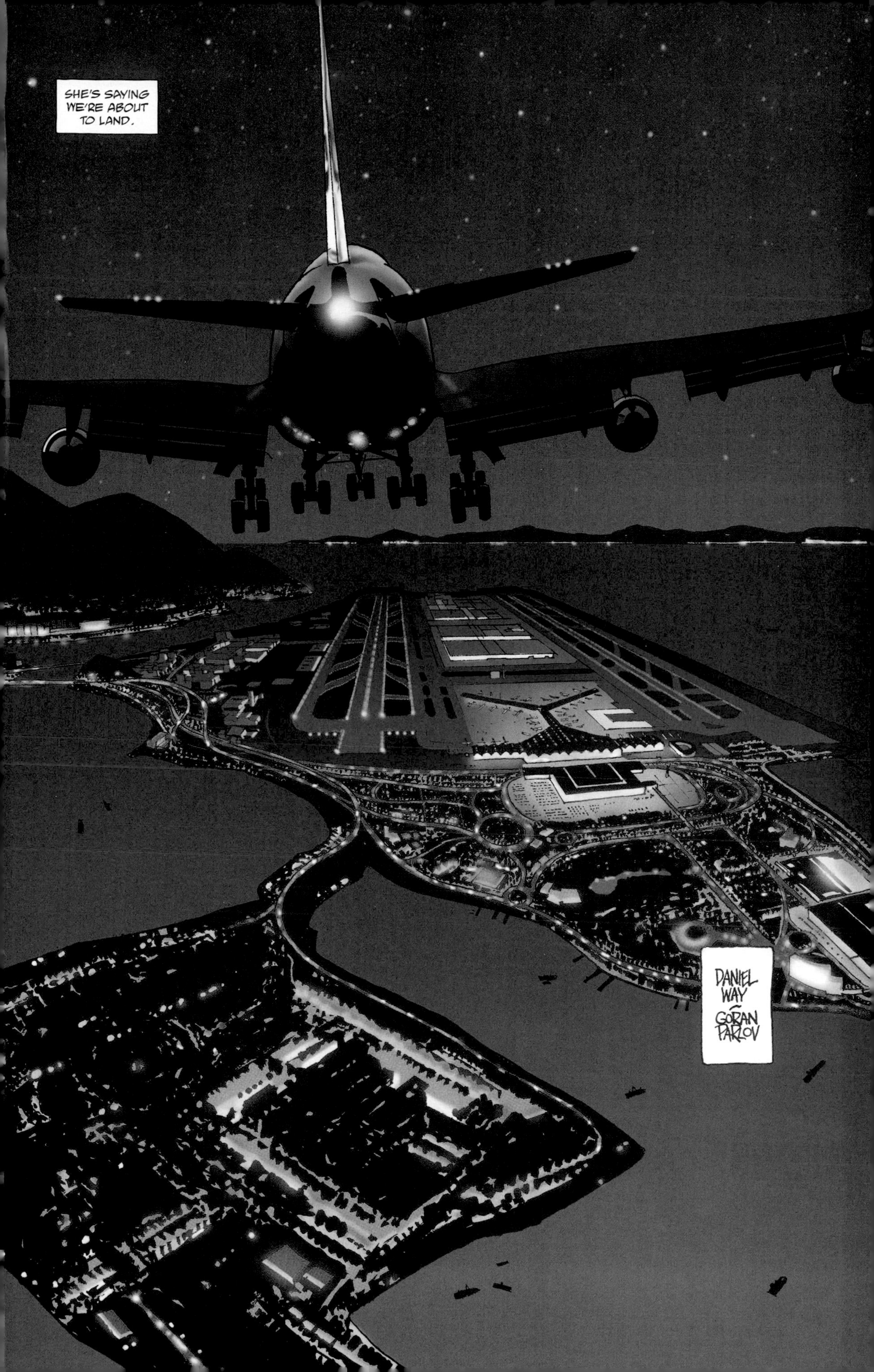
SHE'S SAYING WE'RE ABOUT TO LAND.
DANIEL WAY ~ GORAN PARLOV

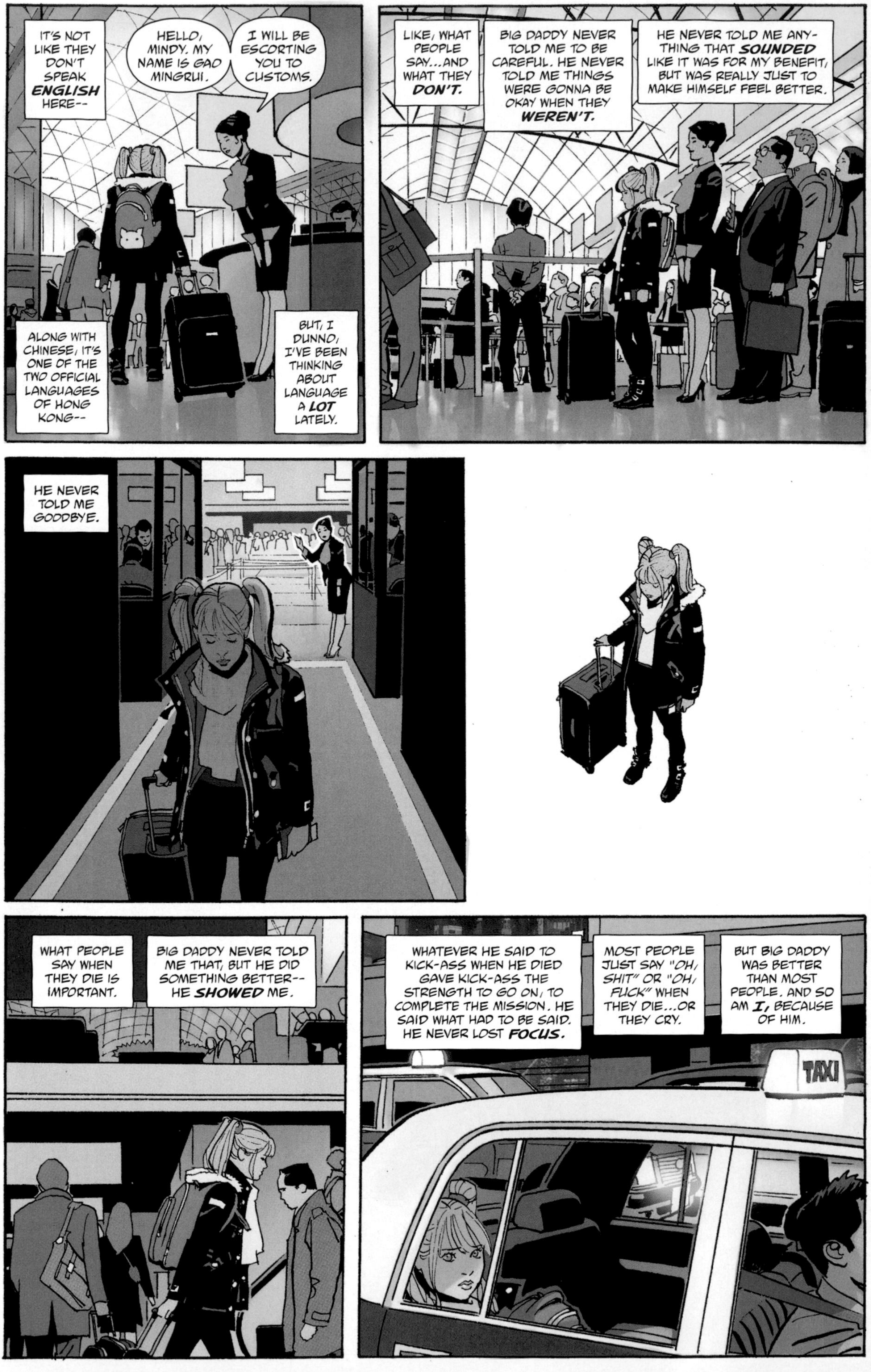
IT'S NOT LIKE THEY DON'T SPEAK ENGLISH HERE--
HELLO, MINDY. MY NAME IS GAO MINGRUI.
I WILL BE ESCORTING YOU TO CUSTOMS.
ALONG WITH CHINESE, IT'S ONE OF THE TWO OFFICIAL LANGUAGES OF HONG KONG--
BUT, I DUNNO, I'VE BEEN THINKING ABOUT LANGUAGE A LOT LATELY.
LIKE, WHAT PEOPLE SAY...AND WHAT THEY DON'T.
BIG DADDY NEVER TOLD ME TO BE CAREFUL. HE NEVER TOLD ME THINGS WERE GONNA BE OKAY WHEN THEY WEREN'T.
HE NEVER TOLD ME ANYTHING THAT SOUNDED LIKE IT WAS FOR MY BENEFIT, BUT WAS REALLY JUST TO MAKE HIMSELF FEEL BETTER.
HE NEVER TOLD ME GOODBYE.
WHAT PEOPLE SAY WHEN THEY DIE IS IMPORTANT.
BIG DADDY NEVER TOLD ME THAT, BUT HE DID SOMETHING BETTER-- HE SHOWED ME.
WHATEVER HE SAID TO KICK-ASS WHEN HE DIED GAVE KICK-ASS THE STRENGTH TO GO ON, TO COMPLETE THE MISSION. HE SAID WHAT HAD TO BE SAID. HE NEVER LOST FOCUS.
MOST PEOPLE JUST SAY "OH, SHIT" OR "OH, FUCK" WHEN THEY DIE...OR THEY CRY.
BUT BIG DADDY WAS BETTER THAN MOST PEOPLE. AND SO AM I, BECAUSE OF HIM.
TAXI

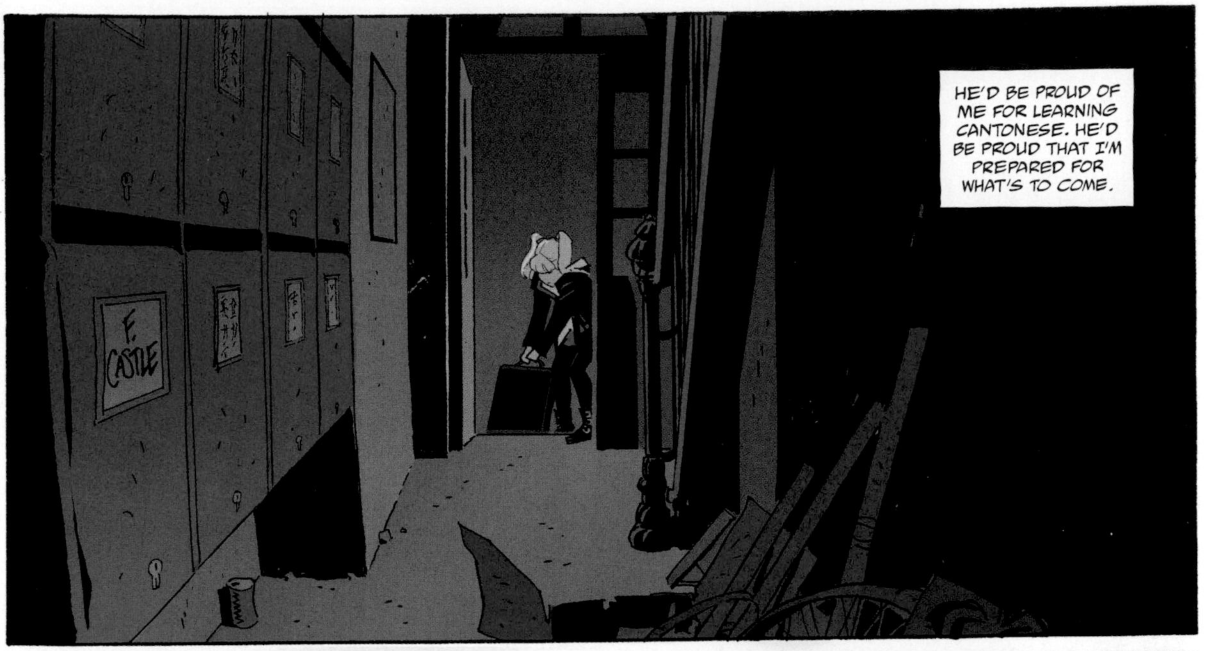
HE'D BE PROUD OF ME FOR LEARNING CANTONESE. HE'D BE PROUD THAT I'M PREPARED FOR WHAT'S TO COME.
F. CASTLE

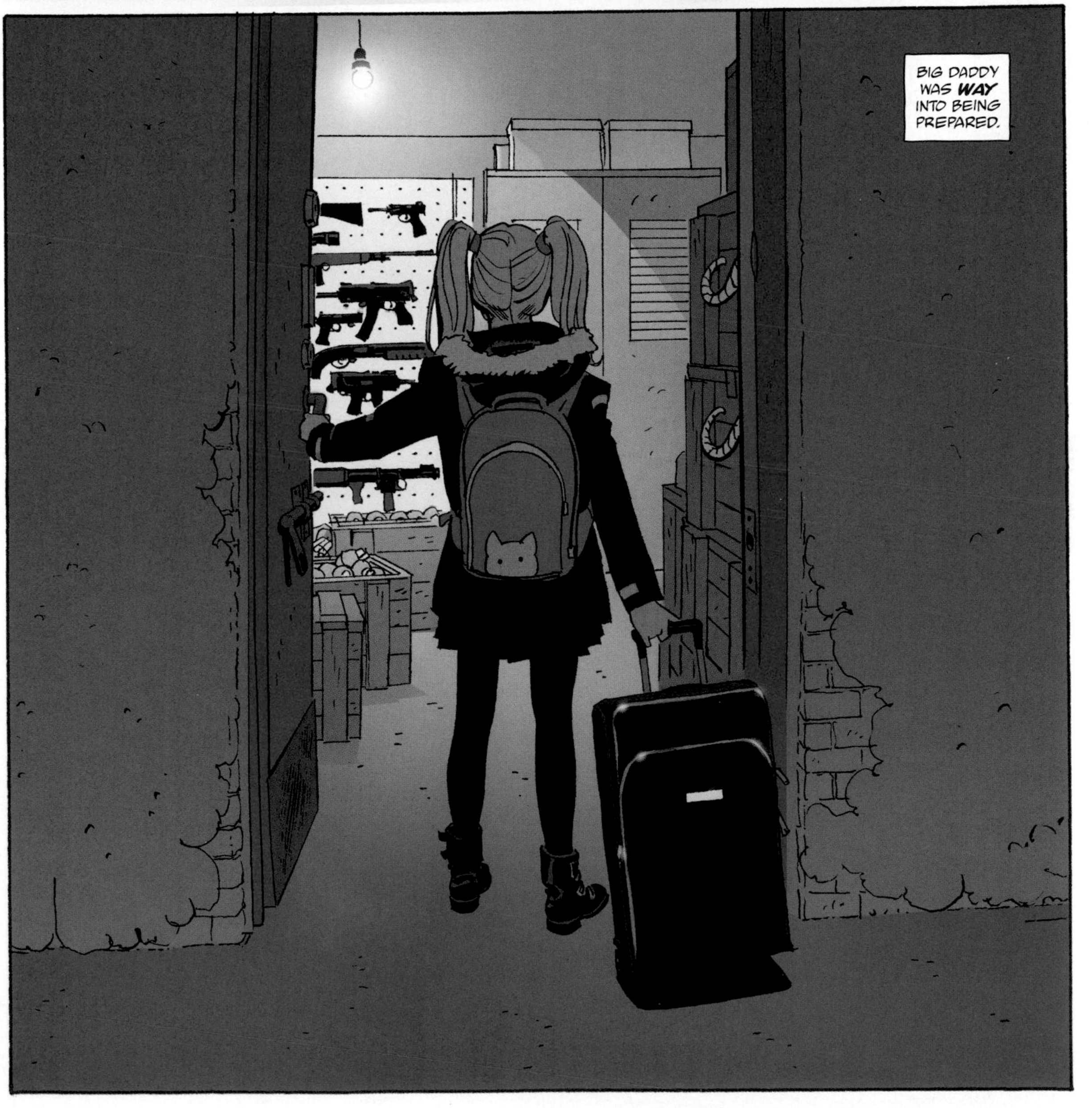
BIG DADDY WAS **WAY** INTO BEING PREPARED.

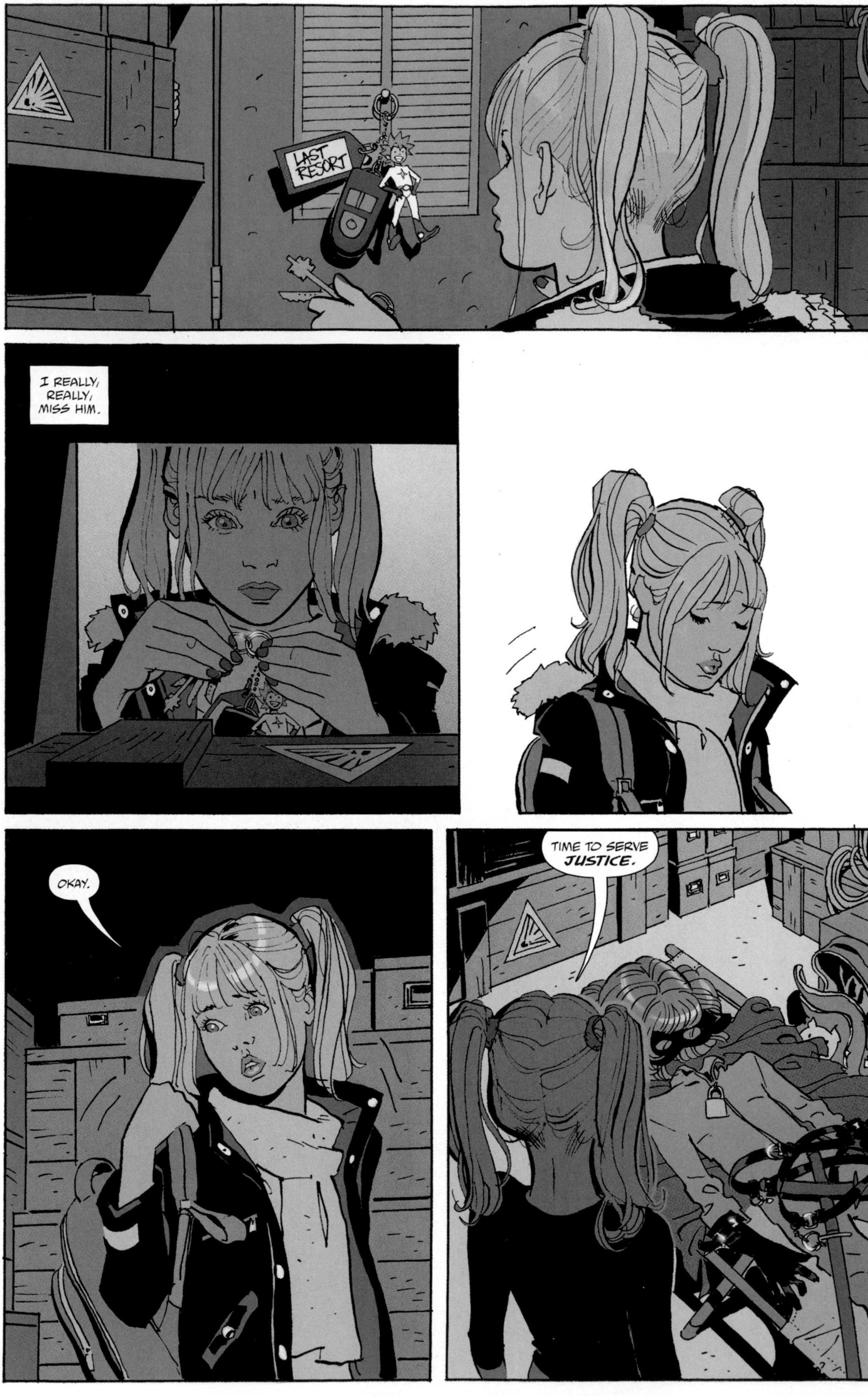
LAST RESORT
I REALLY, REALLY, MISS HIM.
OKAY.
TIME TO SERVE JUSTICE.

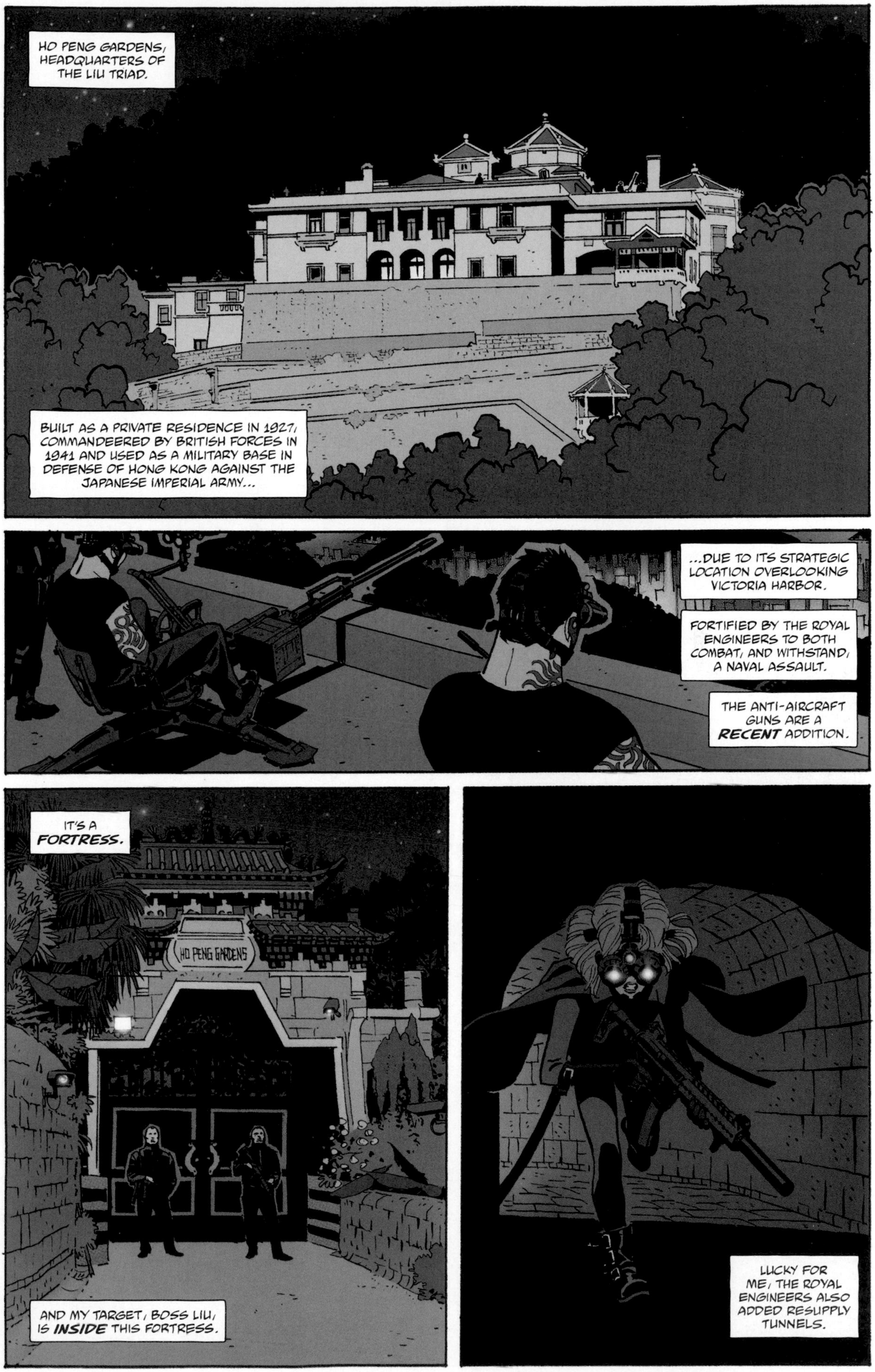
HO PENG GARDENS, HEADQUARTERS OF THE LIU TRIAD.
BUILT AS A PRIVATE RESIDENCE IN 1927, COMMANDEERED BY BRITISH FORCES IN 1941 AND USED AS A MILITARY BASE IN DEFENSE OF HONG KONG AGAINST THE JAPANESE IMPERIAL ARMY...
...DUE TO ITS STRATEGIC LOCATION OVERLOOKING VICTORIA HARBOR.
FORTIFIED BY THE ROYAL ENGINEERS TO BOTH COMBAT, AND WITHSTAND, A NAVAL ASSAULT.
THE ANTI-AIRCRAFT GUNS ARE A **RECENT** ADDITION.
IT'S A **FORTRESS.**
HO PENG GARDENS
AND MY TARGET, BOSS LIU, IS **INSIDE** THIS FORTRESS.
LUCKY FOR ME, THE ROYAL ENGINEERS ALSO ADDED RESUPPLY TUNNELS.

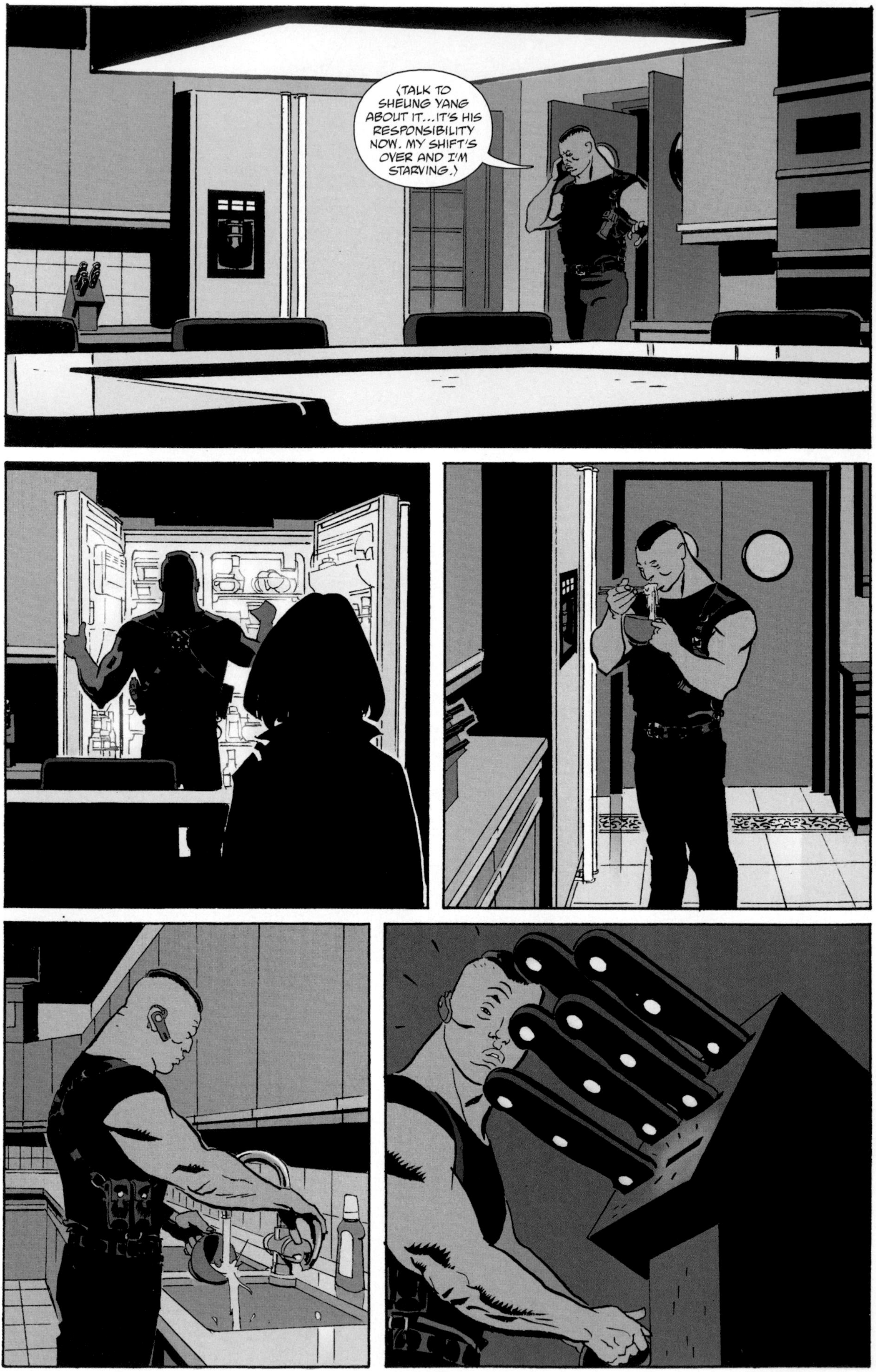
(TALK TO SHEUNG YANG ABOUT IT...IT'S HIS RESPONSIBILITY NOW. MY SHIFT'S OVER AND I'M STARVING.)

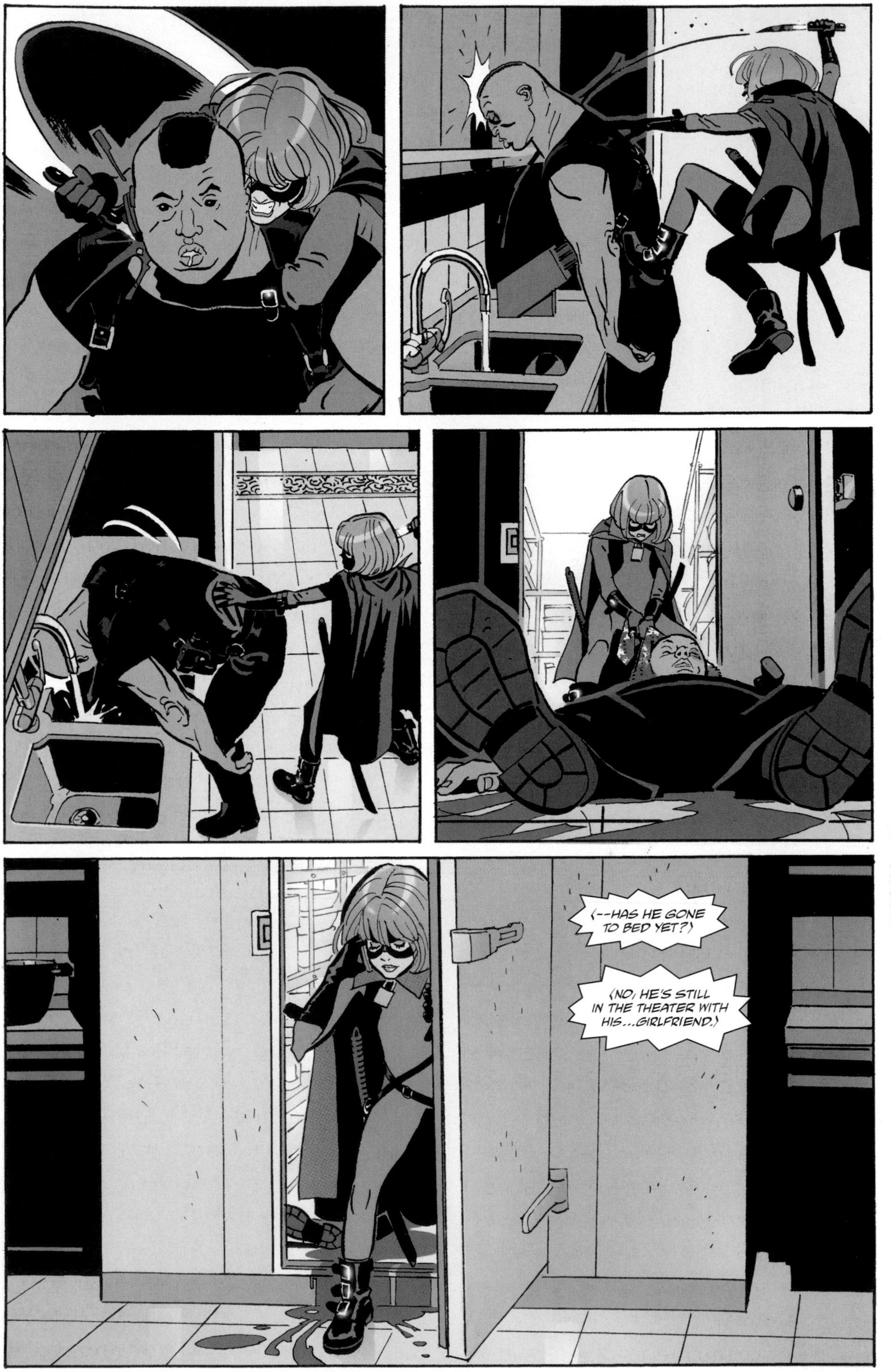
⟨--HAS HE GONE TO BED YET?⟩
⟨NO, HE'S STILL IN THE THEATER WITH HIS...GIRLFRIEND.⟩

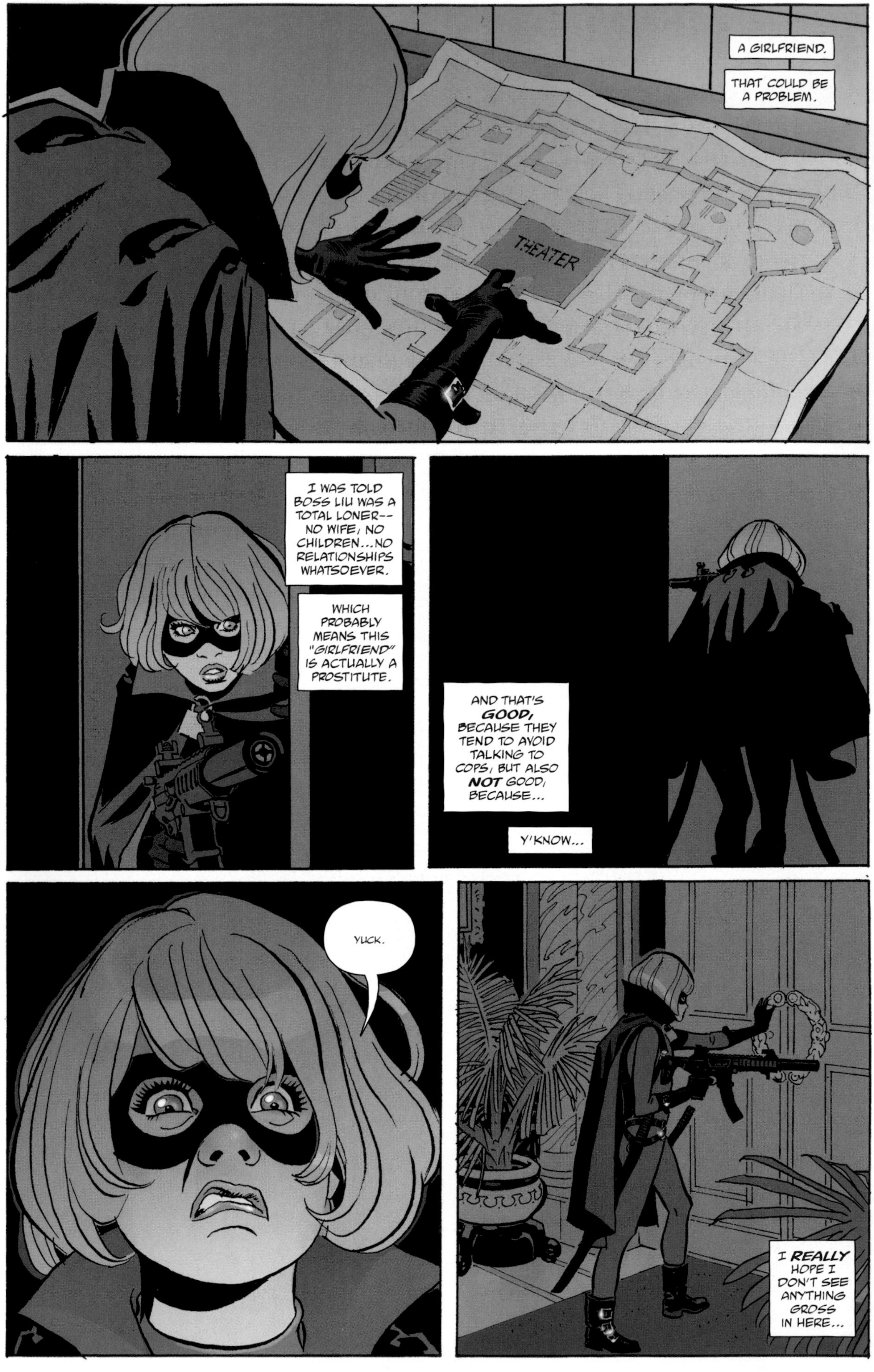

A GIRLFRIEND.
THAT COULD BE A PROBLEM.
THEATER
I WAS TOLD BOSS LIU WAS A TOTAL LONER-- NO WIFE, NO CHILDREN...NO RELATIONSHIPS WHATSOEVER.
WHICH PROBABLY MEANS THIS "GIRLFRIEND" IS ACTUALLY A PROSTITUTE.
AND THAT'S **GOOD,** BECAUSE THEY TEND TO AVOID TALKING TO COPS, BUT ALSO **NOT** GOOD, BECAUSE...
Y'KNOW...
YUCK.
I **REALLY** HOPE I DON'T SEE ANYTHING GROSS IN HERE...

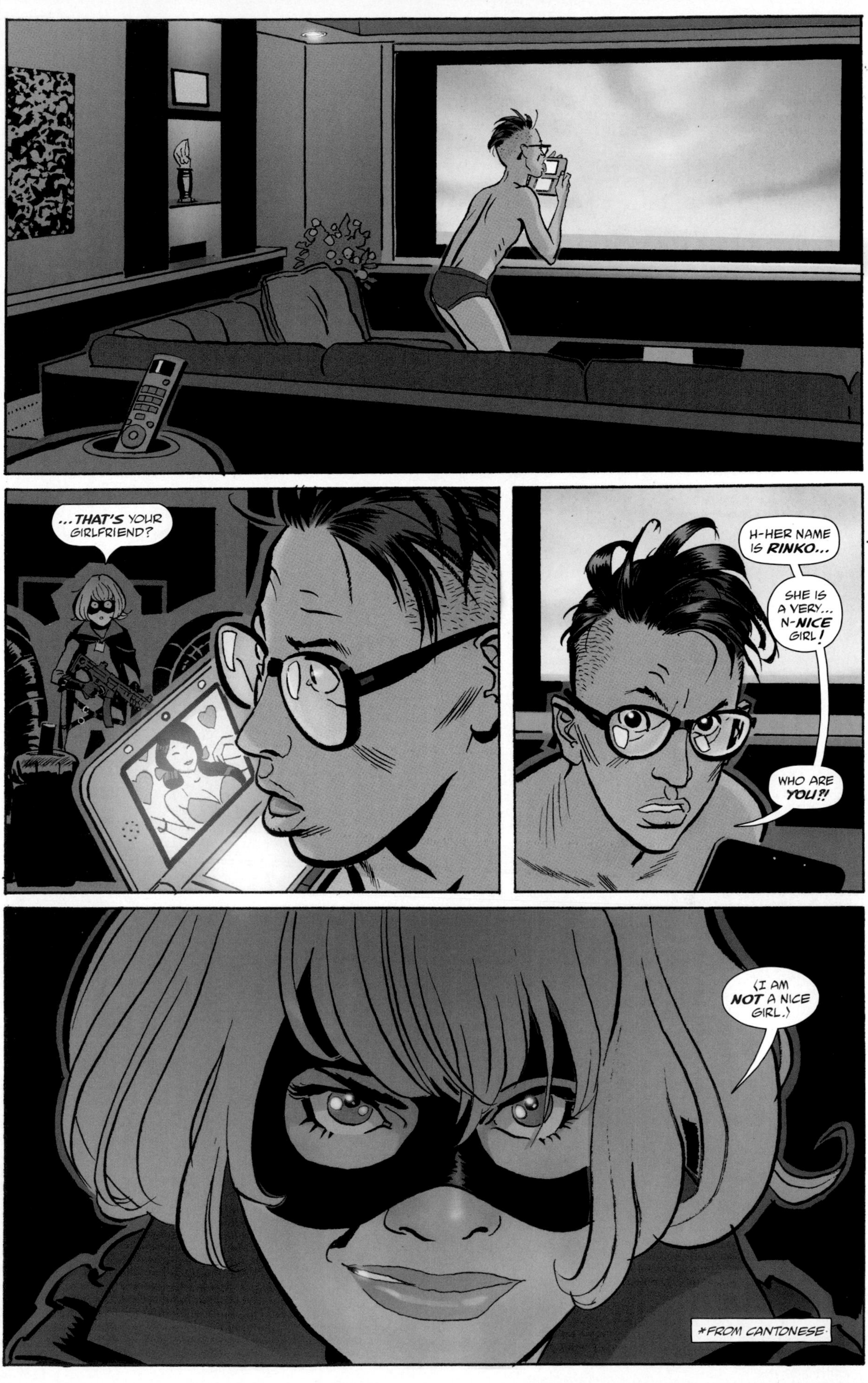
...THAT'S YOUR GIRLFRIEND?
H-HER NAME IS RINKO...
SHE IS A VERY... N-NICE GIRL!
WHO ARE YOU?!
‹I AM NOT A NICE GIRL.›
*FROM CANTONESE.

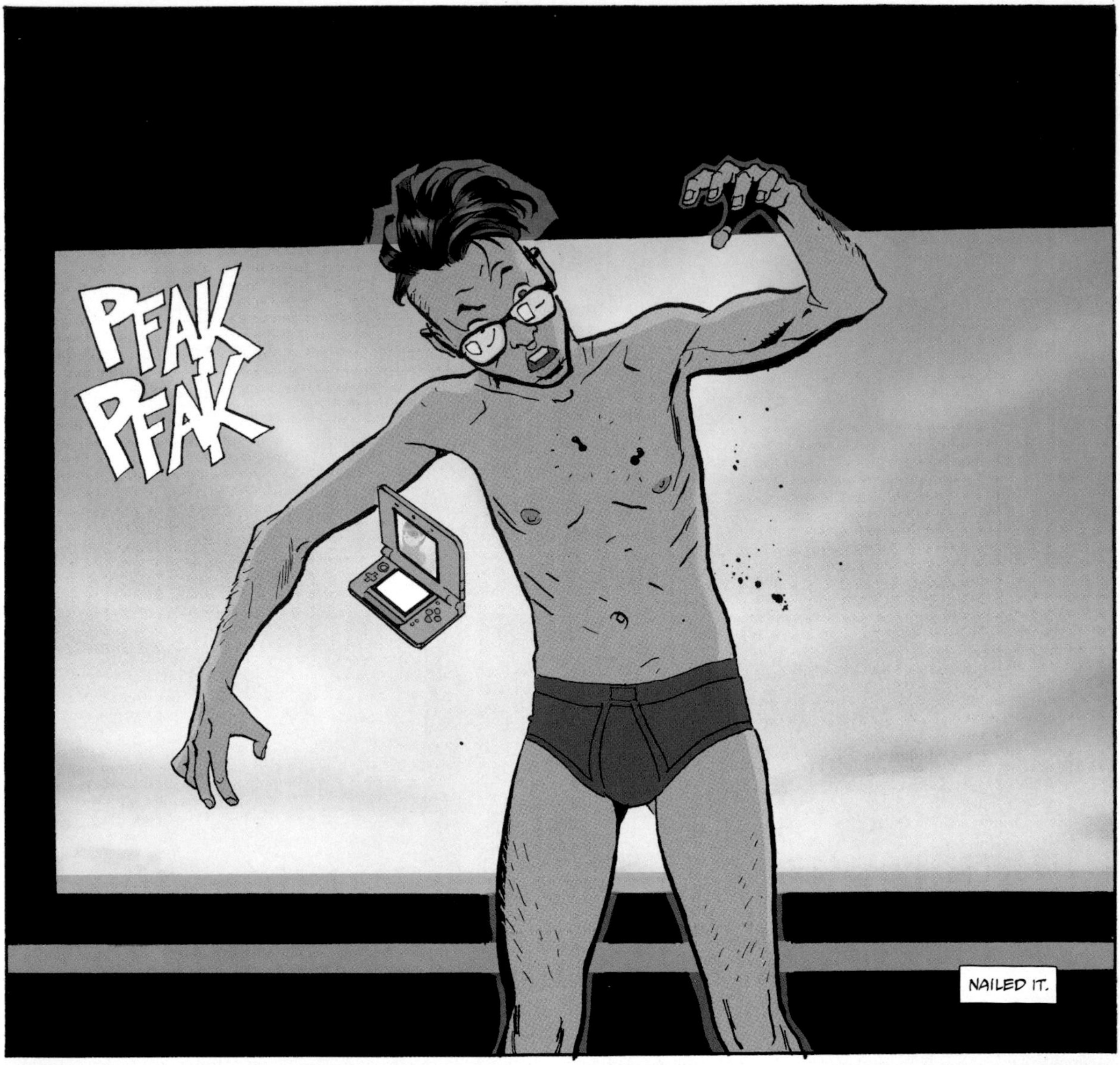
PFAK
PFAK
NAILED IT.

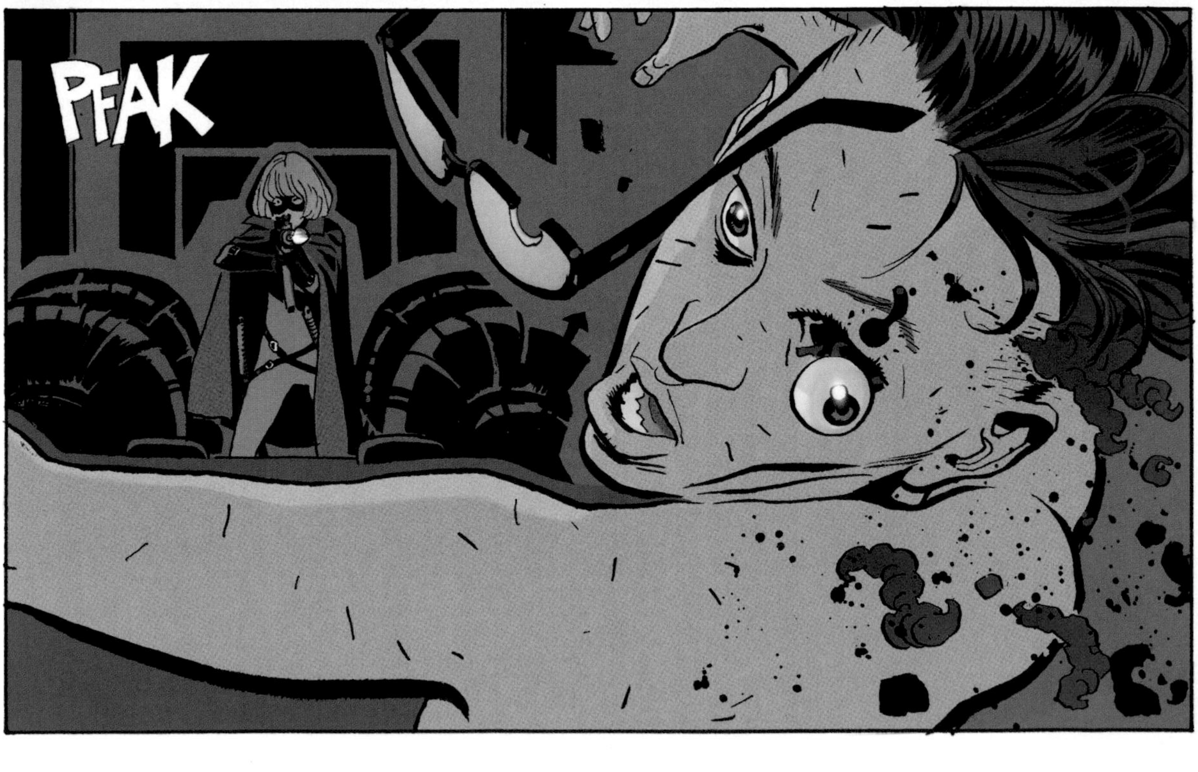
PFAK

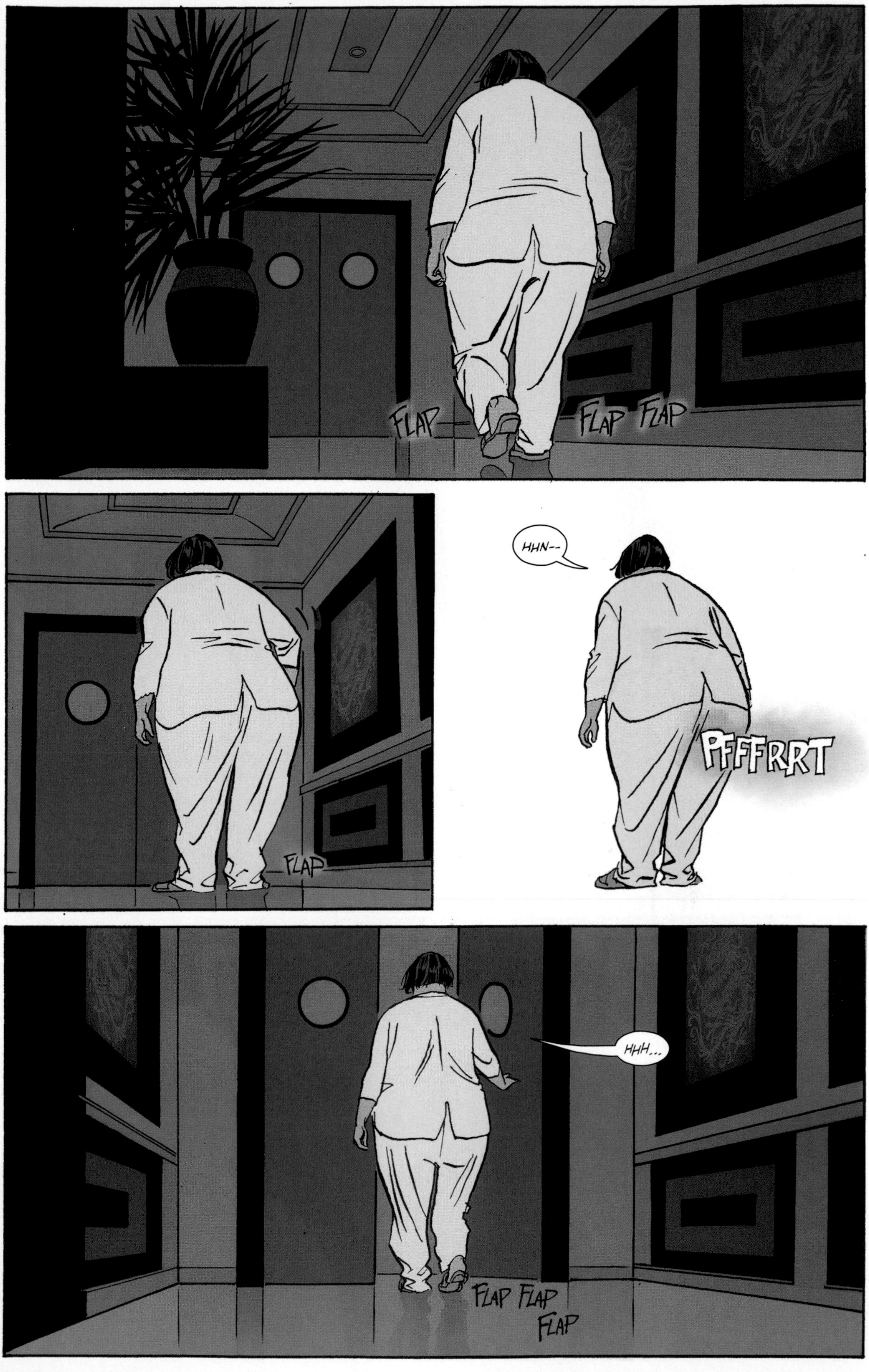
FLAP
FLAP FLAP
FLAP
HHN--
PFFFRRT
HHH...
FLAP FLAP
FLAP

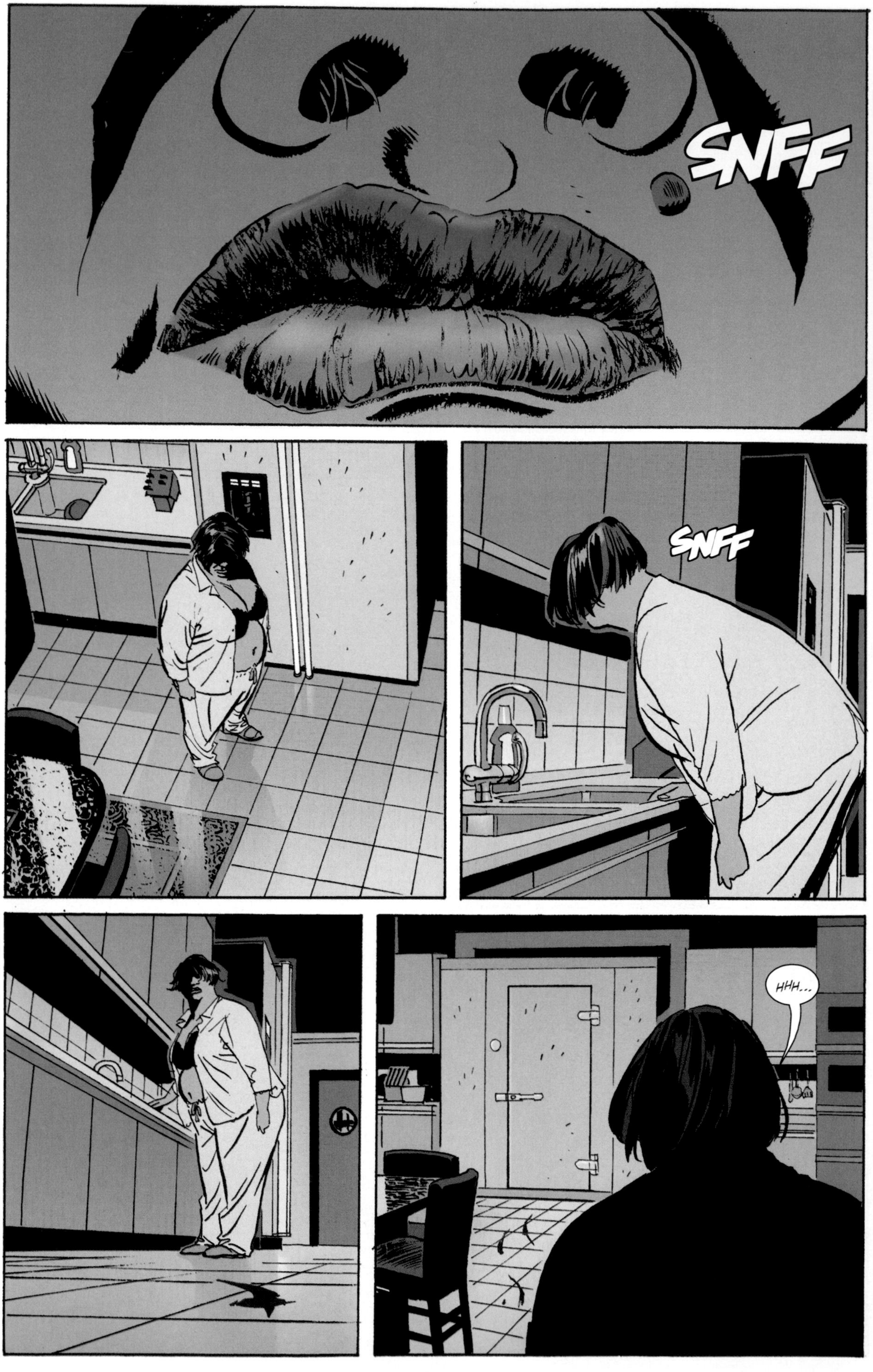
SNFF
SNFF
HHH...

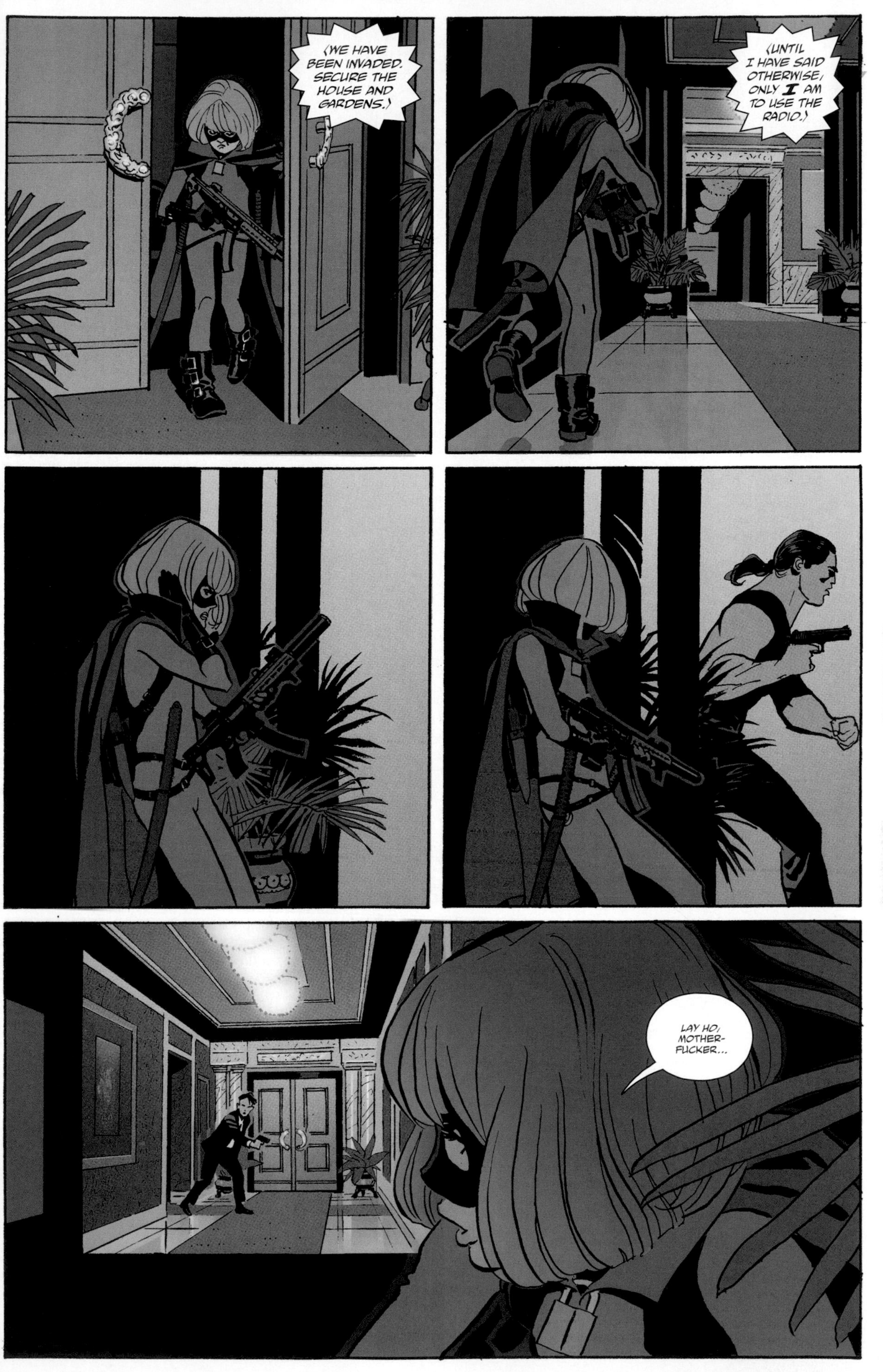
‹WE HAVE BEEN INVADED. SECURE THE HOUSE AND GARDENS.›
‹UNTIL I HAVE SAID OTHERWISE, ONLY I AM TO USE THE RADIO.›
LAY HO, MOTHER-FUCKER...

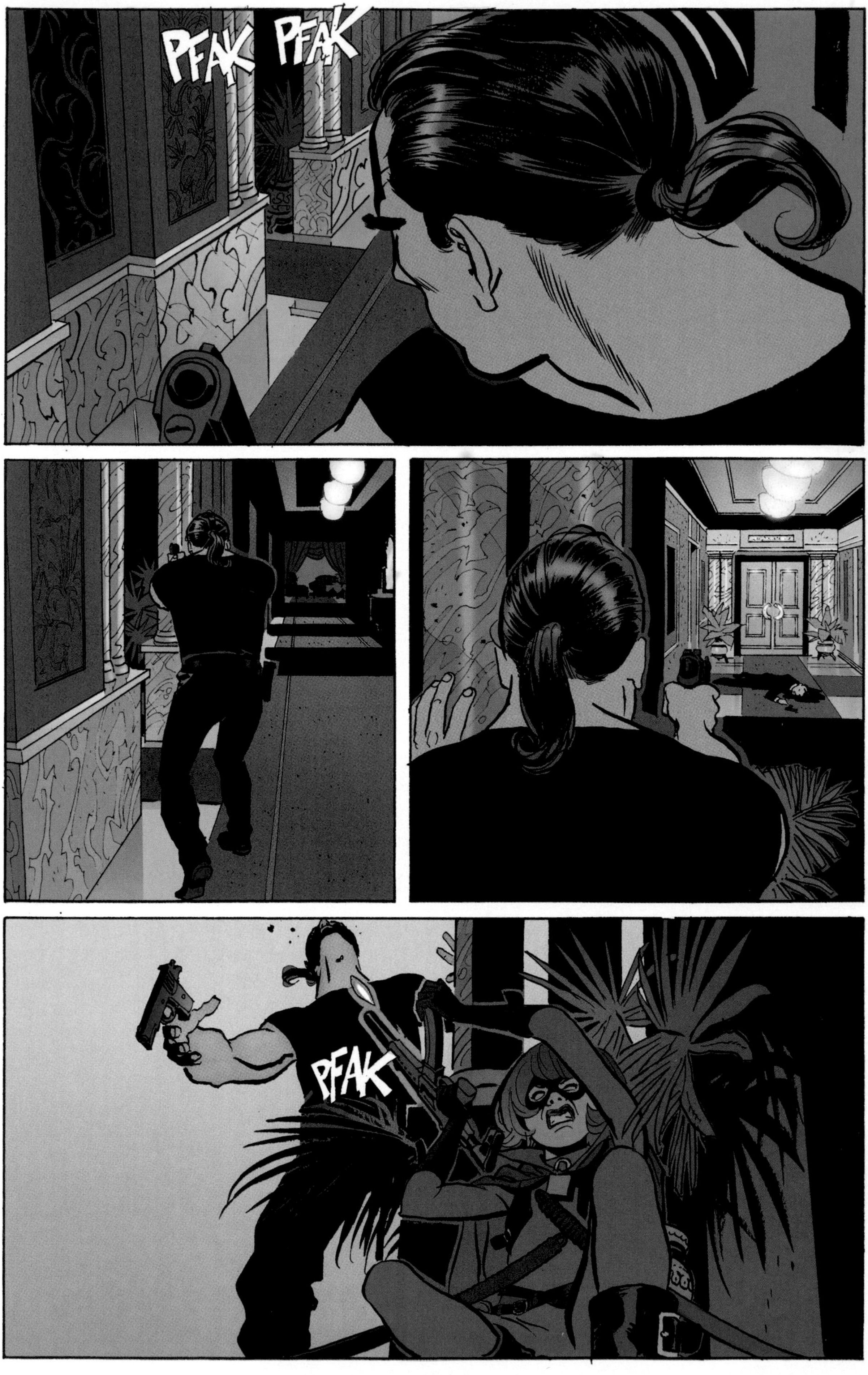
PFAK PFAK
PFAK

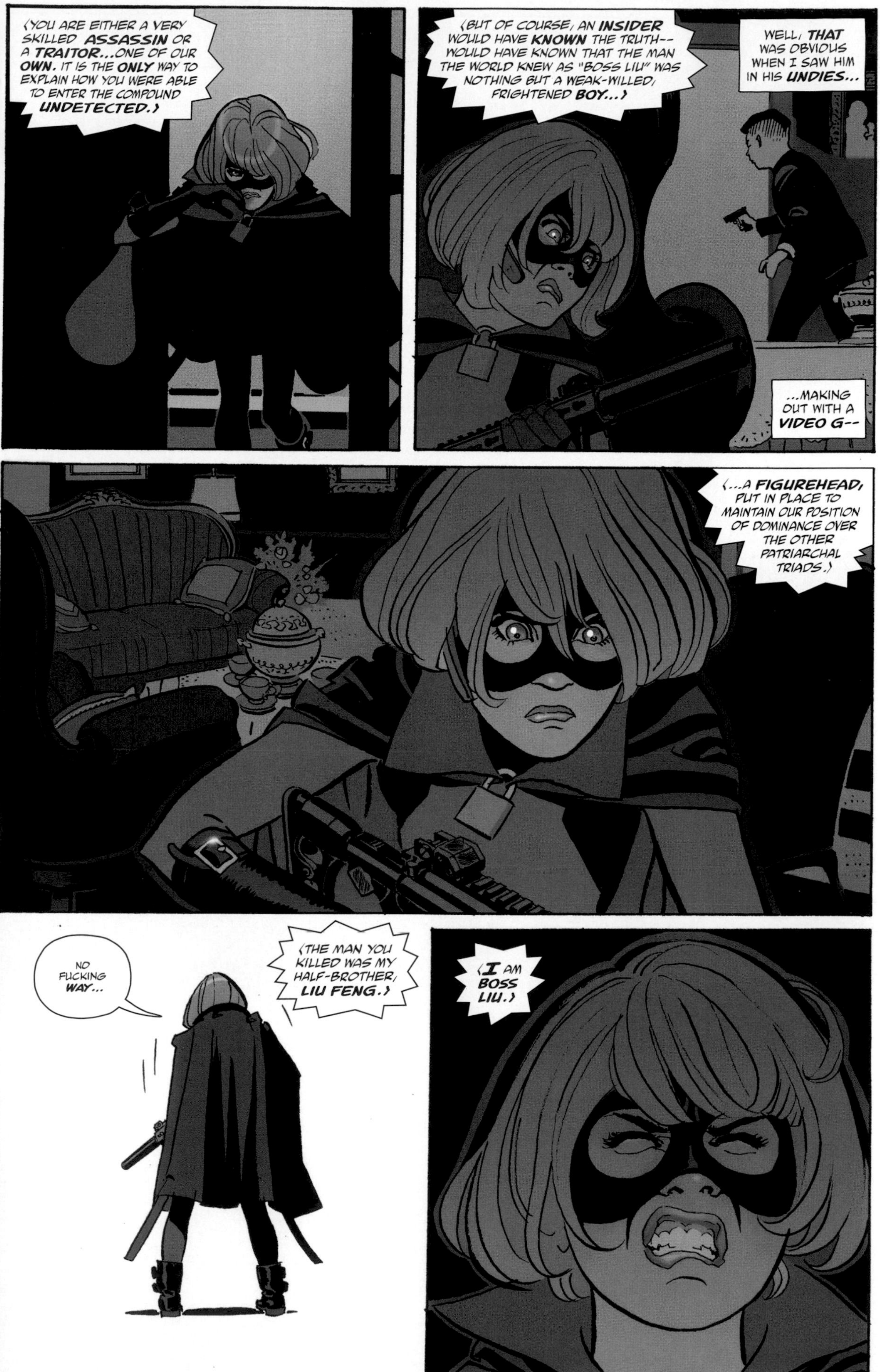

⟨YOU ARE EITHER A VERY SKILLED ASSASSIN OR A TRAITOR...ONE OF OUR OWN. IT IS THE ONLY WAY TO EXPLAIN HOW YOU WERE ABLE TO ENTER THE COMPOUND UNDETECTED.⟩
⟨BUT OF COURSE, AN INSIDER WOULD HAVE KNOWN THE TRUTH-- WOULD HAVE KNOWN THAT THE MAN THE WORLD KNEW AS "BOSS LIU" WAS NOTHING BUT A WEAK-WILLED, FRIGHTENED BOY...⟩
WELL, THAT WAS OBVIOUS WHEN I SAW HIM IN HIS UNDIES...
...MAKING OUT WITH A VIDEO G--
⟨...A FIGUREHEAD, PUT IN PLACE TO MAINTAIN OUR POSITION OF DOMINANCE OVER THE OTHER PATRIARCHAL TRIADS.⟩
NO FUCKING WAY...
⟨THE MAN YOU KILLED WAS MY HALF-BROTHER, LIU FENG.⟩
⟨I AM BOSS LIU.⟩

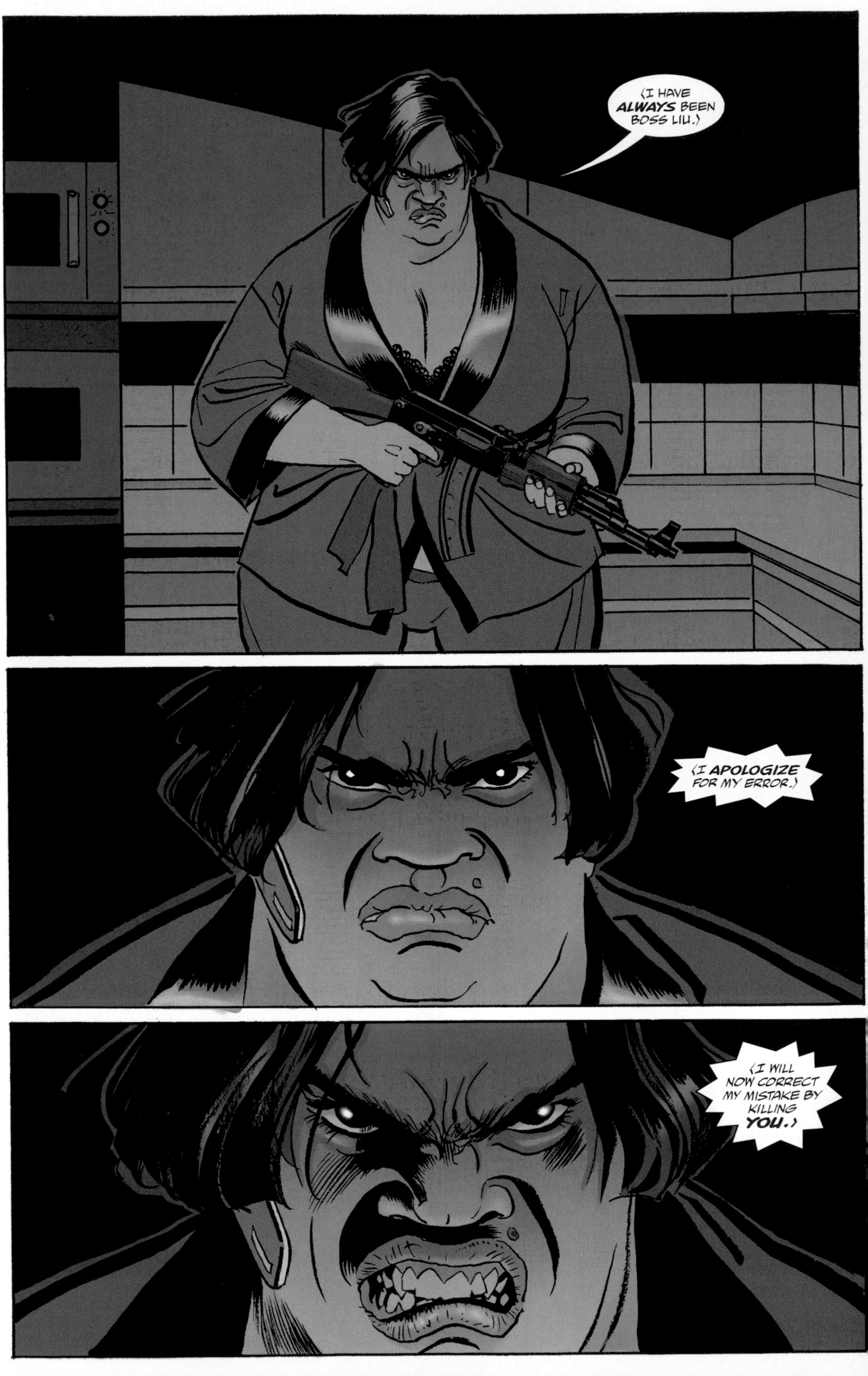
‹I HAVE ALWAYS BEEN BOSS LIU.›
‹I APOLOGIZE FOR MY ERROR.›
‹I WILL NOW CORRECT MY MISTAKE BY KILLING YOU.›

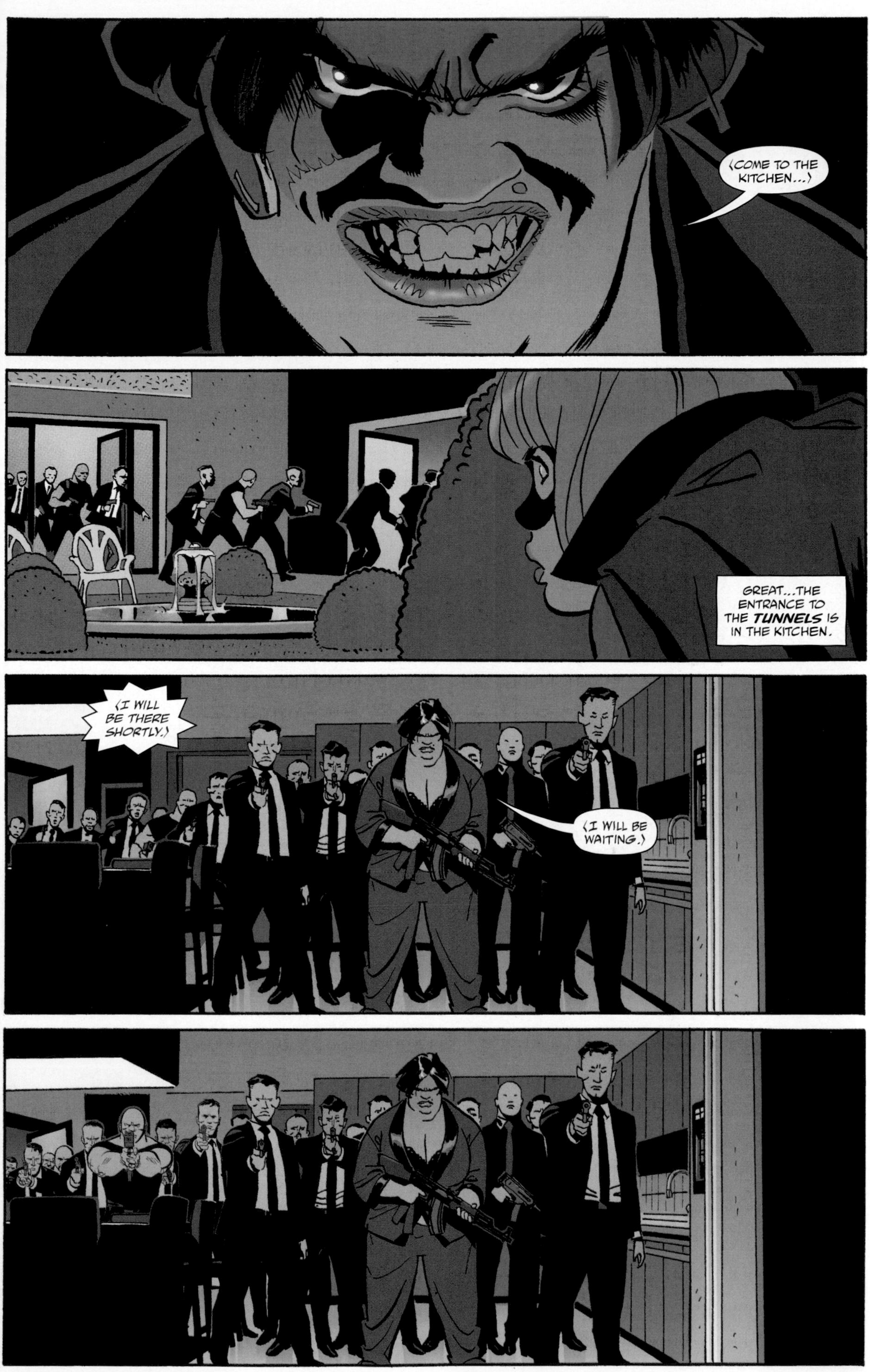
‹COME TO THE KITCHEN...›
GREAT...THE ENTRANCE TO THE TUNNELS IS IN THE KITCHEN.
‹I WILL BE THERE SHORTLY.›
‹I WILL BE WAITING.›

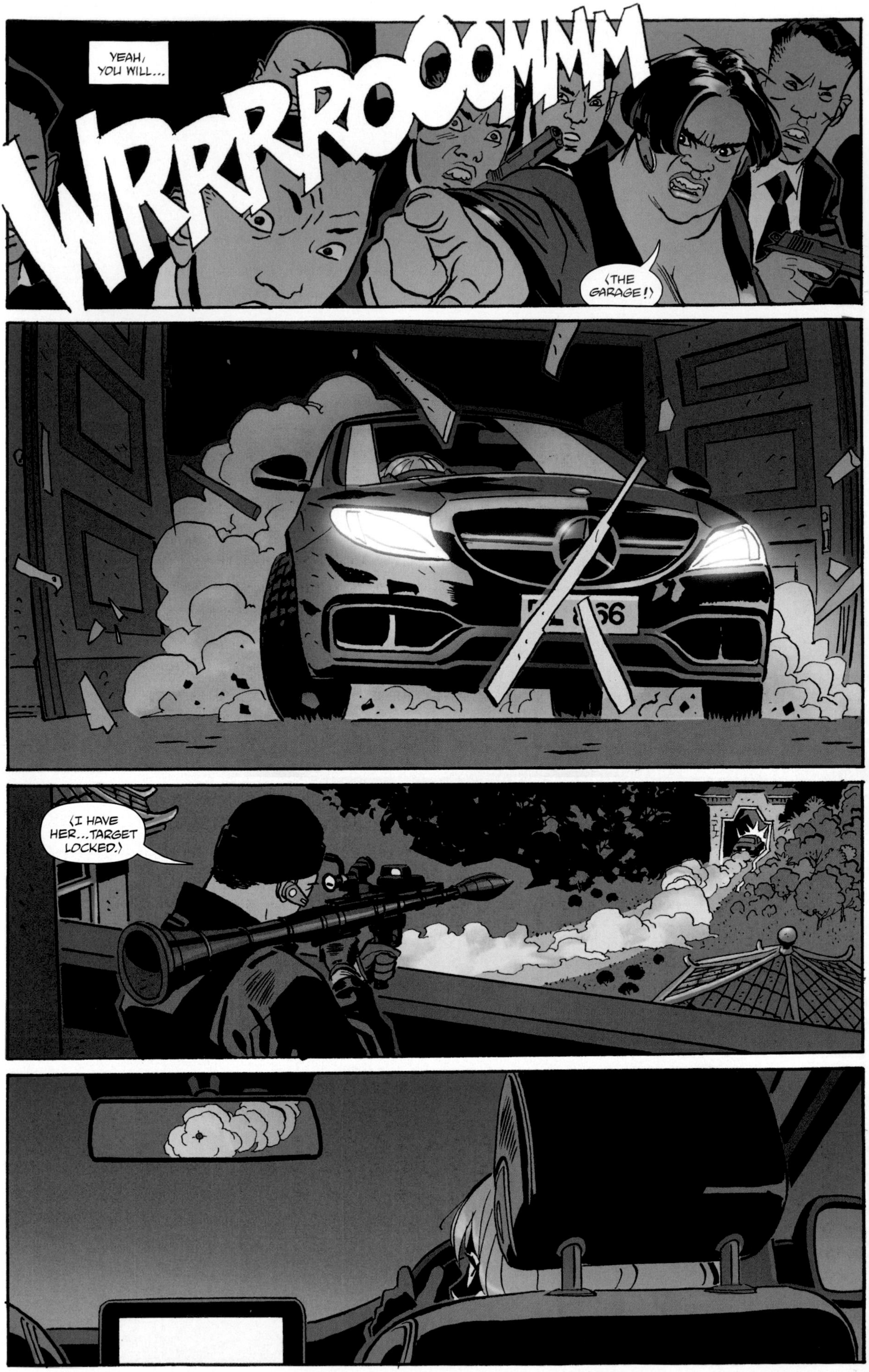
YEAH, YOU WILL...
WRRRROOOMMM
⟨THE GARAGE!⟩
⟨I HAVE HER...TARGET LOCKED.⟩

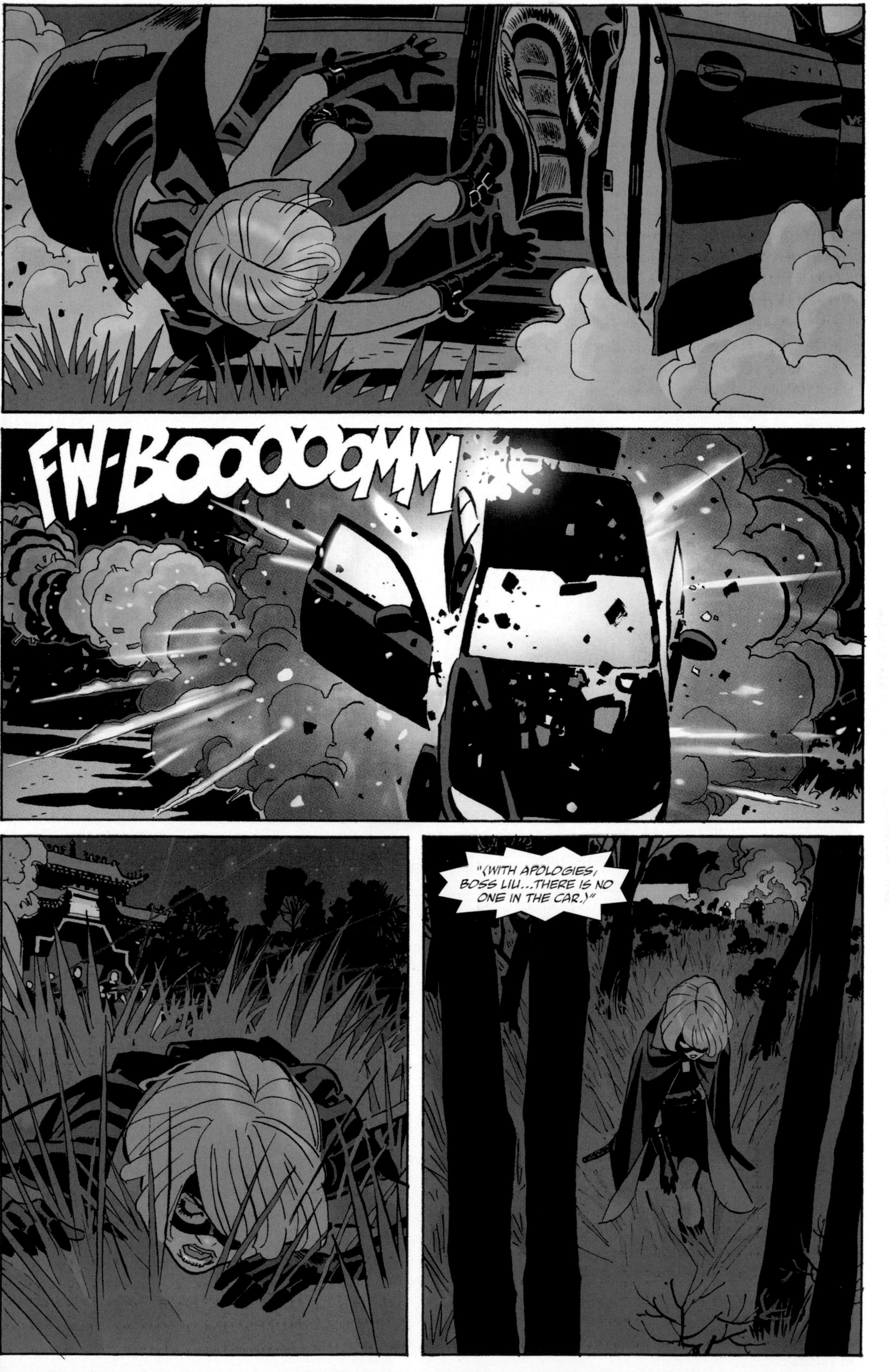
FW-BOOOOOMM
"(WITH APOLOGIES, BOSS LIU...THERE IS NO ONE IN THE CAR.)"

〈OF *COURSE* SHE ESCAPED.〉

〈SHE KNEW THE ROCKET WAS COMING.〉

〈*THIS* IS WHY I ORDERED ALL OF YOU TO *STAY OFF THE RADIO.*〉

〈FIND HER AND BRING HER TO ME.〉

〈AND IF ANYONE...〉

〈ANY-ONE...〉

〈...IS *HELPING* HER...〉

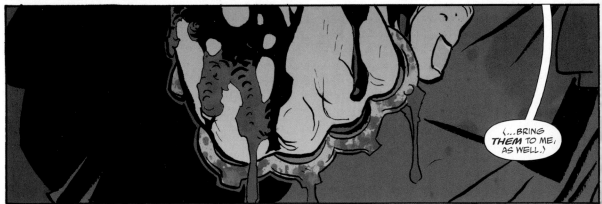

〈...BRING *THEM* TO ME, AS WELL.〉

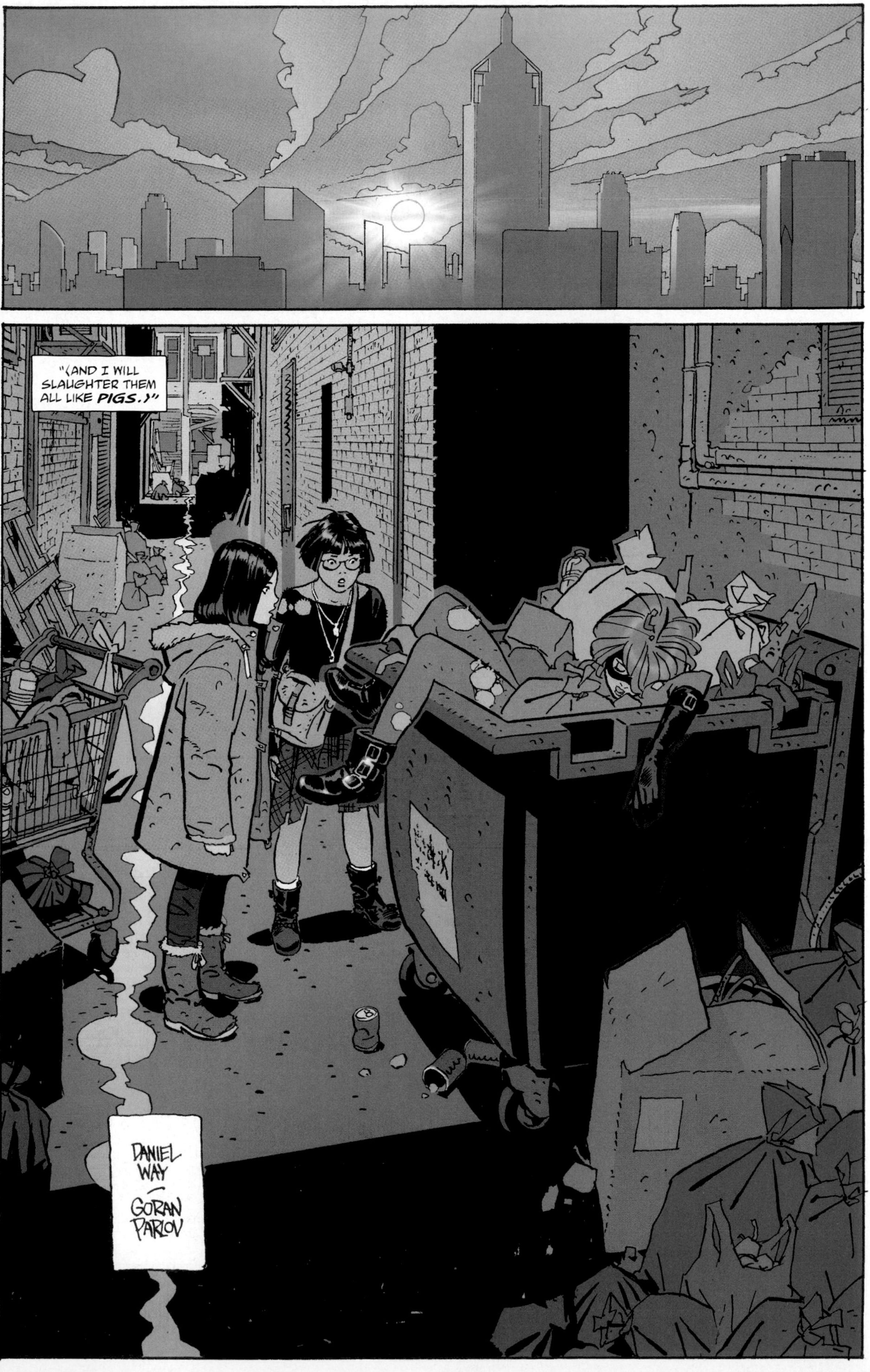
"‹AND I WILL SLAUGHTER THEM ALL LIKE PIGS.›"
DANIEL WAY
—
GORAN PARLOV

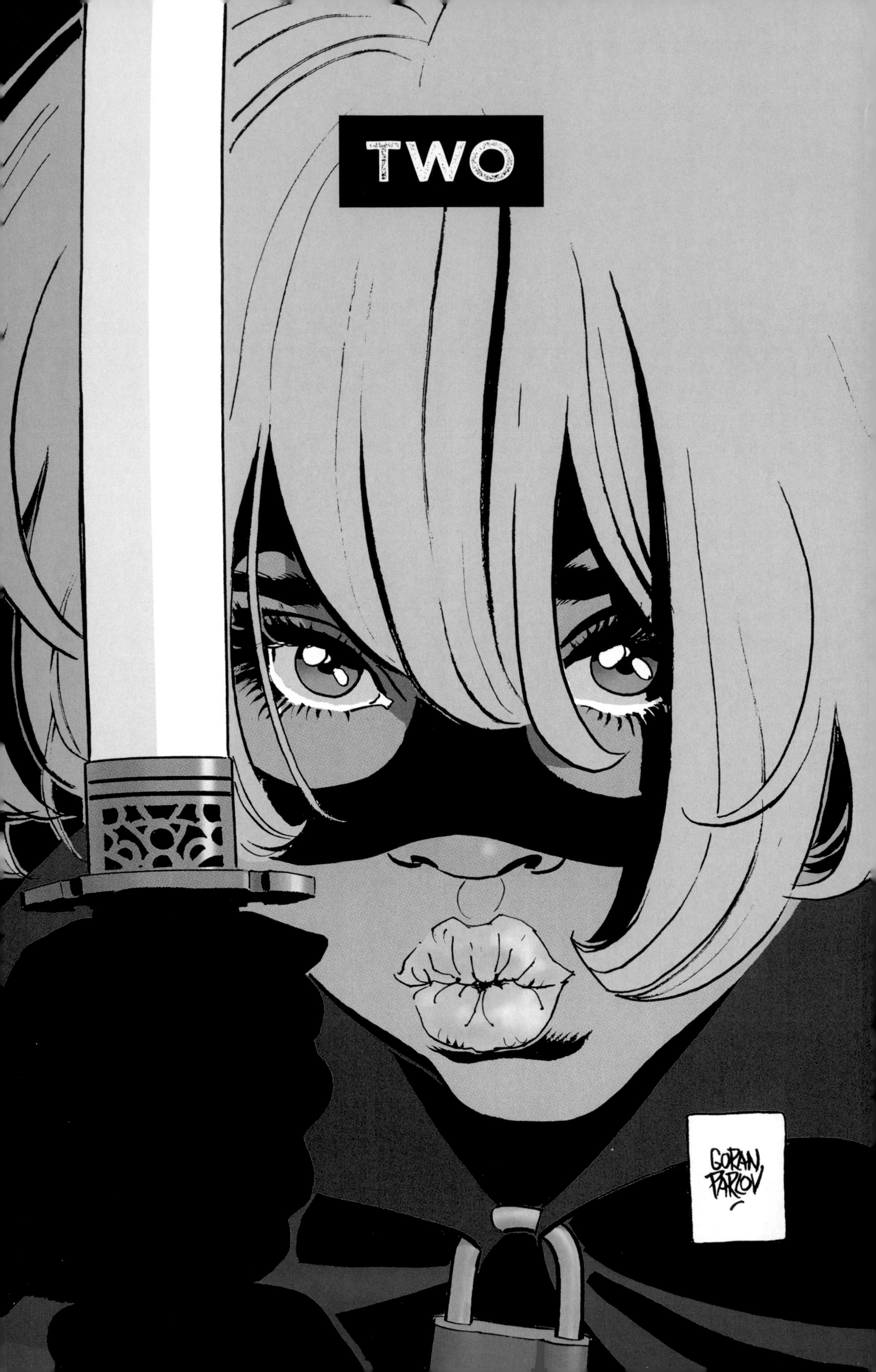
TWO
GORAN PARLOV

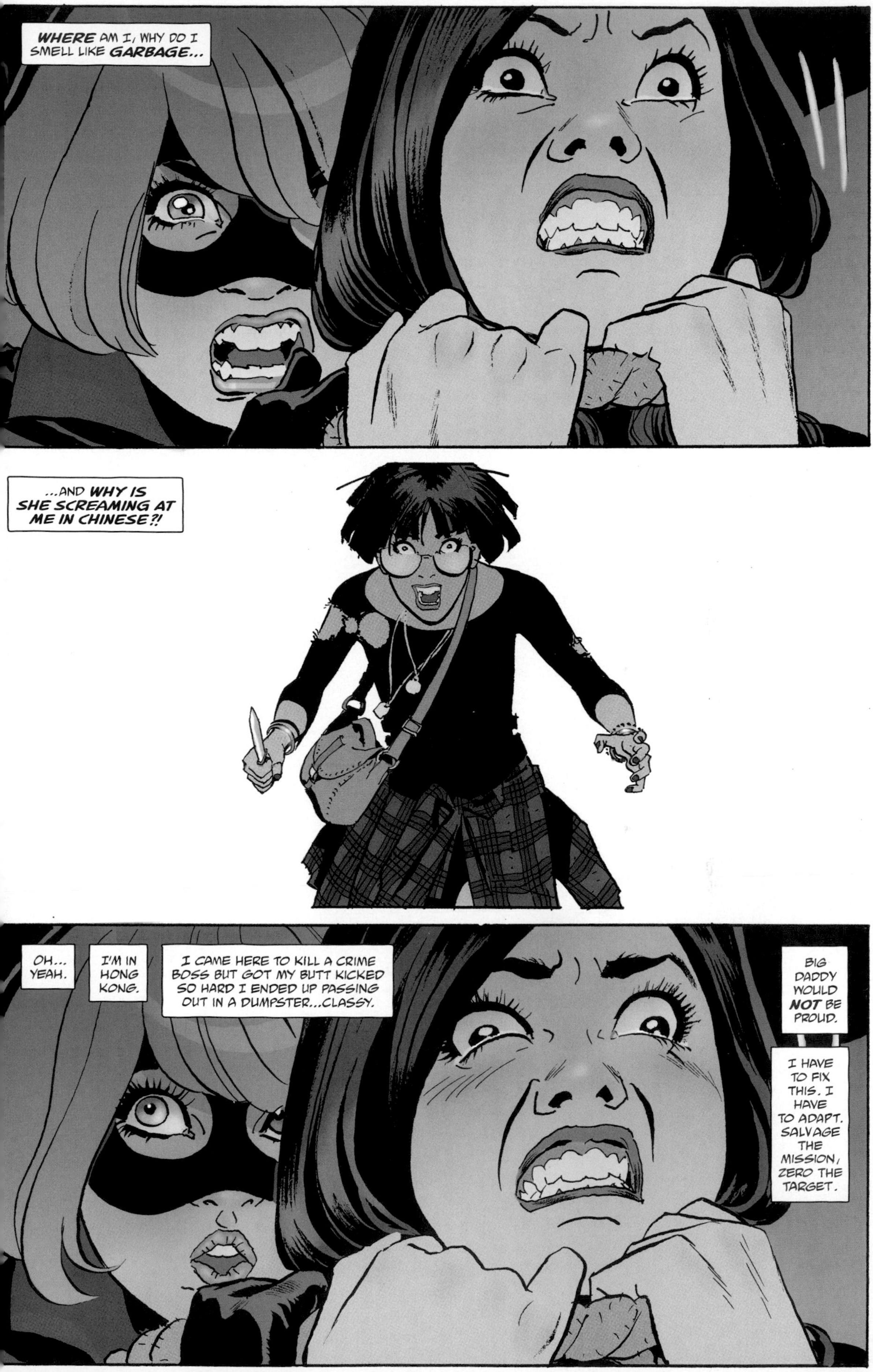

WHERE AM I, WHY DO I SMELL LIKE GARBAGE...
...AND WHY IS SHE SCREAMING AT ME IN CHINESE?!
OH... YEAH.
I'M IN HONG KONG.
I CAME HERE TO KILL A CRIME BOSS BUT GOT MY BUTT KICKED SO HARD I ENDED UP PASSING OUT IN A DUMPSTER...CLASSY.
BIG DADDY WOULD NOT BE PROUD.
I HAVE TO FIX THIS. I HAVE TO ADAPT. SALVAGE THE MISSION, ZERO THE TARGET.

BUT FIRST IT LOOKS LIKE I'M GONNA HAVE TO FUCK UP A BUNCH OF ASIAN KIDS.
DANIEL WAY - GORAN PARLOV

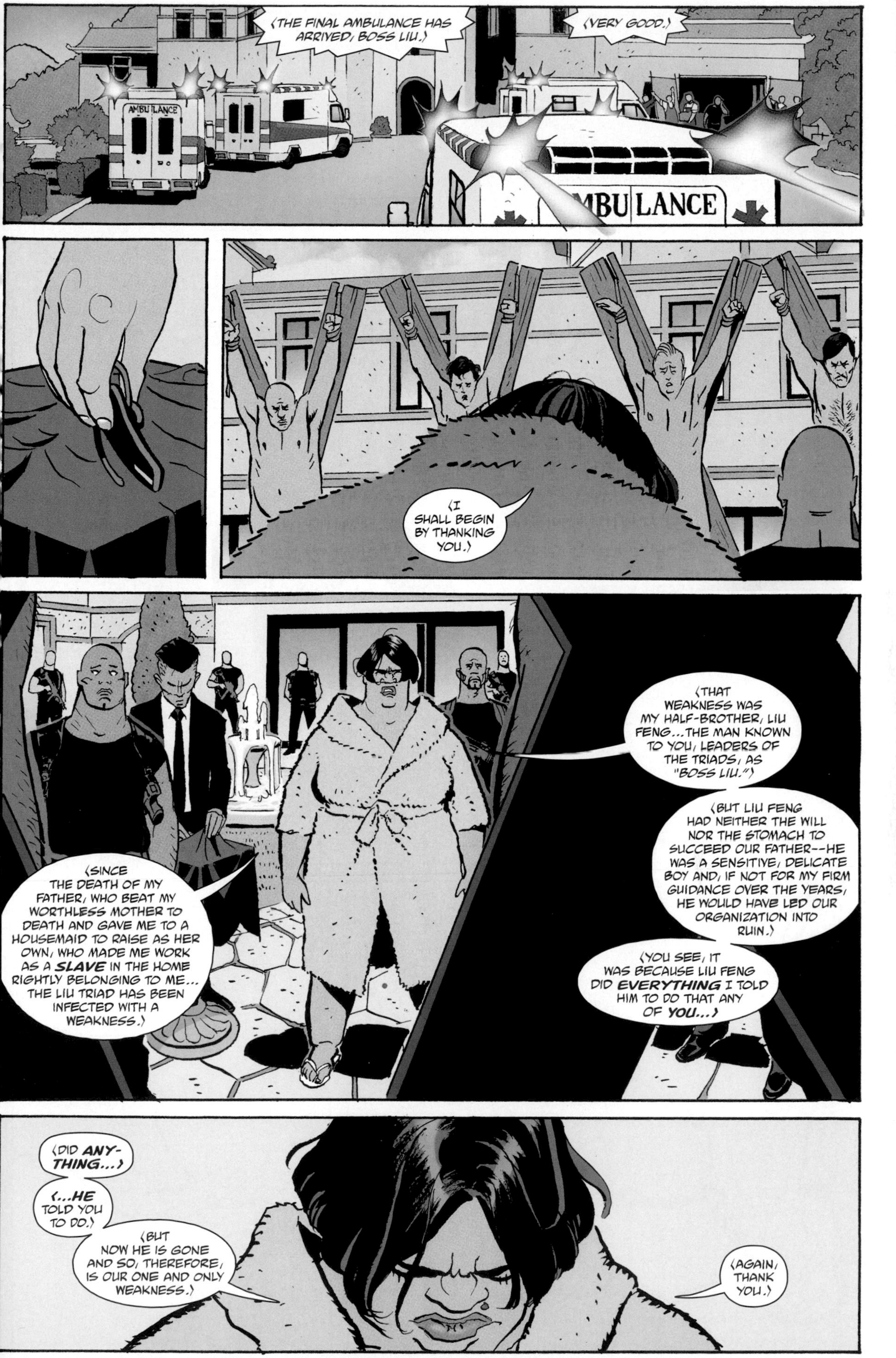

⟨THE FINAL AMBULANCE HAS ARRIVED, BOSS LIU.⟩
⟨VERY GOOD.⟩
AMBULANCE
AMBULANCE
⟨I SHALL BEGIN BY THANKING YOU.⟩
⟨SINCE THE DEATH OF MY FATHER, WHO BEAT MY WORTHLESS MOTHER TO DEATH AND GAVE ME TO A HOUSEMAID TO RAISE AS HER OWN, WHO MADE ME WORK AS A SLAVE IN THE HOME RIGHTLY BELONGING TO ME... THE LIU TRIAD HAS BEEN INFECTED WITH A WEAKNESS.⟩
⟨THAT WEAKNESS WAS MY HALF-BROTHER, LIU FENG...THE MAN KNOWN TO YOU, LEADERS OF THE TRIADS, AS "BOSS LIU."⟩
⟨BUT LIU FENG HAD NEITHER THE WILL NOR THE STOMACH TO SUCCEED OUR FATHER--HE WAS A SENSITIVE, DELICATE BOY AND, IF NOT FOR MY FIRM GUIDANCE OVER THE YEARS, HE WOULD HAVE LED OUR ORGANIZATION INTO RUIN.⟩
⟨YOU SEE, IT WAS BECAUSE LIU FENG DID EVERYTHING I TOLD HIM TO DO THAT ANY OF YOU...⟩
⟨DID ANY-THING...⟩
⟨...HE TOLD YOU TO DO.⟩
⟨BUT NOW HE IS GONE AND SO, THEREFORE, IS OUR ONE AND ONLY WEAKNESS.⟩
⟨AGAIN, THANK YOU.⟩

⟨IT GREATLY AMUSES ME THAT, OF ALL THINGS, A **PENIS** IS REGARDED AS AN ESSENTIAL REQUIREMENT FOR TRIAD LEADERSHIP.⟩

⟨TELL ME, TUNG AN-LO, IS YOUR PENIS THE SECRET TO THE GREAT SUCCESS OF THE FIVE CIRCLES TRIAD?⟩

⟨OR YOURS, CHANG KUEI-SEN, TO THE GREAT SUCCESS OF THE RED JADE TRIAD?⟩

⟨NO, THEY ARE NOT...NOR IS YOURS, JIN CHAO, FOR THAT OF THE GENG YAN TONG.⟩

⟨IN FACT, THE SOLE REASON **ANY** OF YOUR ORGANIZATIONS HAVE HAD **ANY** SUCCESS IS BECAUSE OF THEIR ASSOCIATIONS WITH THE LIU TRIAD.⟩

⟨WITH **ME.**⟩

⟨**I** AM WHAT IS ESSENTIAL.⟩

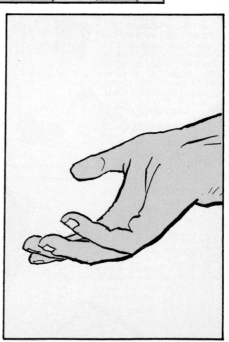

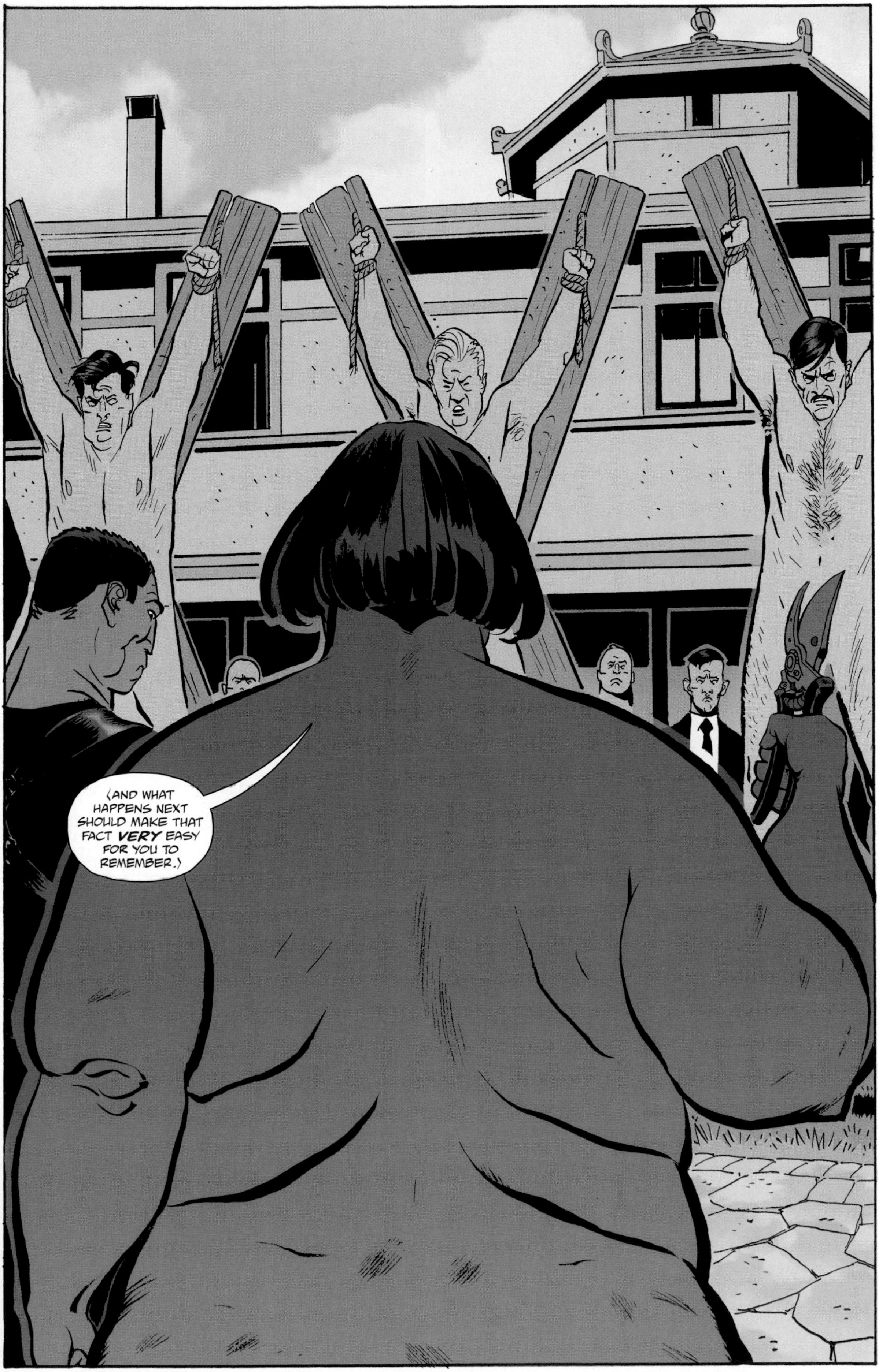
‹AND WHAT HAPPENS NEXT SHOULD MAKE THAT FACT VERY EASY FOR YOU TO REMEMBER.›

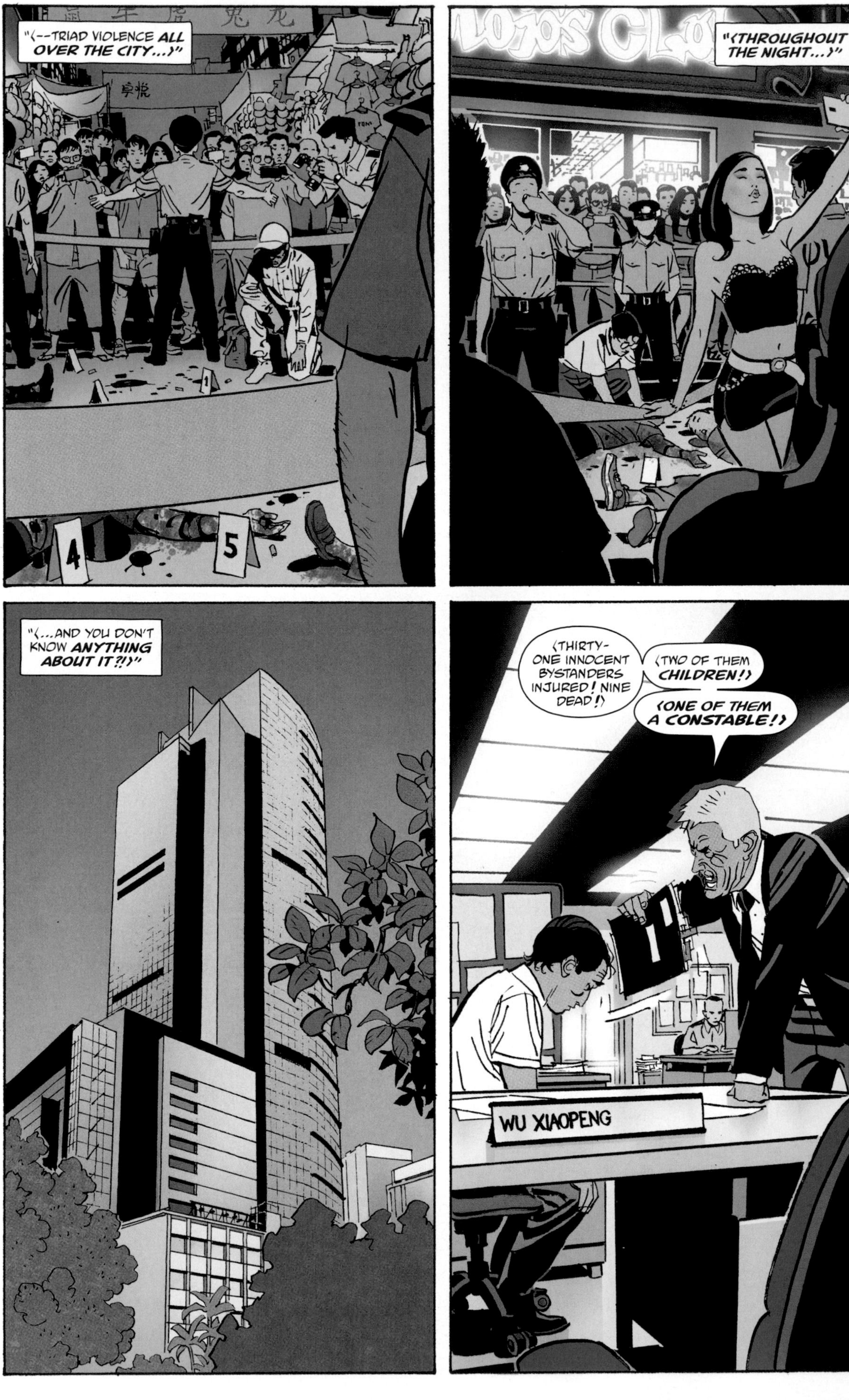
"‹--TRIAD VIOLENCE ALL OVER THE CITY...›"
"‹THROUGHOUT THE NIGHT...›"
"‹...AND YOU DON'T KNOW ANYTHING ABOUT IT?!›"
‹THIRTY-ONE INNOCENT BYSTANDERS INJURED! NINE DEAD!›
‹TWO OF THEM CHILDREN!›
‹ONE OF THEM A CONSTABLE!›
WU XIAOPENG

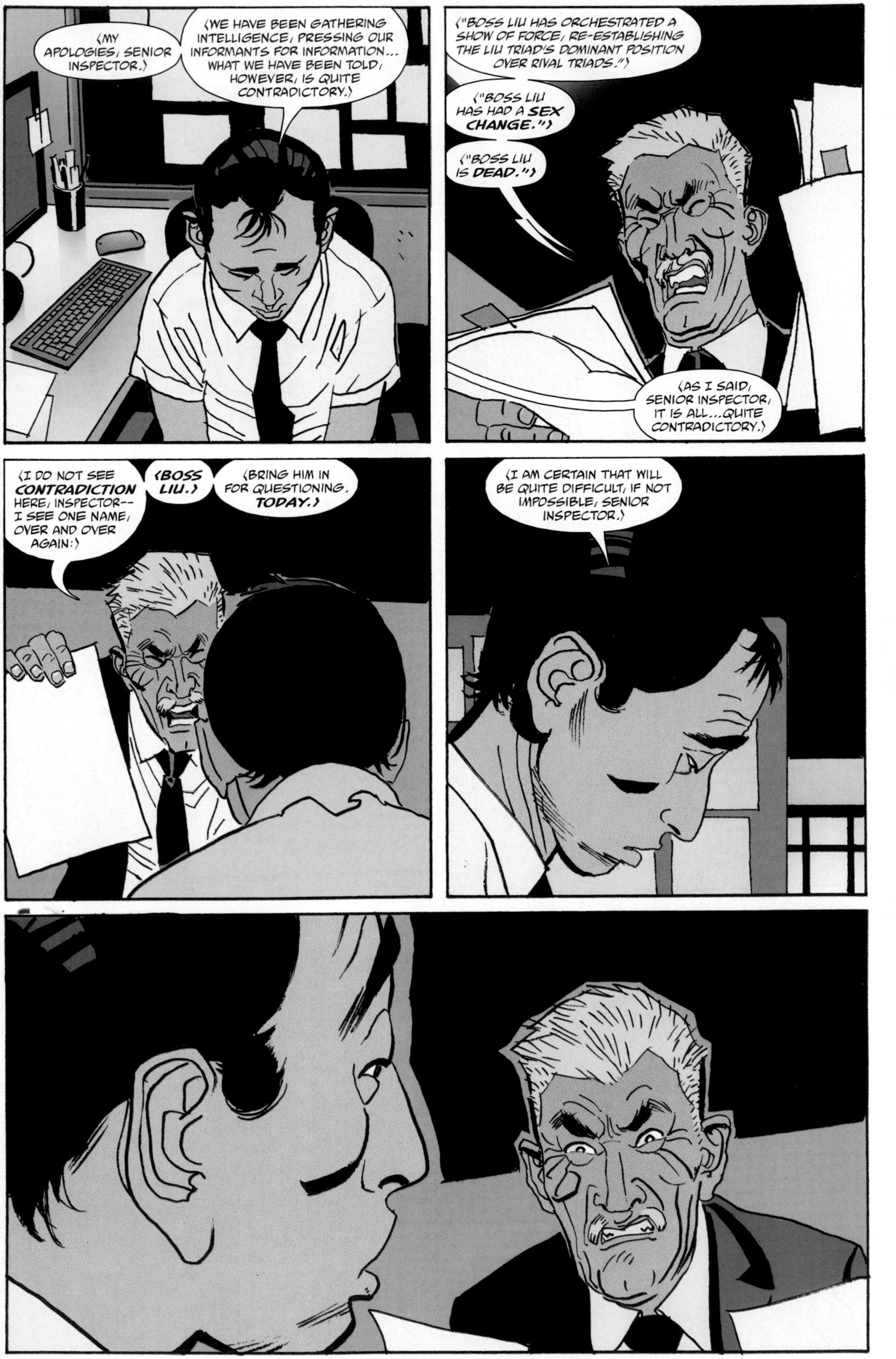

⟨MY APOLOGIES, SENIOR INSPECTOR.⟩
⟨WE HAVE BEEN GATHERING INTELLIGENCE, PRESSING OUR INFORMANTS FOR INFORMATION... WHAT WE HAVE BEEN TOLD, HOWEVER, IS QUITE CONTRADICTORY.⟩
⟨"BOSS LIU HAS ORCHESTRATED A SHOW OF FORCE, RE-ESTABLISHING THE LIU TRIAD'S DOMINANT POSITION OVER RIVAL TRIADS."⟩
⟨"BOSS LIU HAS HAD A SEX CHANGE."⟩
⟨"BOSS LIU IS DEAD."⟩
⟨AS I SAID, SENIOR INSPECTOR, IT IS ALL...QUITE CONTRADICTORY.⟩
⟨I DO NOT SEE CONTRADICTION HERE, INSPECTOR-- I SEE ONE NAME, OVER AND OVER AGAIN:⟩
⟨BOSS LIU.⟩
⟨BRING HIM IN FOR QUESTIONING. TODAY.⟩
⟨I AM CERTAIN THAT WILL BE QUITE DIFFICULT, IF NOT IMPOSSIBLE, SENIOR INSPECTOR.⟩

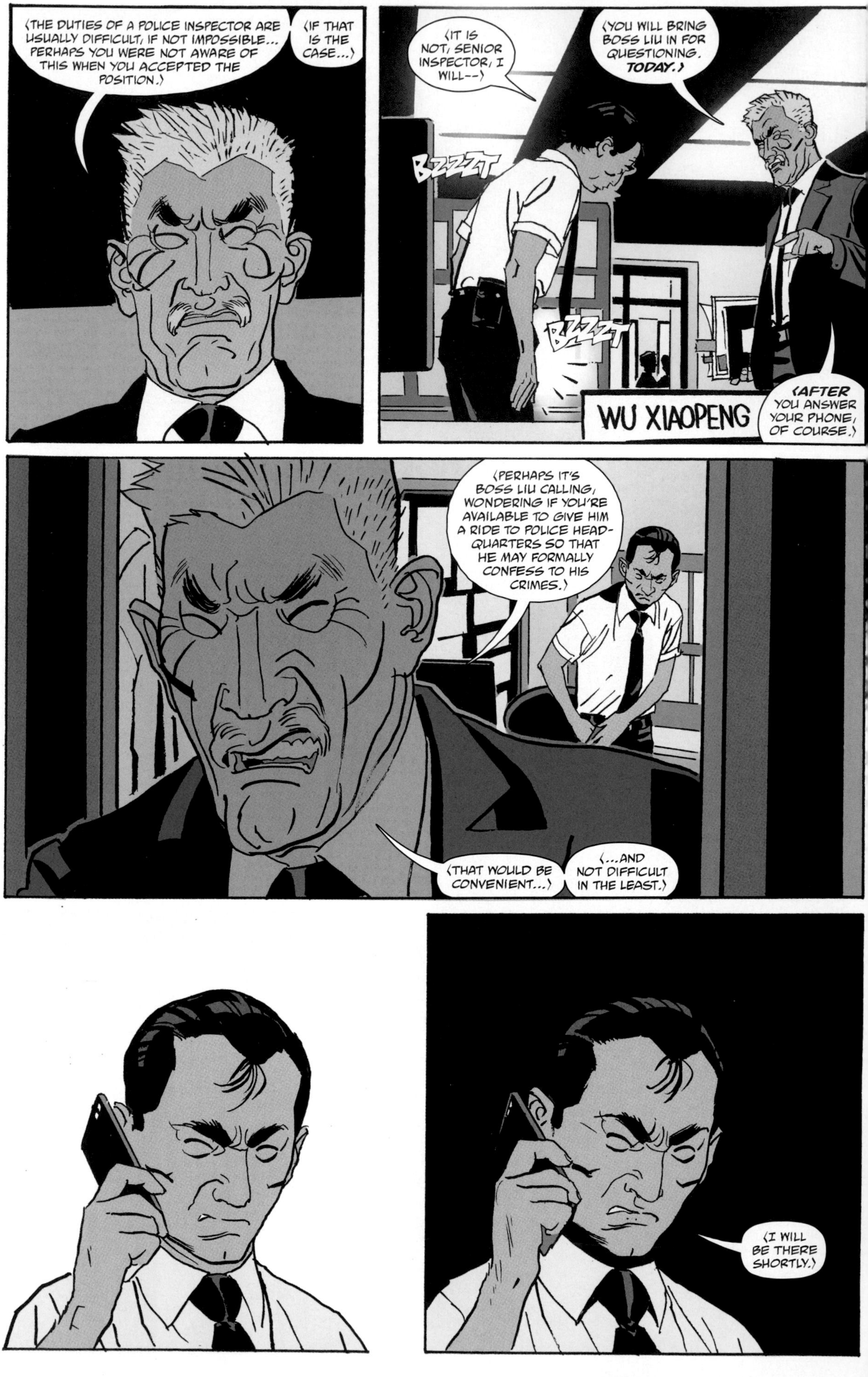
‹THE DUTIES OF A POLICE INSPECTOR ARE USUALLY DIFFICULT, IF NOT IMPOSSIBLE... PERHAPS YOU WERE NOT AWARE OF THIS WHEN YOU ACCEPTED THE POSITION.›
‹IF THAT IS THE CASE...›
‹IT IS NOT, SENIOR INSPECTOR, I WILL--›
‹YOU WILL BRING BOSS LIU IN FOR QUESTIONING. TODAY.›
BZZZT
BZZZT
WU XIAOPENG
‹AFTER YOU ANSWER YOUR PHONE, OF COURSE.›
‹PERHAPS IT'S BOSS LIU CALLING, WONDERING IF YOU'RE AVAILABLE TO GIVE HIM A RIDE TO POLICE HEAD-QUARTERS SO THAT HE MAY FORMALLY CONFESS TO HIS CRIMES.›
‹THAT WOULD BE CONVENIENT...›
‹...AND NOT DIFFICULT IN THE LEAST.›
‹I WILL BE THERE SHORTLY.›

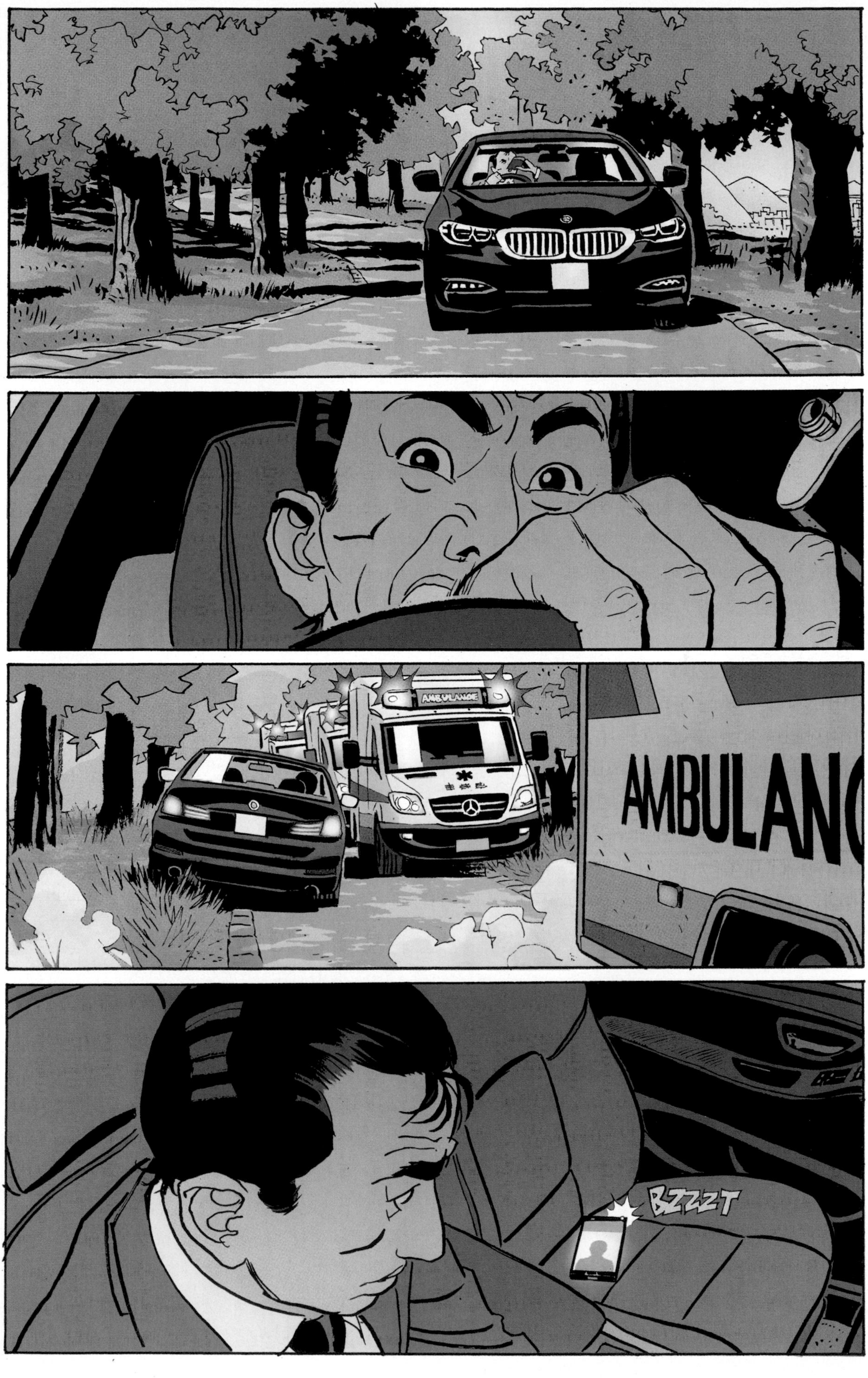
AMBULANCE
AMBULANC
BZZZT

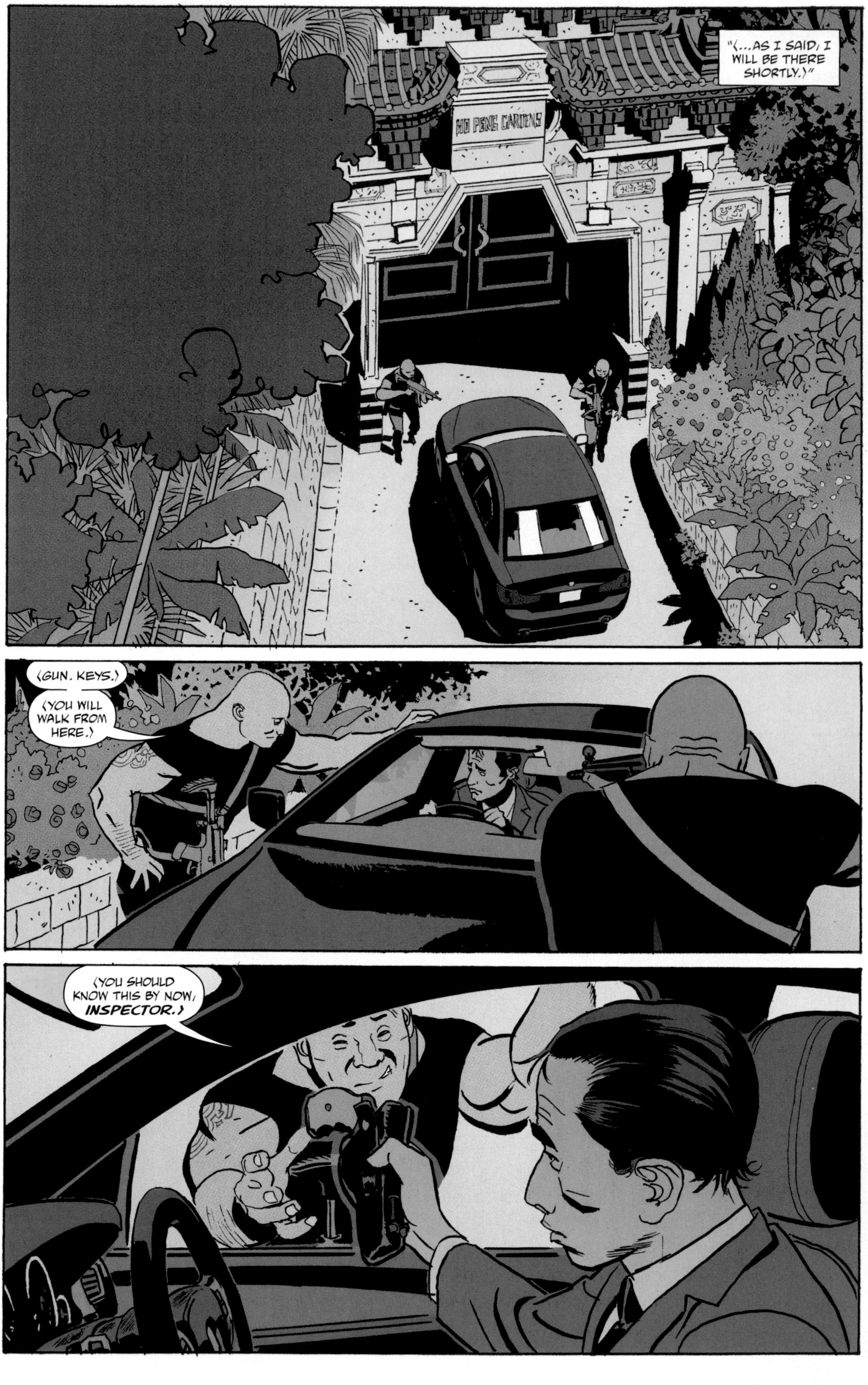
"⟨...AS I SAID, I WILL BE THERE SHORTLY.⟩"
HO PENG GARDENS
⟨GUN. KEYS.⟩
⟨YOU WILL WALK FROM HERE.⟩
⟨YOU SHOULD KNOW THIS BY NOW, **INSPECTOR.**⟩

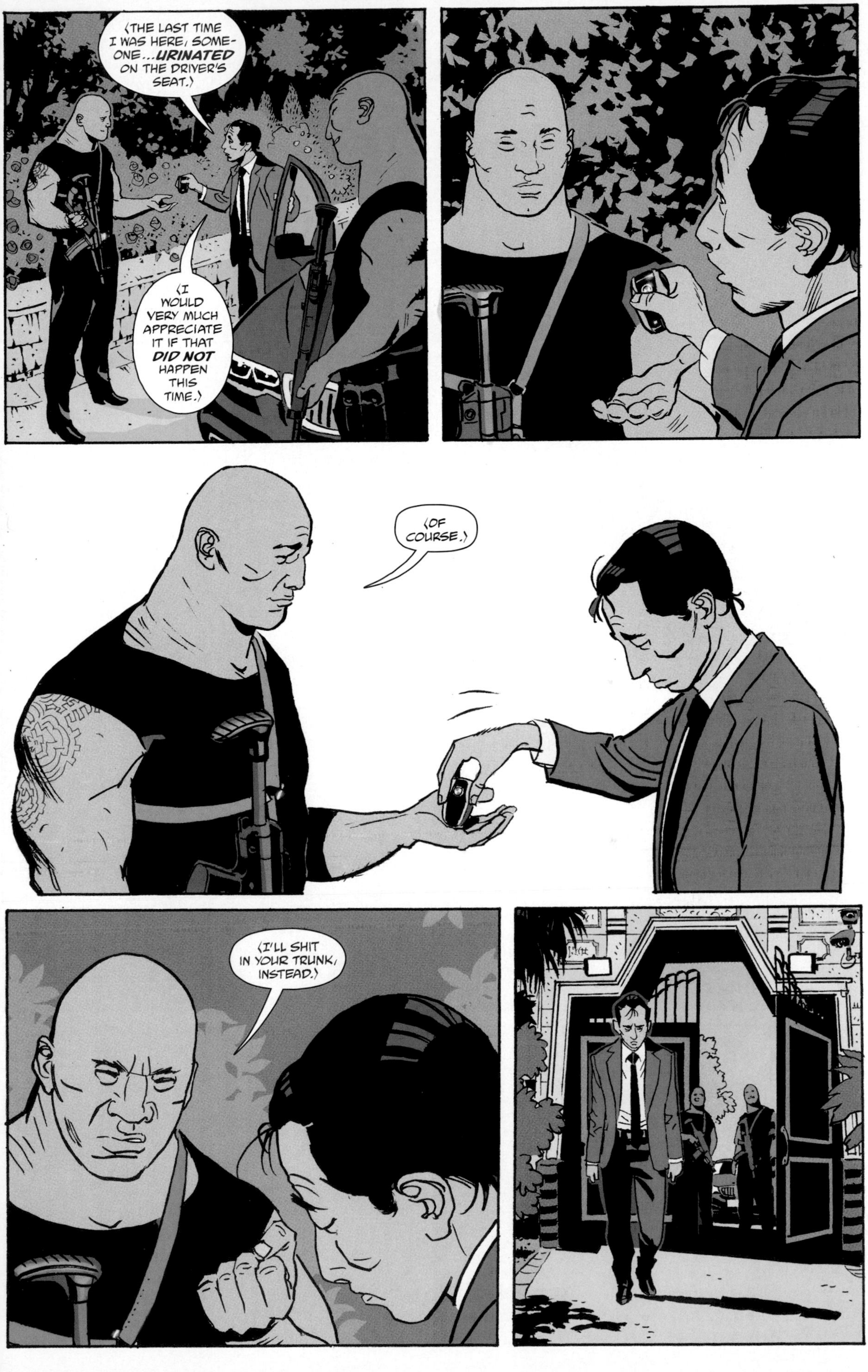
⟨THE LAST TIME I WAS HERE, SOMEONE... **URINATED** ON THE DRIVER'S SEAT.⟩
⟨I WOULD VERY MUCH APPRECIATE IT IF THAT **DID NOT** HAPPEN THIS TIME.⟩
⟨OF COURSE.⟩
⟨I'LL SHIT IN YOUR TRUNK, INSTEAD.⟩

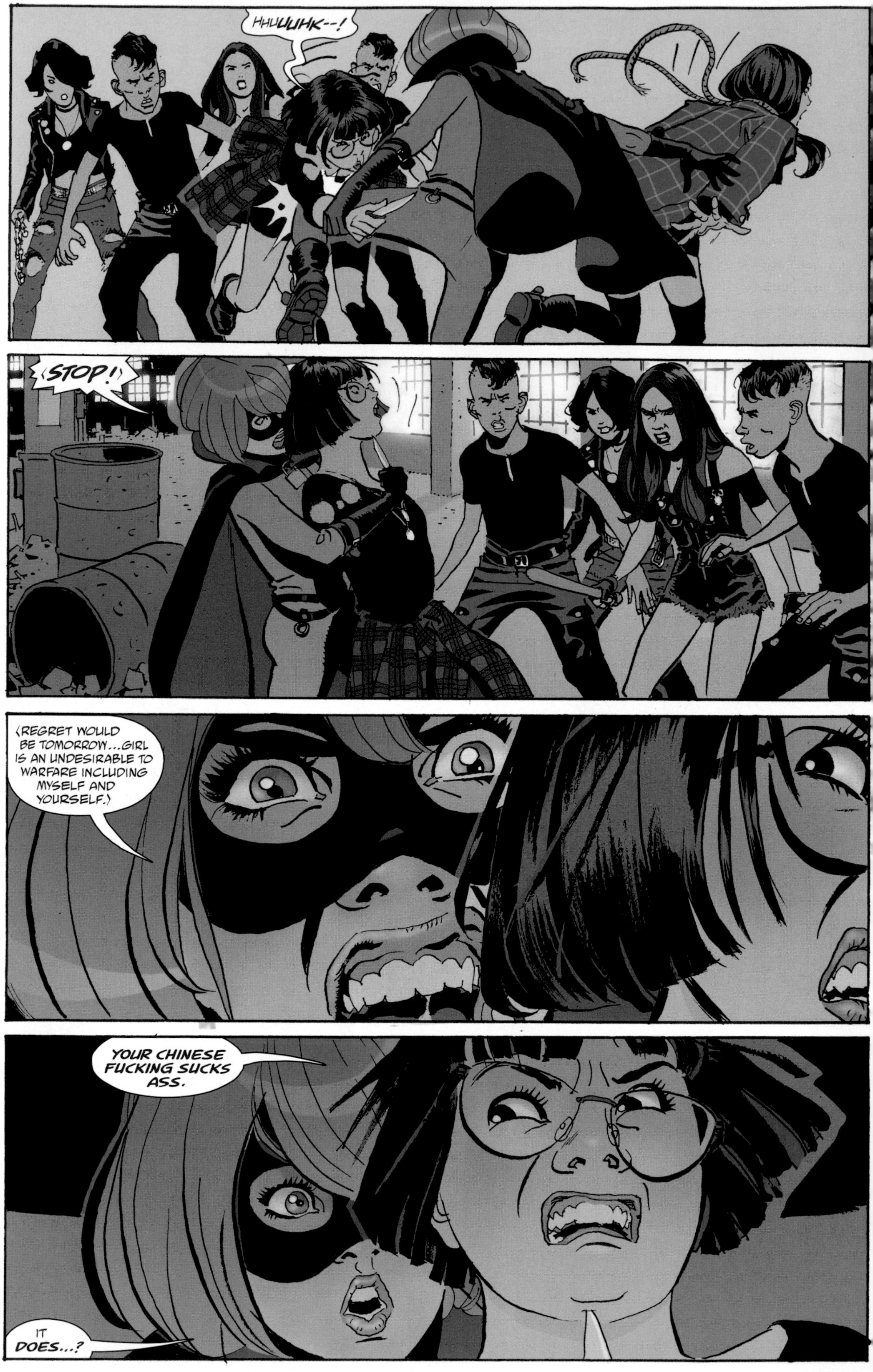
HHUUUHK--!
‹STOP!›
‹REGRET WOULD BE TOMORROW...GIRL IS AN UNDESIRABLE TO WARFARE INCLUDING MYSELF AND YOURSELF.›
YOUR CHINESE FUCKING SUCKS ASS.
IT DOES...?

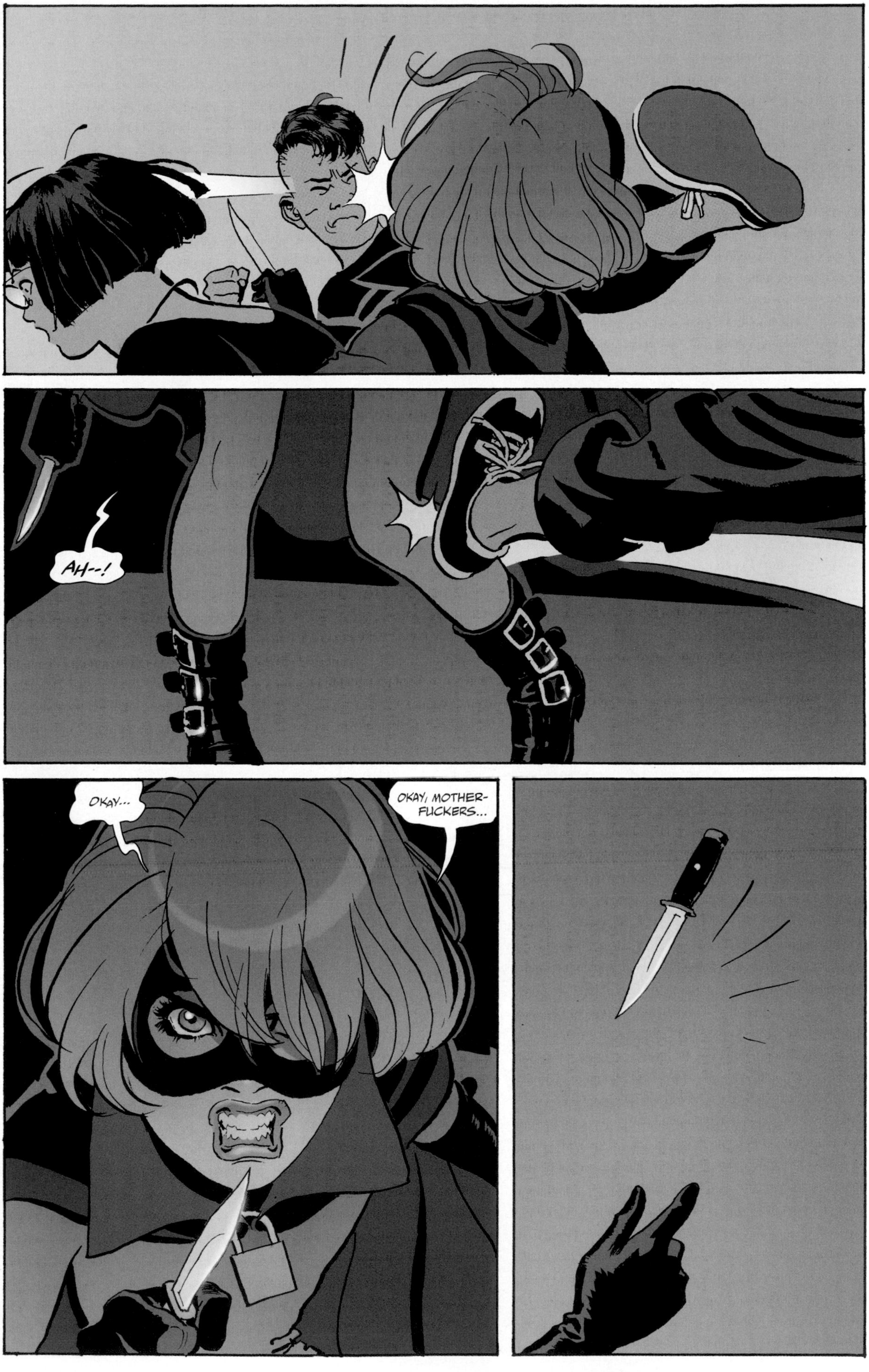
AH--!
OKAY...
OKAY, MOTHER-FUCKERS...

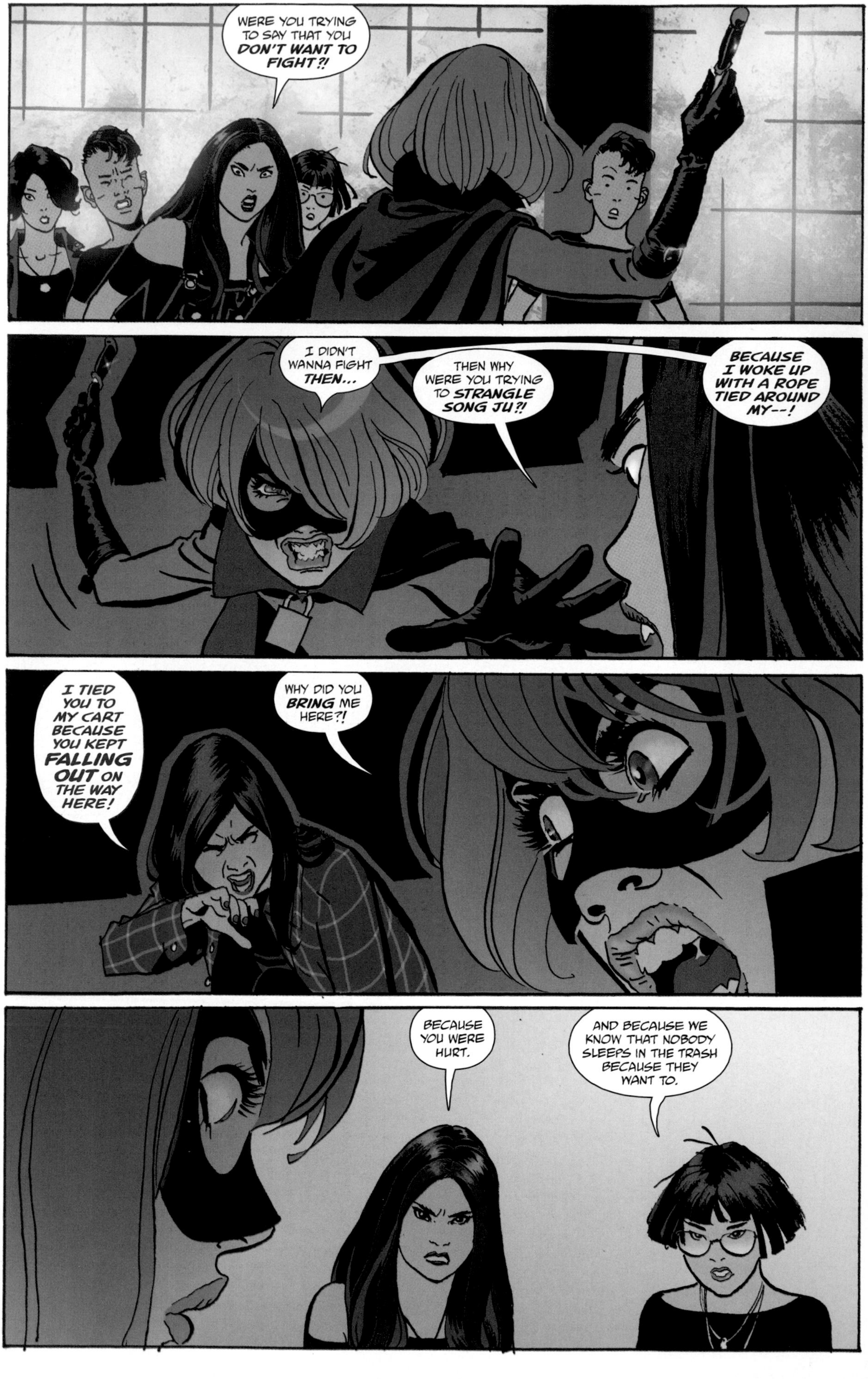
WERE YOU TRYING TO SAY THAT YOU DON'T WANT TO FIGHT?!
I DIDN'T WANNA FIGHT THEN...
THEN WHY WERE YOU TRYING TO STRANGLE SONG JU?!
BECAUSE I WOKE UP WITH A ROPE TIED AROUND MY--!
I TIED YOU TO MY CART BECAUSE YOU KEPT FALLING OUT ON THE WAY HERE!
WHY DID YOU BRING ME HERE?!
BECAUSE YOU WERE HURT.
AND BECAUSE WE KNOW THAT NOBODY SLEEPS IN THE TRASH BECAUSE THEY WANT TO.

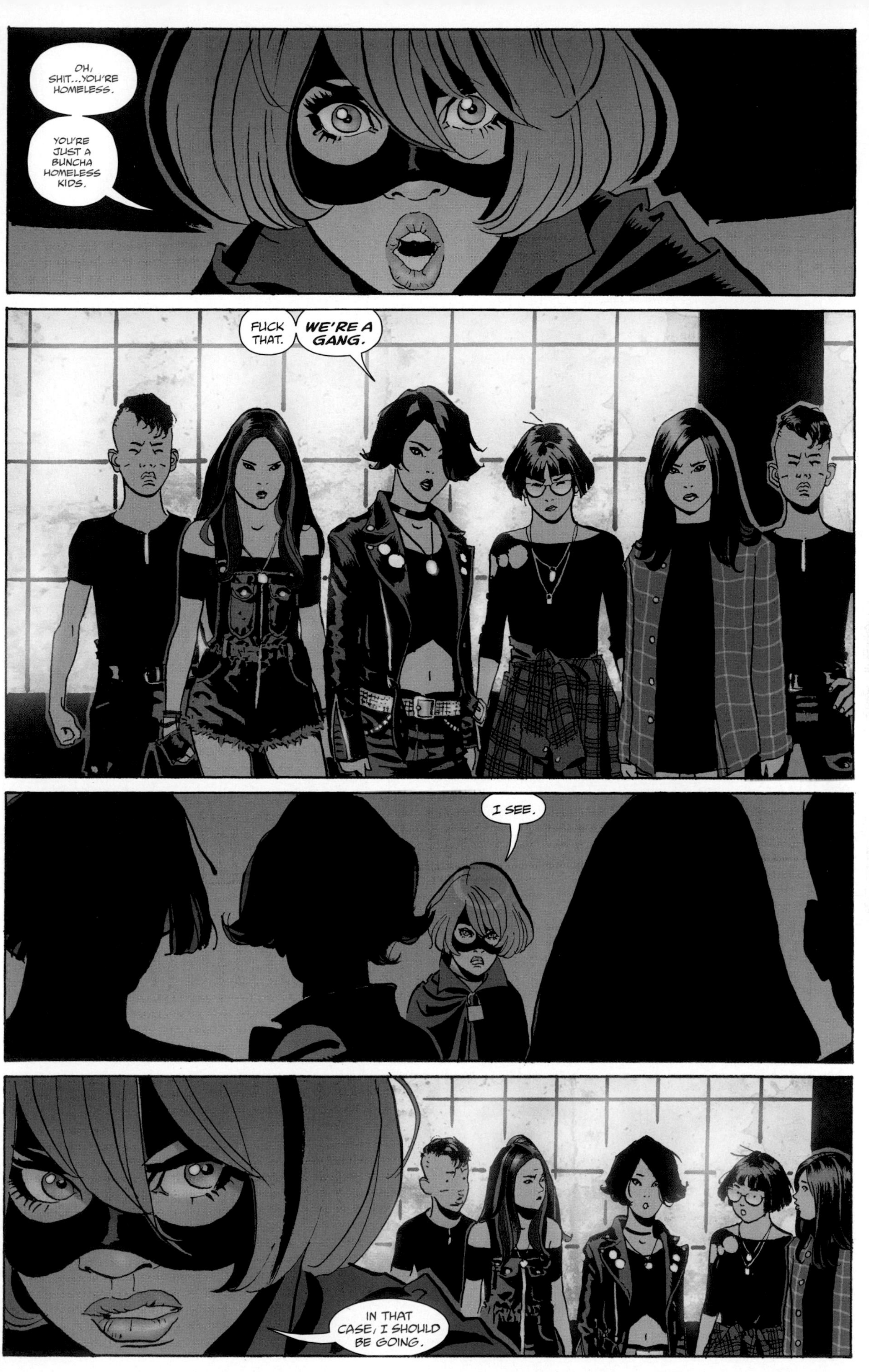
OH, SHIT...YOU'RE HOMELESS.
YOU'RE JUST A BUNCHA HOMELESS KIDS.
FUCK THAT.
WE'RE A GANG.
I SEE.
IN THAT CASE, I SHOULD BE GOING.

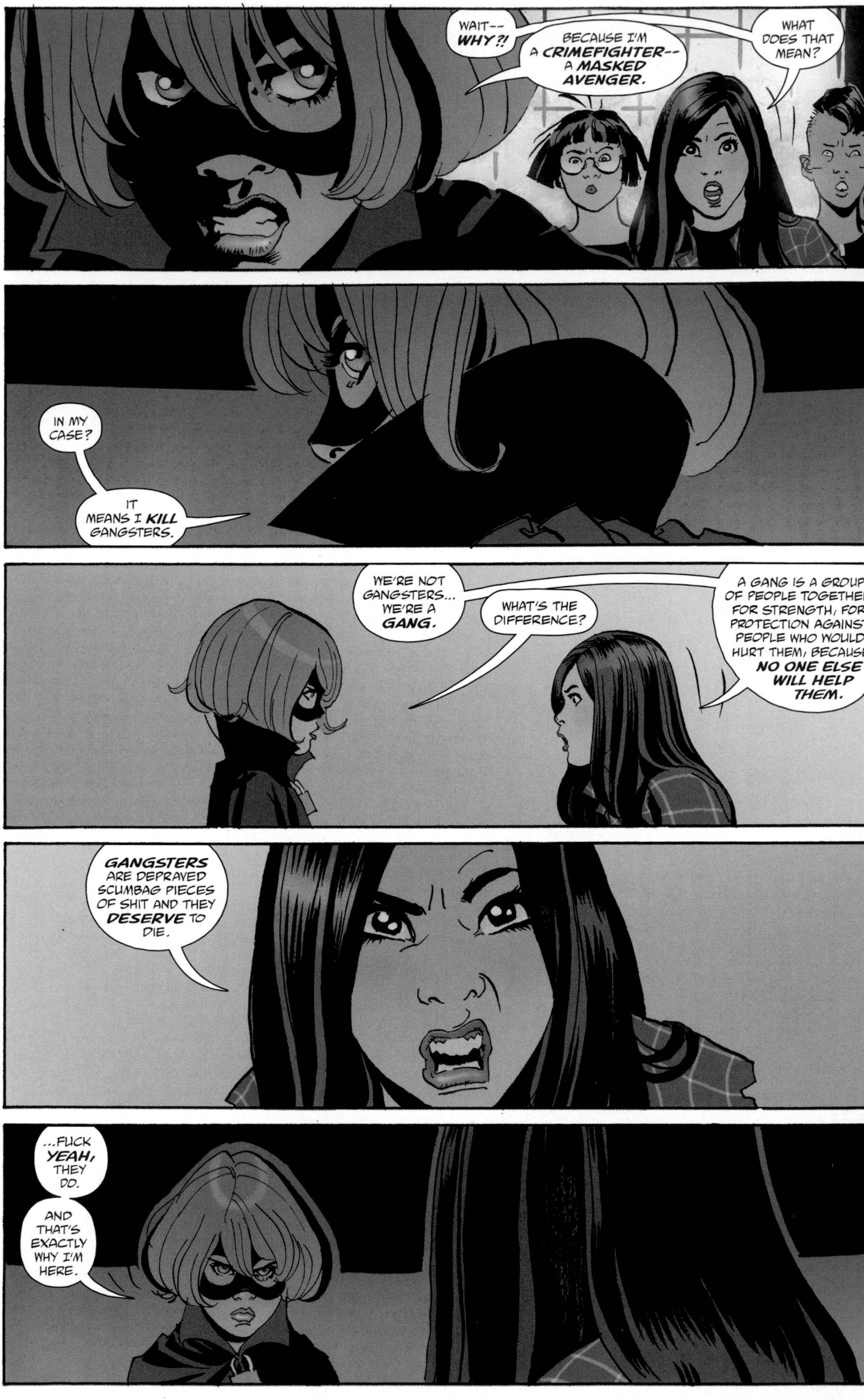
WAIT-- WHY?!
BECAUSE I'M A CRIMEFIGHTER-- A MASKED AVENGER.
WHAT DOES THAT MEAN?
IN MY CASE?
IT MEANS I KILL GANGSTERS.
WE'RE NOT GANGSTERS... WE'RE A GANG.
WHAT'S THE DIFFERENCE?
A GANG IS A GROUP OF PEOPLE TOGETHER FOR STRENGTH, FOR PROTECTION AGAINST PEOPLE WHO WOULD HURT THEM, BECAUSE NO ONE ELSE WILL HELP THEM.
GANGSTERS ARE DEPRAVED SCUMBAG PIECES OF SHIT AND THEY DESERVE TO DIE.
...FUCK YEAH, THEY DO.
AND THAT'S EXACTLY WHY I'M HERE.

"I'M HERE TO KILL THE MOST DEPRAVED SCUMBAG PIECE OF SHIT IN ALL OF HONG KONG."

HWW-URRGK!

⟨THAT... THOSE ARE...⟩

⟨PENISES, YES.⟩

⟨I SEVERED THEM FROM THE BODIES OF MY MALE RIVALS, THEN SENT THEM ON TO THEIR PRIVATE PHYSICIANS.⟩

⟨WHY--?!⟩

⟨BECAUSE I WANTED THEM TO LIVE, NOT BLEED TO DEATH IN MY GARDEN.⟩

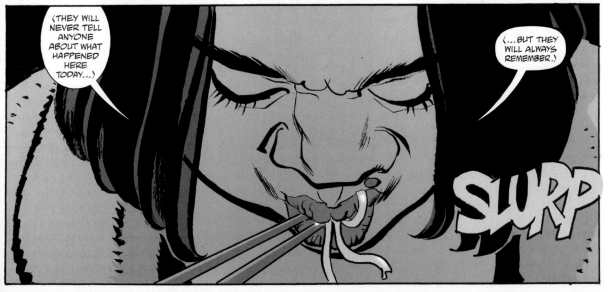

⟨THEY WILL NEVER TELL ANYONE ABOUT WHAT HAPPENED HERE TODAY...⟩

⟨...BUT THEY WILL ALWAYS REMEMBER.⟩

SLURP

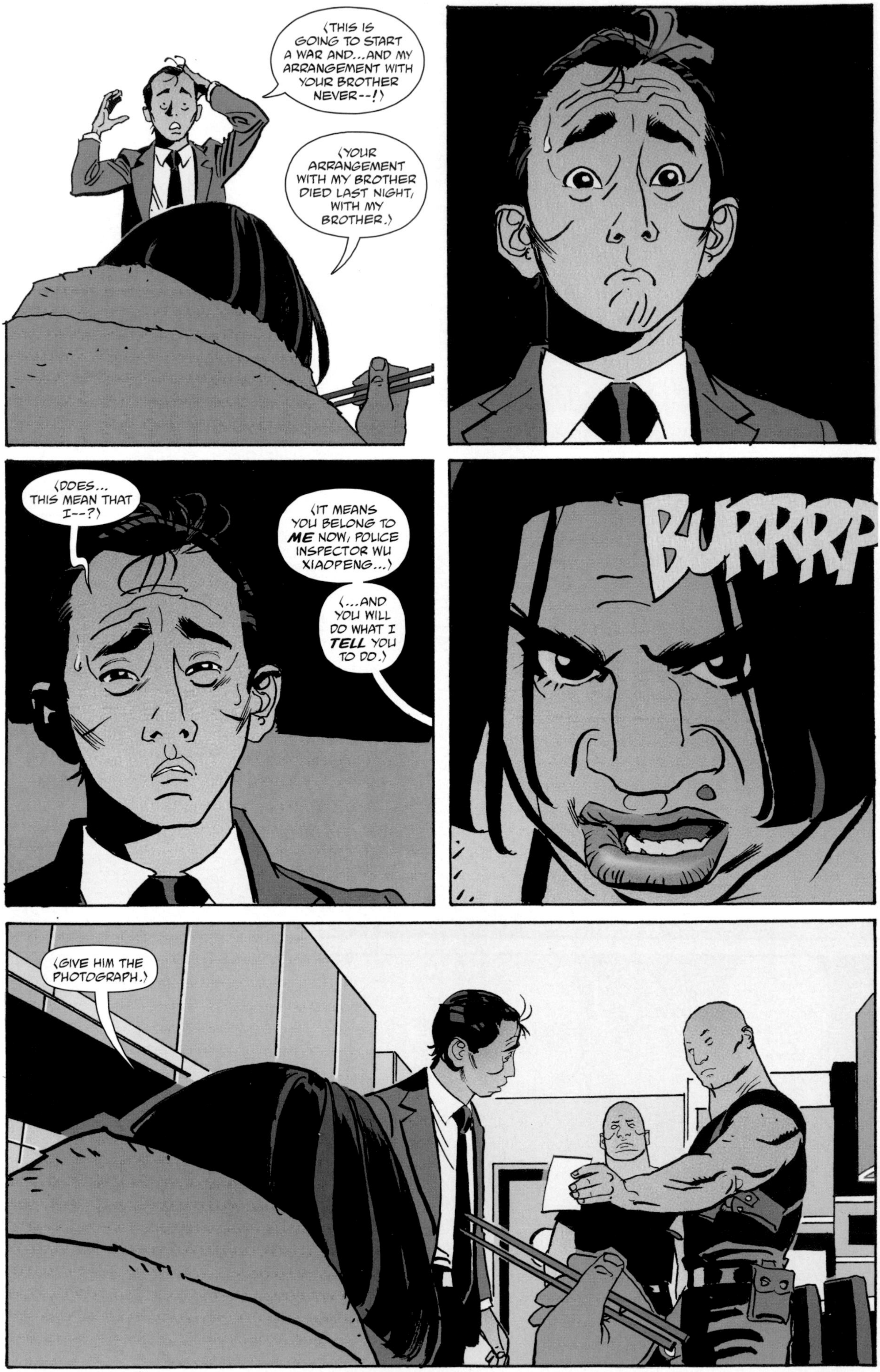
⟨THIS IS GOING TO START A WAR AND...AND MY ARRANGEMENT WITH YOUR BROTHER NEVER--!⟩
⟨YOUR ARRANGEMENT WITH MY BROTHER DIED LAST NIGHT, WITH MY BROTHER.⟩
⟨DOES... THIS MEAN THAT I--?⟩
⟨IT MEANS YOU BELONG TO ME NOW, POLICE INSPECTOR WU XIAOPENG...⟩
⟨...AND YOU WILL DO WHAT I TELL YOU TO DO.⟩
BURRRP
⟨GIVE HIM THE PHOTOGRAPH.⟩

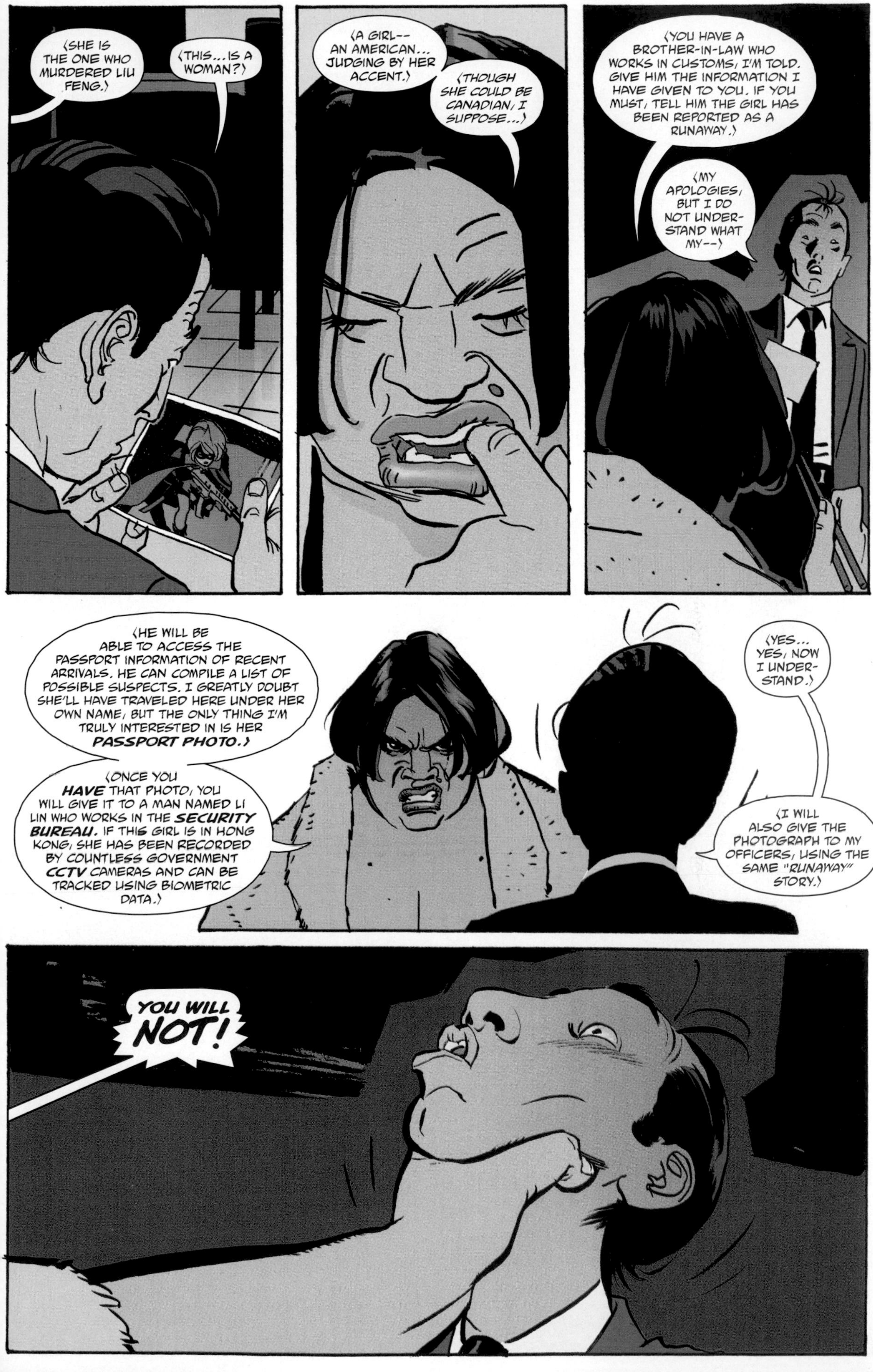

⟨SHE IS THE ONE WHO MURDERED LIU FENG.⟩
⟨THIS...IS A WOMAN?⟩
⟨A GIRL-- AN AMERICAN... JUDGING BY HER ACCENT.⟩
⟨THOUGH SHE COULD BE CANADIAN, I SUPPOSE...⟩
⟨YOU HAVE A BROTHER-IN-LAW WHO WORKS IN CUSTOMS, I'M TOLD. GIVE HIM THE INFORMATION I HAVE GIVEN TO YOU. IF YOU MUST, TELL HIM THE GIRL HAS BEEN REPORTED AS A RUNAWAY.⟩
⟨MY APOLOGIES, BUT I DO NOT UNDER-STAND WHAT MY--⟩
⟨HE WILL BE ABLE TO ACCESS THE PASSPORT INFORMATION OF RECENT ARRIVALS. HE CAN COMPILE A LIST OF POSSIBLE SUSPECTS. I GREATLY DOUBT SHE'LL HAVE TRAVELED HERE UNDER HER OWN NAME, BUT THE ONLY THING I'M TRULY INTERESTED IN IS HER **PASSPORT PHOTO.**⟩
⟨ONCE YOU **HAVE** THAT PHOTO, YOU WILL GIVE IT TO A MAN NAMED LI LIN WHO WORKS IN THE ***SECURITY BUREAU.*** IF THIS GIRL IS IN HONG KONG, SHE HAS BEEN RECORDED BY COUNTLESS GOVERNMENT ***CCTV*** CAMERAS AND CAN BE TRACKED USING BIOMETRIC DATA.⟩
⟨YES... YES, NOW I UNDER-STAND.⟩
⟨I WILL ALSO GIVE THE PHOTOGRAPH TO MY OFFICERS, USING THE SAME "*RUNAWAY*" STORY.⟩
YOU WILL NOT!

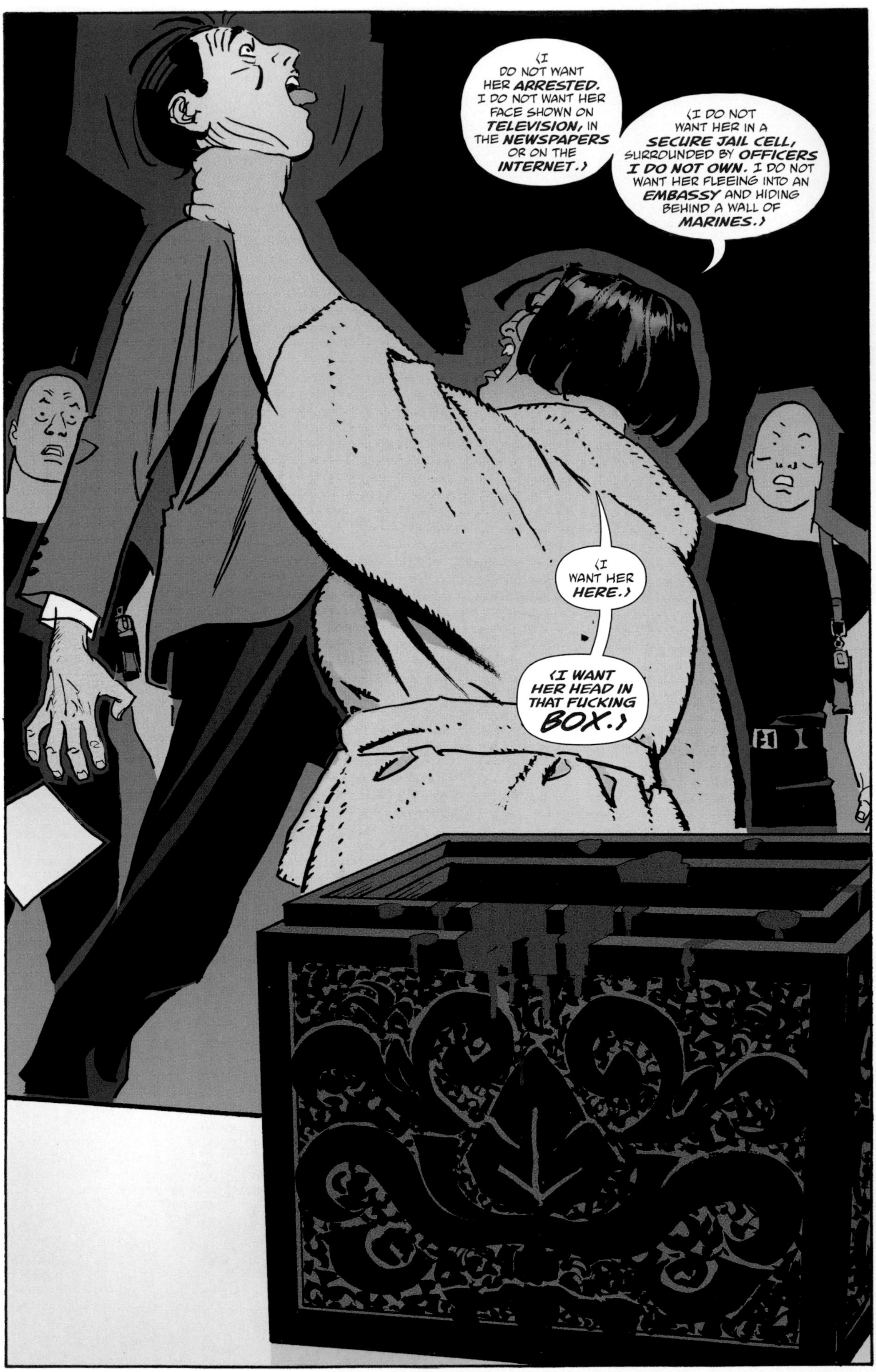
‹I DO NOT WANT HER ARRESTED. I DO NOT WANT HER FACE SHOWN ON TELEVISION, IN THE NEWSPAPERS OR ON THE INTERNET.›
‹I DO NOT WANT HER IN A SECURE JAIL CELL, SURROUNDED BY OFFICERS I DO NOT OWN. I DO NOT WANT HER FLEEING INTO AN EMBASSY AND HIDING BEHIND A WALL OF MARINES.›
‹I WANT HER HERE.›
‹I WANT HER HEAD IN THAT FUCKING BOX.›

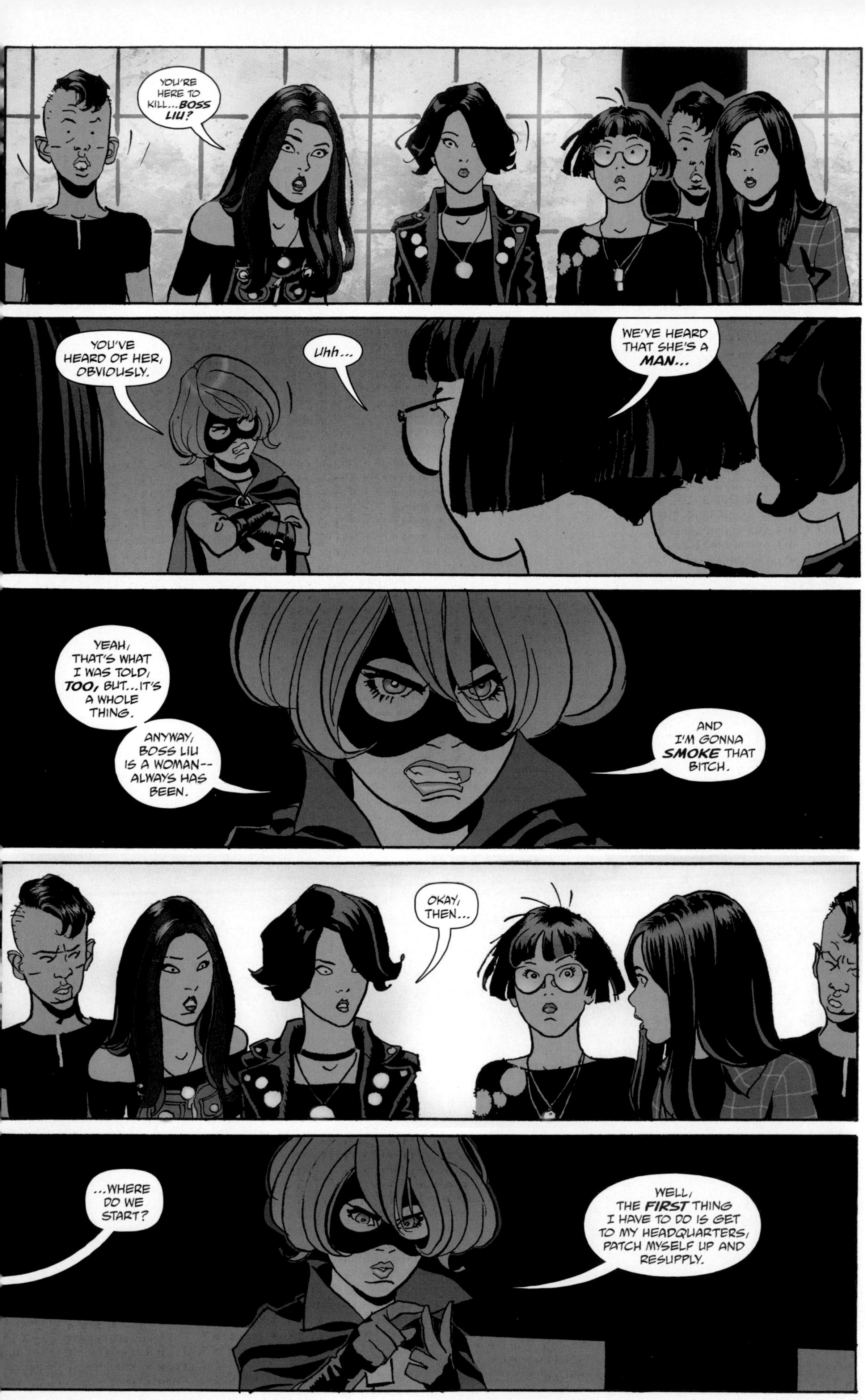
YOU'RE HERE TO KILL...BOSS LIU?
YOU'VE HEARD OF HER, OBVIOUSLY.
Uhh...
WE'VE HEARD THAT SHE'S A MAN...
YEAH, THAT'S WHAT I WAS TOLD, TOO, BUT...IT'S A WHOLE THING.
ANYWAY, BOSS LIU IS A WOMAN-- ALWAYS HAS BEEN.
AND I'M GONNA SMOKE THAT BITCH.
OKAY, THEN...
...WHERE DO WE START?
WELL, THE FIRST THING I HAVE TO DO IS GET TO MY HEADQUARTERS, PATCH MYSELF UP AND RESUPPLY.

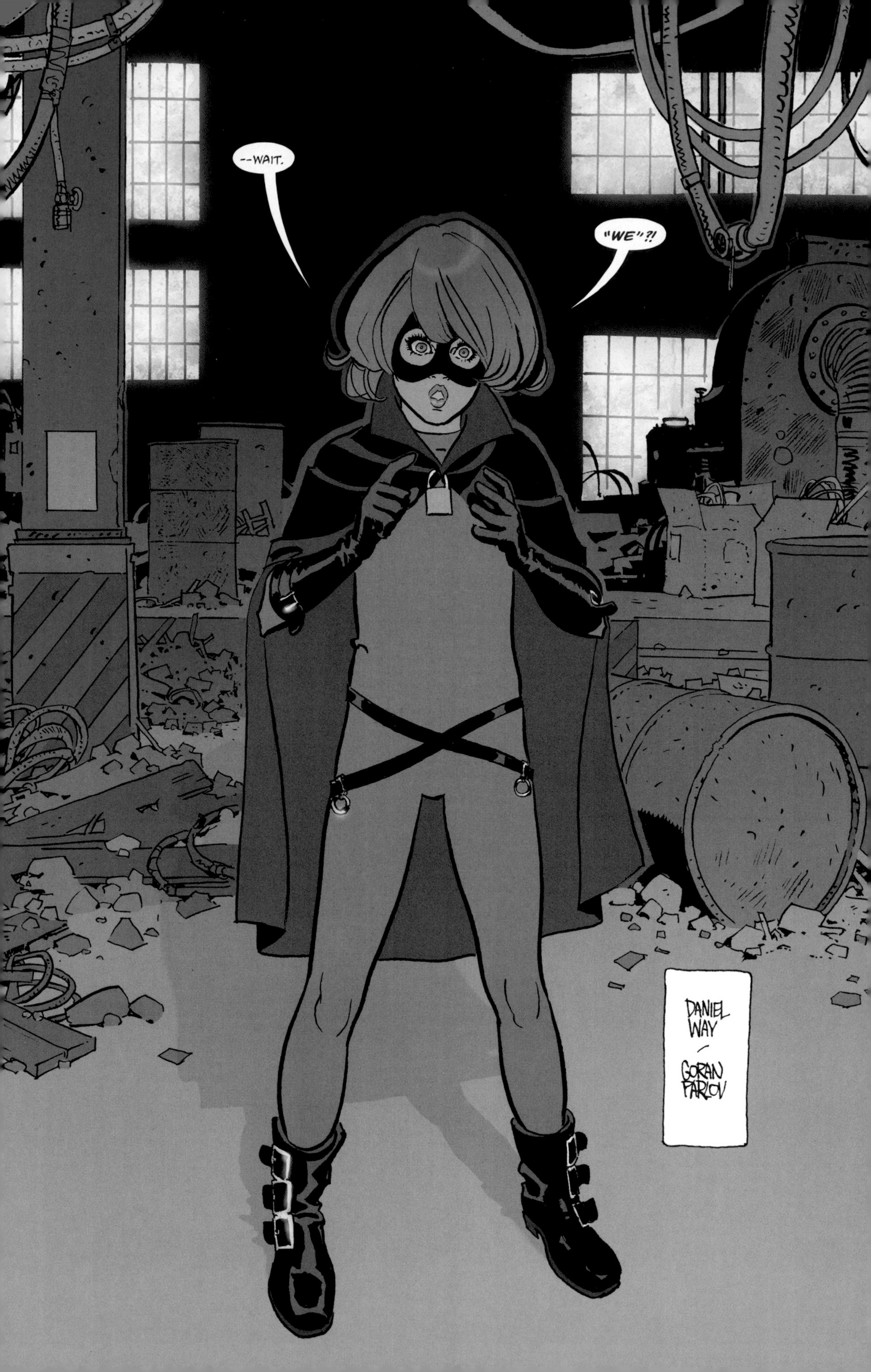
--WAIT.
"WE"?!
DANIEL WAY
/
GORAN PARLOV

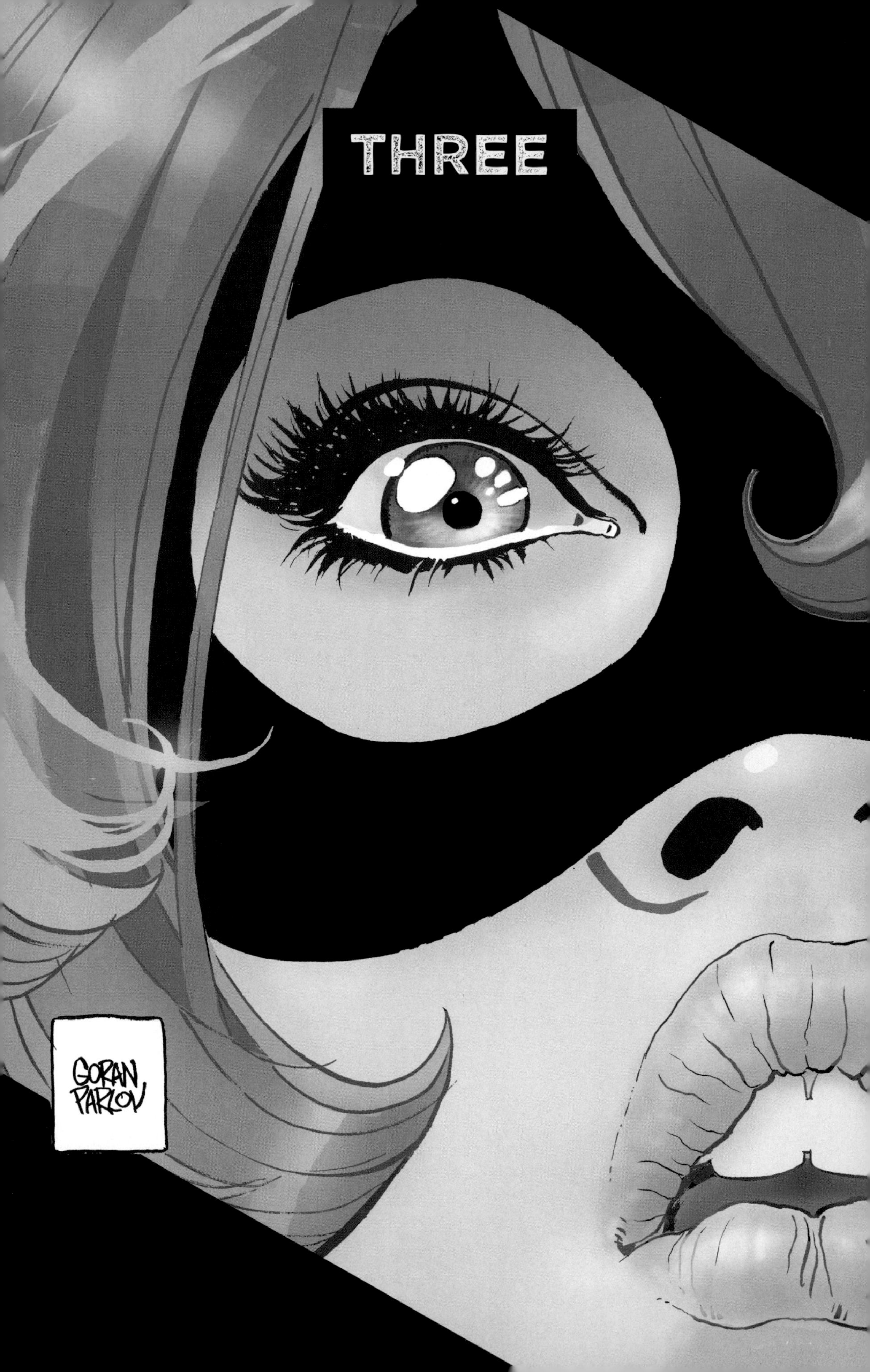
THREE
GORAN PARLOV

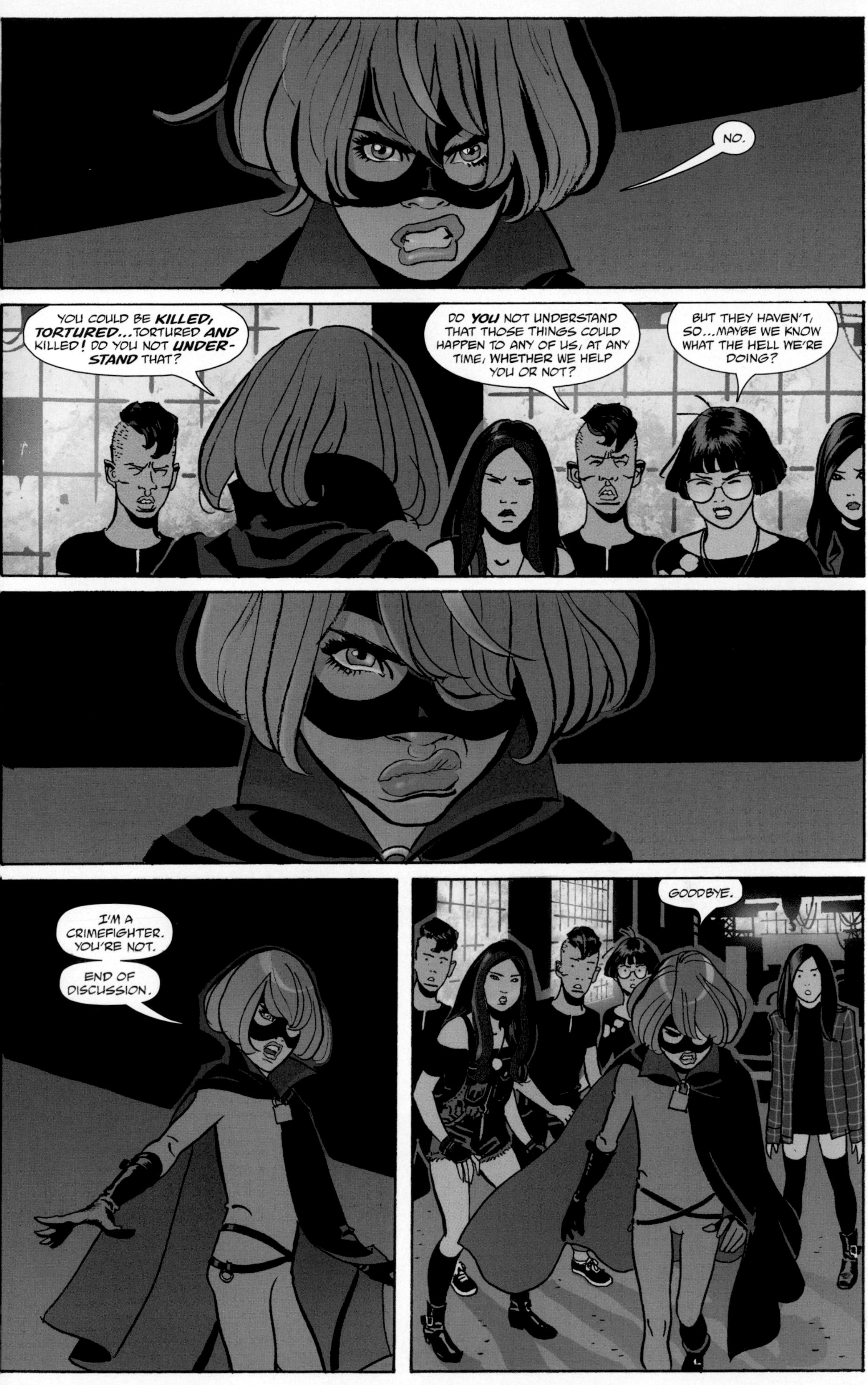
NO.
YOU COULD BE **KILLED, TORTURED...** TORTURED **AND** KILLED! DO YOU NOT **UNDERSTAND** THAT?
DO **YOU** NOT UNDERSTAND THAT THOSE THINGS COULD HAPPEN TO ANY OF US, AT ANY TIME, WHETHER WE HELP YOU OR NOT?
BUT THEY HAVEN'T, SO...MAYBE WE KNOW WHAT THE HELL WE'RE DOING?
I'M A CRIMEFIGHTER. YOU'RE NOT.
END OF DISCUSSION.
GOODBYE.

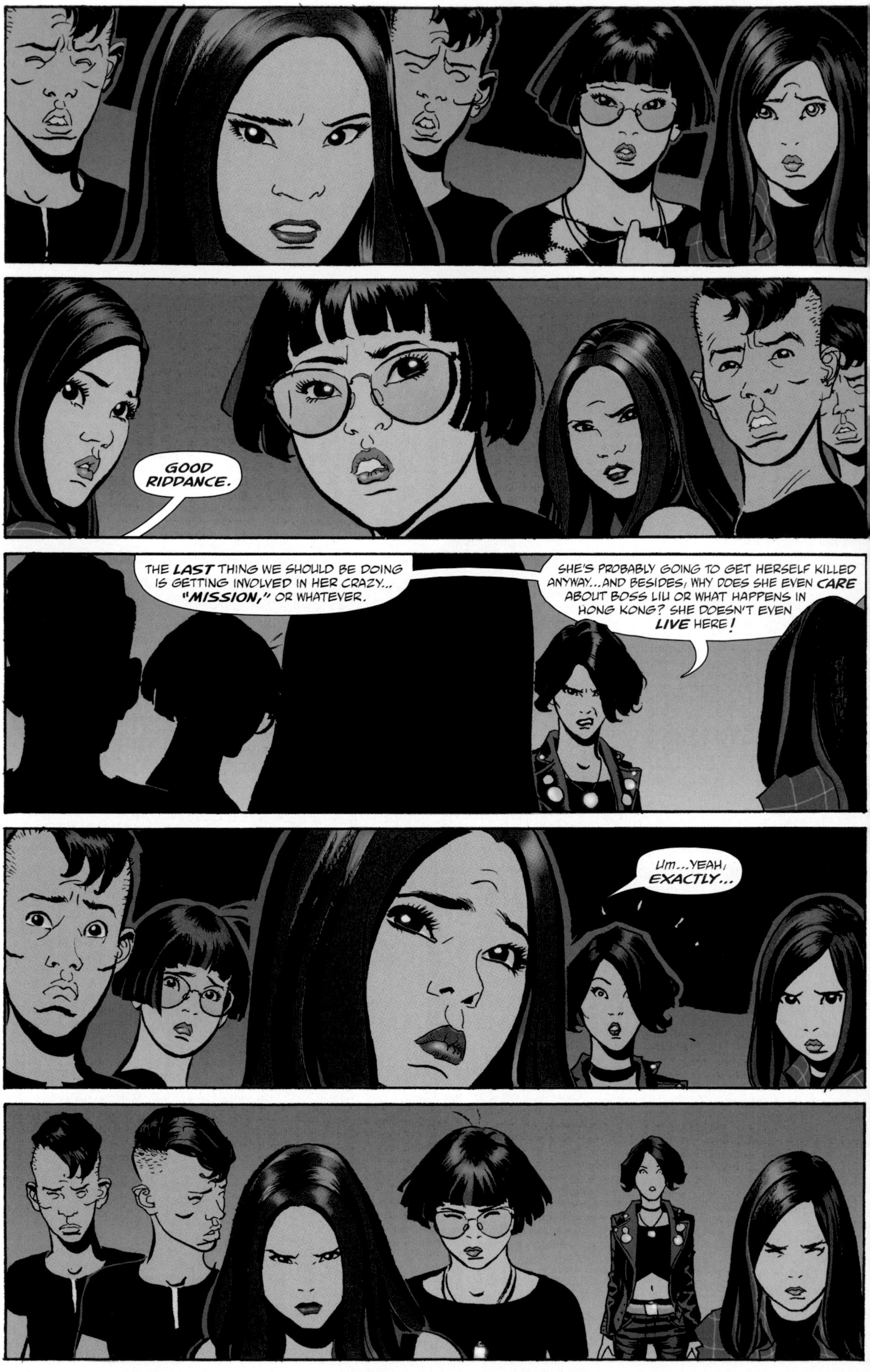
GOOD RIDDANCE.
THE LAST THING WE SHOULD BE DOING IS GETTING INVOLVED IN HER CRAZY... "MISSION," OR WHATEVER.
SHE'S PROBABLY GOING TO GET HERSELF KILLED ANYWAY...AND BESIDES, WHY DOES SHE EVEN CARE ABOUT BOSS LIU OR WHAT HAPPENS IN HONG KONG? SHE DOESN'T EVEN LIVE HERE!
UM...YEAH, EXACTLY...

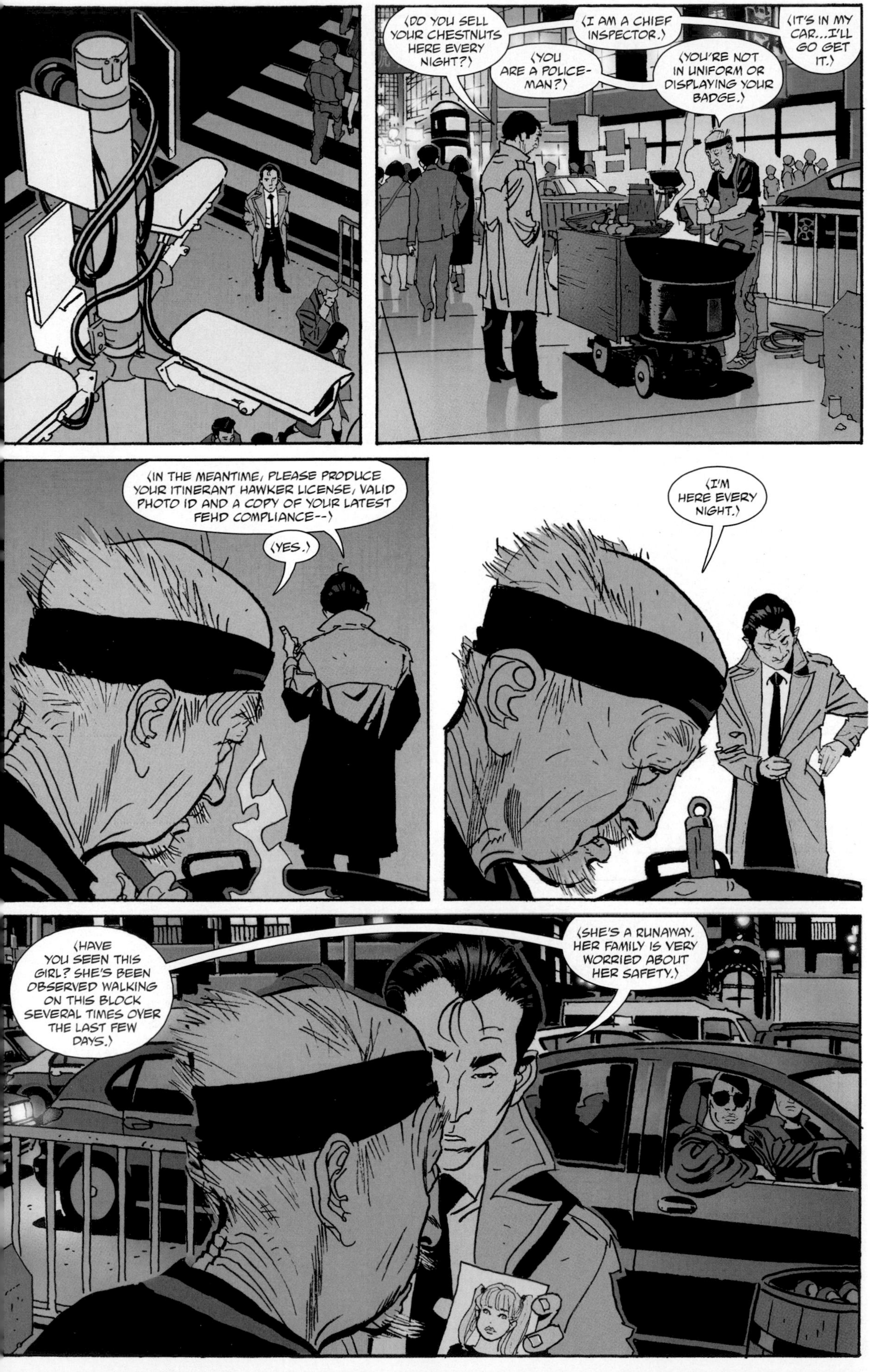
⟨DO YOU SELL YOUR CHESTNUTS HERE EVERY NIGHT?⟩
⟨I AM A CHIEF INSPECTOR.⟩
⟨YOU ARE A POLICE-MAN?⟩
⟨YOU'RE NOT IN UNIFORM OR DISPLAYING YOUR BADGE.⟩
⟨IT'S IN MY CAR...I'LL GO GET IT.⟩
⟨IN THE MEANTIME, PLEASE PRODUCE YOUR ITINERANT HAWKER LICENSE, VALID PHOTO ID AND A COPY OF YOUR LATEST FEHD COMPLIANCE--⟩
⟨YES.⟩
⟨I'M HERE EVERY NIGHT.⟩
⟨HAVE YOU SEEN THIS GIRL? SHE'S BEEN OBSERVED WALKING ON THIS BLOCK SEVERAL TIMES OVER THE LAST FEW DAYS.⟩
⟨SHE'S A RUNAWAY. HER FAMILY IS VERY WORRIED ABOUT HER SAFETY.⟩

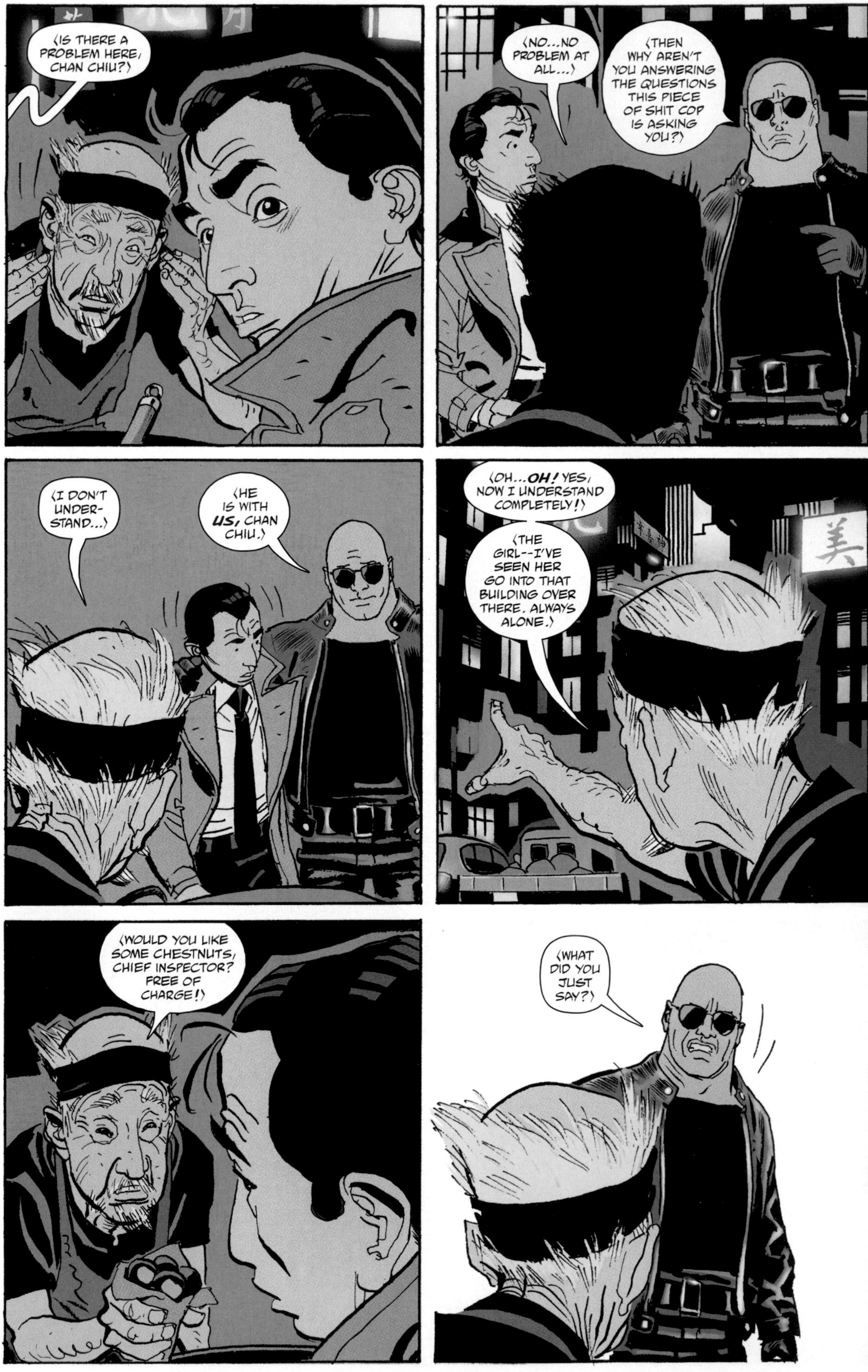
⟨IS THERE A PROBLEM HERE, CHAN CHIU?⟩
⟨NO...NO PROBLEM AT ALL...⟩
⟨THEN WHY AREN'T YOU ANSWERING THE QUESTIONS THIS PIECE OF SHIT COP IS ASKING YOU?⟩
⟨I DON'T UNDER-STAND...⟩
⟨HE IS WITH US, CHAN CHIU.⟩
⟨OH...OH! YES, NOW I UNDERSTAND COMPLETELY!⟩
⟨THE GIRL--I'VE SEEN HER GO INTO THAT BUILDING OVER THERE. ALWAYS ALONE.⟩
⟨WOULD YOU LIKE SOME CHESTNUTS, CHIEF INSPECTOR? FREE OF CHARGE!⟩
⟨WHAT DID YOU JUST SAY?⟩

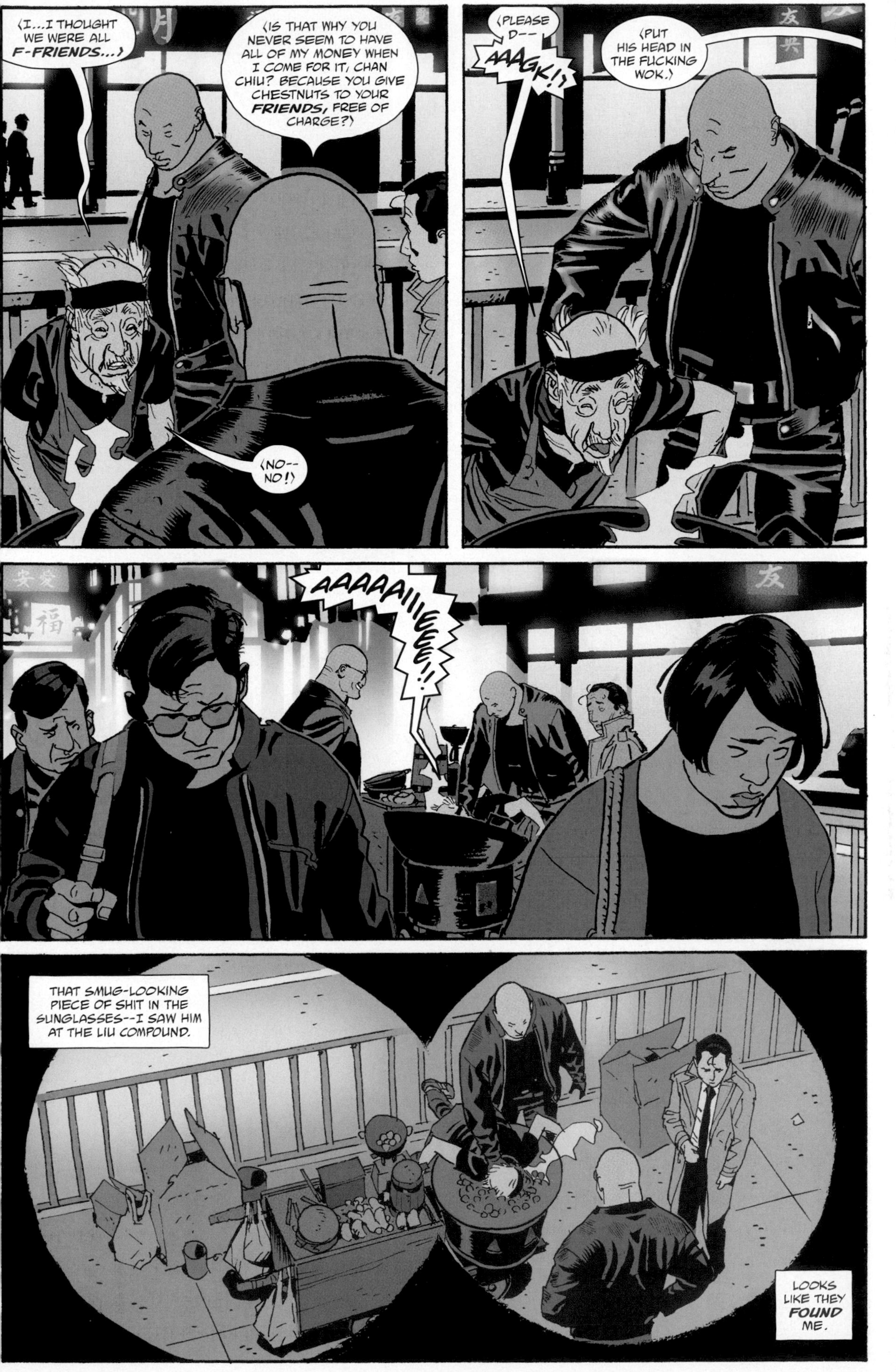

‹I...I THOUGHT WE WERE ALL F-FRIENDS...›
‹IS THAT WHY YOU NEVER SEEM TO HAVE ALL OF MY MONEY WHEN I COME FOR IT, CHAN CHIU? BECAUSE YOU GIVE CHESTNUTS TO YOUR FRIENDS, FREE OF CHARGE?›
‹NO--NO!›
‹PLEASE D--
AAAGK!›
‹PUT HIS HEAD IN THE FUCKING WOK.›
AAAAIIIEEEE!!
THAT SMUG-LOOKING PIECE OF SHIT IN THE SUNGLASSES--I SAW HIM AT THE LIU COMPOUND.
LOOKS LIKE THEY FOUND ME.

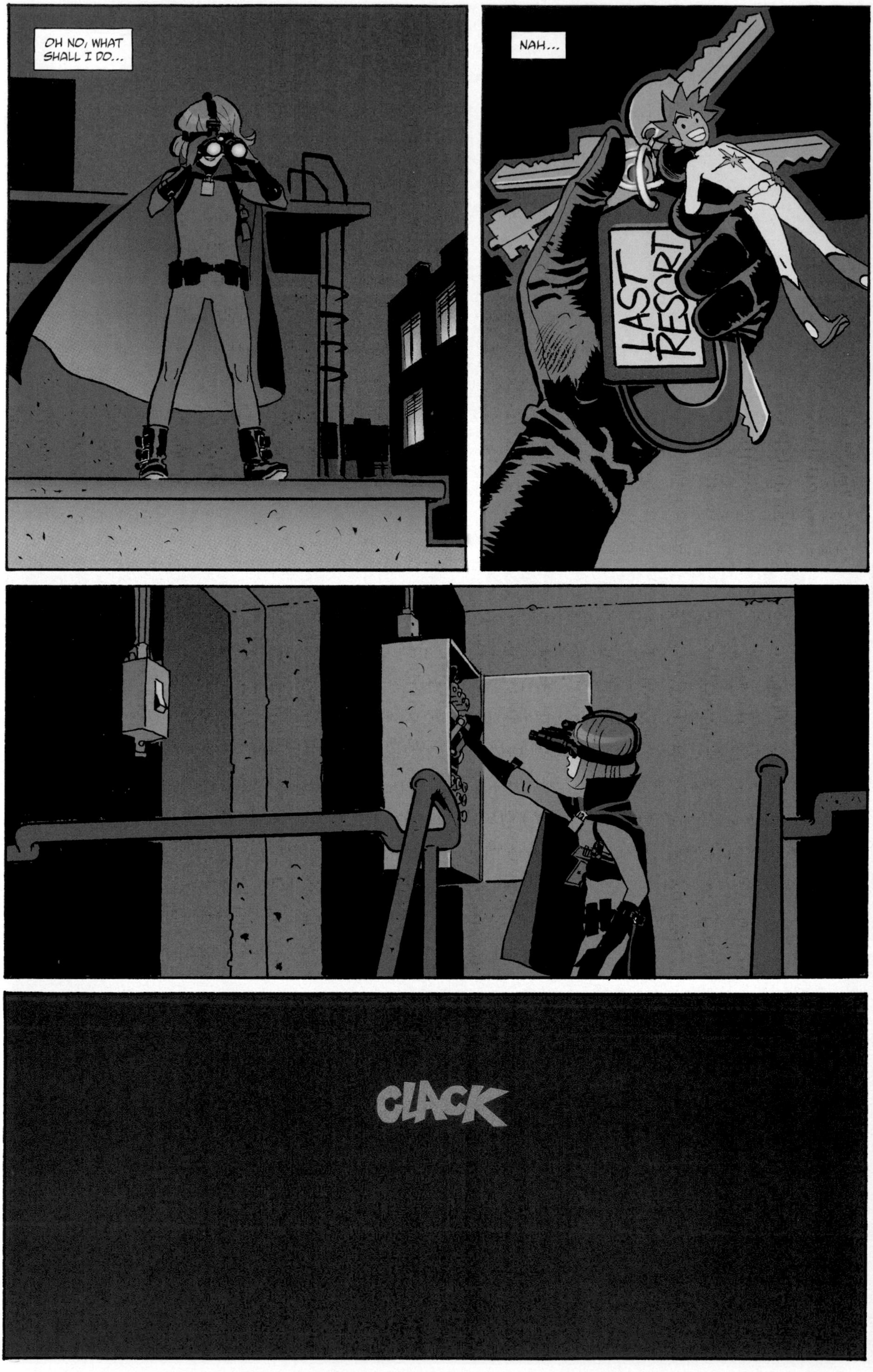
OH NO, WHAT SHALL I DO...
NAH...
LAST RESORT
CLACK

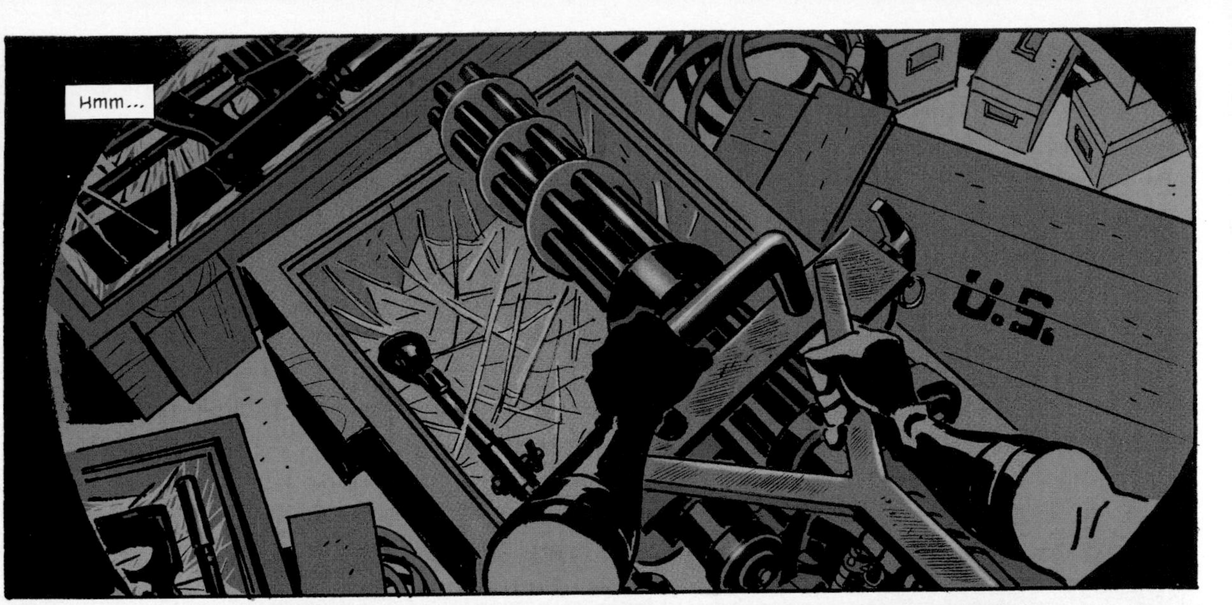
Hmm...
U.S.

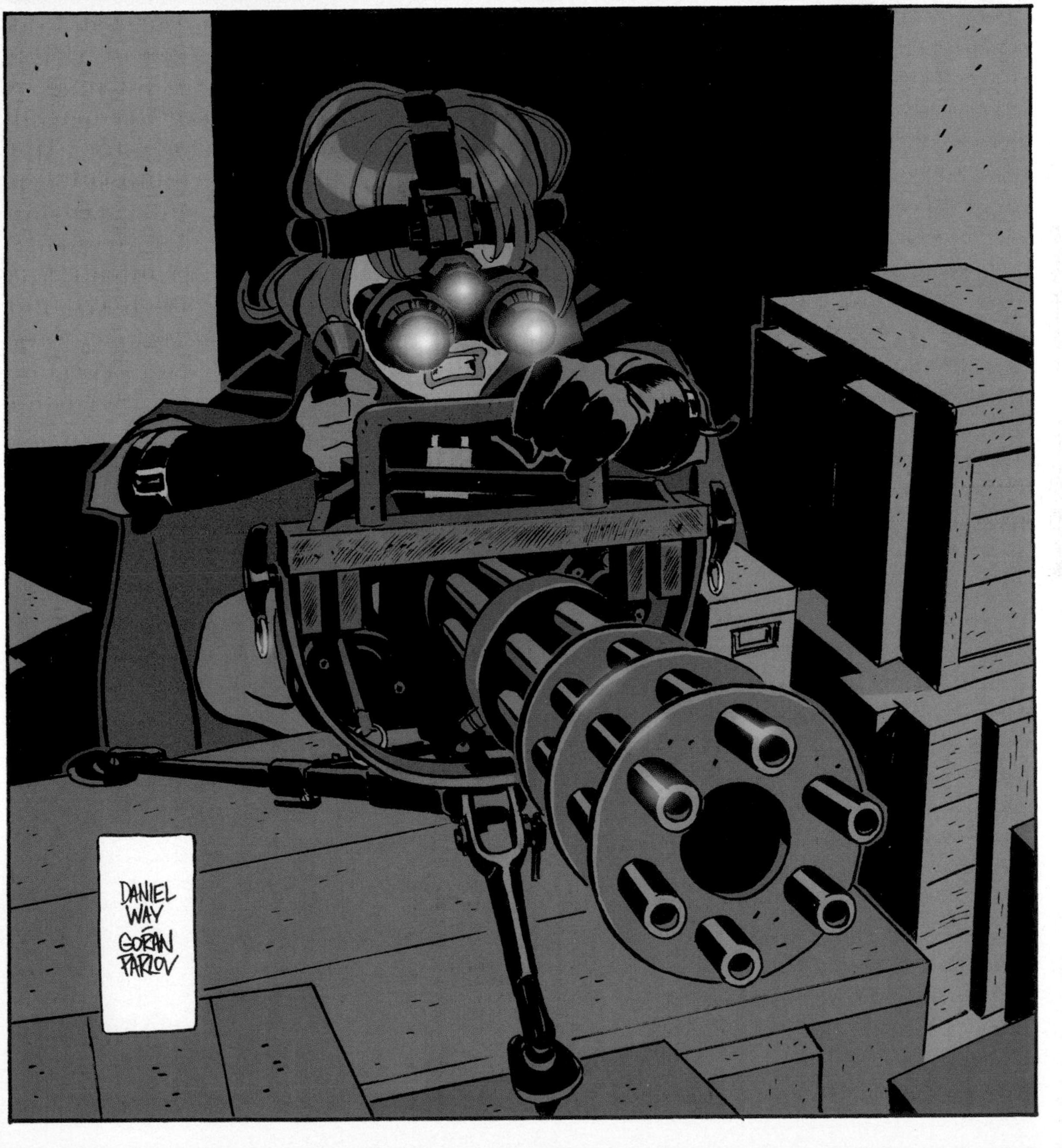
DANIEL
WAY
GORAN
PARLOV

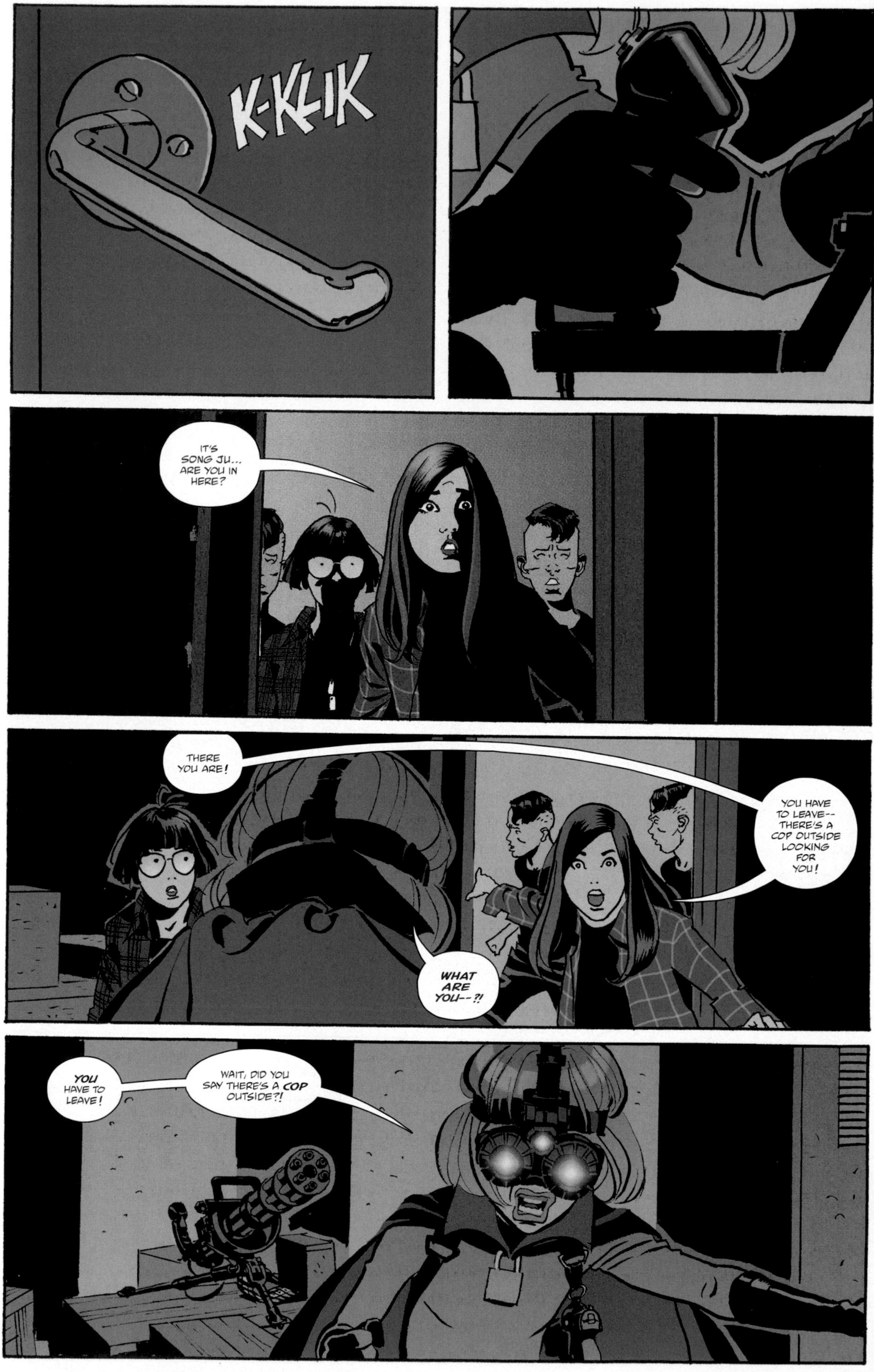
K-KLIK
IT'S SONG JU... ARE YOU IN HERE?
THERE YOU ARE!
YOU HAVE TO LEAVE-- THERE'S A COP OUTSIDE LOOKING FOR YOU!
WHAT ARE YOU--?!
YOU HAVE TO LEAVE!
WAIT, DID YOU SAY THERE'S A COP OUTSIDE?!

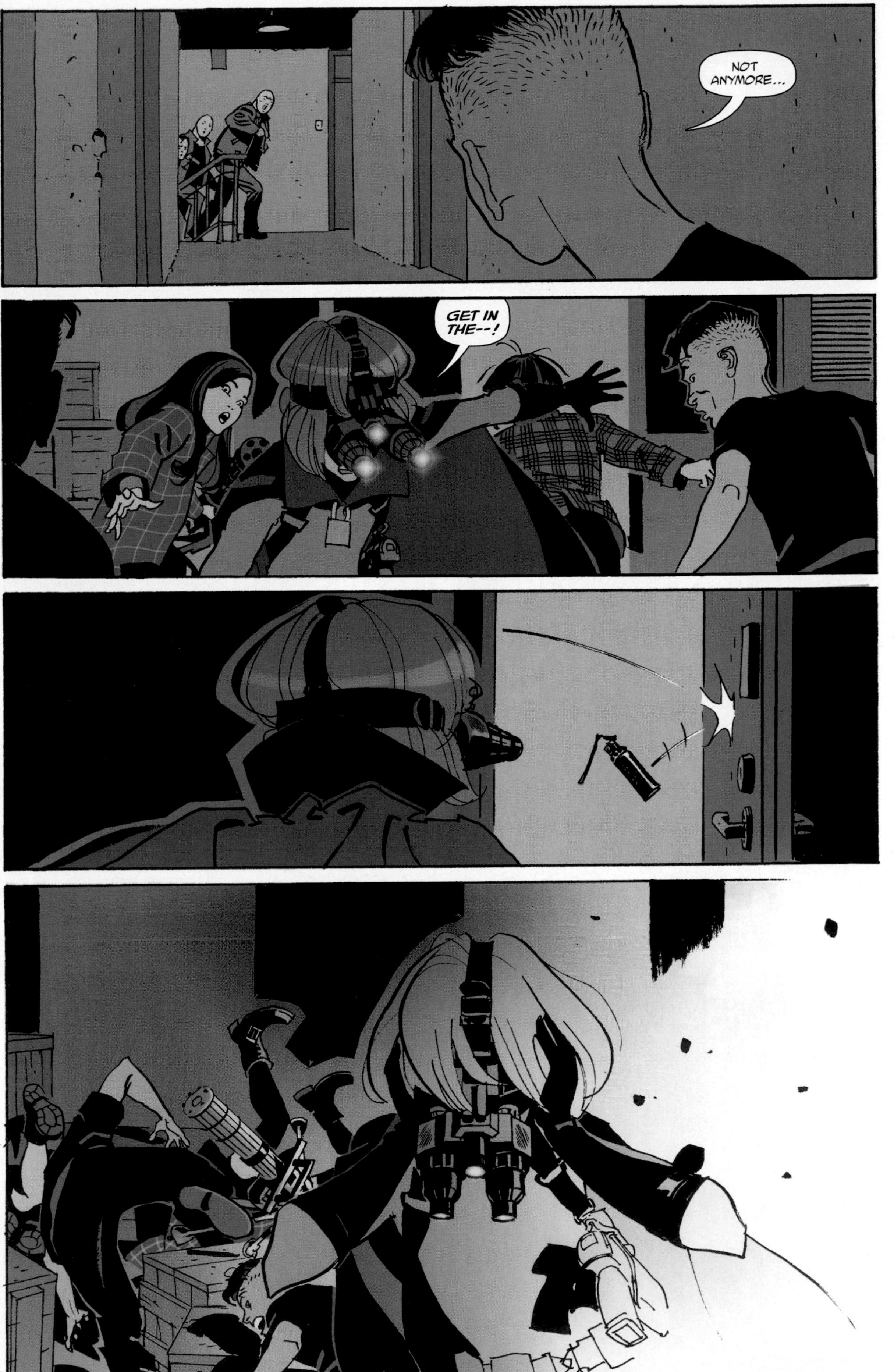
NOT ANYMORE...
GET IN THE--!

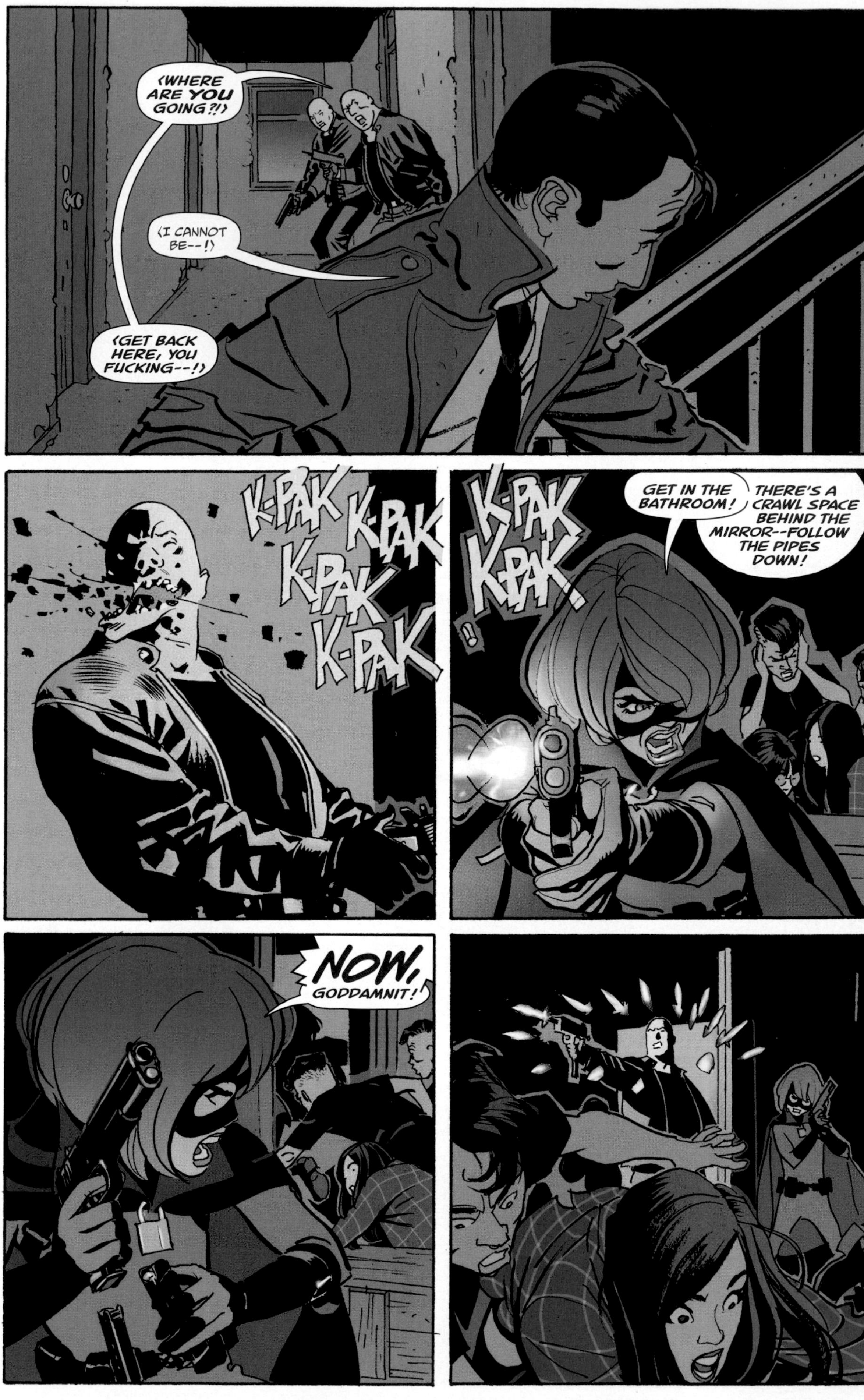

‹WHERE ARE YOU GOING?!›
‹I CANNOT BE--!›
‹GET BACK HERE, YOU FUCKING--!›
K-PAK K-PAK K-PAK K-PAK
K-PAK K-PAK
GET IN THE BATHROOM!
THERE'S A CRAWL SPACE BEHIND THE MIRROR--FOLLOW THE PIPES DOWN!
NOW, GODDAMNIT!

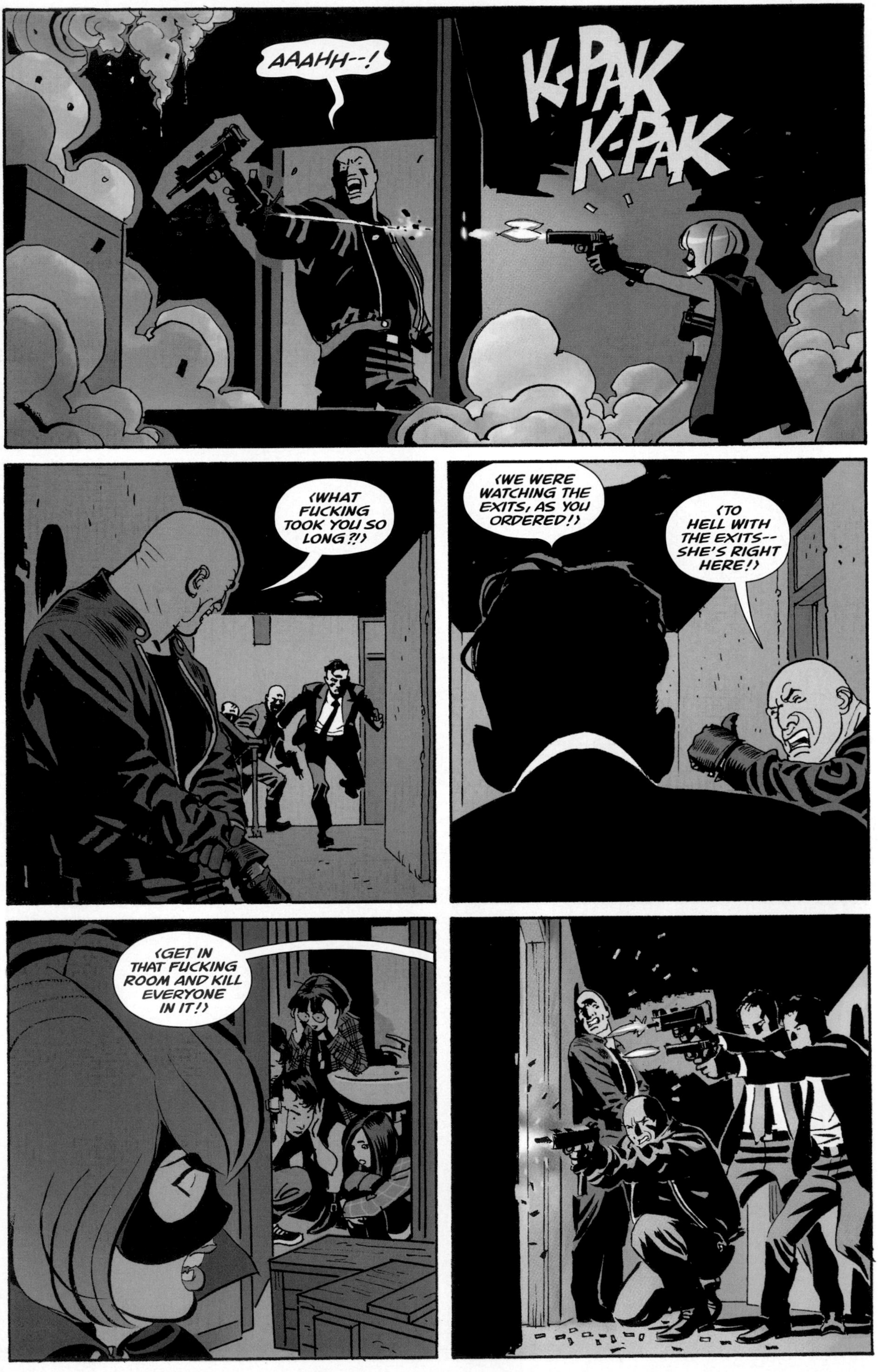
AAAHH--!
K-PAK
K-PAK
‹WHAT FUCKING TOOK YOU SO LONG?!›
‹WE WERE WATCHING THE EXITS, AS YOU ORDERED!›
‹TO HELL WITH THE EXITS-- SHE'S RIGHT HERE!›
‹GET IN THAT FUCKING ROOM AND KILL EVERYONE IN IT!›

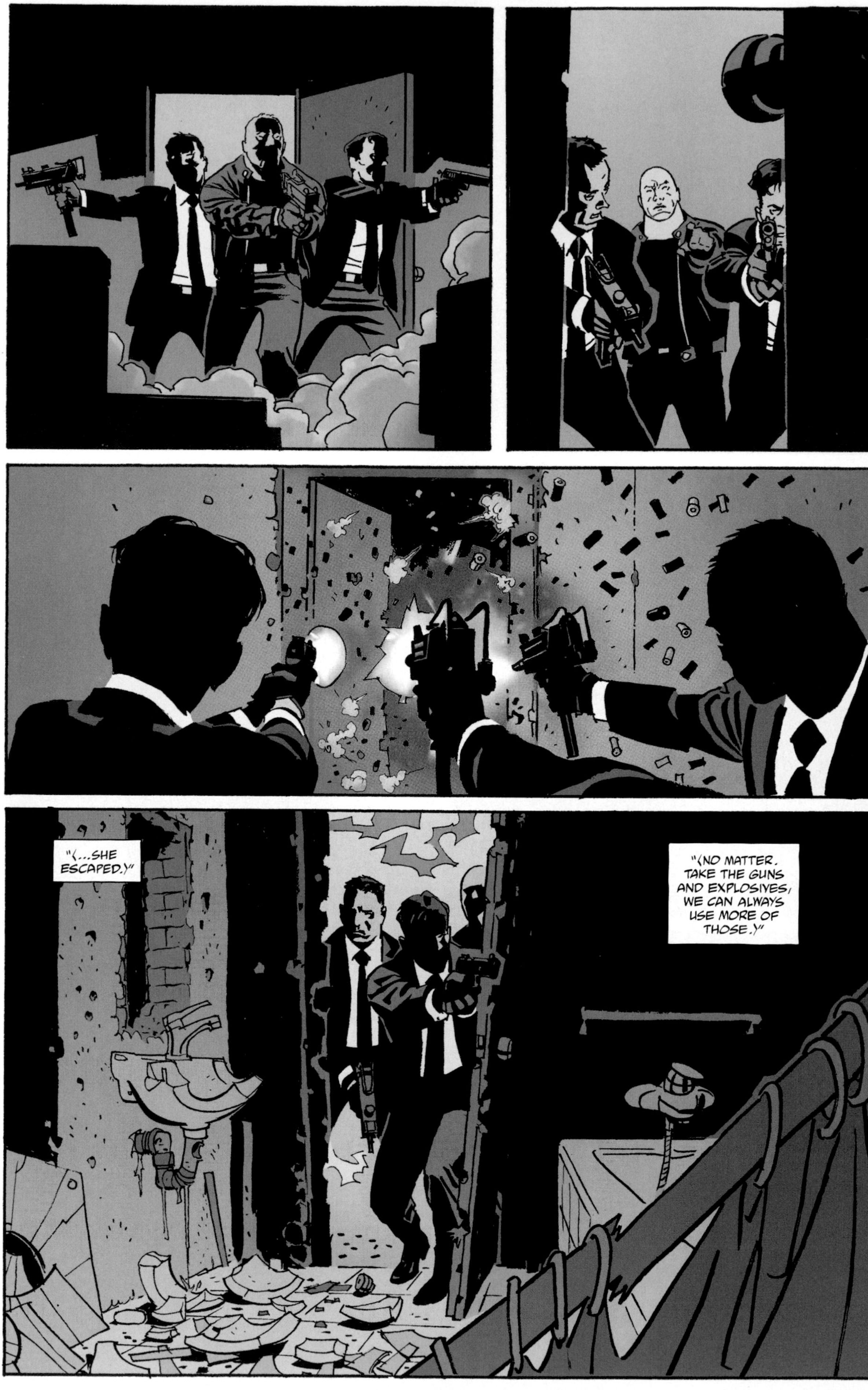
"〈...SHE ESCAPED.〉"
"〈NO MATTER. TAKE THE GUNS AND EXPLOSIVES, WE CAN ALWAYS USE MORE OF THOSE.〉"

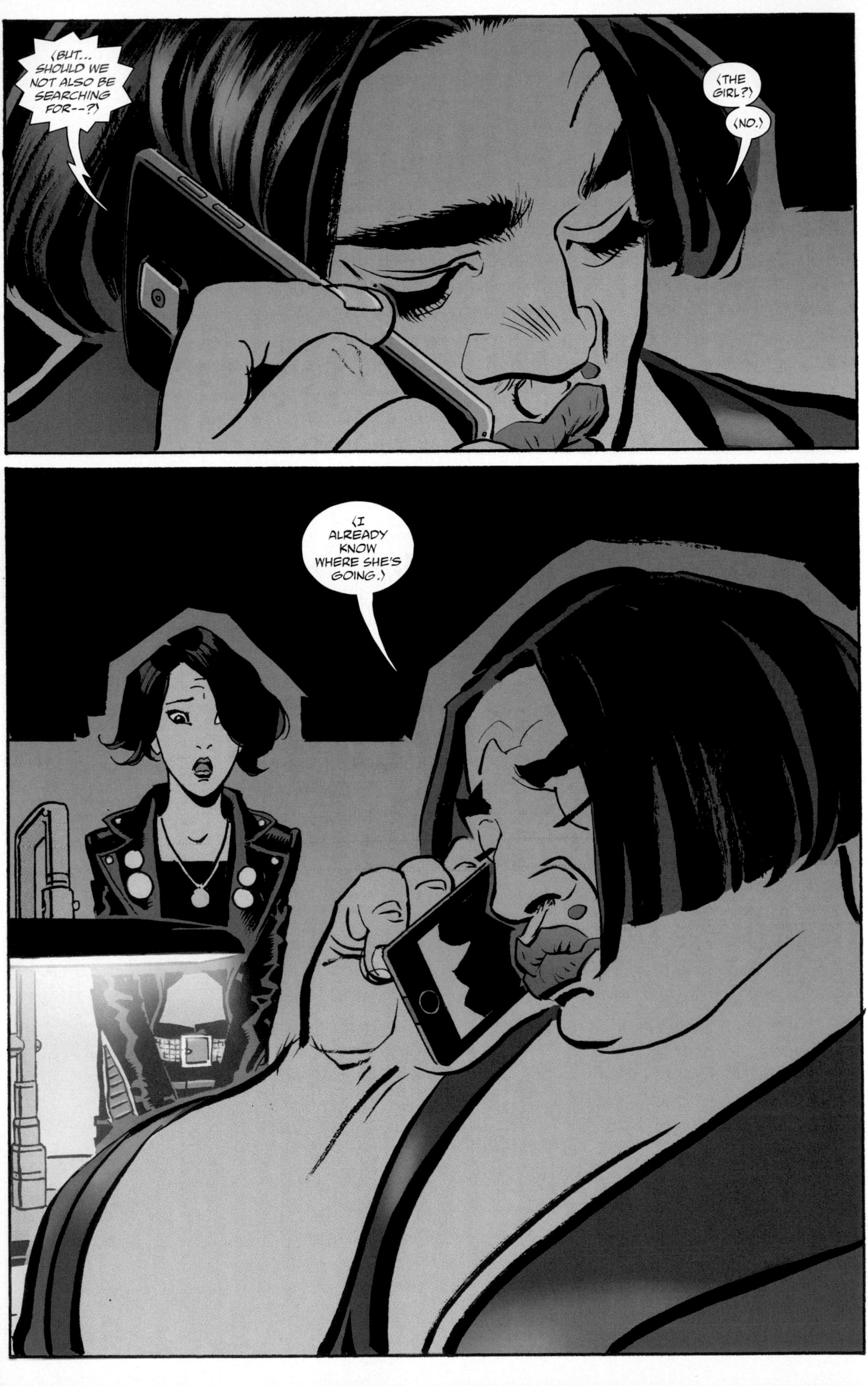

‹BUT... SHOULD WE NOT ALSO BE SEARCHING FOR--?›
‹THE GIRL?›
‹NO.›
‹I ALREADY KNOW WHERE SHE'S GOING.›

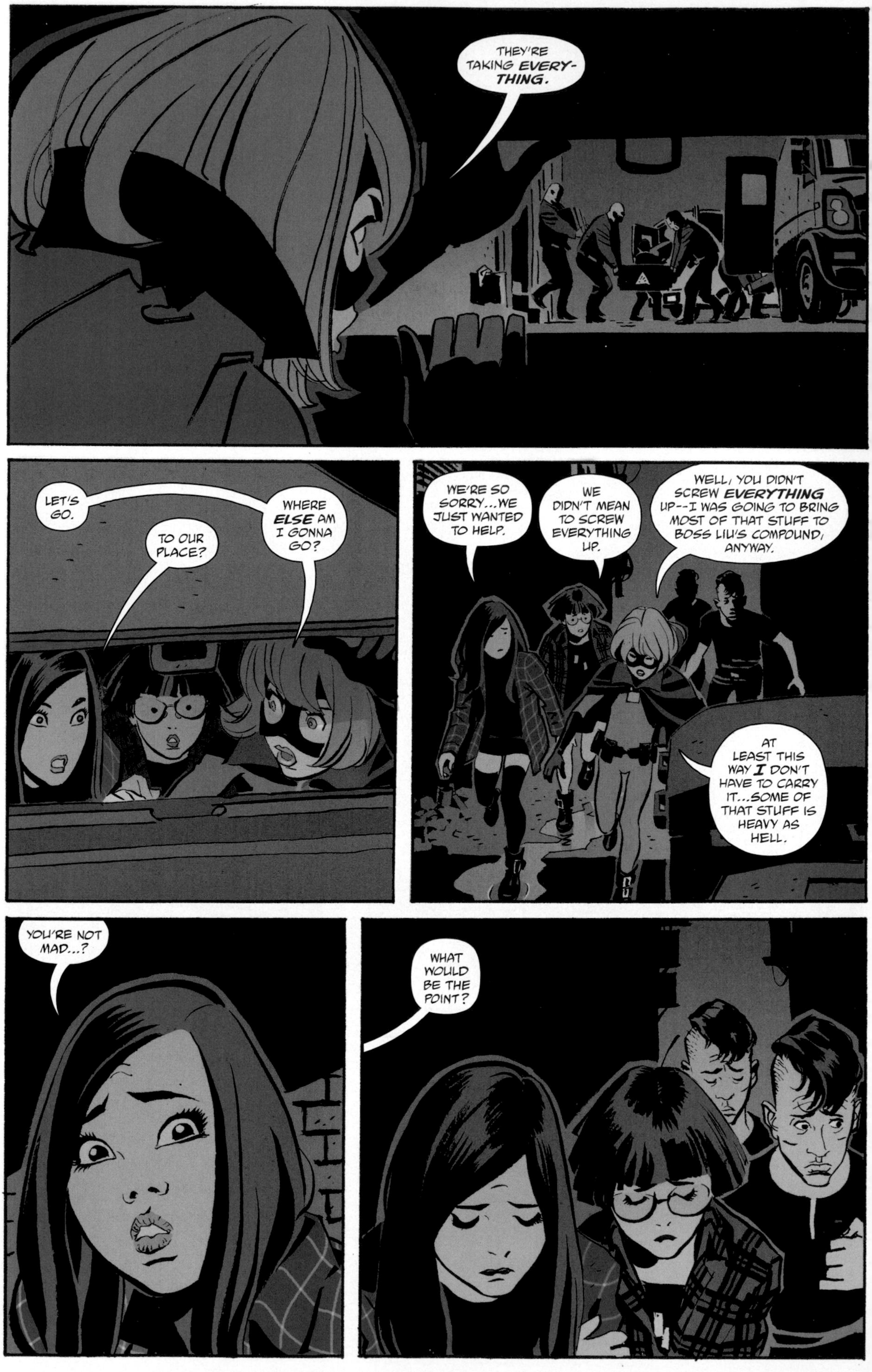
THEY'RE TAKING EVERY-THING.
LET'S GO.
TO OUR PLACE?
WHERE ELSE AM I GONNA GO?
WE'RE SO SORRY...WE JUST WANTED TO HELP.
WE DIDN'T MEAN TO SCREW EVERYTHING UP.
WELL, YOU DIDN'T SCREW EVERYTHING UP--I WAS GOING TO BRING MOST OF THAT STUFF TO BOSS LIU'S COMPOUND, ANYWAY.
AT LEAST THIS WAY I DON'T HAVE TO CARRY IT...SOME OF THAT STUFF IS HEAVY AS HELL.
YOU'RE NOT MAD...?
WHAT WOULD BE THE POINT?

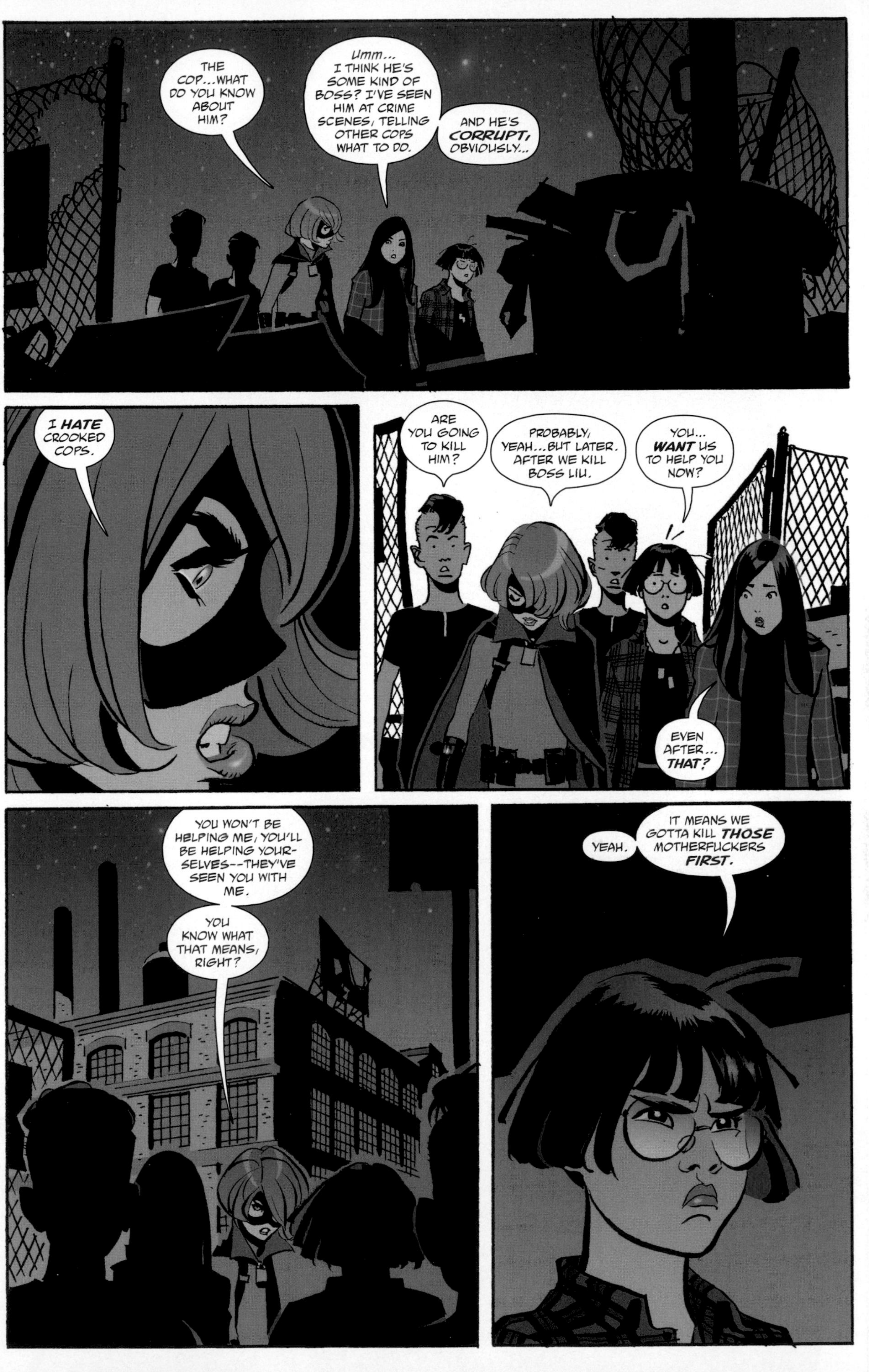

THE COP...WHAT DO YOU KNOW ABOUT HIM?
Umm... I THINK HE'S SOME KIND OF BOSS? I'VE SEEN HIM AT CRIME SCENES, TELLING OTHER COPS WHAT TO DO.
AND HE'S CORRUPT, OBVIOUSLY...
I HATE CROOKED COPS.
ARE YOU GOING TO KILL HIM?
PROBABLY, YEAH...BUT LATER. AFTER WE KILL BOSS LIU.
YOU... WANT US TO HELP YOU NOW?
EVEN AFTER... THAT?
YOU WON'T BE HELPING ME, YOU'LL BE HELPING YOUR-SELVES--THEY'VE SEEN YOU WITH ME.
YOU KNOW WHAT THAT MEANS, RIGHT?
YEAH.
IT MEANS WE GOTTA KILL THOSE MOTHERFUCKERS FIRST.

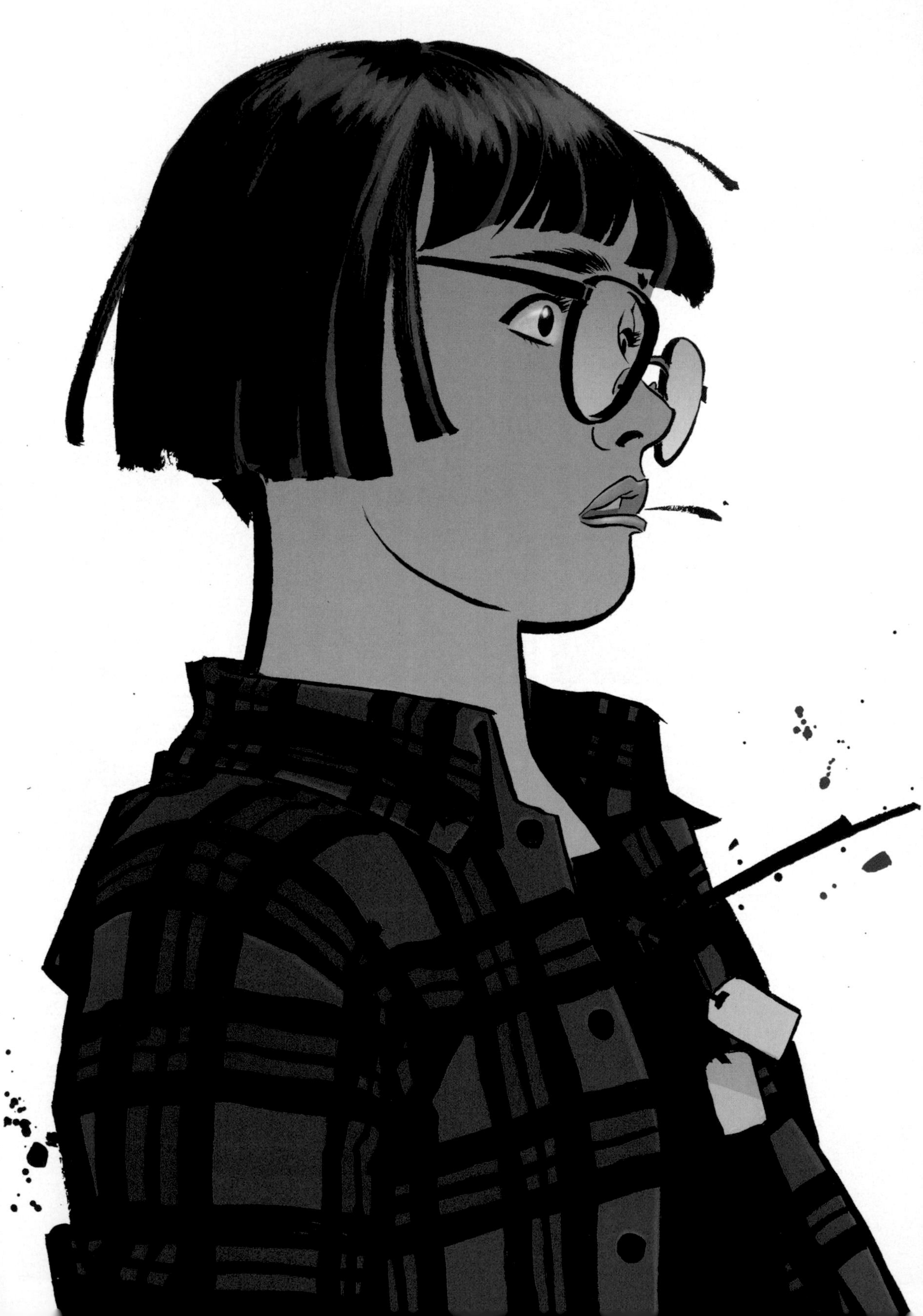

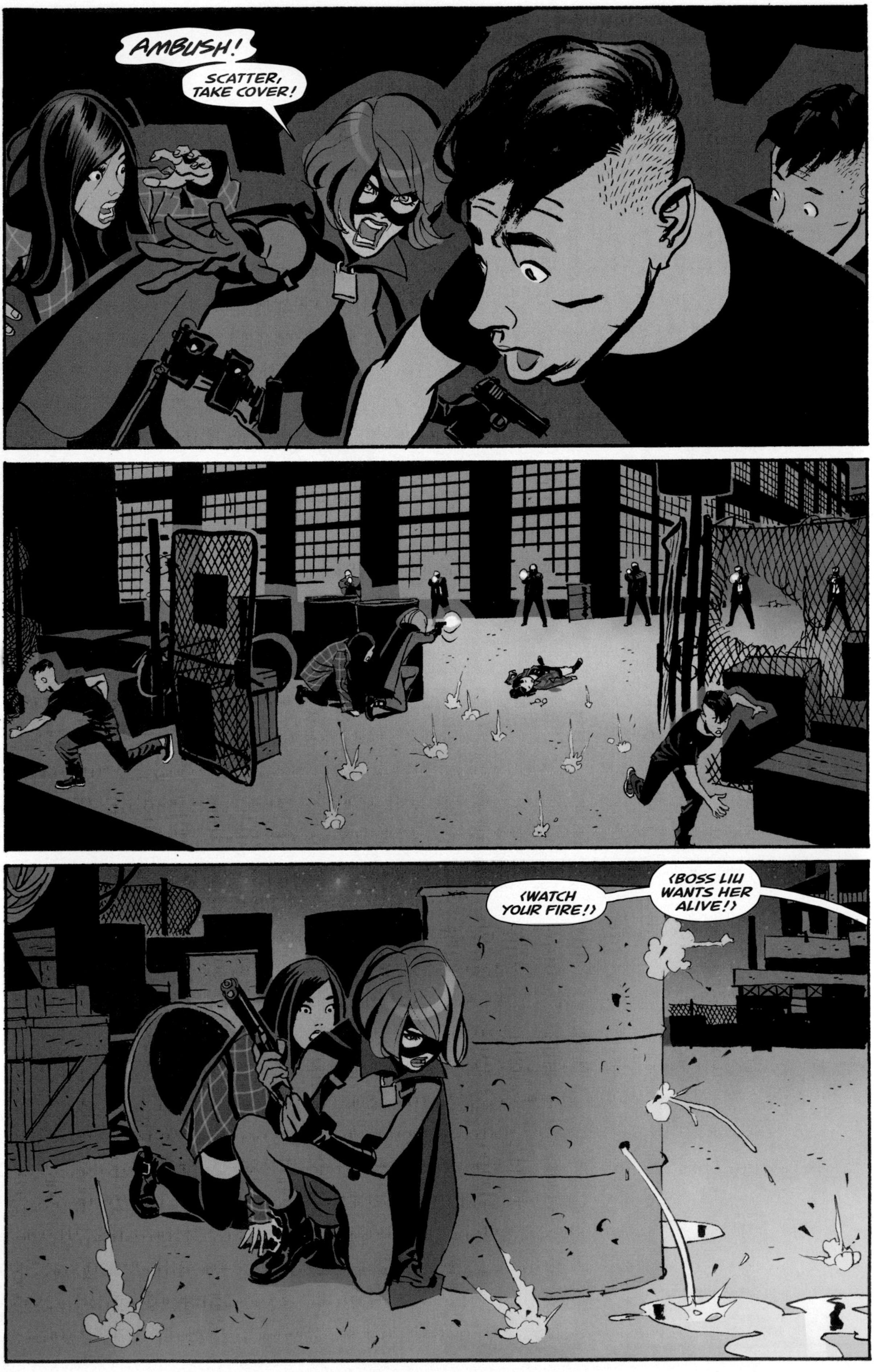
AMBUSH!
SCATTER, TAKE COVER!
‹WATCH YOUR FIRE!›
‹BOSS LIU WANTS HER ALIVE!›

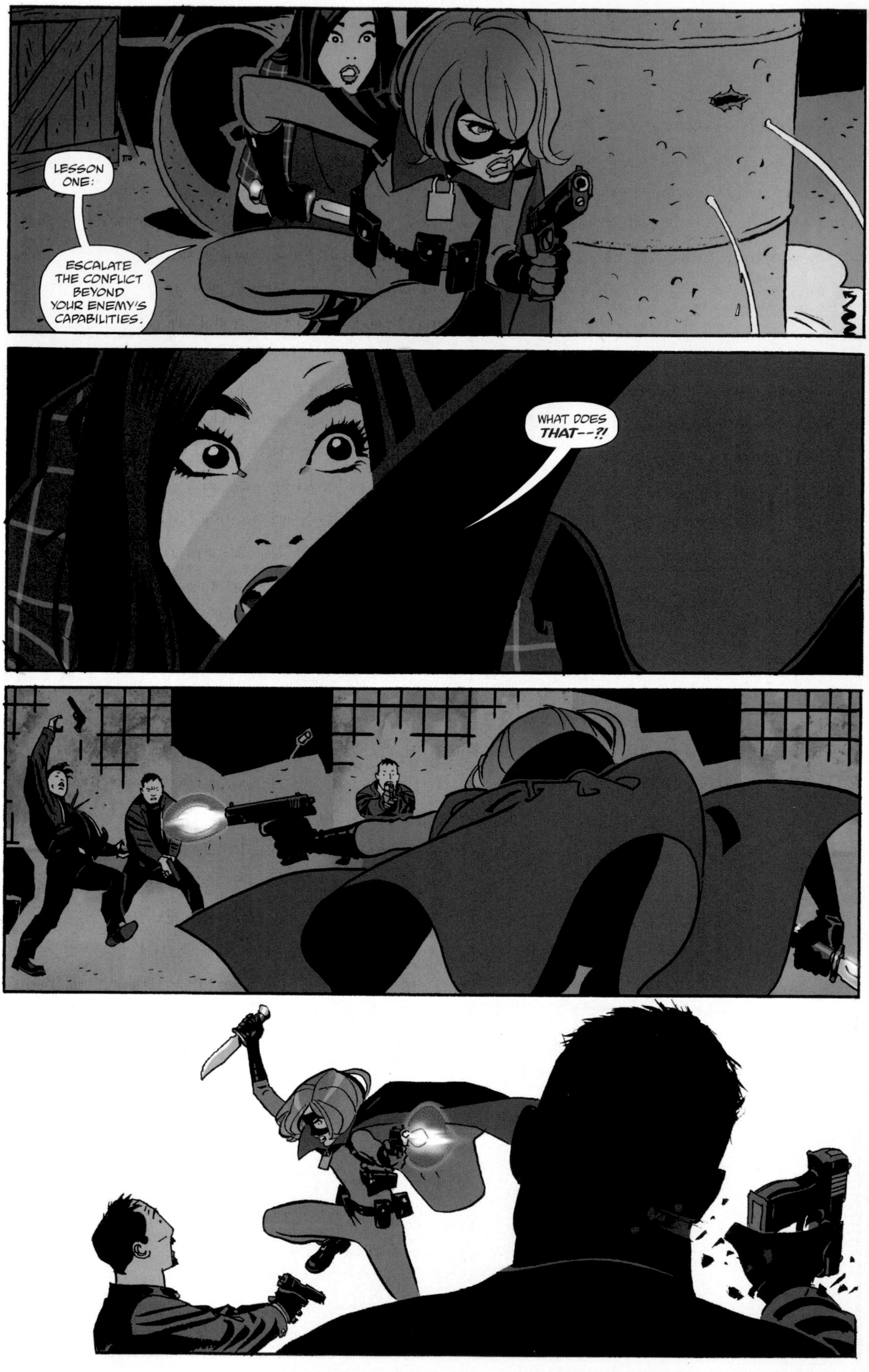
LESSON ONE:
ESCALATE THE CONFLICT BEYOND YOUR ENEMY'S CAPABILITIES.
WHAT DOES THAT--?!

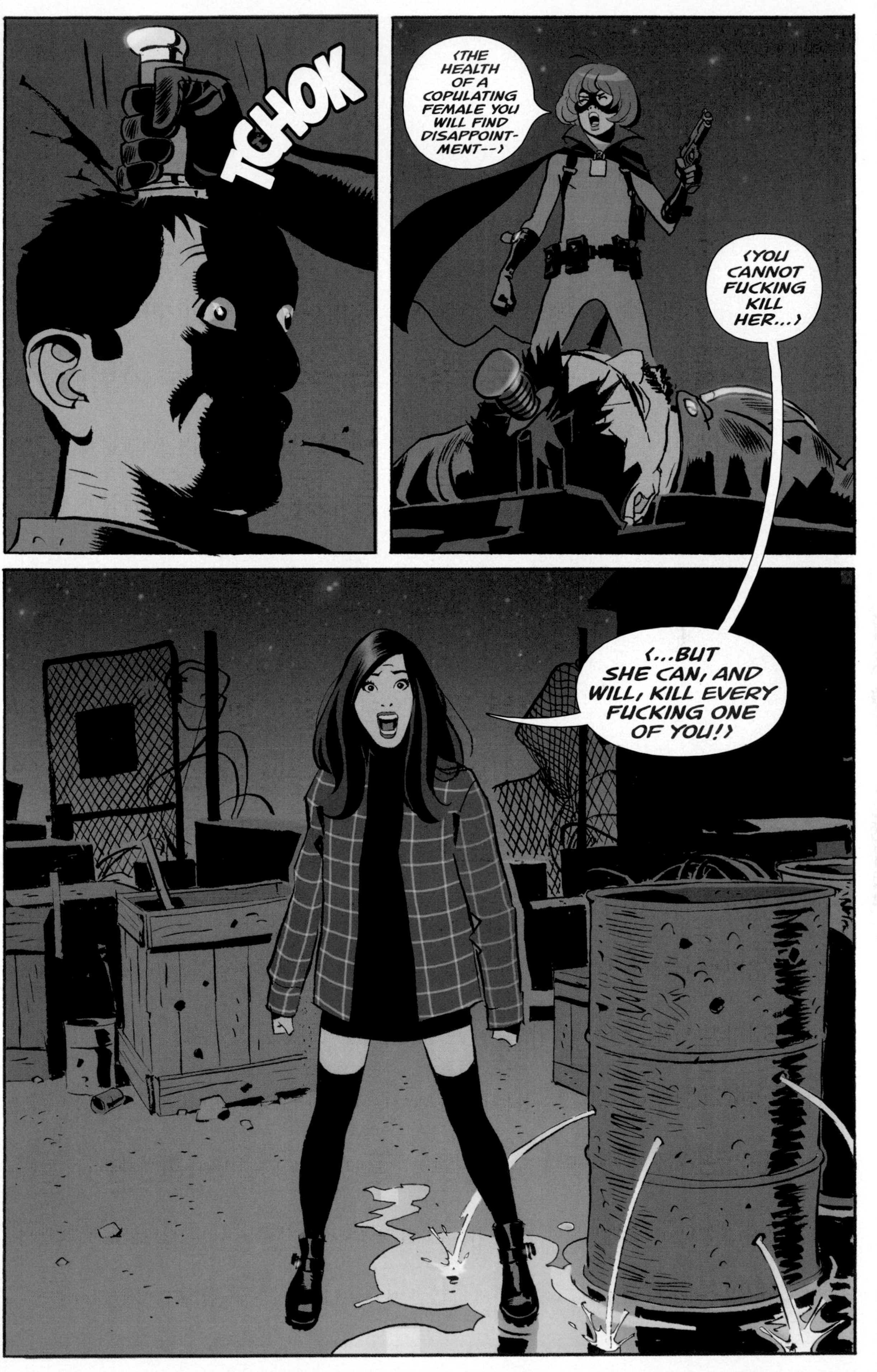
TCHOK
‹THE HEALTH OF A COPULATING FEMALE YOU WILL FIND DISAPPOINT-MENT--›
‹YOU CANNOT FUCKING KILL HER...›
‹...BUT SHE CAN, AND WILL, KILL EVERY FUCKING ONE OF YOU!›

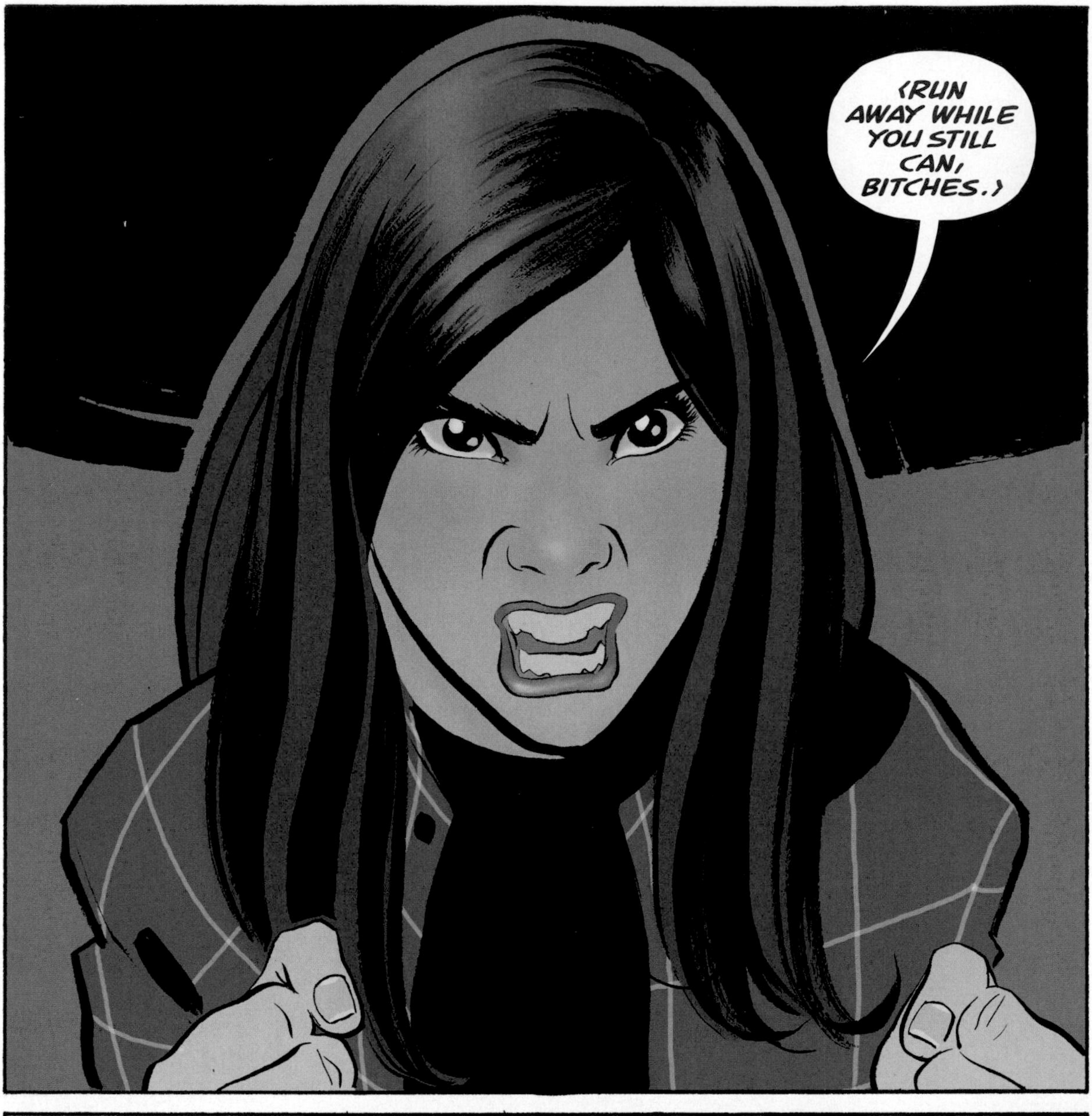
‹RUN AWAY WHILE YOU STILL CAN, BITCHES.›

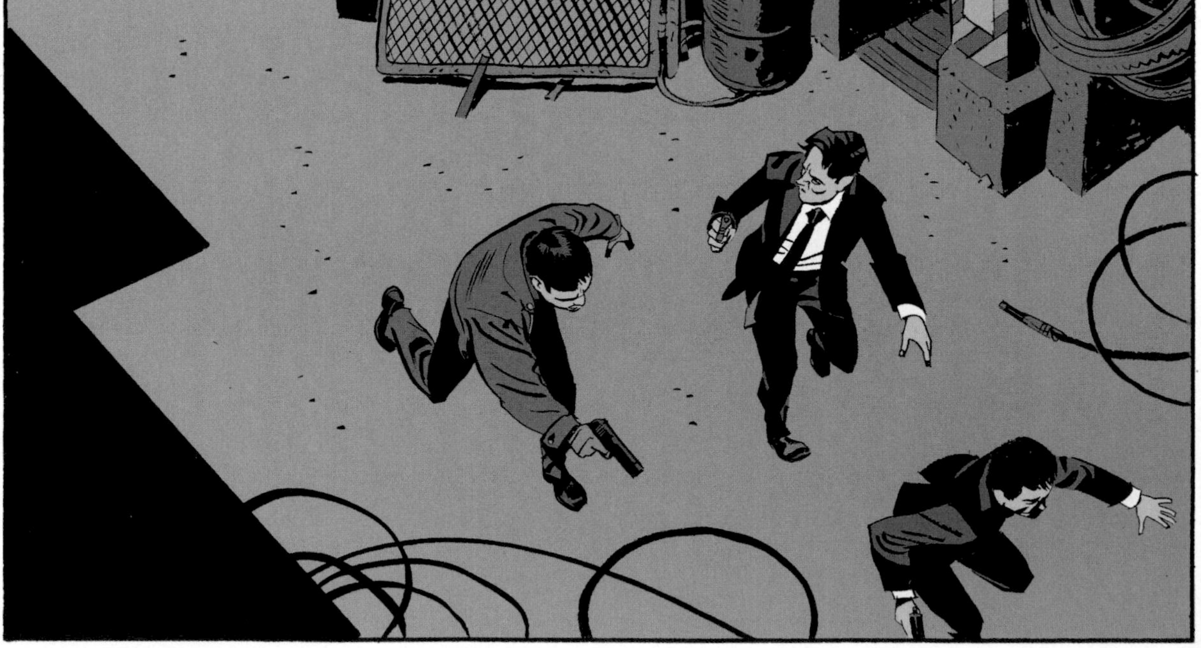

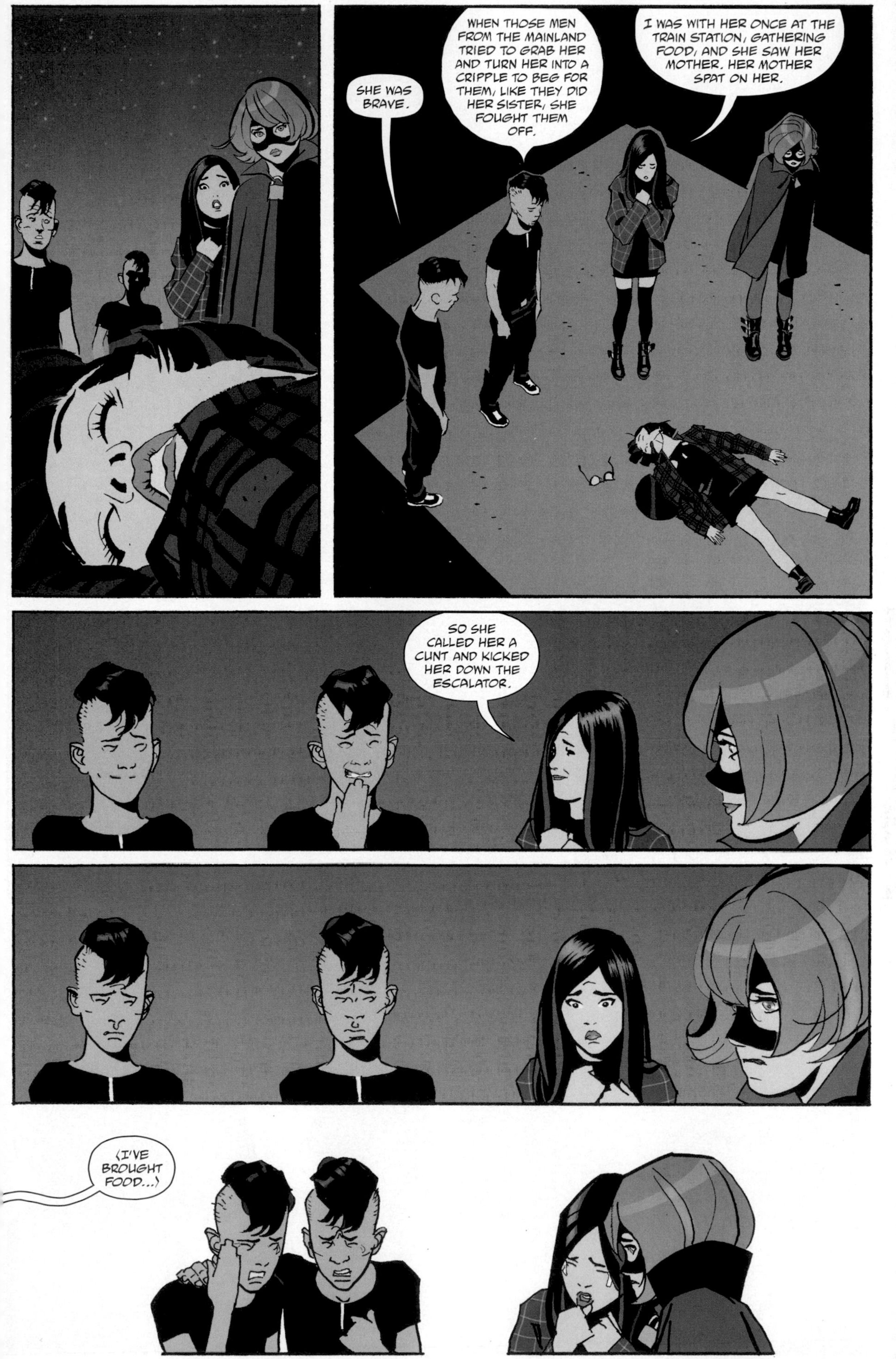
SHE WAS BRAVE.
WHEN THOSE MEN FROM THE MAINLAND TRIED TO GRAB HER AND TURN HER INTO A CRIPPLE TO BEG FOR THEM, LIKE THEY DID HER SISTER, SHE FOUGHT THEM OFF.
I WAS WITH HER ONCE AT THE TRAIN STATION, GATHERING FOOD, AND SHE SAW HER MOTHER. HER MOTHER SPAT ON HER.
SO SHE CALLED HER A CUNT AND KICKED HER DOWN THE ESCALATOR.
‹I'VE BROUGHT FOOD...›

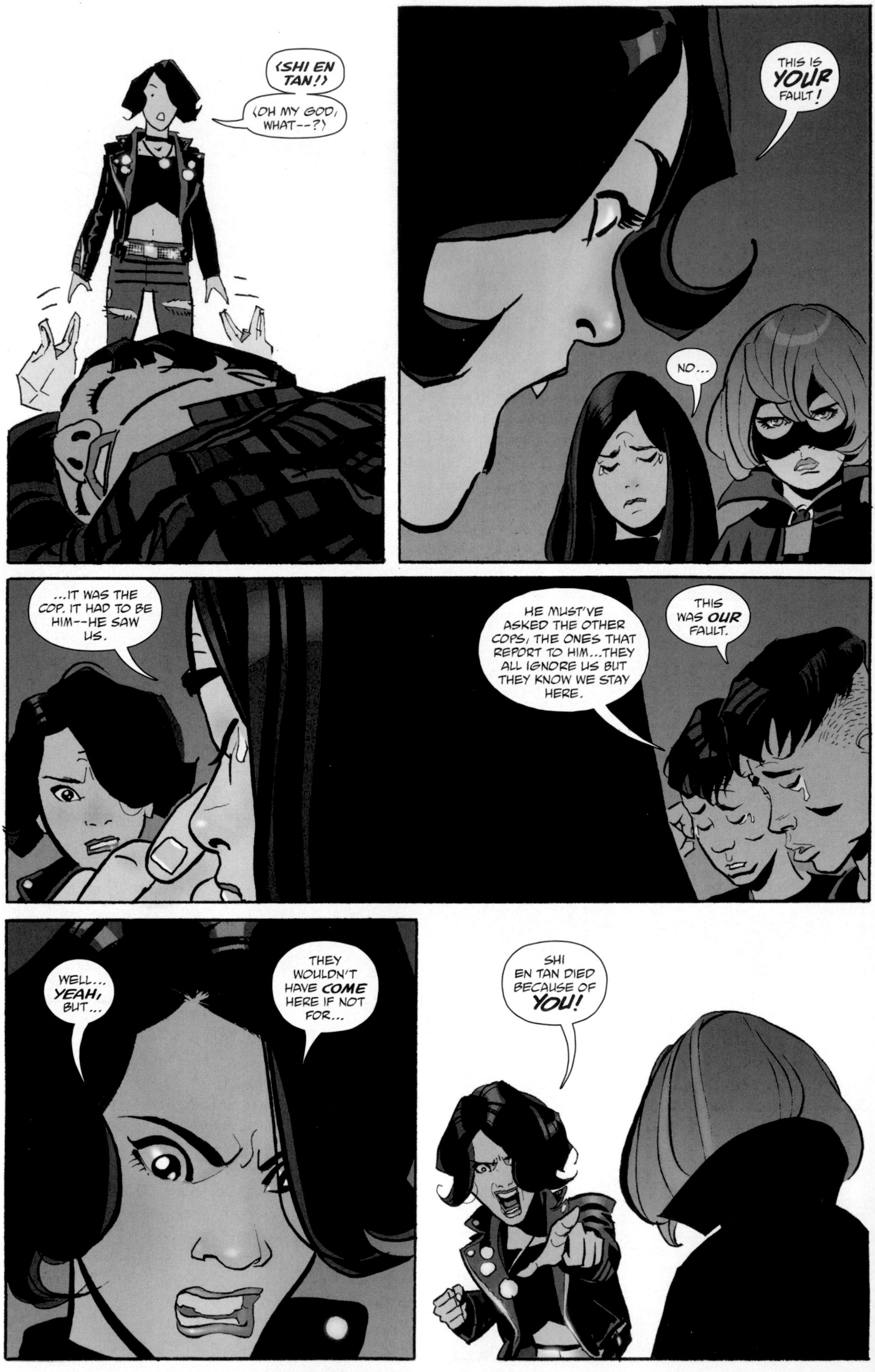

‹SHI EN TAN!›
‹OH MY GOD, WHAT--?›
THIS IS YOUR FAULT!
NO...
...IT WAS THE COP. IT HAD TO BE HIM--HE SAW US.
HE MUST'VE ASKED THE OTHER COPS, THE ONES THAT REPORT TO HIM...THEY ALL IGNORE US BUT THEY KNOW WE STAY HERE.
THIS WAS OUR FAULT.
WELL... YEAH, BUT...
THEY WOULDN'T HAVE COME HERE IF NOT FOR...
SHI EN TAN DIED BECAUSE OF YOU!

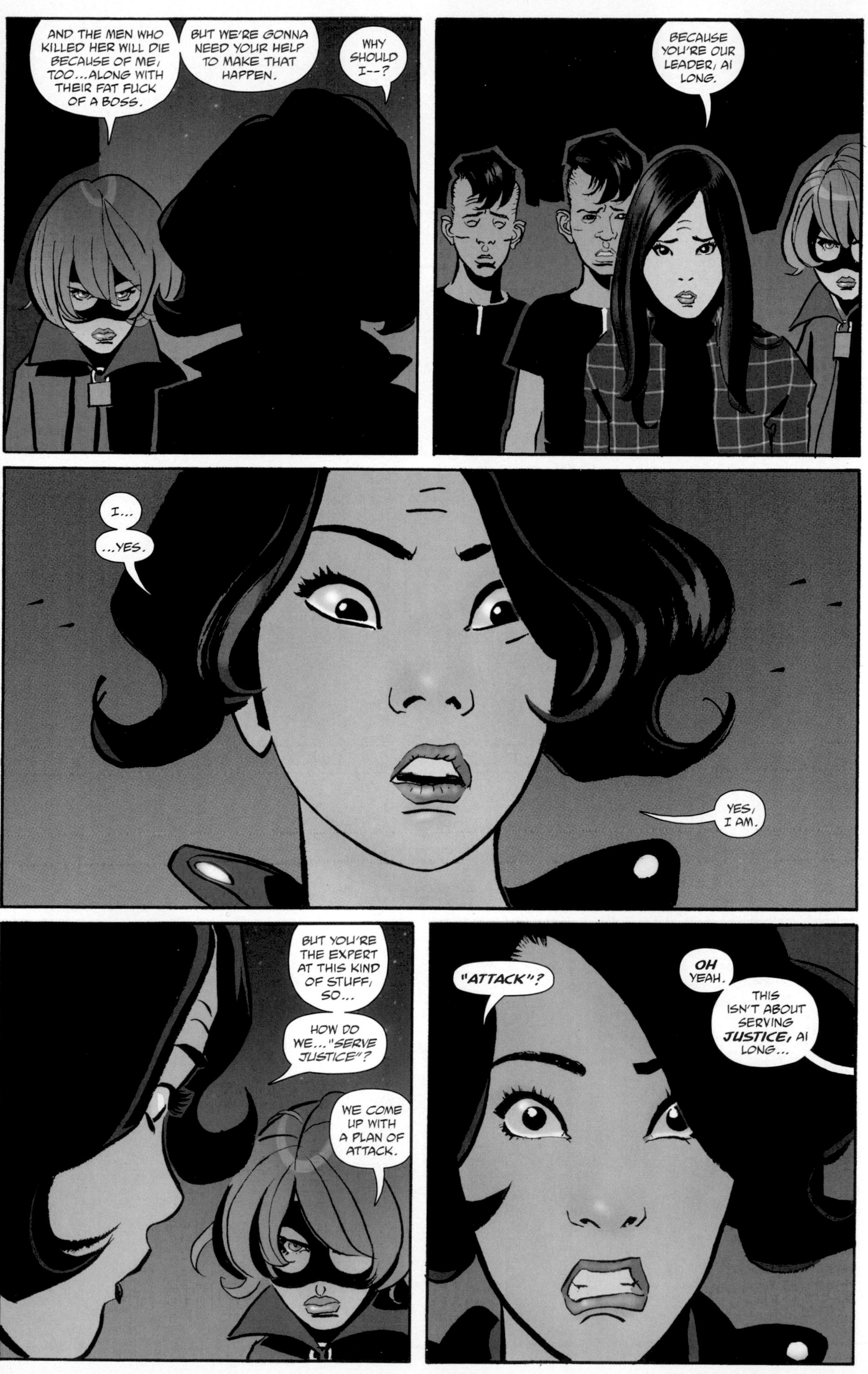
AND THE MEN WHO KILLED HER WILL DIE BECAUSE OF ME, TOO...ALONG WITH THEIR FAT FUCK OF A BOSS.
BUT WE'RE GONNA NEED YOUR HELP TO MAKE THAT HAPPEN.
WHY SHOULD I--?
BECAUSE YOU'RE OUR LEADER, AI LONG.
I...
...YES.
YES, I AM.
BUT YOU'RE THE EXPERT AT THIS KIND OF STUFF, SO...
HOW DO WE..."SERVE JUSTICE"?
WE COME UP WITH A PLAN OF ATTACK.
"ATTACK"?
OH YEAH.
THIS ISN'T ABOUT SERVING JUSTICE, AI LONG...

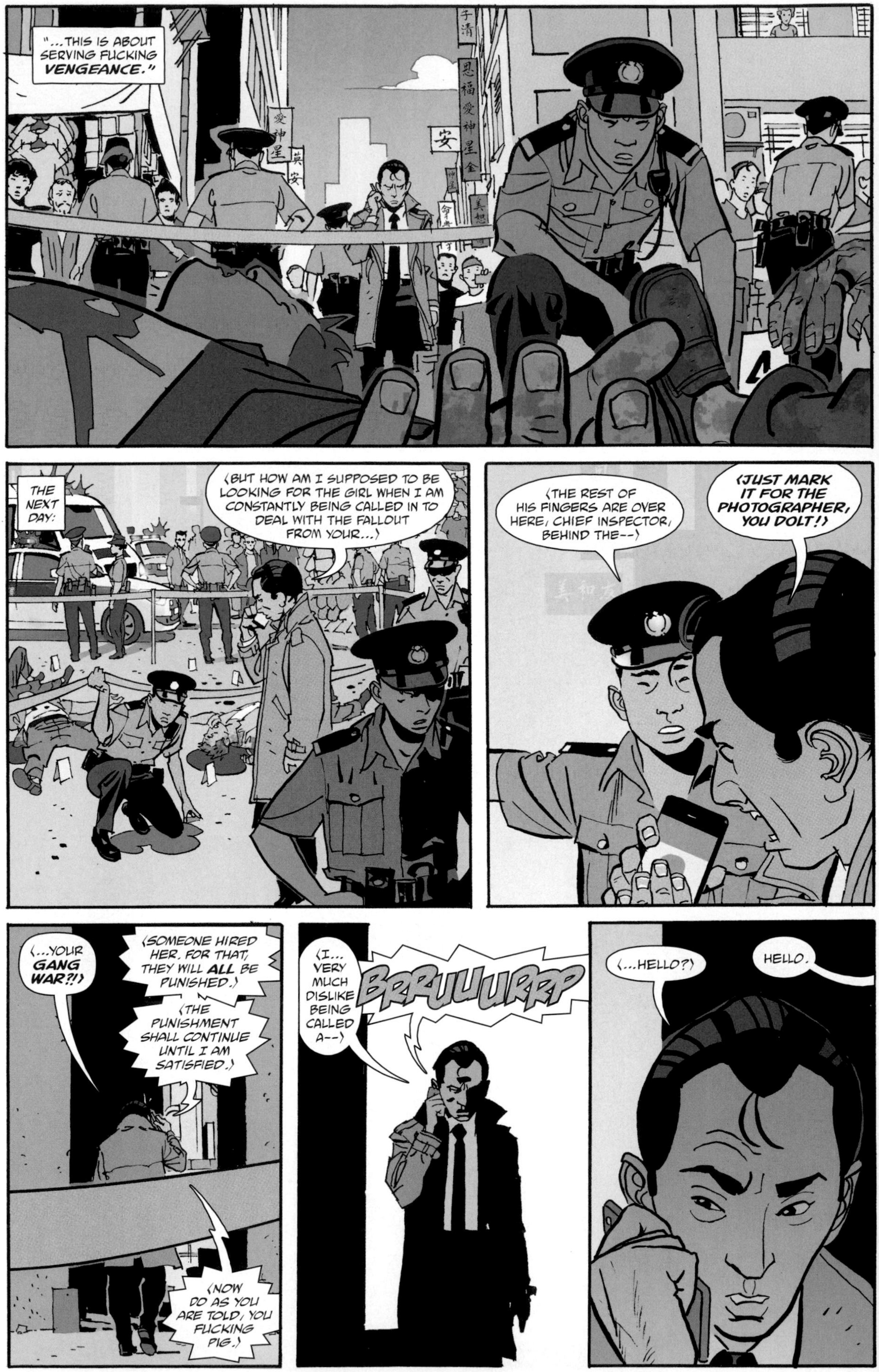

"...THIS IS ABOUT SERVING FUCKING VENGEANCE."
THE NEXT DAY:
⟨BUT HOW AM I SUPPOSED TO BE LOOKING FOR THE GIRL WHEN I AM CONSTANTLY BEING CALLED IN TO DEAL WITH THE FALLOUT FROM YOUR...⟩
⟨THE REST OF HIS FINGERS ARE OVER HERE, CHIEF INSPECTOR, BEHIND THE--⟩
⟨JUST MARK IT FOR THE PHOTOGRAPHER, YOU DOLT!⟩
⟨...YOUR GANG WAR?!⟩
⟨SOMEONE HIRED HER. FOR THAT, THEY WILL ALL BE PUNISHED.⟩
⟨THE PUNISHMENT SHALL CONTINUE UNTIL I AM SATISFIED.⟩
⟨NOW DO AS YOU ARE TOLD, YOU FUCKING PIG.⟩
⟨I... VERY MUCH DISLIKE BEING CALLED A--⟩
BRRUUURRP
⟨...HELLO?⟩
HELLO.

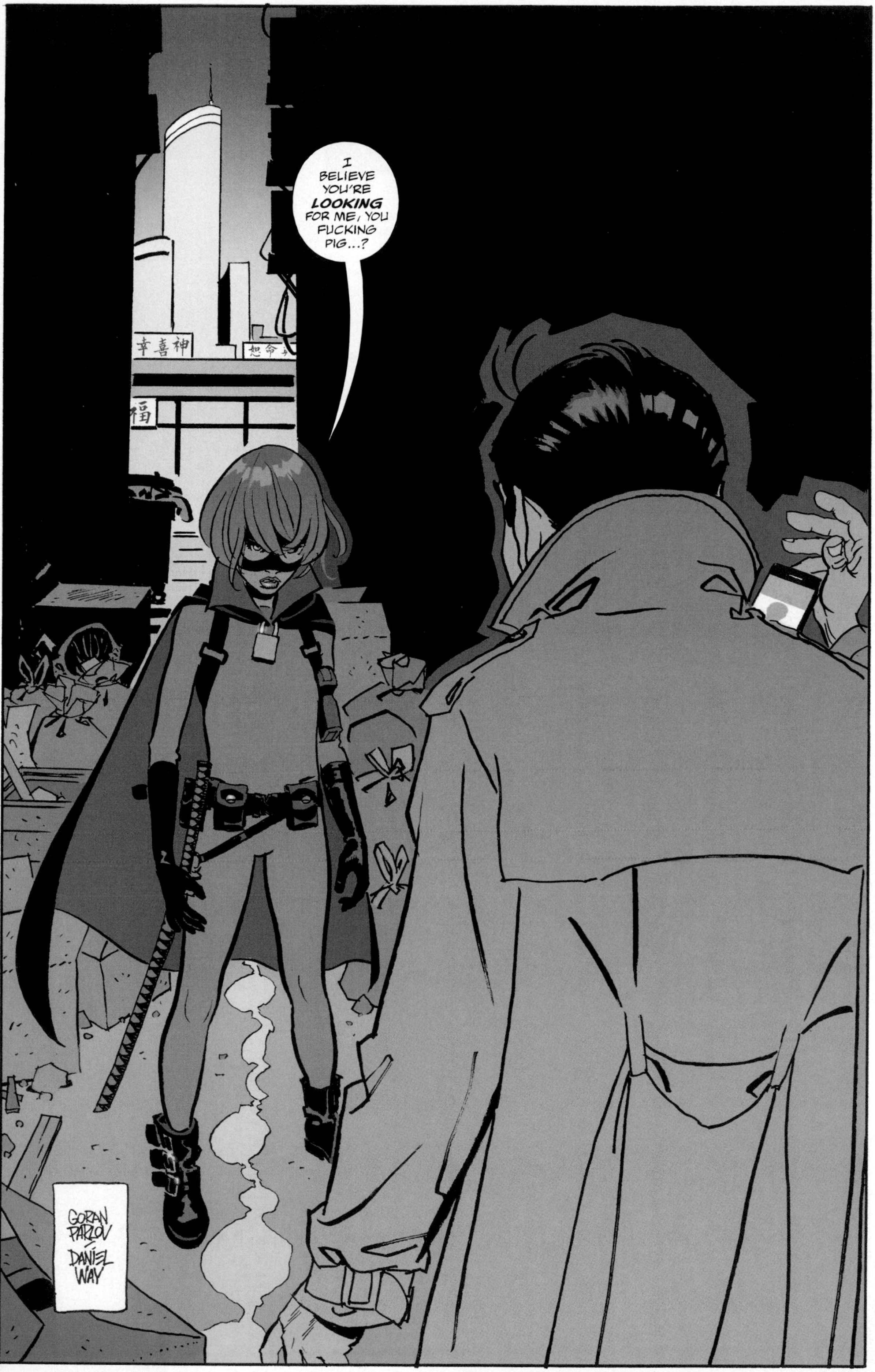
I BELIEVE YOU'RE **LOOKING** FOR ME, YOU FUCKING PIG...?
GORAN PARLOV - DANIEL WAY

FOUR

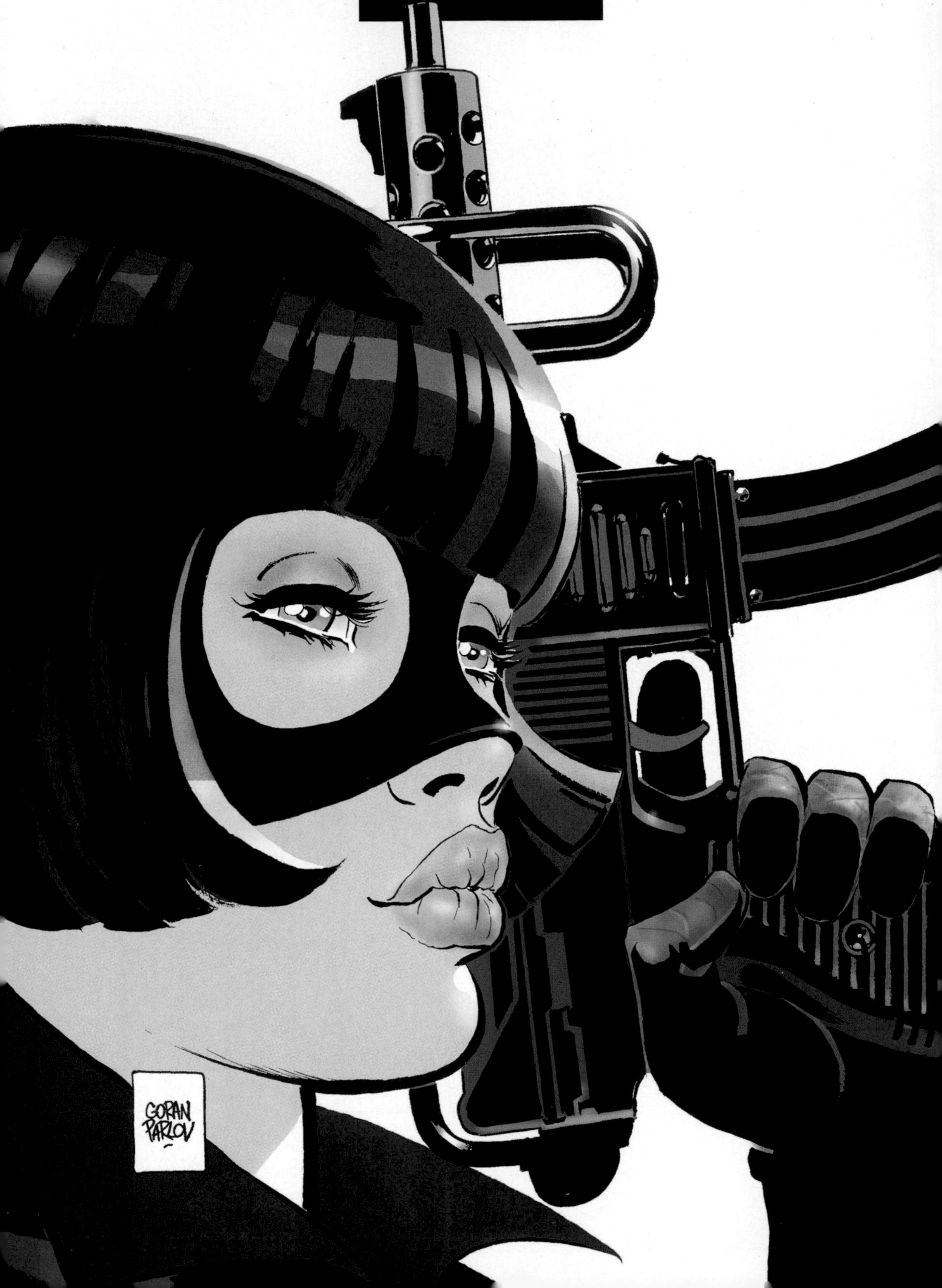
GORAN PARLOV

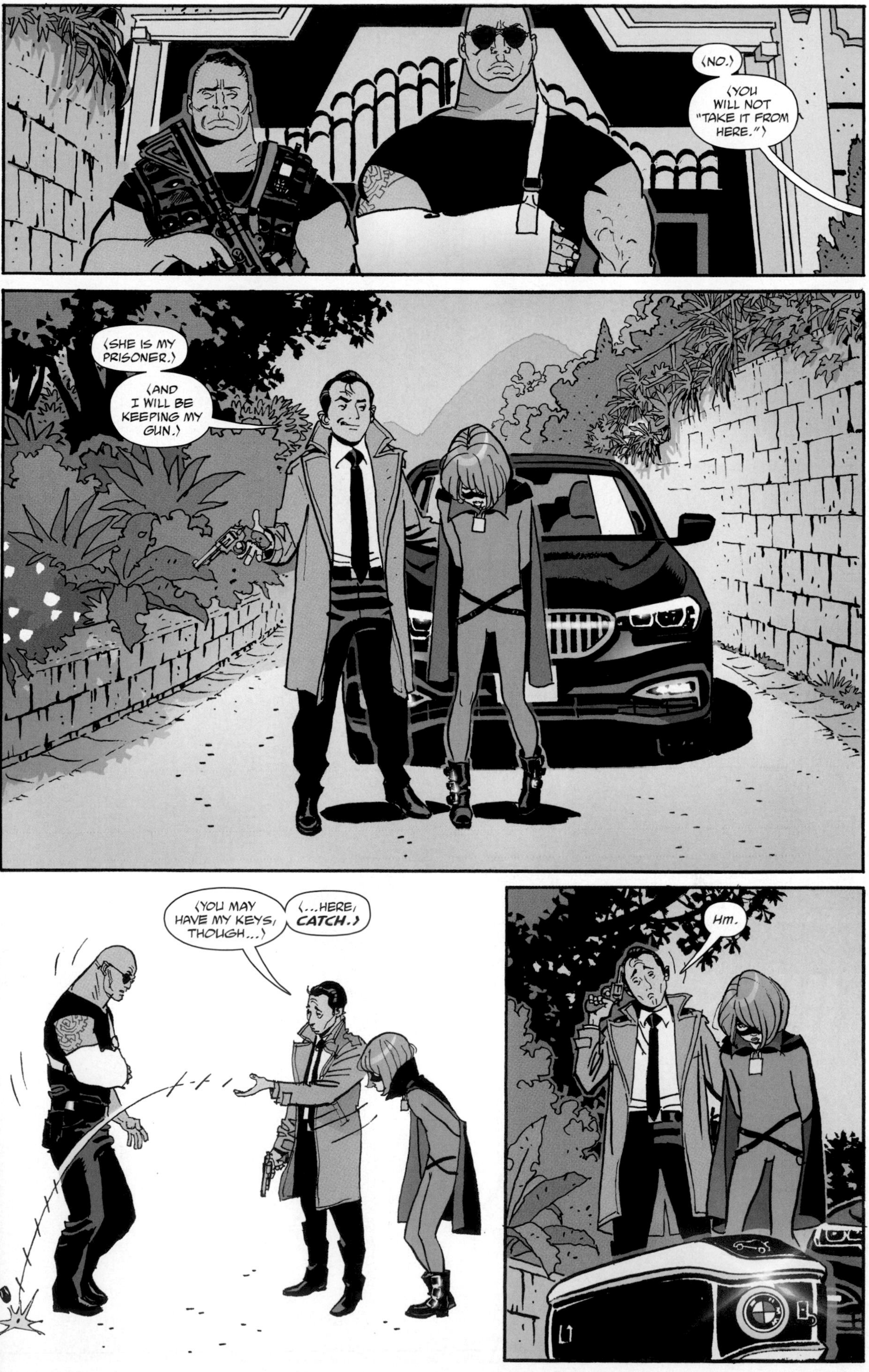
‹NO.›
‹YOU WILL NOT "TAKE IT FROM HERE."›
‹SHE IS MY PRISONER.›
‹AND I WILL BE KEEPING MY GUN.›
‹YOU MAY HAVE MY KEYS, THOUGH...›
‹...HERE, CATCH.›
Hm.

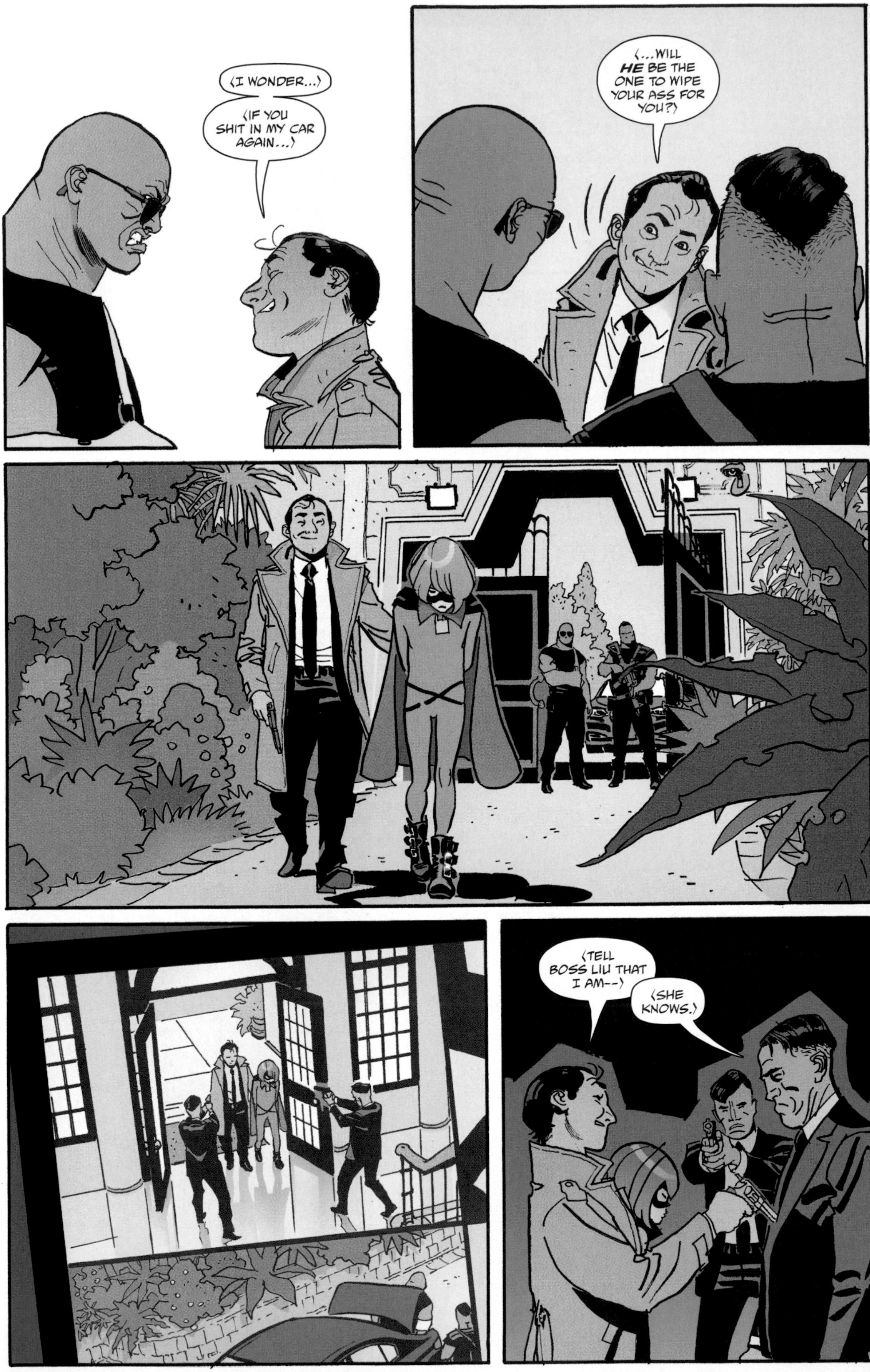

⟨I WONDER...⟩
⟨IF YOU SHIT IN MY CAR AGAIN...⟩
⟨...WILL HE BE THE ONE TO WIPE YOUR ASS FOR YOU?⟩
⟨TELL BOSS LIU THAT I AM--⟩
⟨SHE KNOWS.⟩

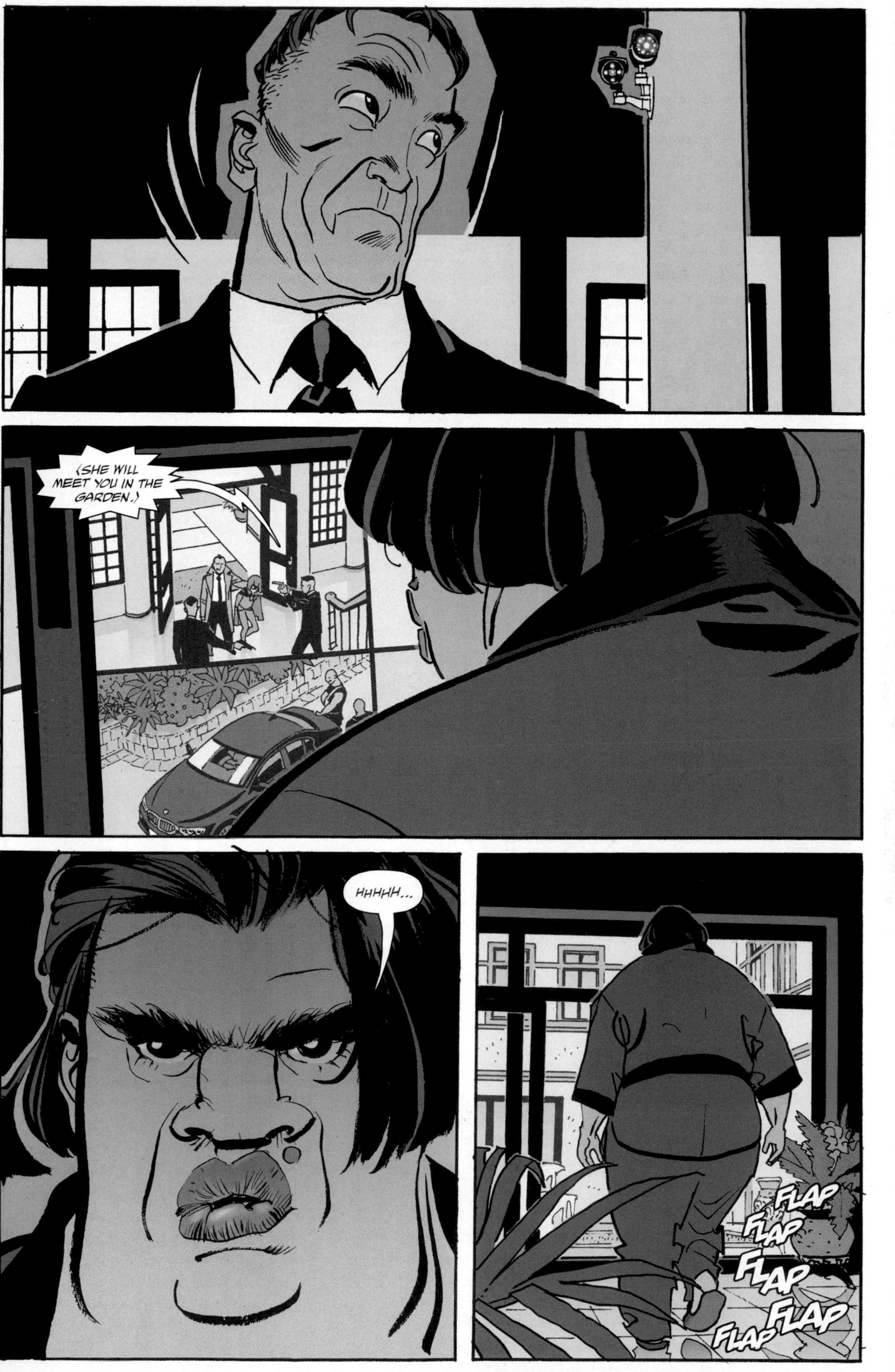

‹SHE WILL MEET YOU IN THE GARDEN.›
HHHHH...
FLAP
FLAP
FLAP
FLAP
FLAP

⟨WHY DOES HE HAVE A GUN?⟩

⟨I BELIEVE IT HAS BEEN *AMPLY* PROVEN THAT YOUR MEN OFFER YOU NO PROTECTION AGAINST THIS YOUNG ASSASSIN, BOSS LIU.⟩

⟨I THEREFORE FEEL IT IS MY RESPONSIBILITY, AS THE ONLY ONE WHO COULD APPREHEND HER, TO MAKE CERTAIN SHE NOT BE ALLOWED TO--⟩

⟨GIVE IT TO ME.⟩

⟨BUT...⟩

⟨...WITH RESPECT, BOSS LIU, IT IS MY *SERVICE WEAPON.*⟩

⟨*DO* YOU RESPECT ME, CHIEF INSPECTOR WU XIAOPENG?⟩

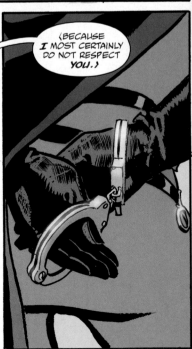

⟨BECAUSE *I* MOST CERTAINLY DO NOT RESPECT *YOU.*⟩

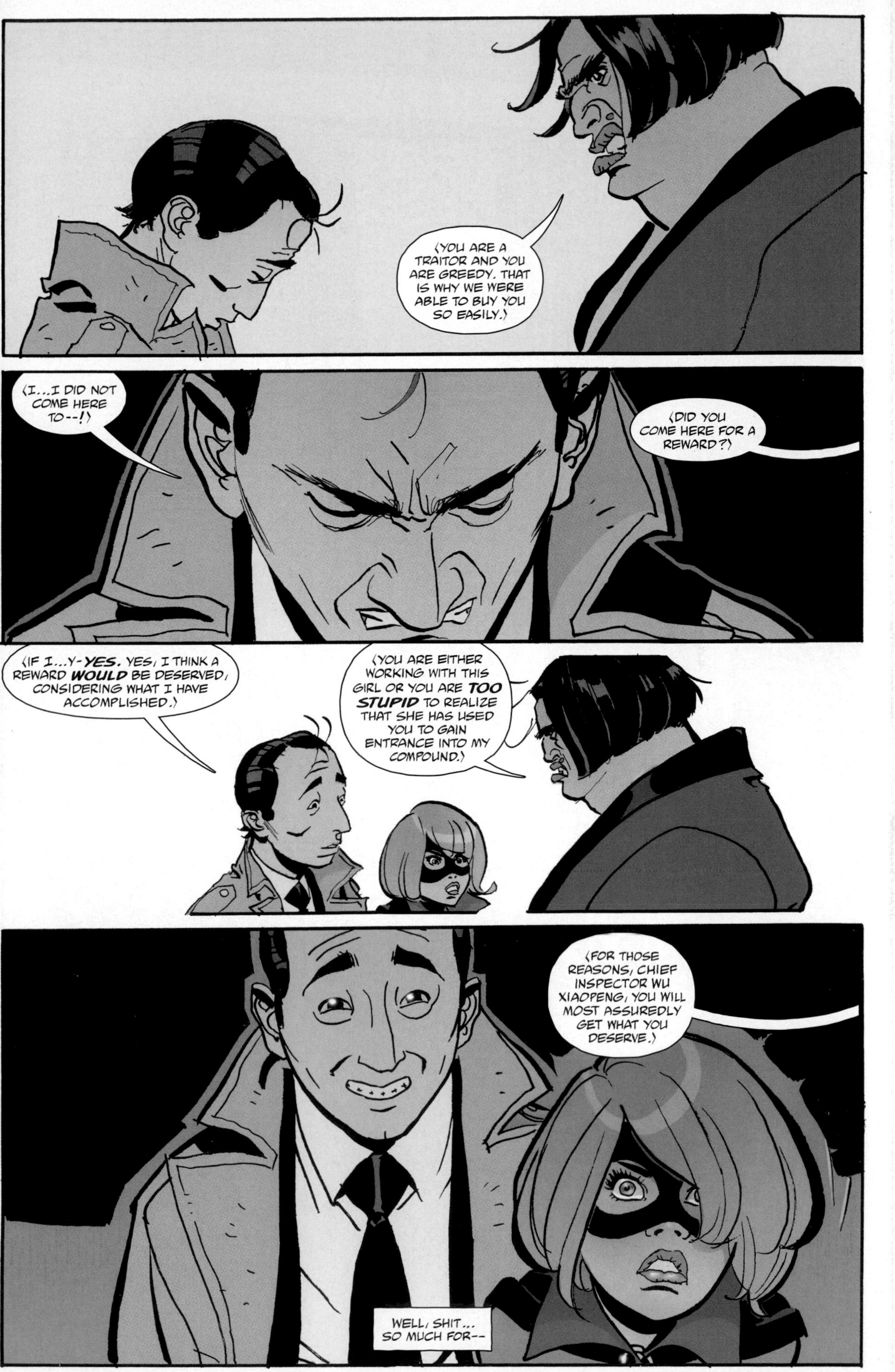
‹YOU ARE A TRAITOR AND YOU ARE GREEDY. THAT IS WHY WE WERE ABLE TO BUY YOU SO EASILY.›
‹I...I DID NOT COME HERE TO--!›
‹DID YOU COME HERE FOR A REWARD?›
‹IF I...Y-YES. YES, I THINK A REWARD WOULD BE DESERVED, CONSIDERING WHAT I HAVE ACCOMPLISHED.›
‹YOU ARE EITHER WORKING WITH THIS GIRL OR YOU ARE TOO STUPID TO REALIZE THAT SHE HAS USED YOU TO GAIN ENTRANCE INTO MY COMPOUND.›
‹FOR THOSE REASONS, CHIEF INSPECTOR WU XIAOPENG, YOU WILL MOST ASSUREDLY GET WHAT YOU DESERVE.›
WELL, SHIT... SO MUCH FOR--

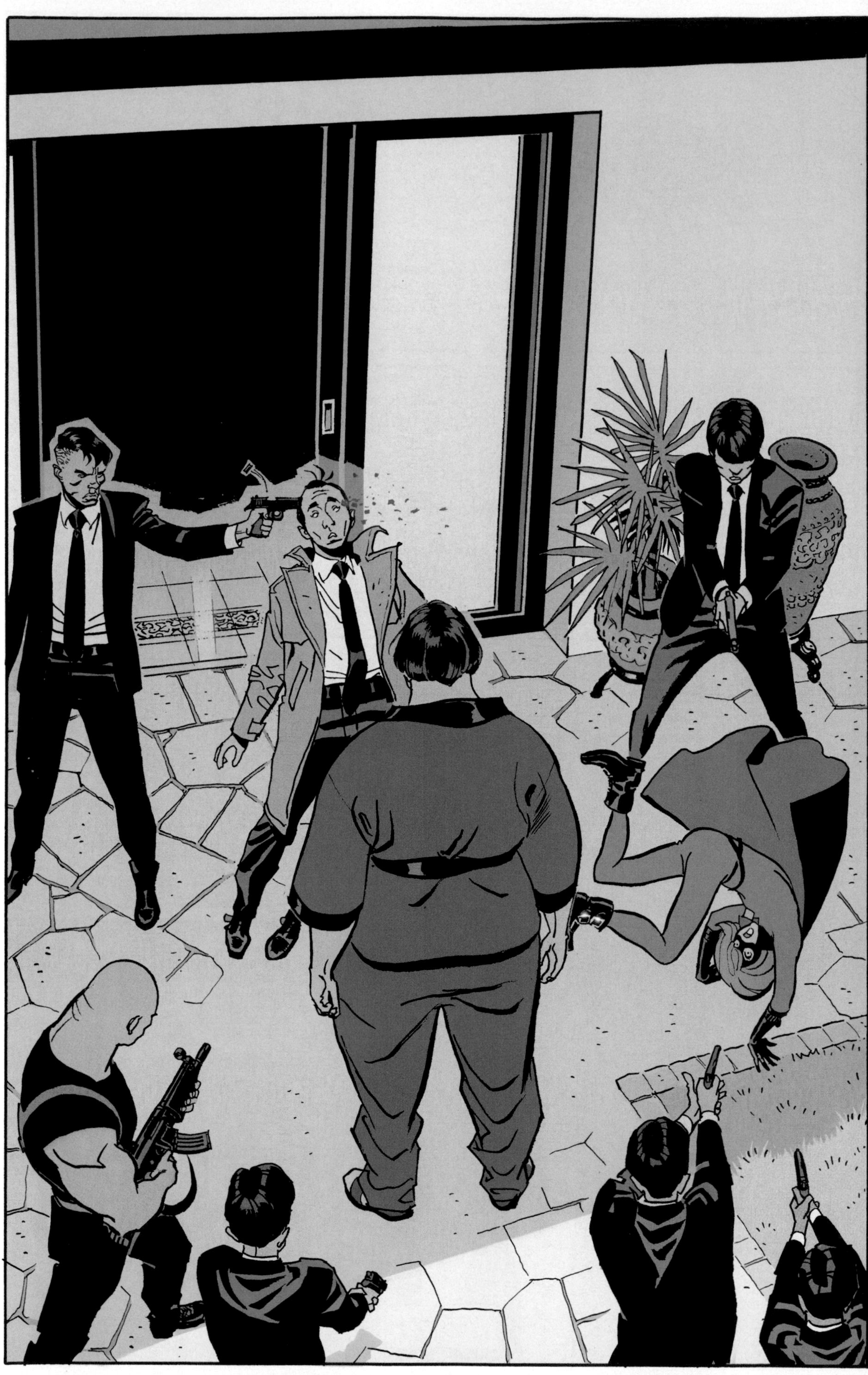

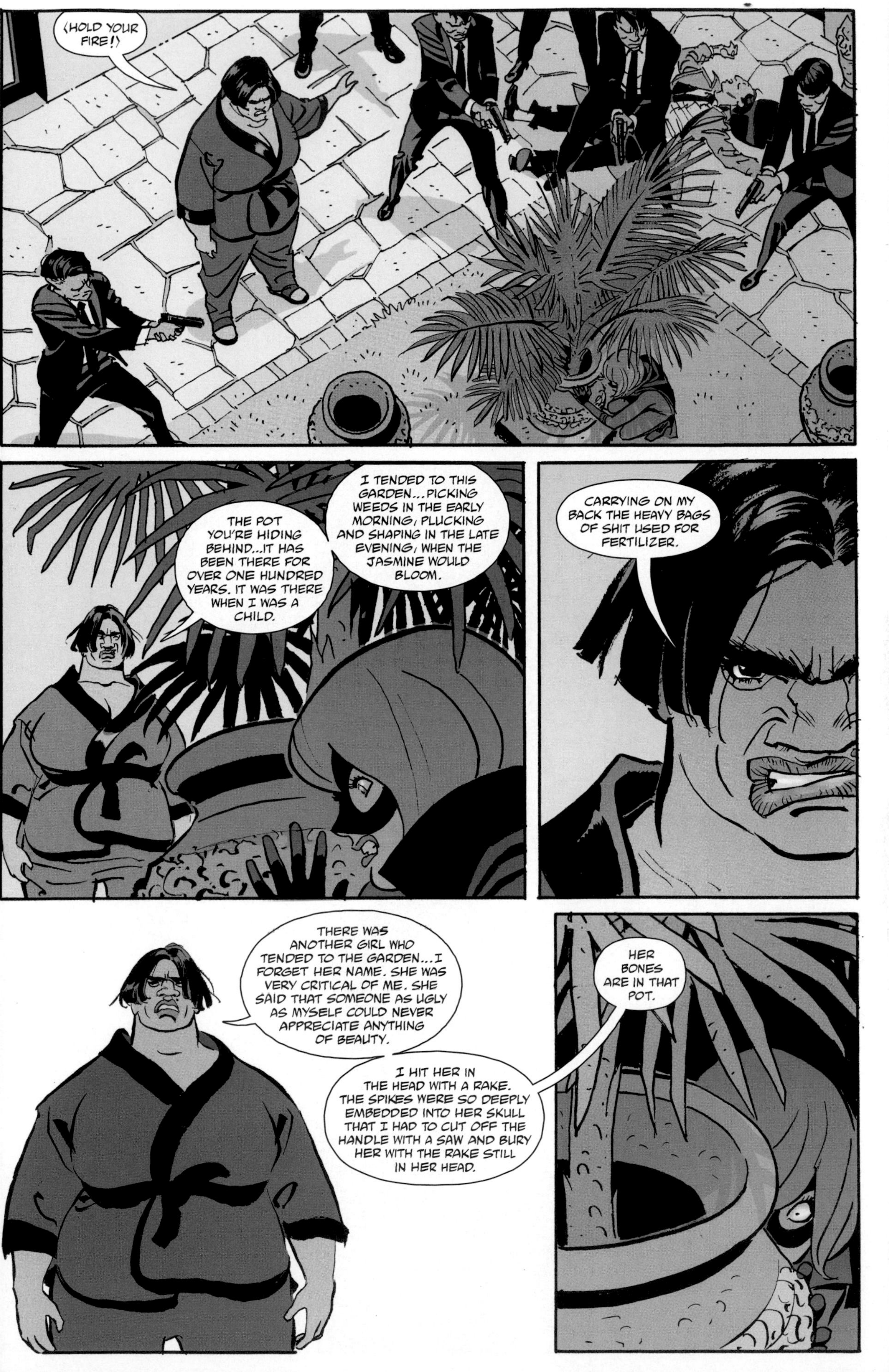
‹HOLD YOUR FIRE!›
THE POT YOU'RE HIDING BEHIND...IT HAS BEEN THERE FOR OVER ONE HUNDRED YEARS. IT WAS THERE WHEN I WAS A CHILD.
I TENDED TO THIS GARDEN...PICKING WEEDS IN THE EARLY MORNING; PLUCKING AND SHAPING IN THE LATE EVENING, WHEN THE JASMINE WOULD BLOOM.
CARRYING ON MY BACK THE HEAVY BAGS OF SHIT USED FOR FERTILIZER.
THERE WAS ANOTHER GIRL WHO TENDED TO THE GARDEN...I FORGET HER NAME. SHE WAS VERY CRITICAL OF ME. SHE SAID THAT SOMEONE AS UGLY AS MYSELF COULD NEVER APPRECIATE ANYTHING OF BEAUTY.
I HIT HER IN THE HEAD WITH A RAKE. THE SPIKES WERE SO DEEPLY EMBEDDED INTO HER SKULL THAT I HAD TO CUT OFF THE HANDLE WITH A SAW AND BURY HER WITH THE RAKE STILL IN HER HEAD.
HER BONES ARE IN THAT POT.

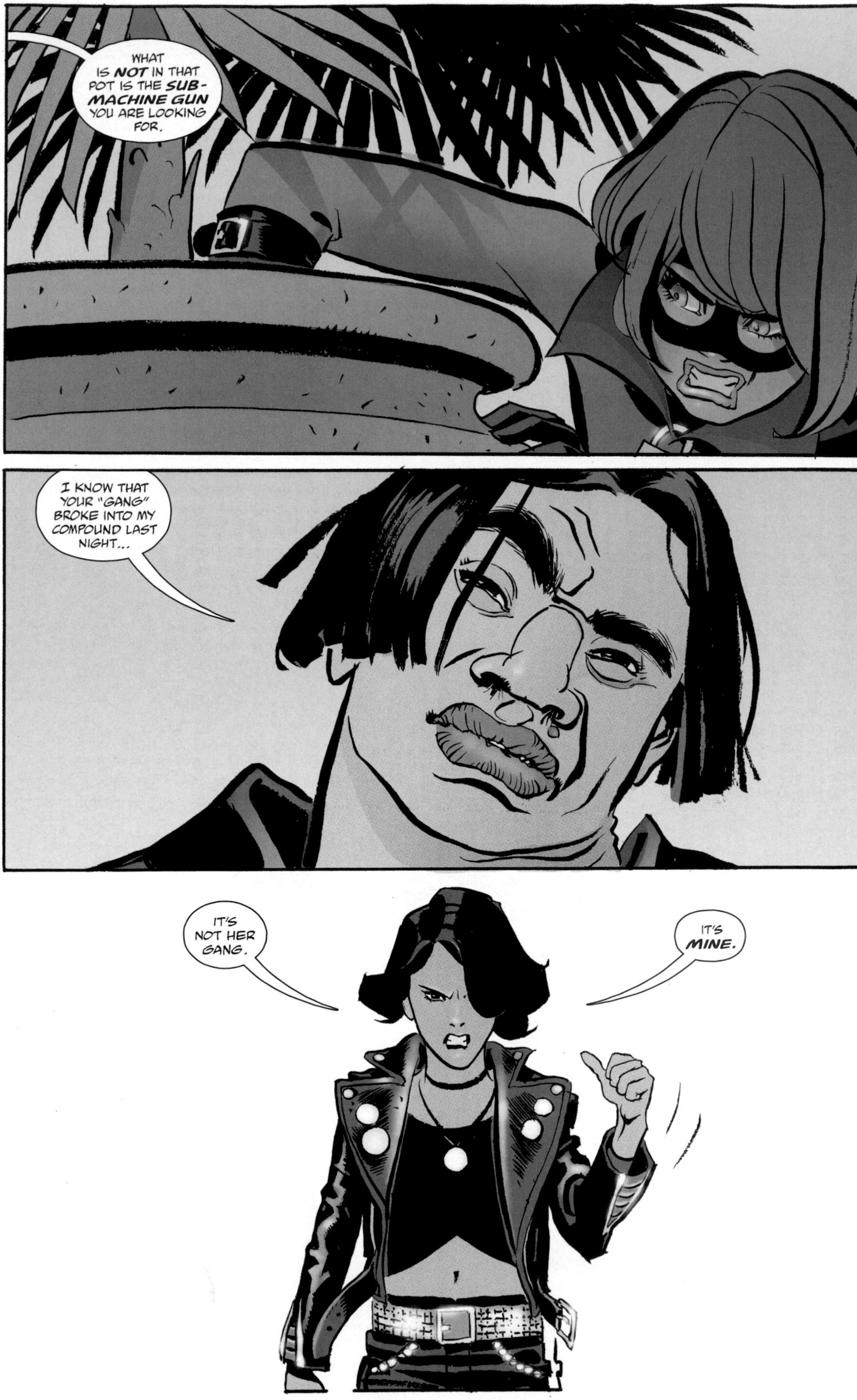

WHAT IS NOT IN THAT POT IS THE SUB-MACHINE GUN YOU ARE LOOKING FOR.
I KNOW THAT YOUR "GANG" BROKE INTO MY COMPOUND LAST NIGHT...
IT'S NOT HER GANG.
IT'S MINE.

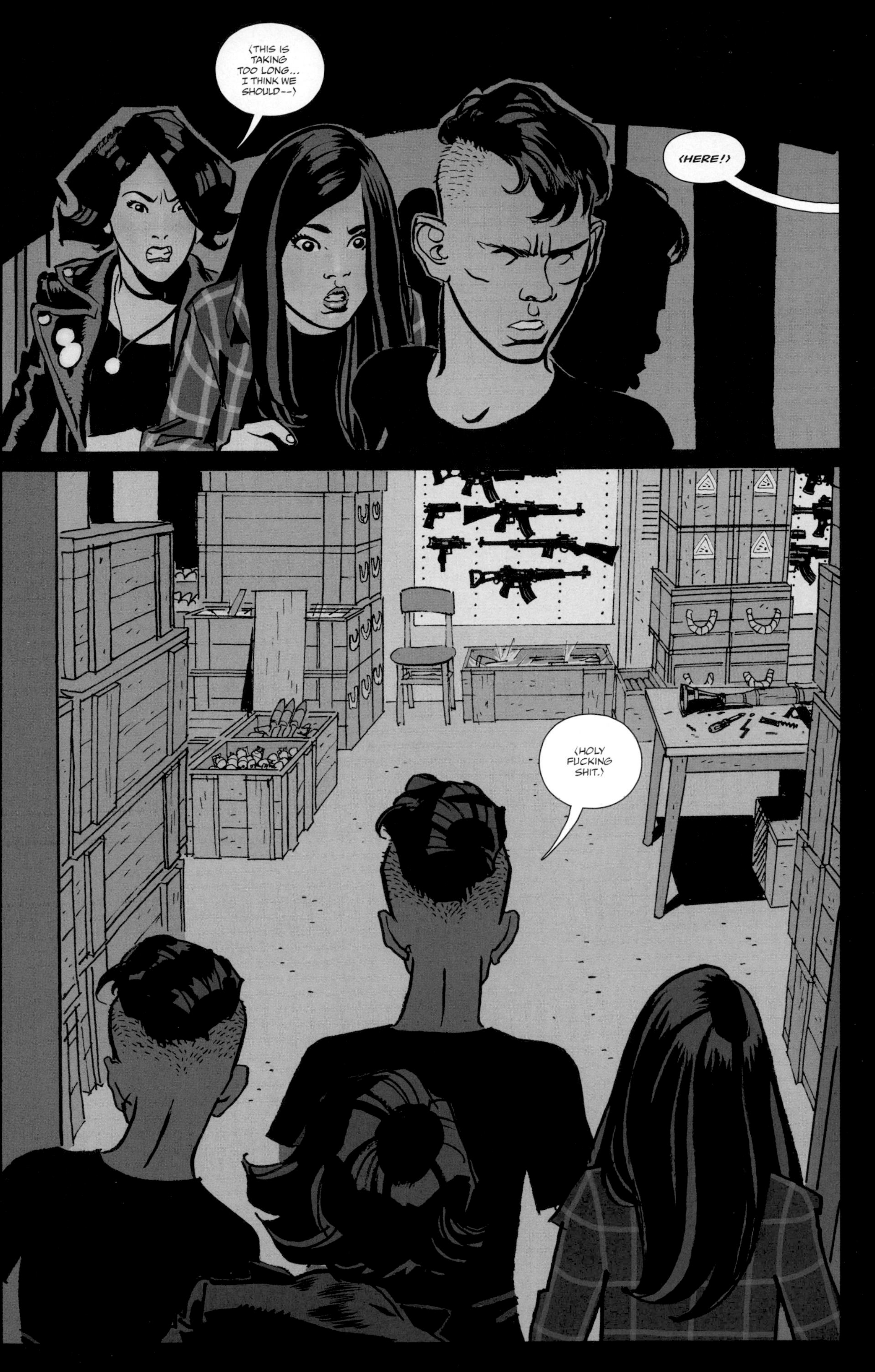
‹THIS IS TAKING TOO LONG... I THINK WE SHOULD--›
‹HERE!›
‹HOLY FUCKING SHIT.›

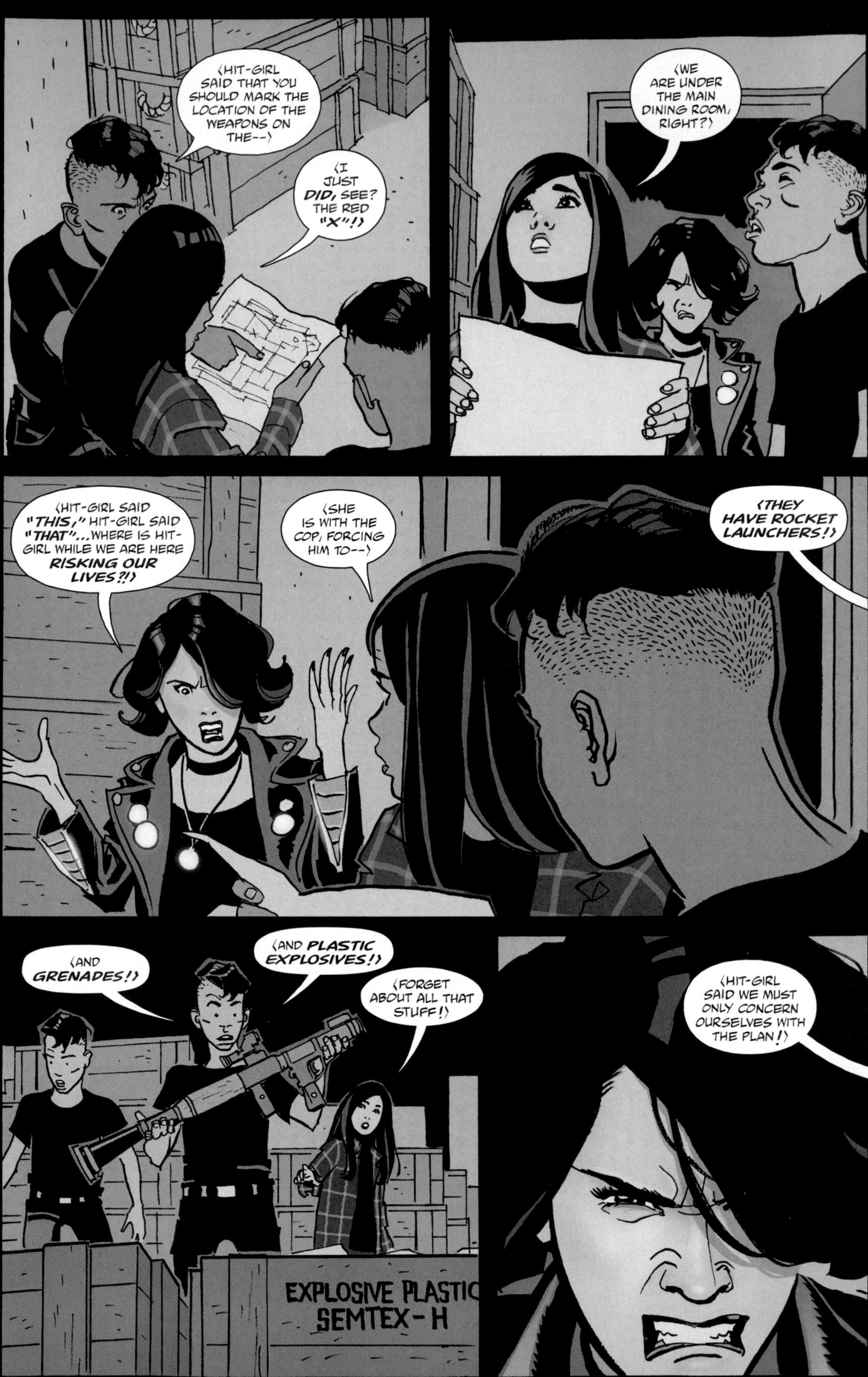

⟨HIT-GIRL SAID THAT YOU SHOULD MARK THE LOCATION OF THE WEAPONS ON THE--⟩
⟨I JUST DID, SEE? THE RED "X"!⟩
⟨WE ARE UNDER THE MAIN DINING ROOM, RIGHT?⟩
⟨HIT-GIRL SAID "THIS," HIT-GIRL SAID "THAT"... WHERE IS HIT-GIRL WHILE WE ARE HERE RISKING OUR LIVES?!⟩
⟨SHE IS WITH THE COP, FORCING HIM TO--⟩
⟨THEY HAVE ROCKET LAUNCHERS!⟩
⟨AND GRENADES!⟩
⟨AND PLASTIC EXPLOSIVES!⟩
⟨FORGET ABOUT ALL THAT STUFF!⟩
EXPLOSIVE PLASTIC
SEMTEX-H
⟨HIT-GIRL SAID WE MUST ONLY CONCERN OURSELVES WITH THE PLAN!⟩

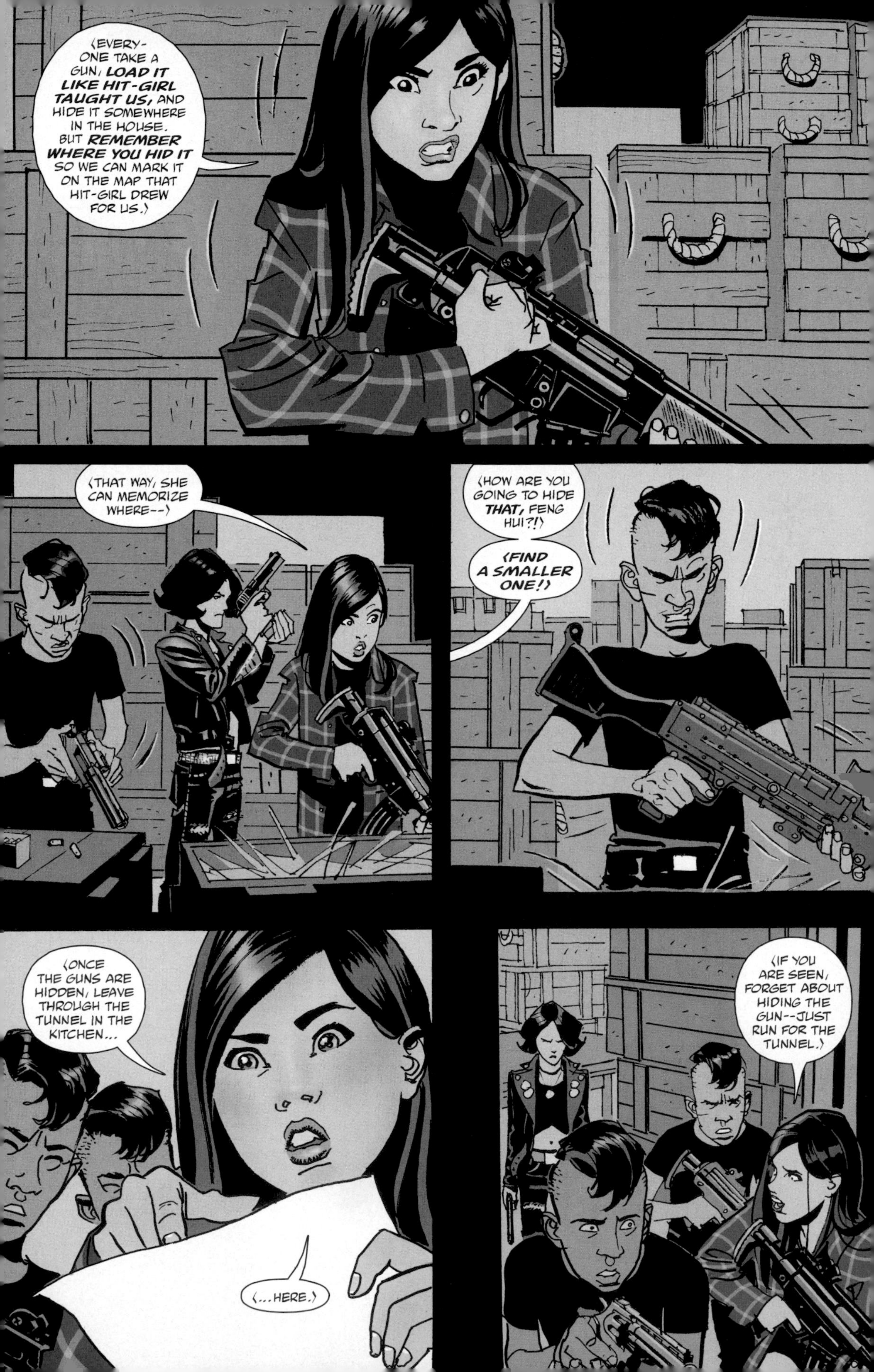
⟨EVERY-ONE TAKE A GUN, **LOAD IT LIKE HIT-GIRL TAUGHT US,** AND HIDE IT SOMEWHERE IN THE HOUSE. BUT **REMEMBER WHERE YOU HID IT** SO WE CAN MARK IT ON THE MAP THAT HIT-GIRL DREW FOR US.⟩
⟨THAT WAY, SHE CAN MEMORIZE WHERE--⟩
⟨HOW ARE YOU GOING TO HIDE **THAT,** FENG HUI?!⟩
⟨FIND A SMALLER ONE!⟩
⟨ONCE THE GUNS ARE HIDDEN, LEAVE THROUGH THE TUNNEL IN THE KITCHEN...
⟨...HERE.⟩
⟨IF YOU ARE SEEN, FORGET ABOUT HIDING THE GUN--JUST RUN FOR THE TUNNEL.⟩

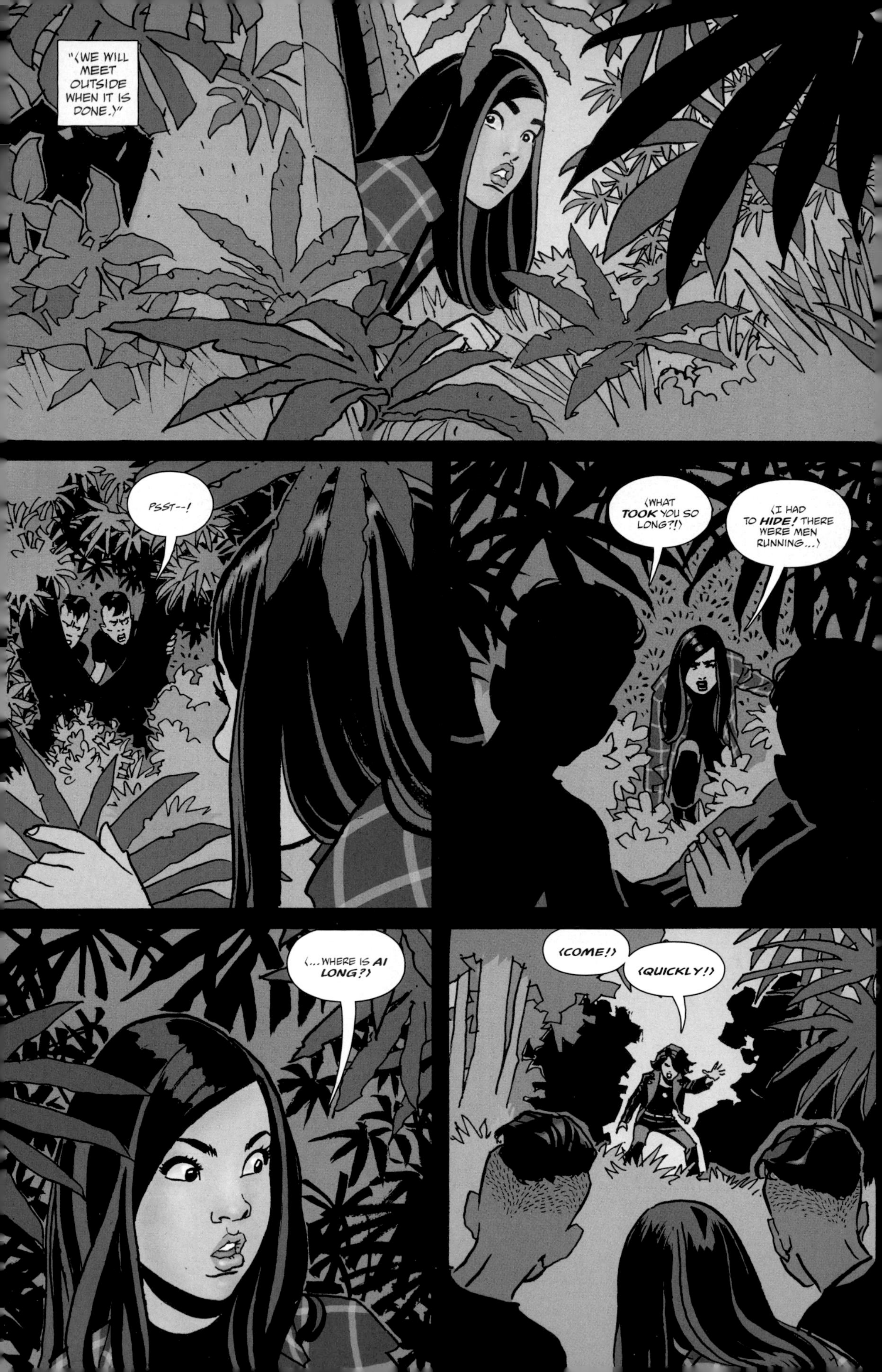
"⟨WE WILL MEET OUTSIDE WHEN IT IS DONE.⟩"
PSST--!
⟨WHAT TOOK YOU SO LONG?!⟩
⟨I HAD TO HIDE! THERE WERE MEN RUNNING...⟩
⟨...WHERE IS AI LONG?⟩
⟨COME!⟩
⟨QUICKLY!⟩

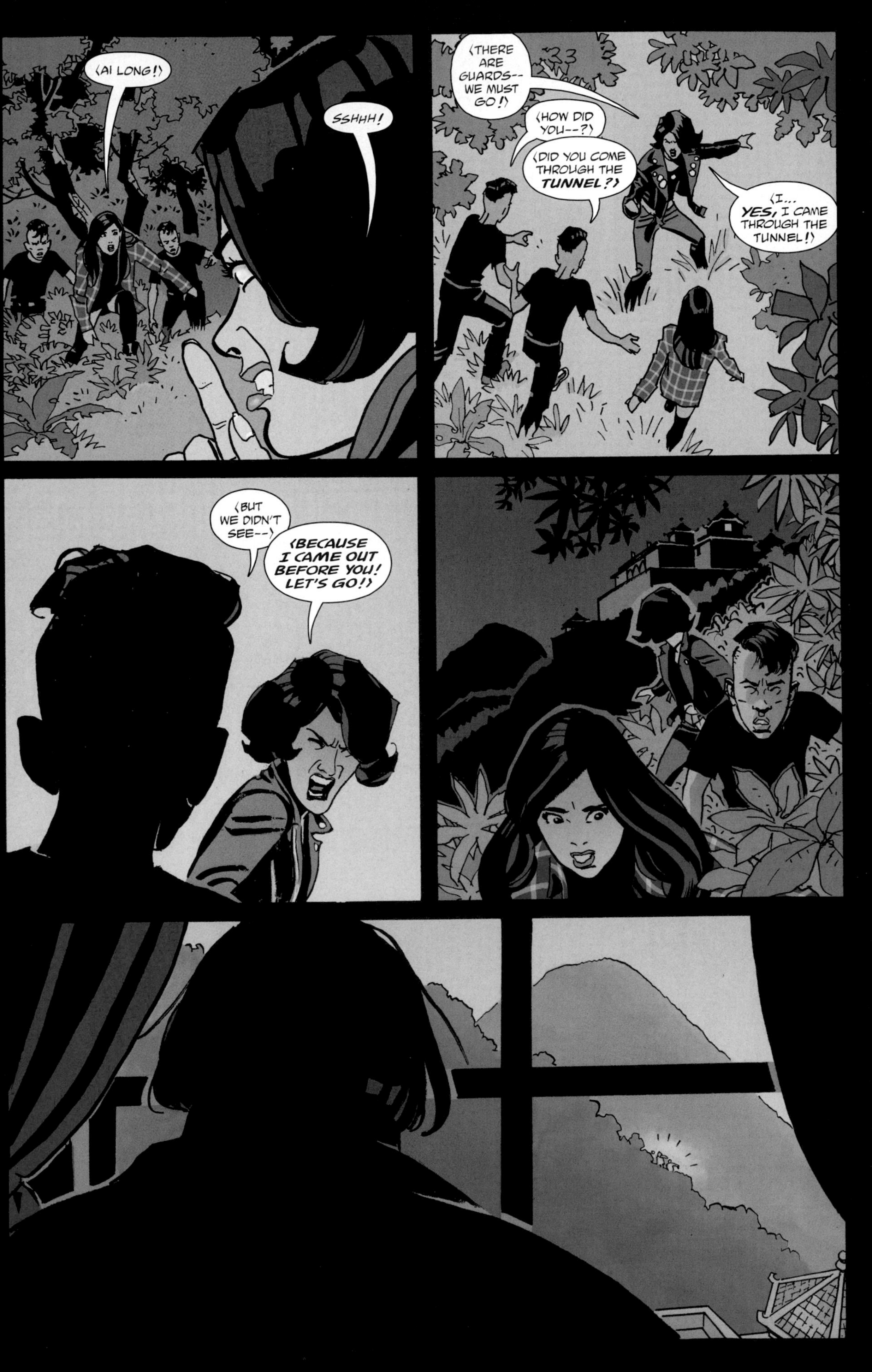
⟨AI LONG!⟩
SSHHH!
⟨THERE ARE GUARDS-- WE MUST GO!⟩
⟨HOW DID YOU--?⟩
⟨DID YOU COME THROUGH THE TUNNEL?⟩
⟨I... YES, I CAME THROUGH THE TUNNEL!⟩
⟨BUT WE DIDN'T SEE--⟩
⟨BECAUSE I CAME OUT BEFORE YOU! LET'S GO!⟩

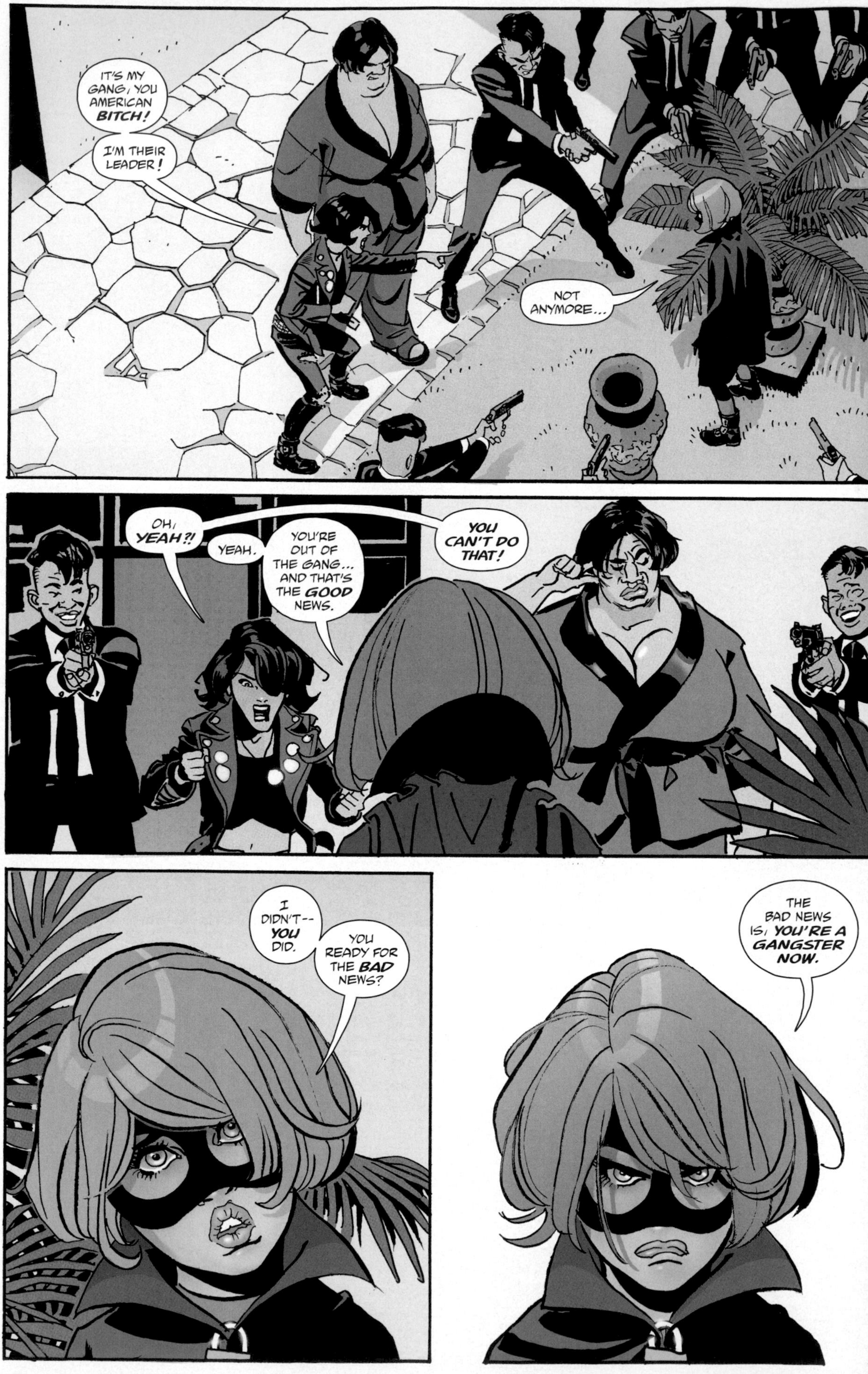
IT'S MY GANG, YOU AMERICAN BITCH!
I'M THEIR LEADER!
NOT ANYMORE...
OH, YEAH?!
YEAH.
YOU'RE OUT OF THE GANG... AND THAT'S THE GOOD NEWS.
YOU CAN'T DO THAT!
I DIDN'T--
YOU DID.
YOU READY FOR THE BAD NEWS?
THE BAD NEWS IS, YOU'RE A GANGSTER NOW.

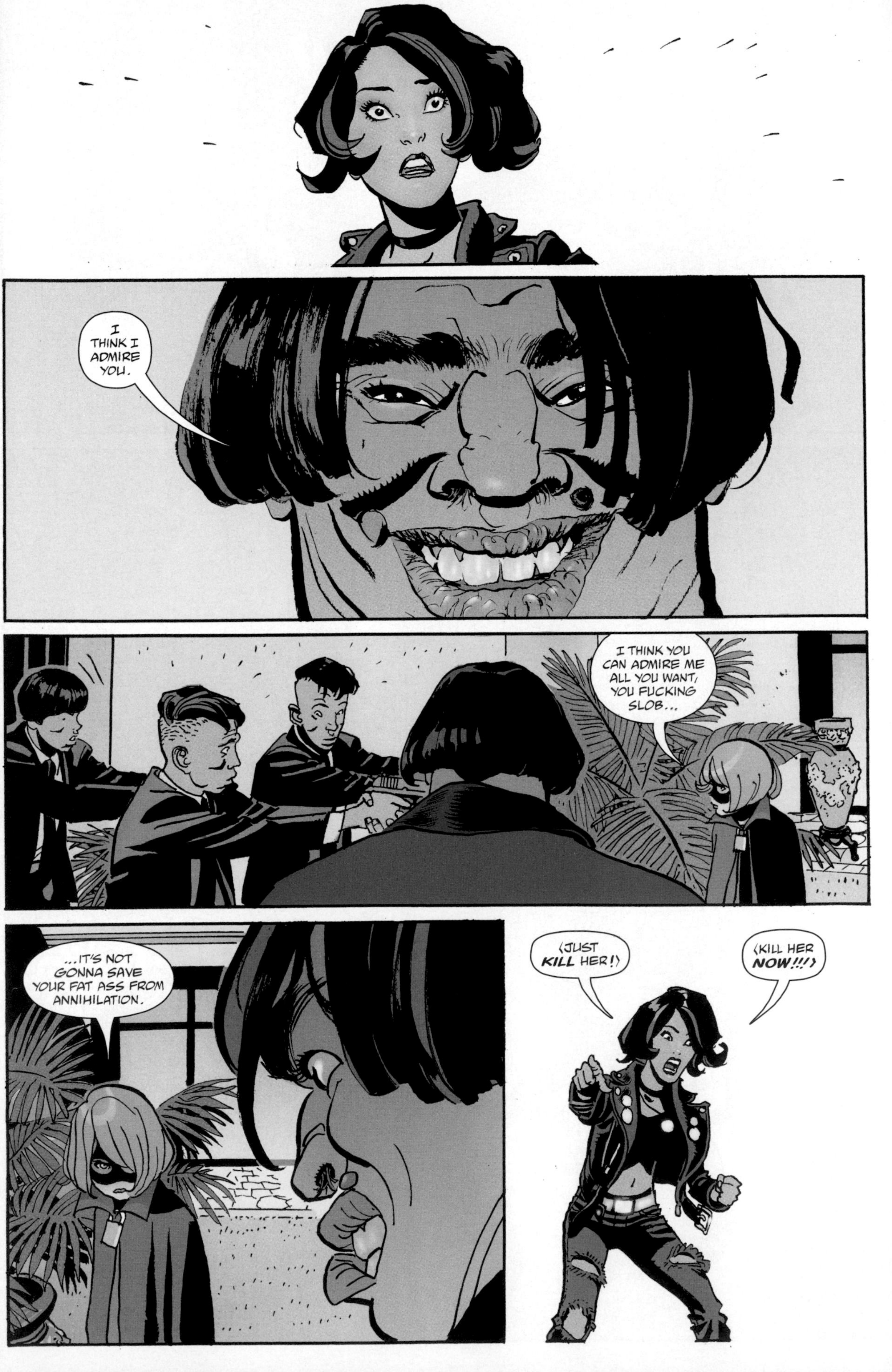
I THINK I ADMIRE YOU.
I THINK YOU CAN ADMIRE ME ALL YOU WANT, YOU FUCKING SLOB...
...IT'S NOT GONNA SAVE YOUR FAT ASS FROM ANNIHILATION.
‹JUST **KILL** HER!›
‹KILL HER **NOW!!!**›

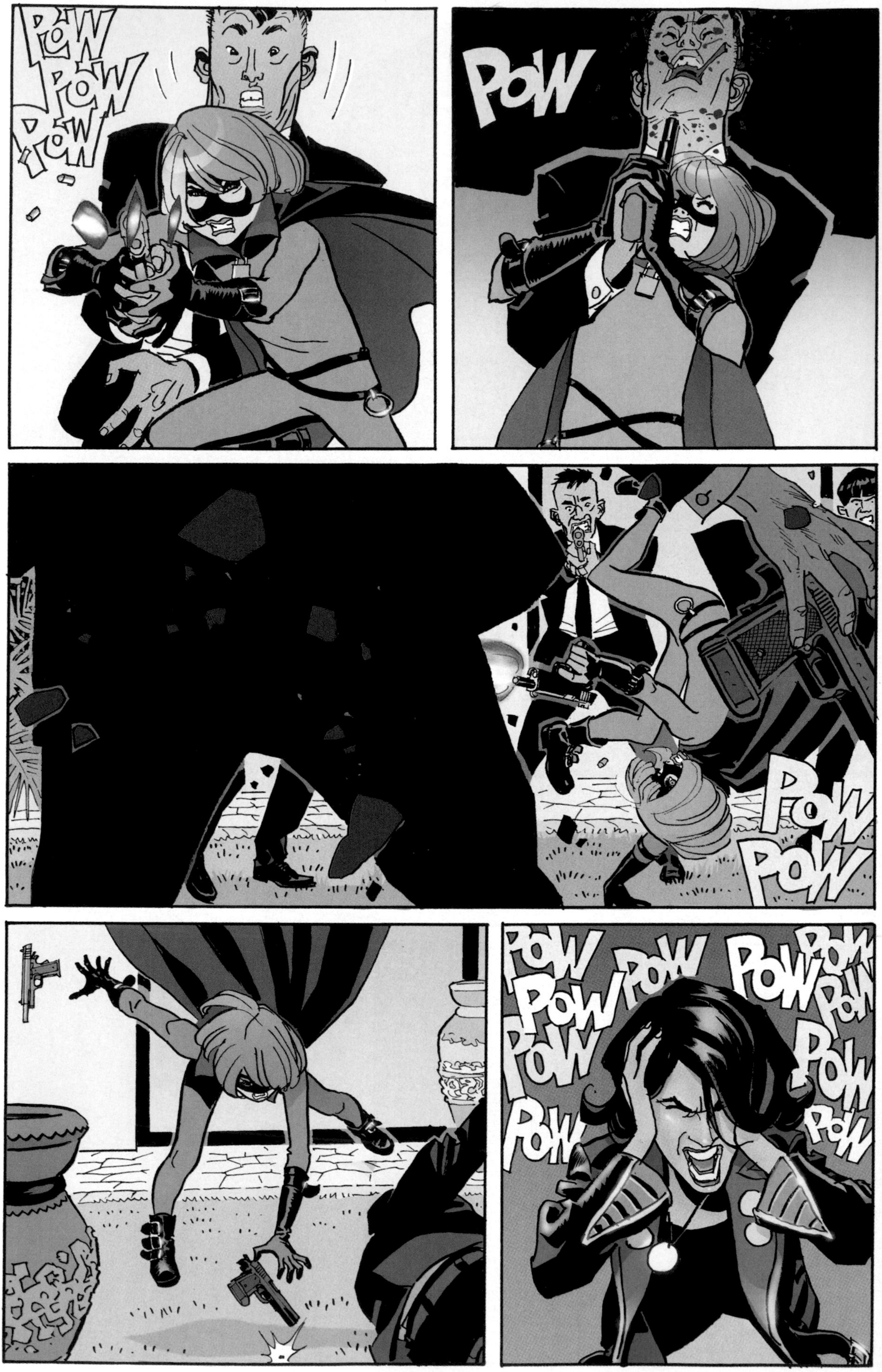
POW
POW
POW
POW
POW
POW
POW
POW
POW
POW
POW
POW
POW
POW
POW
POW
POW
POW
POW
POW
POW

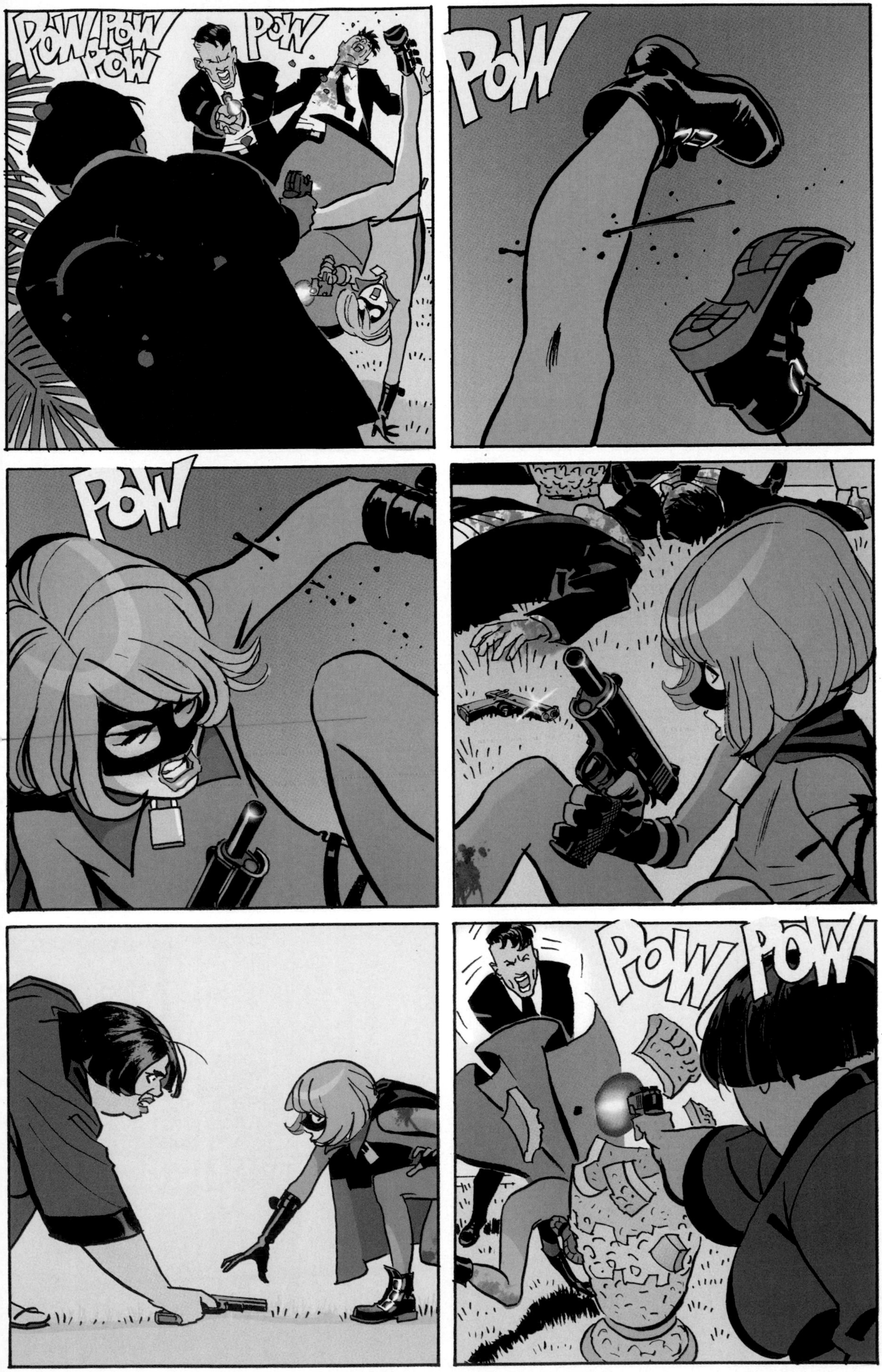

POW POW POW
POW
POW
POW
POW POW

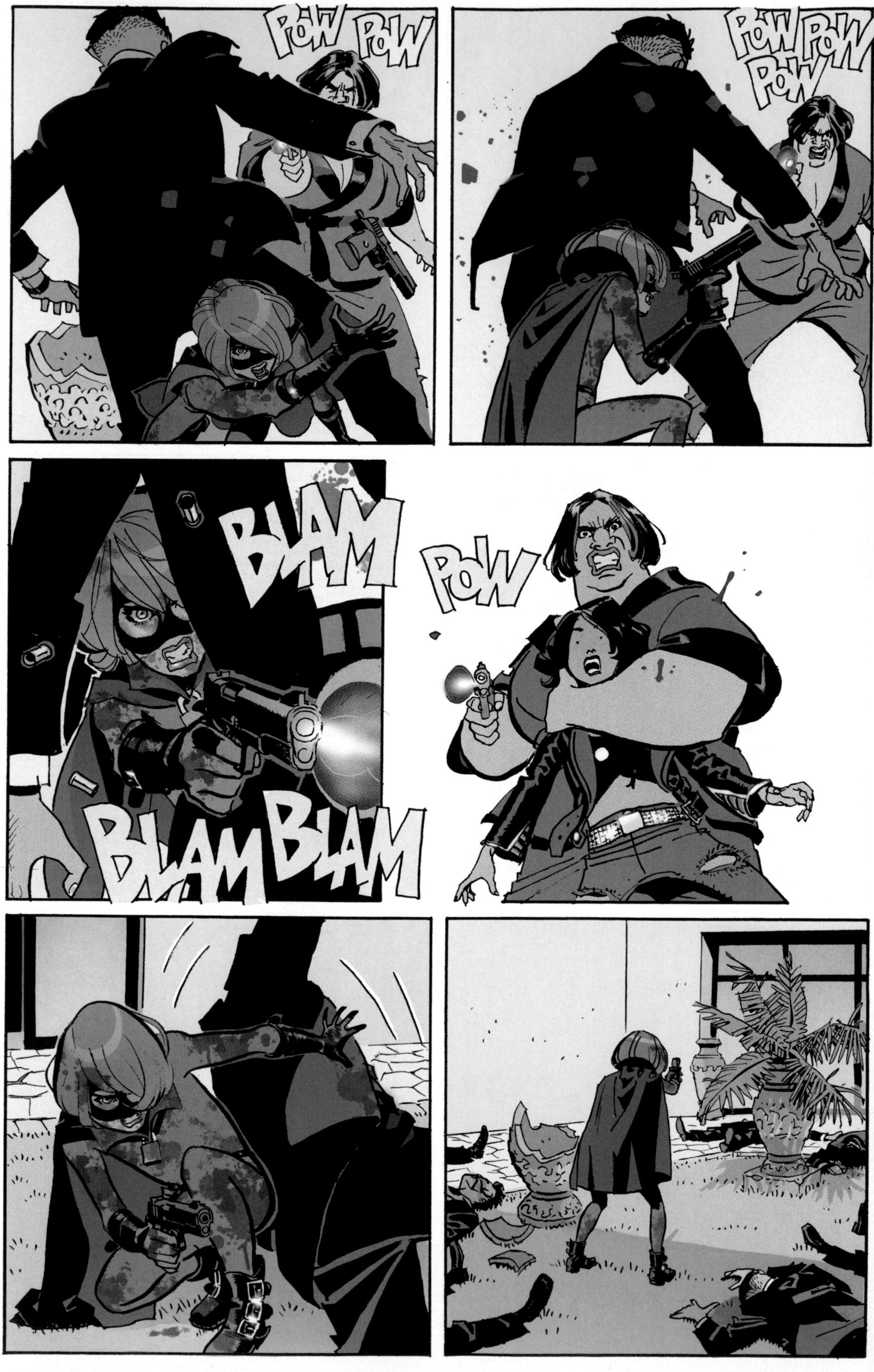
POW POW
POW POW
POW
BLAM
POW
BLAM BLAM

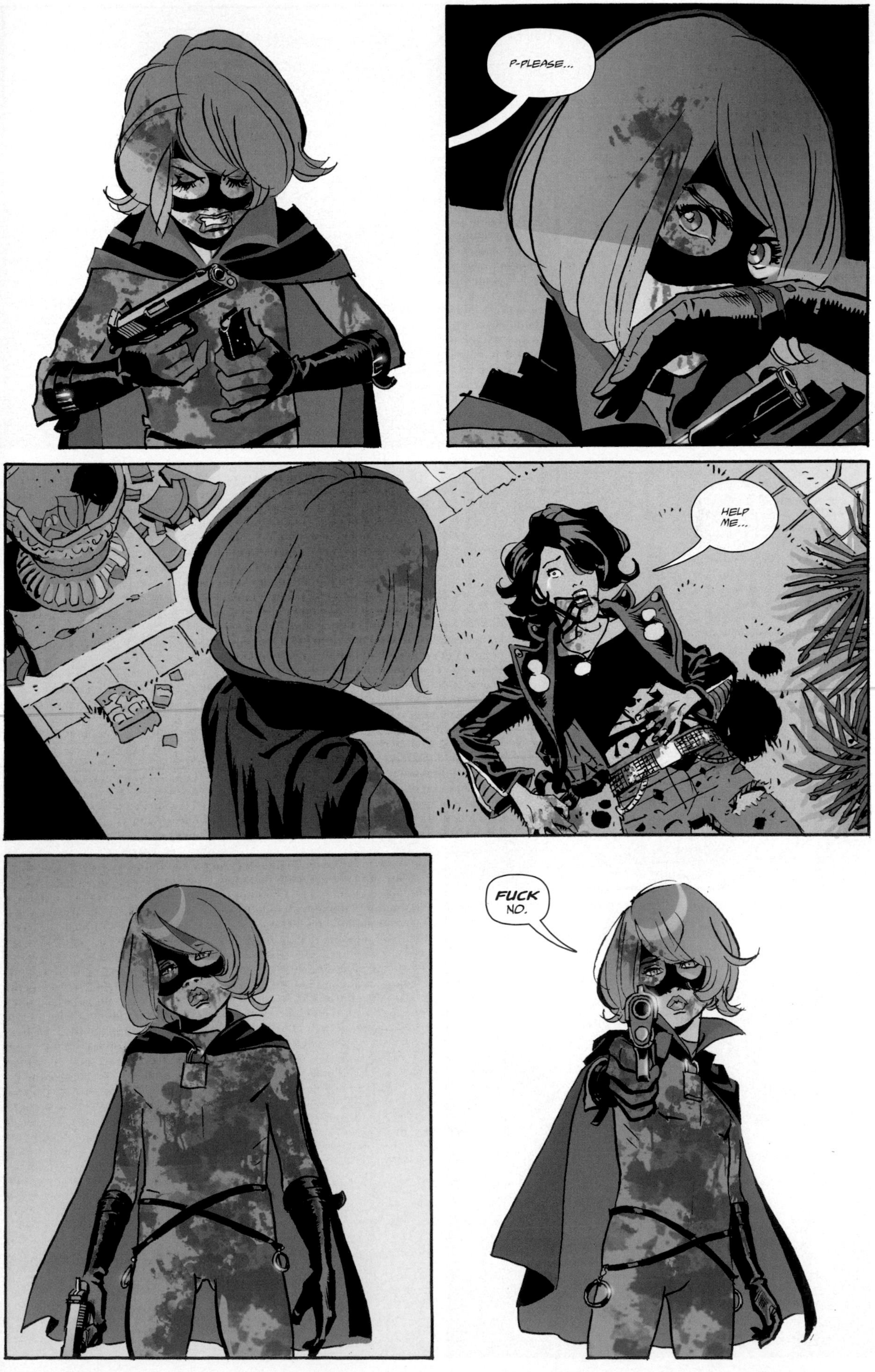
P-PLEASE...
HELP ME...
FUCK NO.

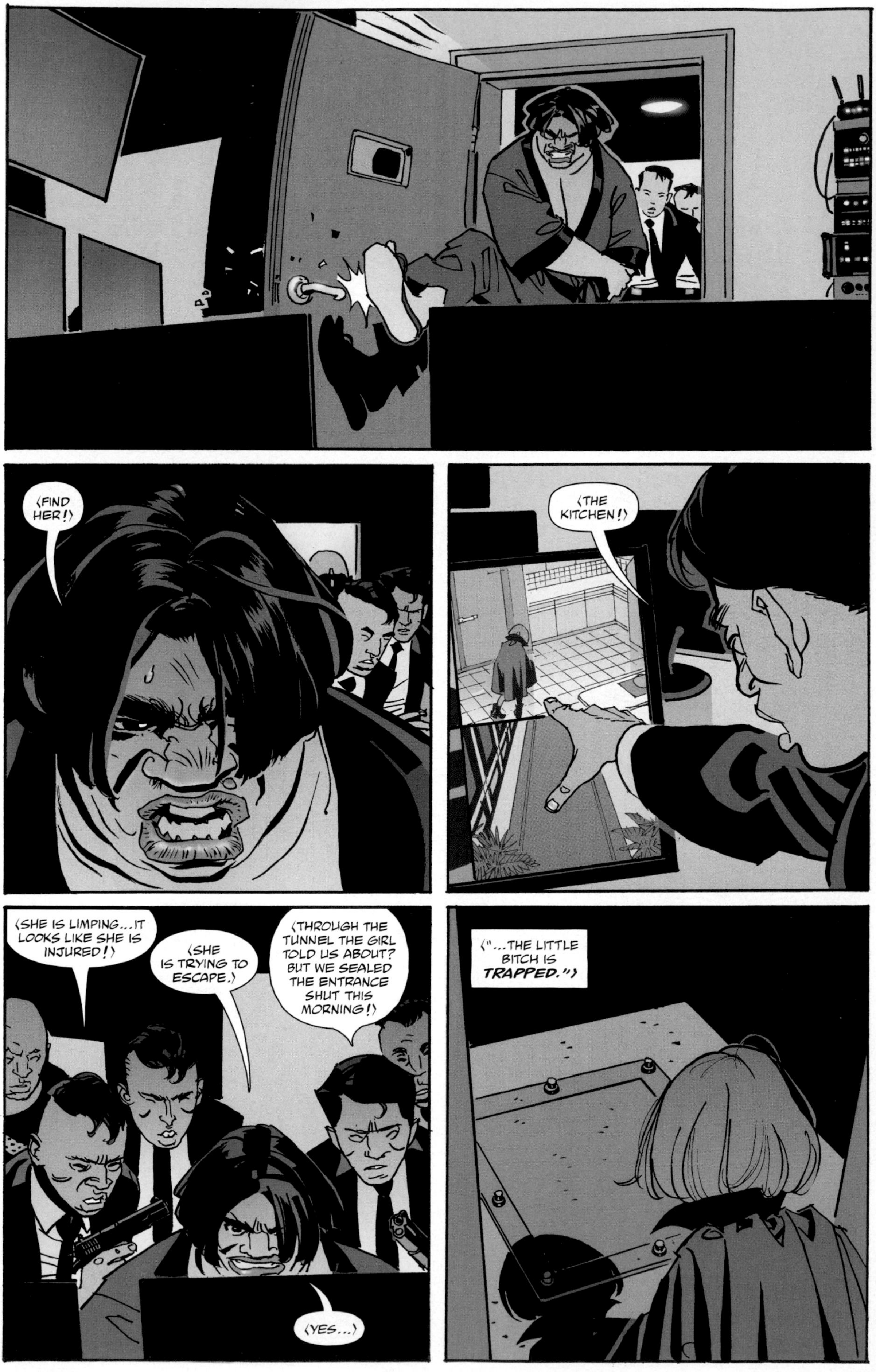

‹FIND HER!›
‹THE KITCHEN!›
‹SHE IS LIMPING... IT LOOKS LIKE SHE IS INJURED!›
‹SHE IS TRYING TO ESCAPE.›
‹THROUGH THE TUNNEL THE GIRL TOLD US ABOUT? BUT WE SEALED THE ENTRANCE SHUT THIS MORNING!›
‹YES...›
‹"...THE LITTLE BITCH IS **TRAPPED.**"›

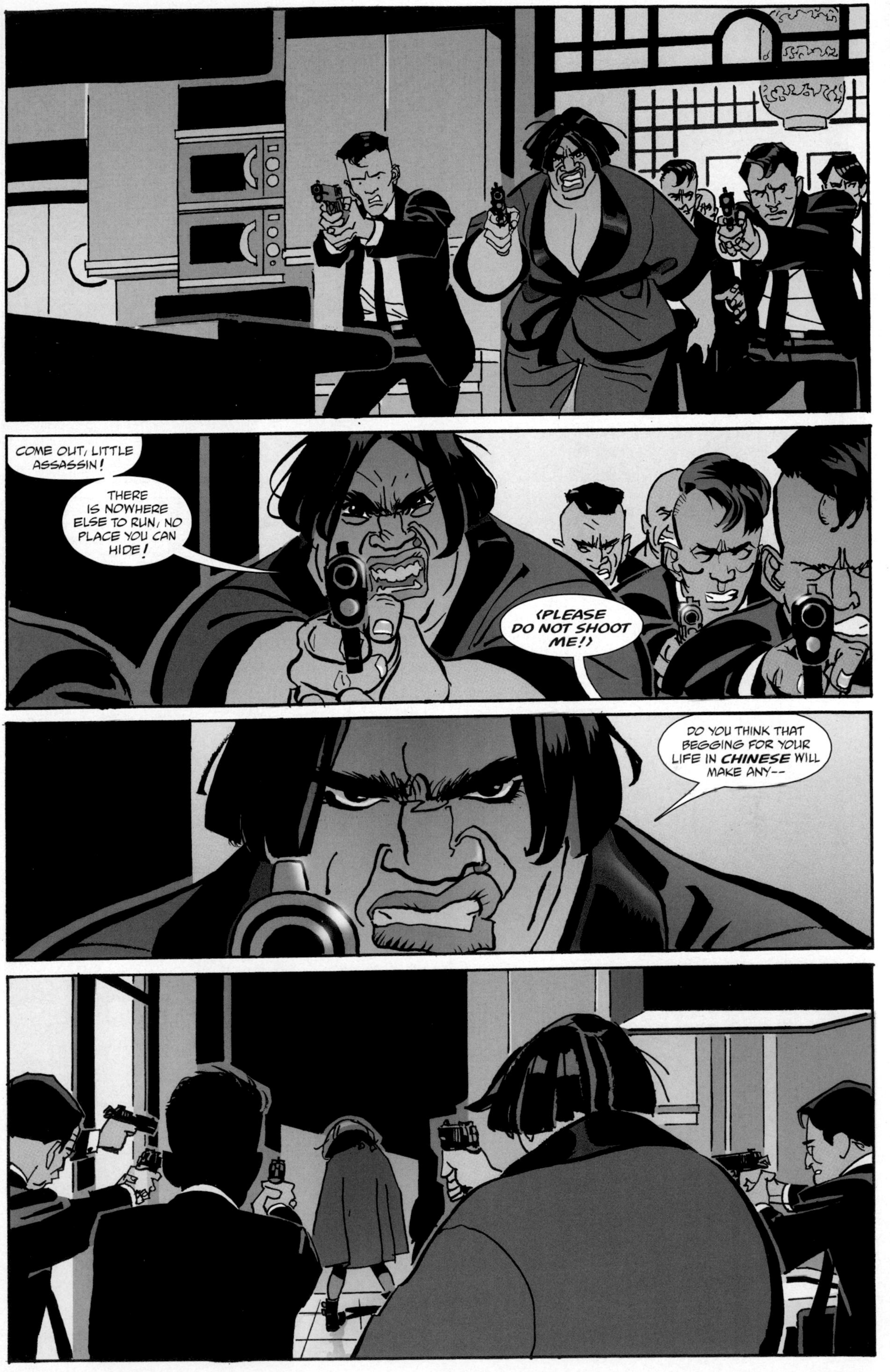
COME OUT, LITTLE ASSASSIN!
THERE IS NOWHERE ELSE TO RUN, NO PLACE YOU CAN HIDE!
‹PLEASE DO NOT SHOOT ME!›
DO YOU THINK THAT BEGGING FOR YOUR LIFE IN CHINESE WILL MAKE ANY--

⟨SH-SHE MADE ME PUT ON HER CLOTHES...⟩

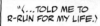

"⟨...TOLD ME TO R-RUN FOR MY LIFE.⟩

"⟨I...I NEED TO GO TO THE HOSPITAL...⟩"

⟨WHERE IS SHE?!⟩

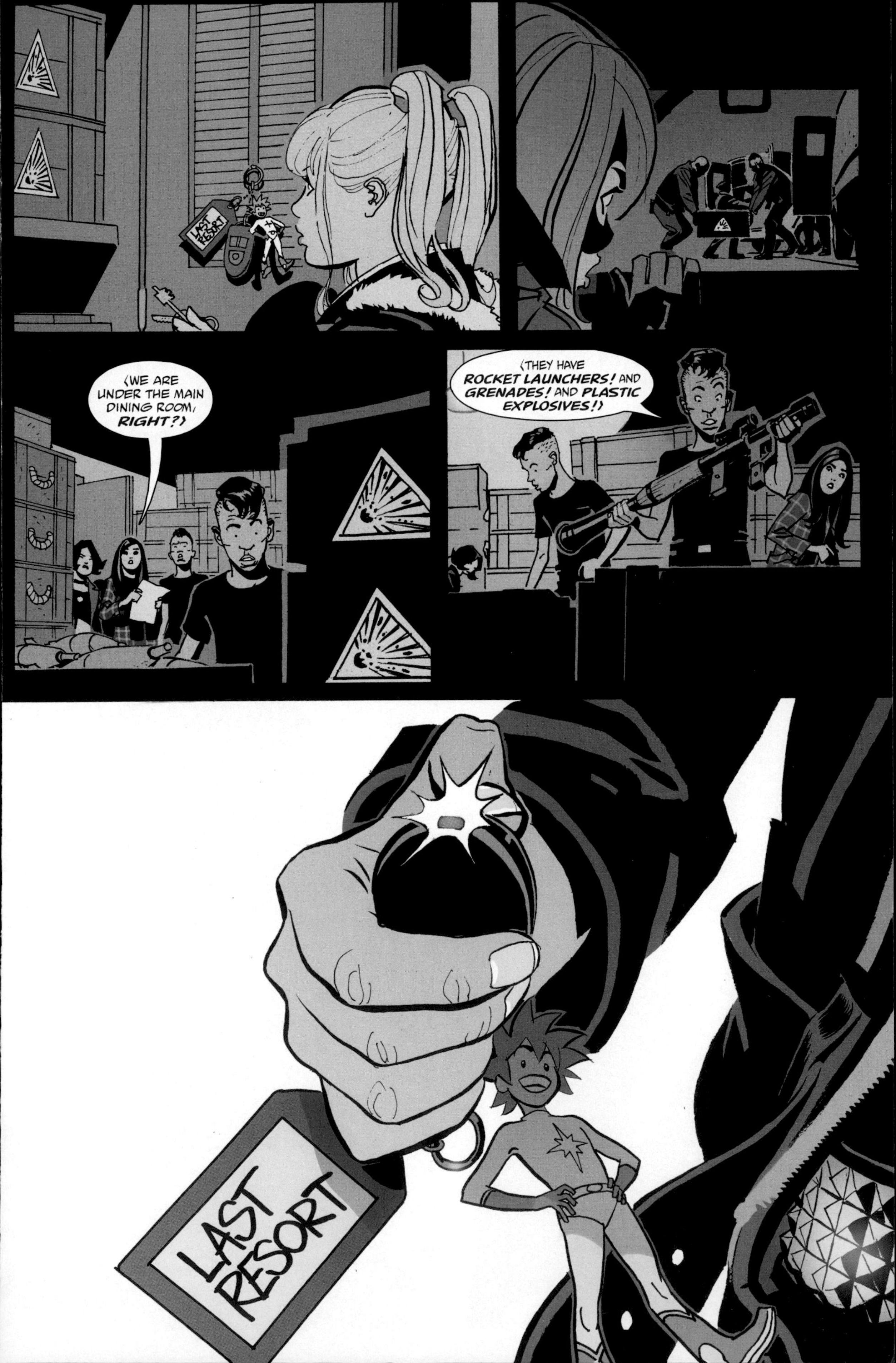

LAST RESORT
⟨WE ARE UNDER THE MAIN DINING ROOM, RIGHT?⟩
⟨THEY HAVE ROCKET LAUNCHERS! AND GRENADES! AND PLASTIC EXPLOSIVES!⟩
LAST RESORT

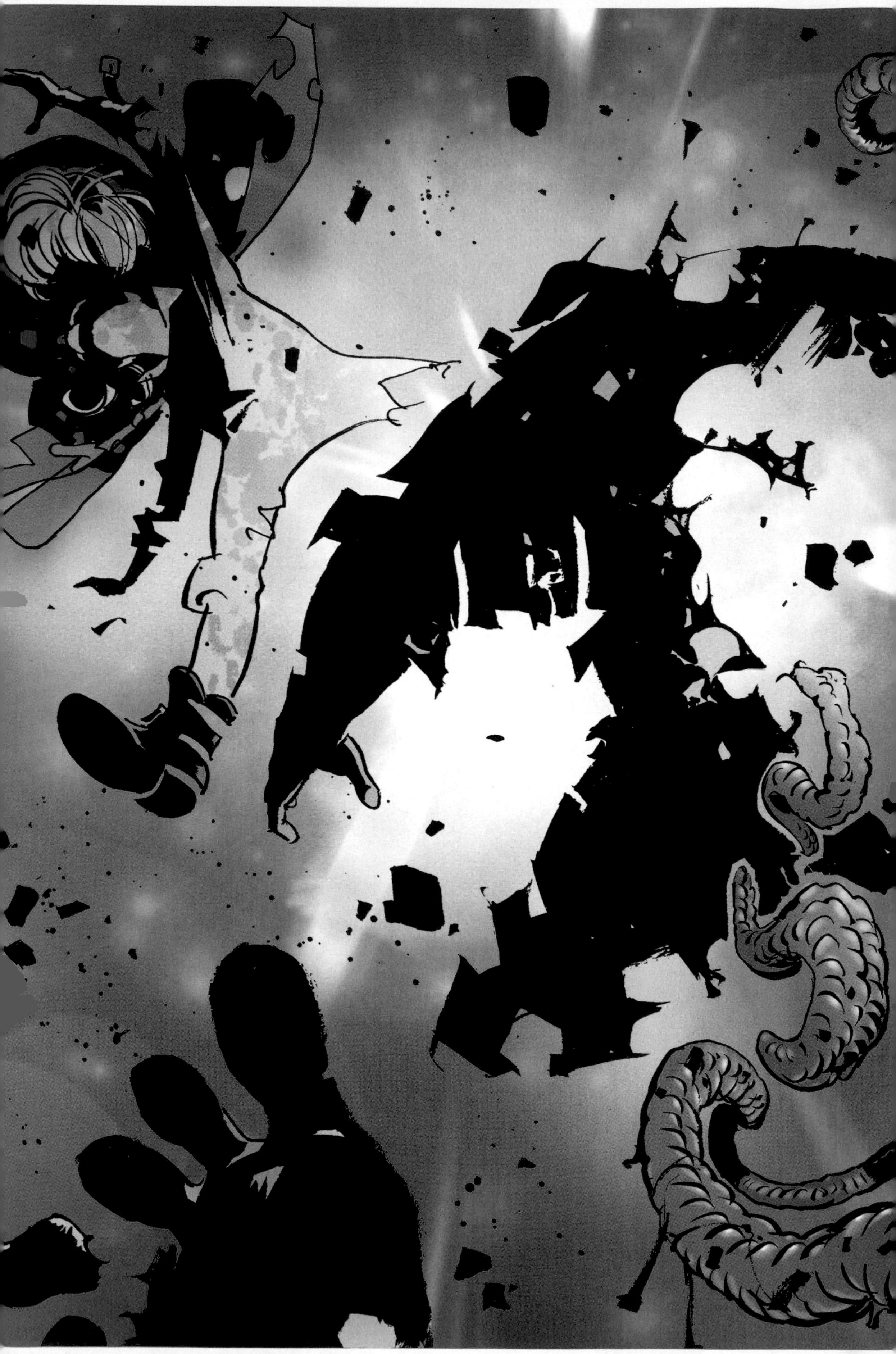

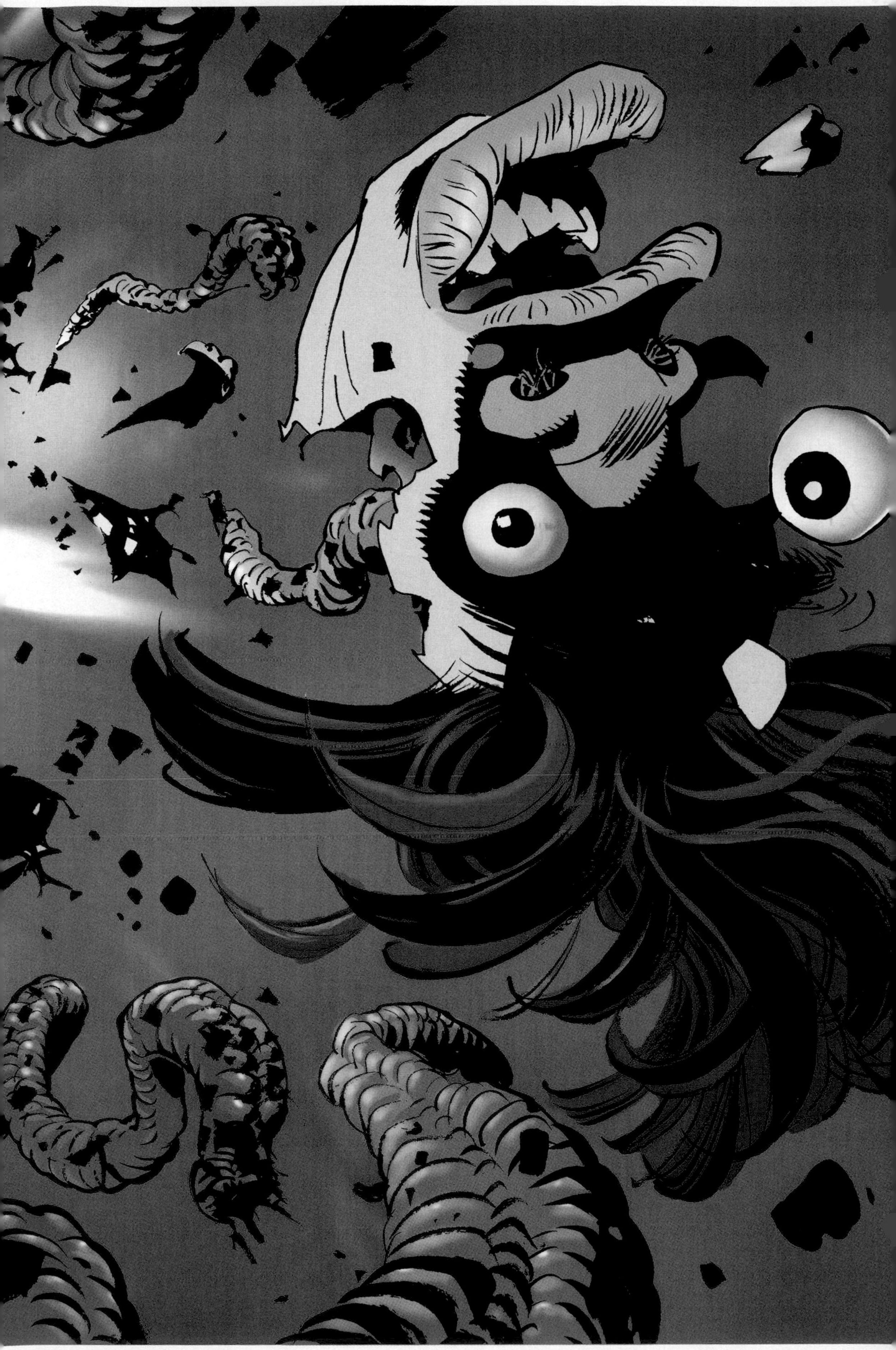

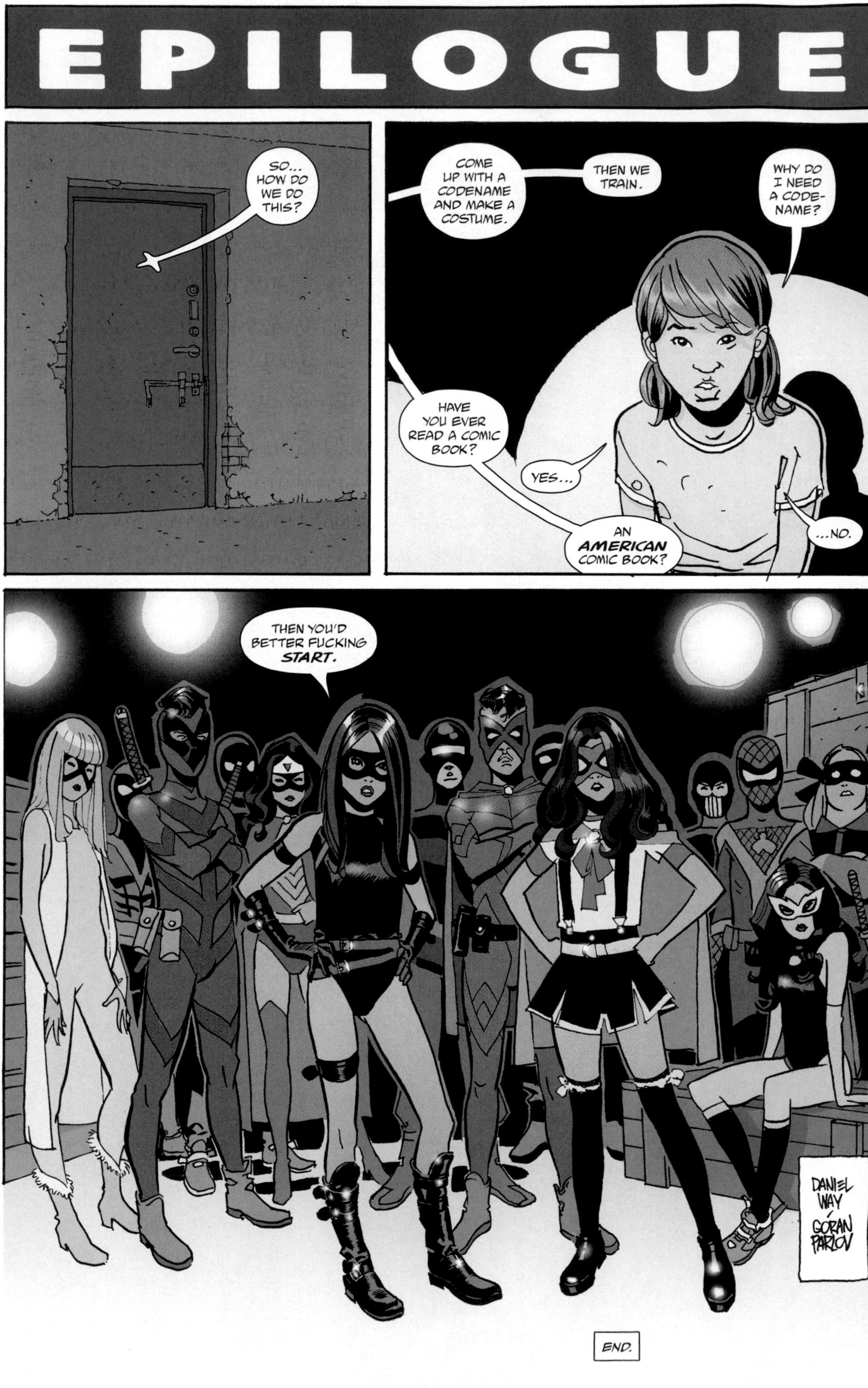
EPILOGUE
SO... HOW DO WE DO THIS?
COME UP WITH A CODENAME AND MAKE A COSTUME.
THEN WE TRAIN.
WHY DO I NEED A CODE-NAME?
HAVE YOU EVER READ A COMIC BOOK?
YES...
AN AMERICAN COMIC BOOK?
...NO.
THEN YOU'D BETTER FUCKING START.
DANIEL WAY / GORAN PARLOV
END.

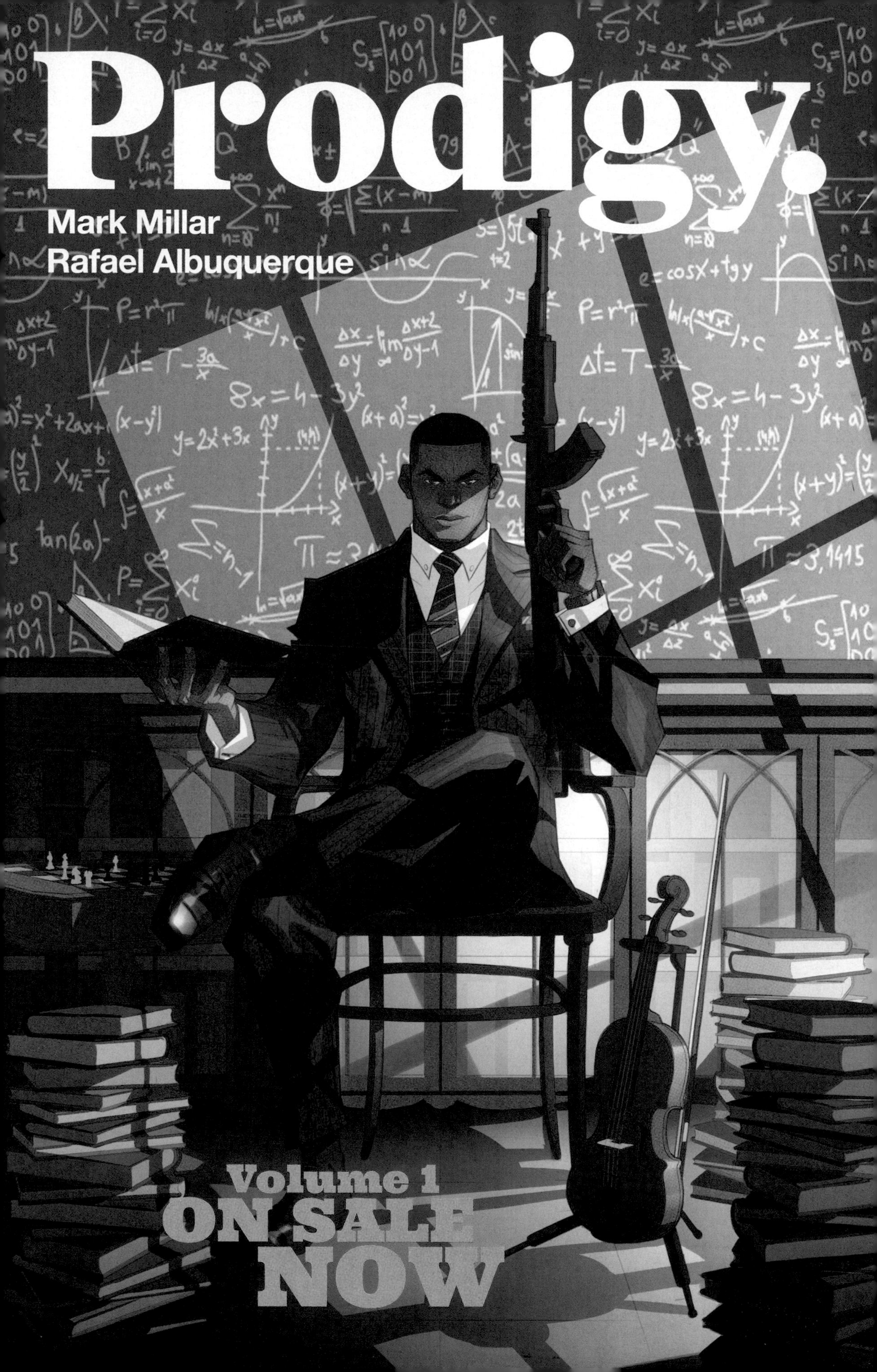
Prodigy.
Mark Millar
Rafael Albuquerque
Volume 1
ON SALE
NOW

VARIANT COVER

CLAIRE ROE

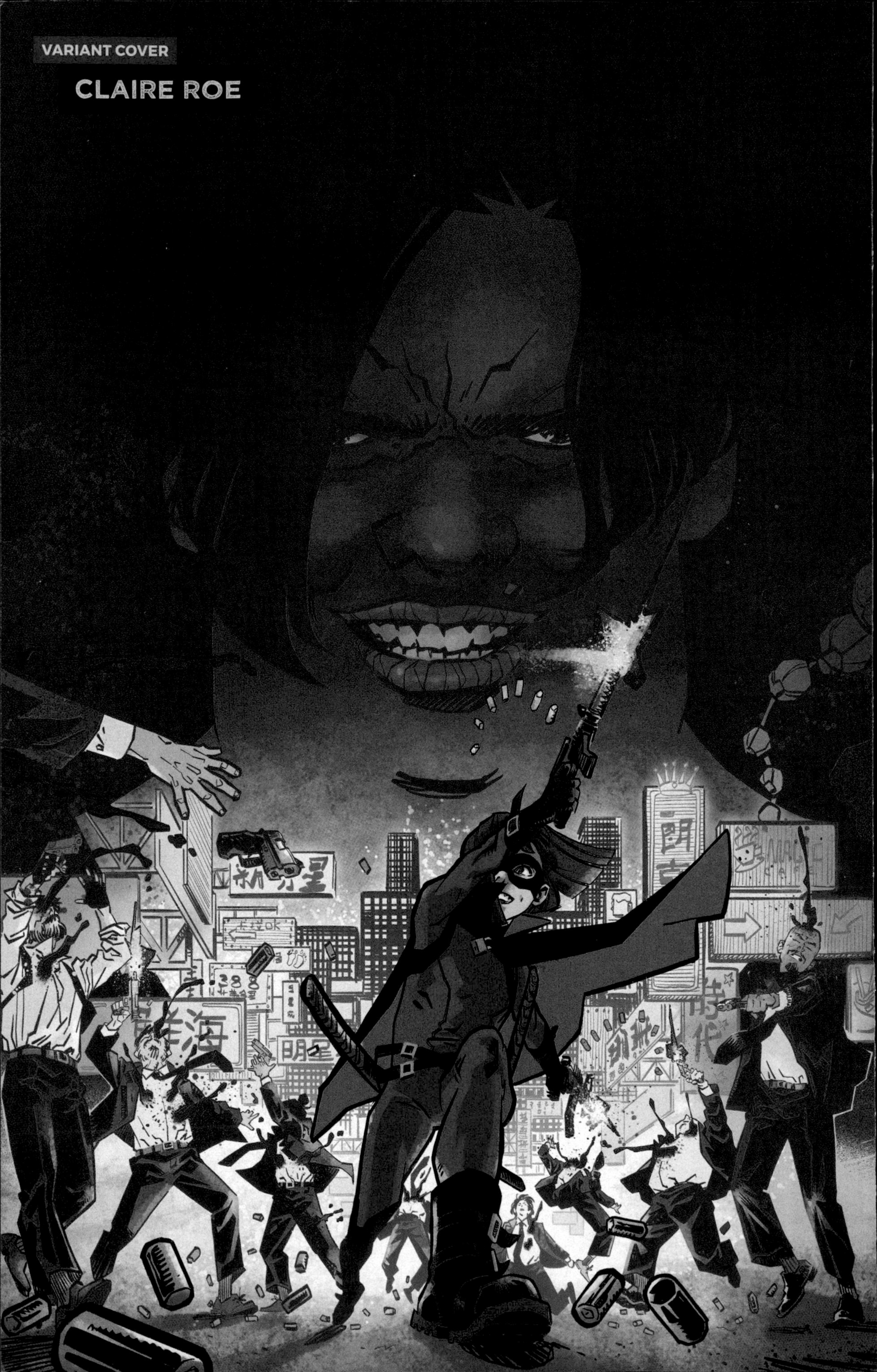

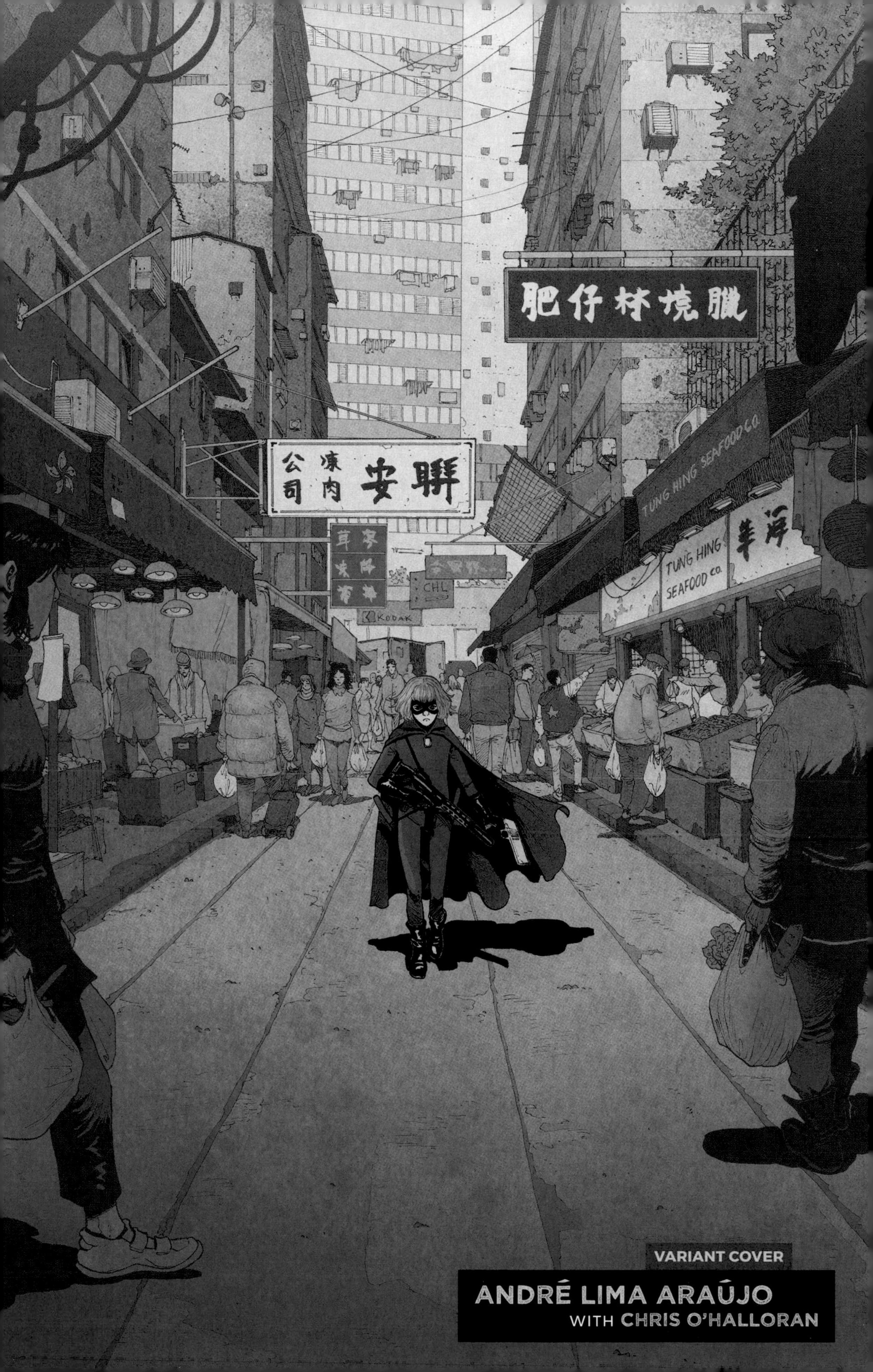
肥仔林焼臘
聯安
凍肉
公司
TUNG HING SEAFOOD CO.
TUNG HING SEAFOOD CO.
CHL
KODAK

VARIANT COVER

ANDRÉ LIMA ARAÚJO
WITH **CHRIS O'HALLORAN**

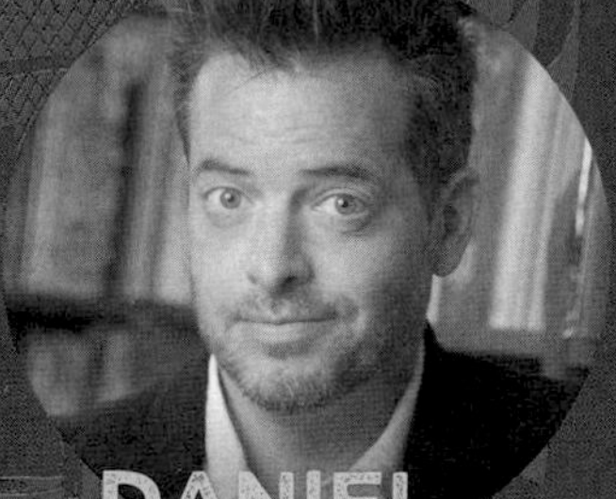

DANIEL WAY

A New York Times bestselling author, Daniel Way got his start in 2000 when he was awarded the prestigious Xeric Grant for Violent Lifestyle, his first attempt at comic book writing. He's also written **DEADPOOL**, the character with whom he is most closely associated, due to his historic 65-issue run on that title. He still takes on the occasional project for mainstream publishers, such as the **HIT-GIRL** series for Image Comics/ Mark Millar. In addition to his work in comics, Mr. Way has also worked in video games (Activision's **DEADPOOL**) and film, having recently consulted on the **DEADPOOL** feature at the personal request of the film's director. In addition to his writing accomplishments, Daniel Way is the co-founder and director of GeekCraft Expo, a collection of curated, geek-themed handmade markets held across North America. He lives in Hawaii.

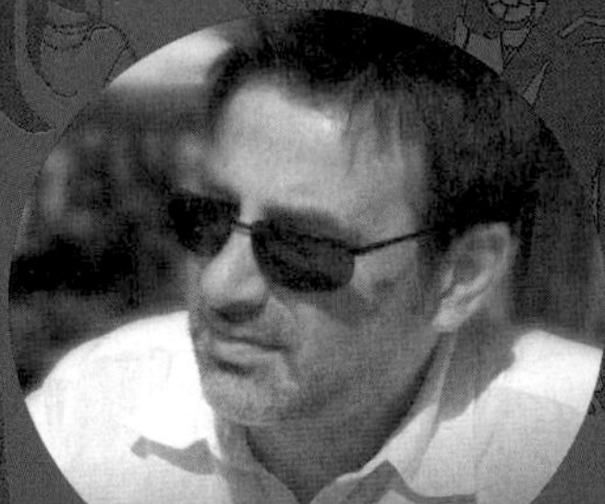

GORAN PARLOV

was born in Pula, Croatia. After graduating from the Art Academy in Zagreb, Goran moved to Italy, where he began his career as a comic book artist. His first published work was for Italy's Sergio Bonelli Editore, which included art for **TEX** – one of the most popular characters in Italian comics. Other assignments included the **NICK RAIDER** and **MAGICO VENTO** series.

Goran began working for the American market in the early 2000s, with credits including **OUTLAW NATION** and **Y: THE LAST MAN** for Vertigo; **TERMINATOR 3** for Beckett Comics; and **BLACK WIDOW**, **THE PUNISHER: MAX**, and **FURY: MAX** for Marvel. He co-created Mark Millar's Starlight, now owned by Netflix.

After living in Milan for almost a decade, Goran returned to Croatia, where he now resides in Zagreb.

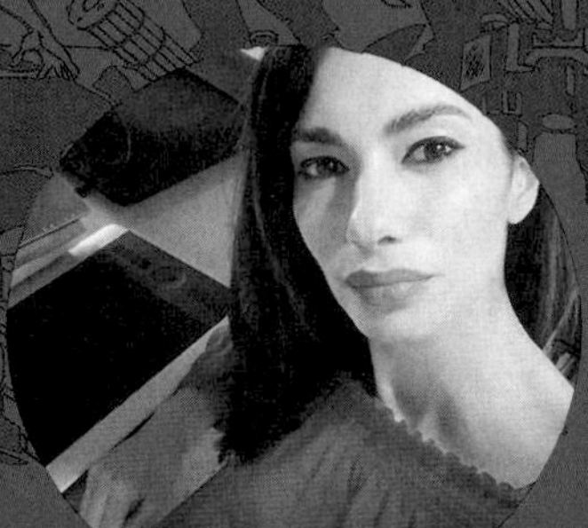

GIADA MARCHISIO

is an Italian colorist. After completing her studies at the International School of Comics and the iMasterArt, she began working as an illustrator for Rizzoli.

Before working in comics, she was a ballet dancer for the Scala theatre in Milan. Later, she entered the world of comics in 2017 as a colorist for the Sergio Bonelli Editore with **DRAGONERO**, until she began working with Marvel – coloring Goran Parlov's covers on **THE PLATOON: THE ORIGINS OF THE PUNISHER**, **THE SPECTACULAR SPIDER-MAN**, **BACKUP #300**, **THE CANARY** and **MARVEL COMICS #1000 BLOODBATH**. With other artists, she has worked on **ASTONISHING X-MEN**, **CLOAK AND DAGGER** season 1 and 2, and **AVENGERS #700**.

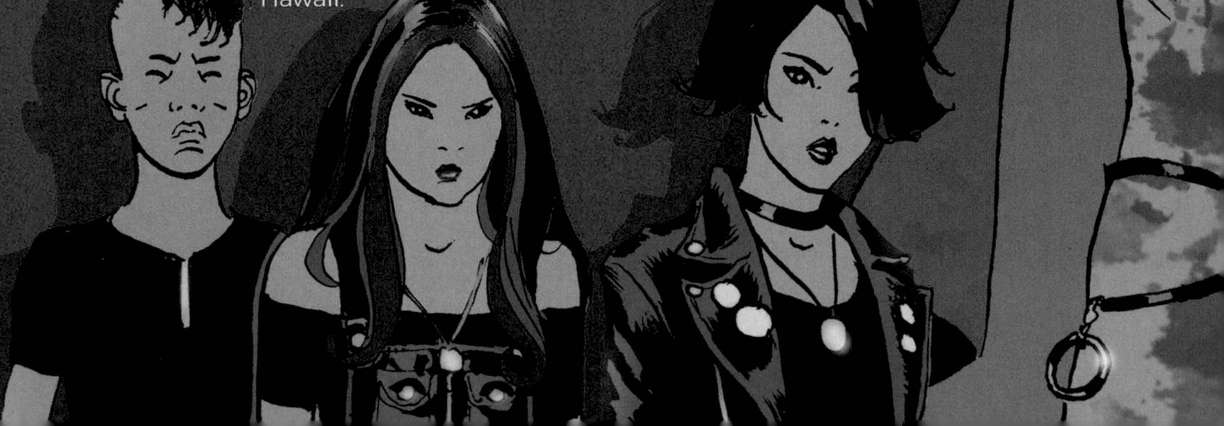

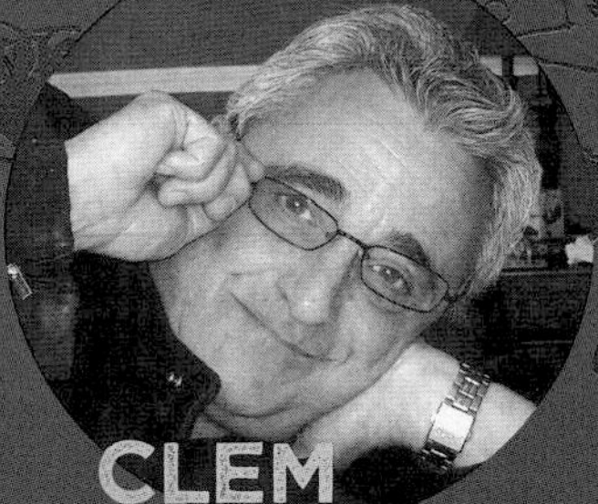

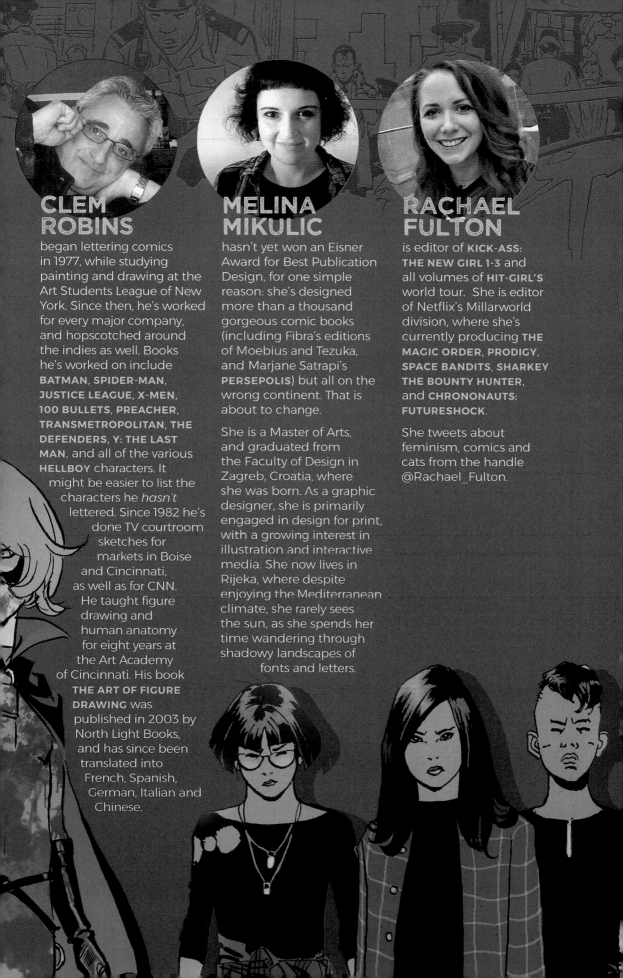

CLEM ROBINS

began lettering comics in 1977, while studying painting and drawing at the Art Students League of New York. Since then, he's worked for every major company, and hopscotched around the indies as well. Books he's worked on include **BATMAN**, **SPIDER-MAN**, **JUSTICE LEAGUE**, **X-MEN**, **100 BULLETS**, **PREACHER**, **TRANSMETROPOLITAN**, **THE DEFENDERS**, **Y: THE LAST MAN**, and all of the various **HELLBOY** characters. It might be easier to list the characters he *hasn't* lettered. Since 1982 he's done TV courtroom sketches for markets in Boise and Cincinnati, as well as for CNN. He taught figure drawing and human anatomy for eight years at the Art Academy of Cincinnati. His book **THE ART OF FIGURE DRAWING** was published in 2003 by North Light Books, and has since been translated into French, Spanish, German, Italian and Chinese.

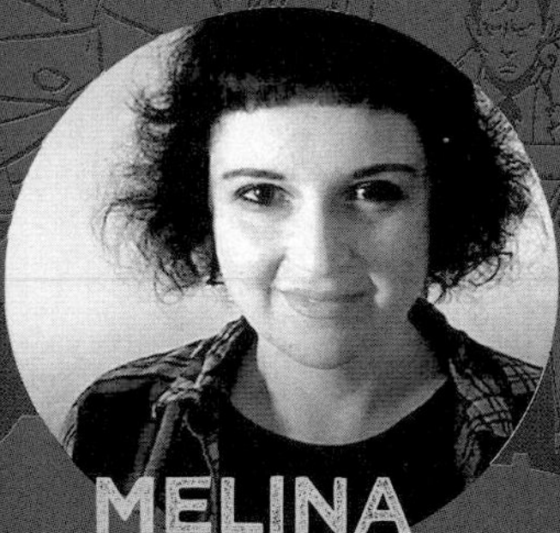

MELINA MIKULIC

hasn't yet won an Eisner Award for Best Publication Design, for one simple reason: she's designed more than a thousand gorgeous comic books (including Fibra's editions of Moebius and Tezuka, and Marjane Satrapi's **PERSEPOLIS**) but all on the wrong continent. That is about to change.

She is a Master of Arts, and graduated from the Faculty of Design in Zagreb, Croatia, where she was born. As a graphic designer, she is primarily engaged in design for print, with a growing interest in illustration and interactive media. She now lives in Rijeka, where despite enjoying the Mediterranean climate, she rarely sees the sun, as she spends her time wandering through shadowy landscapes of fonts and letters.

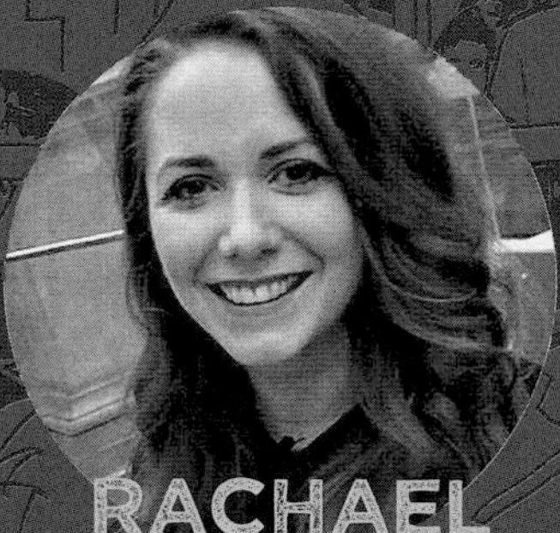

RACHAEL FULTON

is editor of **KICK-ASS: THE NEW GIRL 1-3** and all volumes of **HIT-GIRL'S** world tour. She is editor of Netflix's Millarworld division, where she's currently producing **THE MAGIC ORDER**, **PRODIGY**, **SPACE BANDITS**, **SHARKEY THE BOUNTY HUNTER**, and **CHRONONAUTS: FUTURESHOCK**.

She tweets about feminism, comics and cats from the handle @Rachael_Fulton.

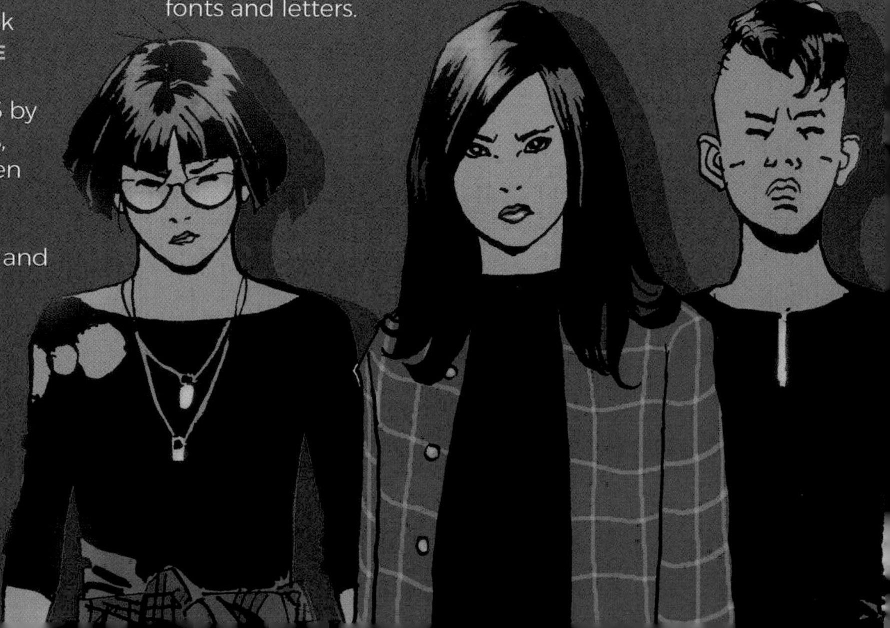

The CO
KICK-ASS
SER

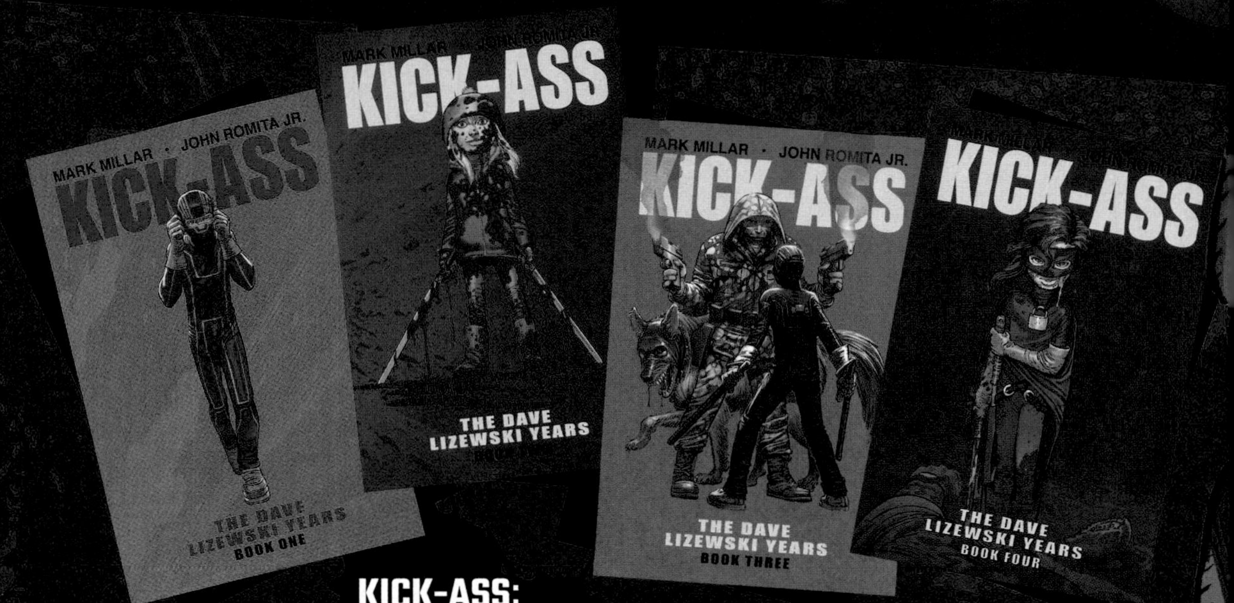
MARK MILLAR • JOHN ROMITA JR.
KICK-ASS
THE DAVE LIZEWSKI YEARS
BOOK ONE
KICK-ASS
THE DAVE LIZEWSKI YEARS
MARK MILLAR • JOHN ROMITA JR.
KICK-ASS
THE DAVE LIZEWSKI YEARS
BOOK THREE
KICK-ASS
THE DAVE LIZEWSKI YEARS
BOOK FOUR

KICK-ASS: THE DAVE LIZEWSKI YEARS
Vol 1-4

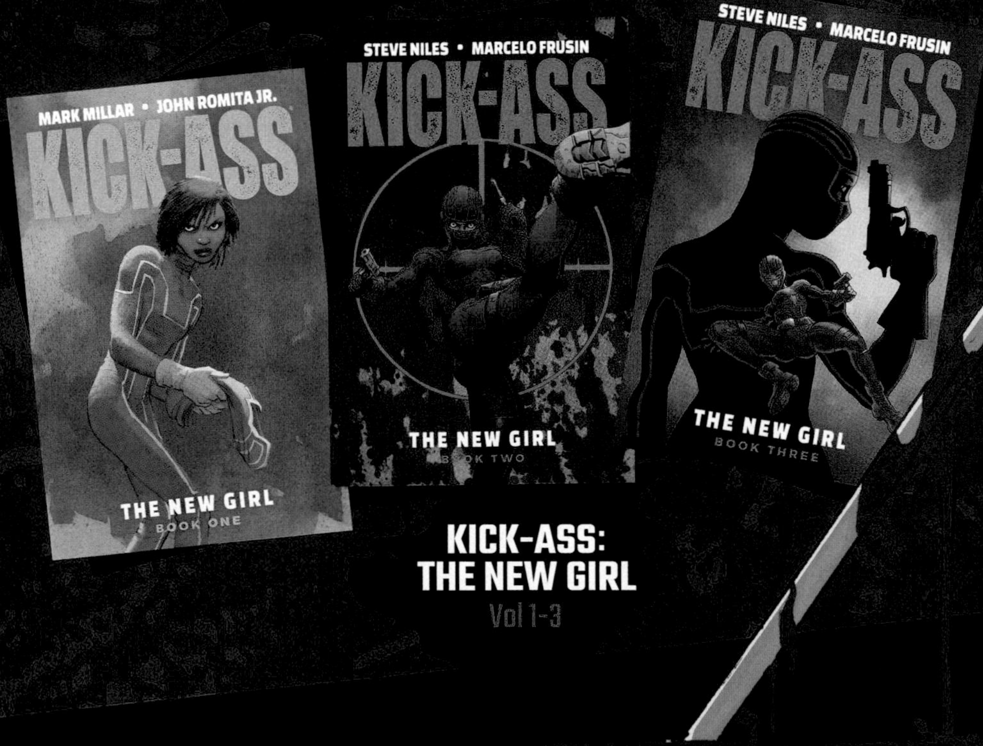
MARK MILLAR • JOHN ROMITA JR.
KICK-ASS
THE NEW GIRL
BOOK ONE
STEVE NILES • MARCELO FRUSIN
KICK-ASS
THE NEW GIRL
BOOK TWO
STEVE NILES • MARCELO FRUSIN
KICK-ASS
THE NEW GIRL
BOOK THREE

KICK-ASS: THE NEW GIRL
Vol 1-3

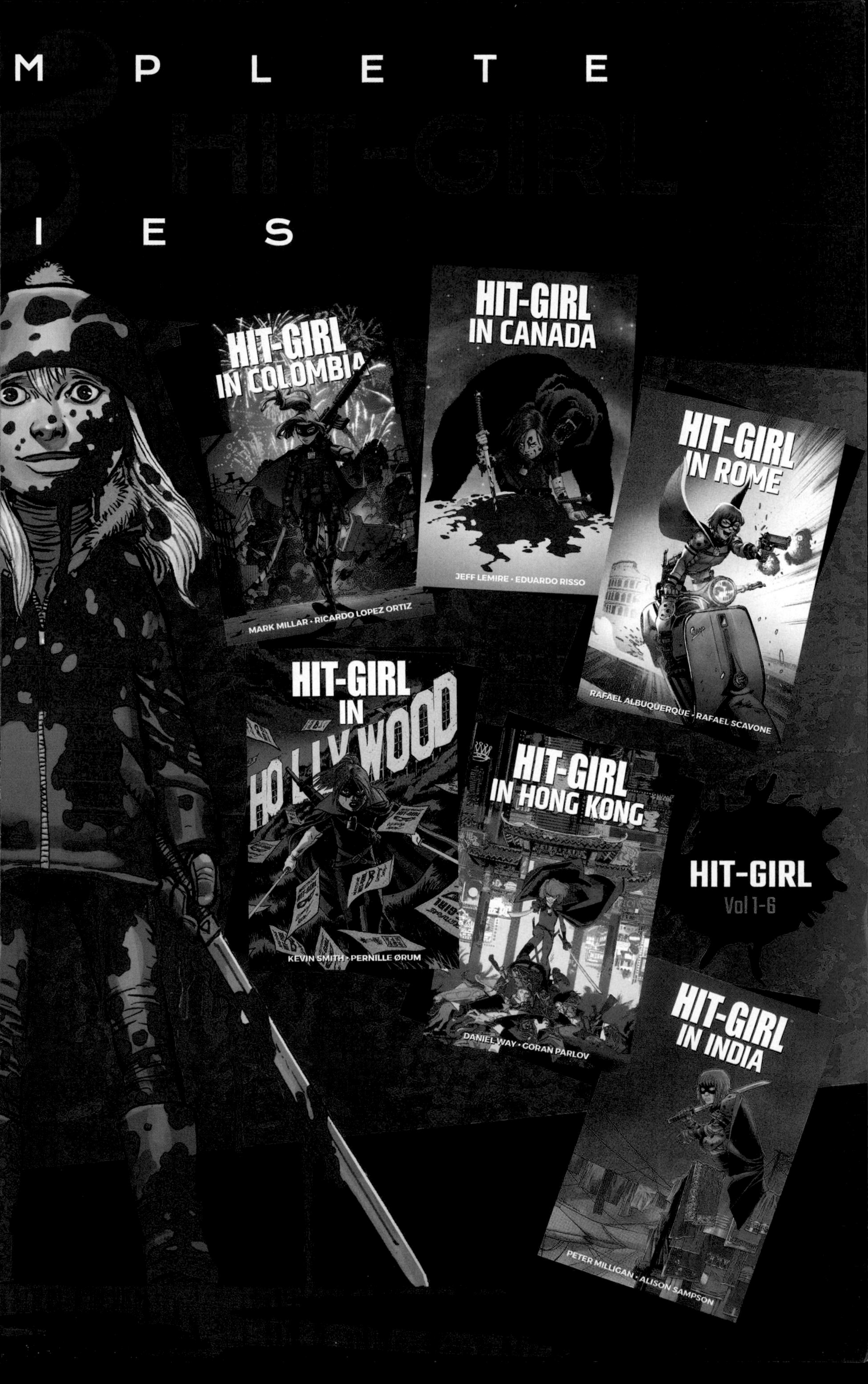

M P L E T E
HIT-GIRL
I E S
HIT-GIRL IN COLOMBIA
MARK MILLAR · RICARDO LOPEZ ORTIZ
HIT-GIRL IN CANADA
JEFF LEMIRE · EDUARDO RISSO
HIT-GIRL IN ROME
RAFAEL ALBUQUERQUE · RAFAEL SCAVONE
HIT-GIRL IN HOLLYWOOD
KEVIN SMITH · PERNILLE ØRUM
HIT-GIRL IN HONG KONG
DANIEL WAY · GORAN PARLOV
HIT-GIRL
Vol 1-6
HIT-GIRL IN INDIA
PETER MILLIGAN · ALISON SAMPSON

BOOKS BY

EMPRESS
MARK MILLAR
STUART IMMONEN
with WADE VON GRAWBADGER & IVE SVORCINA
ICON

EMPRESS
Art by Stuart Immonen

Huck
MARK MILLAR
RAFAEL ALBUQUERQUE
DAVE McCAIG
BOOK 1:
ALL-AMERICAN

HUCK
Art by Rafael Albuquerque

MILLAR MURPHY
CHRONONAUTS
#1
$3.50

CHRONONAUTS
Art by Sean Gordon Murphy

MARK MILLAR DUNCAN FEGREDO
MPH
image
$14.99

MPH
Art by Duncan Fegredo

MARK MILLAR · FRANK QUITELY
JUPITER'S
LEGACY
BOOK ONE

JUPITER'S LEGACY 1 & 2
Art by Frank Quitely

MILLAR · TORRES · GIANFELICE
JUPITER'S
CIRCLE
BOOK ONE

JUPITER'S CIRCLE 1 & 2
Art by Wilfredo Torres

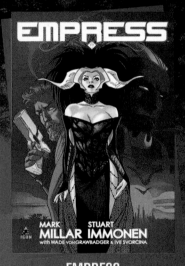

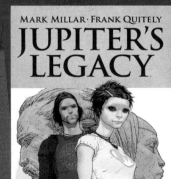

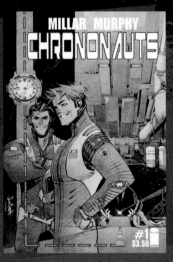

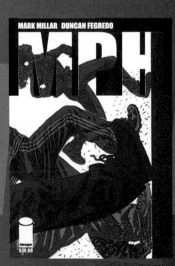

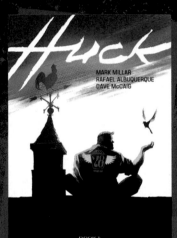

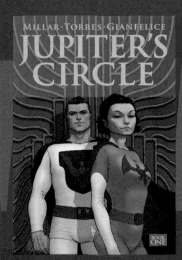

MARK MILLAR

STARLIGHT
Art by Goran Parlov

SUPER CROOKS
Art by Leinil Yu

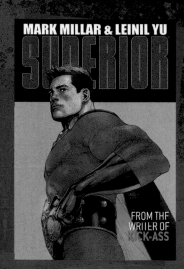

SUPERIOR
Art by Leinil Yu

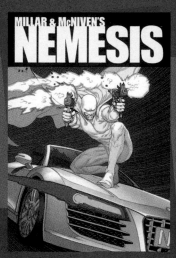

NEMESIS
Art by Steve McNiven

AMERICAN JESUS
Art by Peter Gross

THE MAGIC ORDER
Art by Olivier Coipel